The Sources of
Antislavery Constitutionalism
in America, 1760–1848

The Sources of
Antislavery Constitutionalism
in America, 1760-1848

William M. Wiecek

Cornell University Press
ITHACA AND LONDON

KF4545
S5 W53

Cornell University Press gratefully acknowledges a grant from the Andrew W. Mellon Foundation that aided in bringing this book to publication.

First published 1977 by Cornell University Press.
Published in the United Kingdom by Cornell University Press Ltd., 2-4 Brook Street, London W1Y 1AA.

International Standard Book Number 0-8014-1089-4
Library of Congress Catalog Card Number 77-6169
Printed in the United States of America by York Composition Co., Inc.
Librarians: Library of Congress cataloging information appears on the last page of the book.

For Michael, Sophie, and Kristen

The law will never make men free; it is men who have got to make the law free.

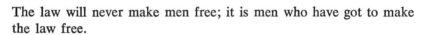

—Henry David Thoreau
"Slavery in Massachusetts" (1854)

Preface

In 1760 the institution of slavery in the British colonies enjoyed undisputed legitimacy. No colonials considered it inherently illegitimate, although some, especially Quakers in the middle colonies, attacked it on moral grounds. By 1848 some American abolitionists contended that slavery was everywhere illegitimate, while a larger number, as well as many nonabolitionists, believed that the federal government could properly restrict the spread of slavery into the territories. In addition, many northerners believed that the free states could repel the intrusion of slavery into their jurisdictions. The passage from the constitutional world of 1760 to that of 1848, with respect to slavery, is the subject of this study.

Antislavery constitutionalism developed from nontechnical, popular origins that lay outside courts and legislatures. Constitutional development was (and is) not a monopoly of a hieratic caste of judges and lawyers. It has its beginnings in the American people, and its first expressions are to be found in documents less formal than decisions and statutes. Alvan Stewart perceived this when he wrote:

The great secret of successful prosecution of the anti slavery conquest is yet unrevealed, and where revealed is not believed. The simplicity of means is so amazing, men will not believe it. It is *the great every-man power, the one-man power, the common-man power, the unlearned-man power.* Every honest antislavery man has the power of converting some of his neighbors to our glorious principles, in the next five weeks by talking, by tract, newspaper, or pamphlet.[1]

1. Alvan Stewart, "The Great Every-man Power" (undated), in Luther R. Marsh, ed., *Writings and Speeches of Alvan Stewart, on Slavery* (New York: A. B. Burdick, 1860), 401 (italics in original).

"Constitutional meaning and protection have to embody and reflect a great deal besides case law," Howard Jay Graham has said. "Extrajudicial factors have been and are the keys to Everyman's Constitution."[2] This study is an exploration of those extrajudicial factors, the true sources of antislavery constitutionalism in America.

The assistance of many persons and institutions has made this book possible. I received financial aid that supported summer research trips and a sabbatical leave and paid the costs of typing and photocopying from the National Endowment for the Humanities (Younger Humanist Award and summer research fellowship); the University of Missouri–Columbia (grants from the Assistant Professor Research Fund and the Faculty Research Council); the John Carter Brown Library, Brown University; the Newberry Library, Chicago.

Librarians, archivists, and their staffs were always helpful and hospitable. At the University of Missouri–Columbia, Anne Edwards, Betty Ellington Parrigin, and the staffs of the Rare Book Division of Ellis Memorial Library and the State Historical Society of Missouri kindly dug out materials and secured interlibrary loan requests. Other individual librarians who helped were William Ewing, formerly Curator of Manuscripts, and William Joyce at the William L. Clements Library, University of Michigan–Ann Arbor; Thomas R. Adams and Samuel Hough at the John Carter Brown Library; Archie Motley of the Manuscripts Division, Chicago Historical Society; Lawrence W. Towner and Arthur Miller of the Newberry Library; and Marion Brophy at the New York State Historical Association, Cooperstown. Staffs at the following made research trips a pleasure: the Manuscripts Division, Library of Congress; the National Archives; the New-York Historical Society; the New York Public Library; the Manuscripts Division of the Libraries of Columbia University; the Pennsylvania Historical Society; the Boston Public Library; the Massachusetts Historical Society; Houghton Library, Harvard; and the Schlesinger Library, Radcliffe.

The University of Chicago has granted permission to quote from and adapt my article *"Somerset:* Lord Mansfield and the Legitimacy

2. Howard Jay Graham, *Everyman's Constitution: Historical Essays on the Fourteenth Amendment, the "Conspiracy Theory," and American Constitutionalism* (Madison: State Historical Society of Wisconsin, 1968), 588.

of Slavery in the Anglo-American World," originally published in the *University of Chicago Law Review*. I wish also to record my gratitude to the holders of all archival material cited herein (including that read on microfilm) for permission to do research in their holdings and quote from them.

Colleagues at the University of Missouri–Columbia read parts of this study and provided helpful criticism: Charles F. Mullett, William F. Fratcher, Thomas B. Alexander, and Robert Ruigh. The Nineteenth-Century Studies Group and the History Department's Faculty Seminar provided a learned audience for early versions of several chapters.

Scholars elsewhere, in an act of incredible generosity, read an eight-hundred-page draft manuscript and gave me the benefit of lengthy written and verbal critiques: Louis S. Gerteis of the University of Missouri–St. Louis, Stanley I. Kutler of the University of Wisconsin–Madison, George M. Dennison of Colorado State University, Phillip S. Paludan of the University of Kansas, Herman Belz of the University of Maryland–College Park, and Howard Jay Graham of Walla Walla, Washington. None of these persons is responsible for any statements or opinions expressed in this study.

My greatest scholarly debt is owed to Dean Stanley N. Katz of the University of Chicago Law School, a friend, scholar, and historian who has been a source of encouragement over the years.

WILLIAM M. WIECEK

Columbia, Missouri

Contents

Abbreviations

AA-SS	American Anti-Slavery Society
A&FA-SS	American and Foreign Anti-Slavery Society
ACS	American Colonization Society
Annals	*Annals of Congress* [debates in Congress, 1789–1824]
Birney Letters	Dwight L. Dumond, ed., *Letters of James Gillespie Birney 1831–1857* (New York: D. Appleton-Century, 1938)
Elliot, *Debates*	Jonathan Elliot, comp., *Debates in the Several State Conventions on the Adoption of the Federal Constitution* . . . (Philadelphia: Lippincott, 1901)
Farrand, *Records*	Max Farrand, ed., *The Records of the Federal Convention of 1787*, rev. ed. (New Haven: Yale University Press, 1937)
Federalist	Jacob E. Cooke, ed., *The Federalist* (Middletown, Conn.: Wesleyan University Press, 1961)
LC	Library of Congress
N-EA-SS	New-England Anti-Slavery Society
N-YHS	New-York Historical Society
NYSA-SS	New York State Anti-Slavery Society
Wm. & M. Q.	*William and Mary Quarterly* (3d ser.)

*The Sources of
Antislavery Constitutionalism
in America, 1760–1848*

Introduction

The slavery controversy was the most important single influence on American constitutional development before the Civil War. It underlay the struggle for sectional advantage that took place during the six crises of the union: 1783–1788, 1819–1821, 1832, 1846–1850, 1854, and 1860–1861. There were other great constitutional controversies in the antebellum period: creation of a national government, establishment of judicial review, charter of a national bank, restriction of speech. Each had its day and shaped our constitution, but none proved to be as lasting or as divisive as the ongoing effort to restrict or protect the enslavement of black people. In the end, the slavery controversy proved its potency by destroying the union.

Five of the crises of the union directly involved the expansion or security of slavery outside the existing slave states. Leaving aside the Nullification crisis of 1832, all the crises of the union after the first occurred when southerners perceived a threat to the security of slavery at times when the nation was about to expand again into the western empire. The crises occurred because some question about the place of slavery in the western empire had not yet been resolved, and all but the last were settled by a constitutional compromise of that question.

Because slavery had been regulated by law in all the mainland colonies during the eighteenth century,[1] Americans in the early years of national independence neither questioned its legitimacy in the states

1. William M. Wiecek, "The Statutory Law of Slavery and Race in the Thirteen Mainland Colonies of British America," *Wm. & M. Q.*, 34 (1977), 258–280, surveys the statutory component of this regulation.

where it survived nor believed that the federal government could abolish it in those states. This assumption will be called the "federal consensus." Its correlative tenets were: (1) only the states could abolish or in any way regulate slavery within their jurisdictions; (2) the federal government had no power over slavery in the states. It followed that the only proper posture of the national government with respect to slavery was strict laissez faire, except for one problem (the international slave trade) over which it had explicit constitutional powers, another (fugitive slaves) arguably within its regulatory ambit, and a third (slave insurrections) implicitly so. The crises of the union did not directly involve the security of slavery in the extant states; they related only to slavery in the territories or new states. No one, until the emergence of radical constitutional abolitionists in the 1840s, thought to challenge the federal consensus.

The consensus was threatened, however, by a momentous shift in outlook that took place within the antislavery movement around 1830—the appearance of immediatism. Before the 1830s, organized antislavery was moderate in spirit, gradualistic, and oriented to grappling with slavery at the state and local level. When the American Anti-Slavery Society was founded in 1833 around the demand for the immediate abolition of slavery, and when it directed its interests more conspicuously toward federal action than its predecessors had done, defenders of slavery sensed a challenge to the security of slavery in the extant states. The AA-SS repeatedly denied that it harbored any such intention, but it failed to convince slavery's champions.

The federal consensus assumed the legitimacy of slavery in the states where it existed. In 1838, five years after the founding of the AA-SS, a coterie of abolitionists adopted the position that slavery was everywhere illegitimate. They rejected the federal consensus and tried, unsuccessfully, to have the AA-SS repudiate it. This group will be referred to as the radical constitutionalists, "radical" because they rejected the consensus, "constitutionalists" because they sought to abolish slavery by constitutional action.

The radicals' challenge, together with a disagreement over the wisdom of organizing an antislavery third party, split the organized movement. In addition to the radicals, two other abolitionist groups emerged in the 1840s: Garrisonians and moderate constitutionalists. Both, in differing ways, supported the consensus. The Garrisonians by

1844 maintained that the Constitution supported slavery and was a proslavery compact. They therefore condemned it, urged disunion and personal disallegiance, and denounced the Liberty party, which had become the vehicle for supporters of antislavery third-party action. Moderate constitutionalists defended the consensus, but demanded that the federal government be divorced from any support of slavery. They hoped that the removal of federal support, coupled with vigorous antislavery political involvement either through the Liberty party or in one of the regular parties, would render slavery so vulnerable that the states would abolish it of their own accord.

The moderates in 1846 to 1848 coalesced with nonabolitionists from the regular parties on a platform of opposition to the extension of slavery into the new territories acquired in the Mexican War. The catalyst for this fusion was the Wilmot Proviso, first introduced in 1846, which would have forbidden the establishment of slavery in any of the erstwhile Mexican territories. The Proviso also marked the transit of abolitionist constitutionalism from one era to another. Before the Proviso, the controversy over slavery was waged over a wide range of issues, of which the problem of slavery in the territories was only one among several. After 1846, however, the extension of slavery into the territories became the overriding issue, eclipsing all others in national politics except that of fugitive slaves, which was decidedly subordinate. Constitutional development after 1848 was so radically different from what had gone before, and its political configurations so changed, that it must be the subject of separate investigation. Hence the terminal date of this study.

Except for the Garrisonians, who looked only backward, abolitionists tried to describe what the Constitution had been, what it was in their present, and what it could or should become, and they sometimes did these three things simultaneously, confusing past and future in a fused "is." Aileen Kraditor assumes agreement among modern historians that the Garrisonian interpretation of the Constitution is the "correct one," but that judgment requires severe qualification.[2] Garrisonians and defenders of slavery were correct in seeing a tra-

2. Aileen S. Kraditor, *Means and Ends in American Abolitionism: Garrison and His Critics on Strategy and Tactics, 1834–1850* (New York: Pantheon, 1969), 216; see also a more qualified statement of this view in Staughton Lynd, "The Abolitionist Critique of the United States Constitution," in Martin Duberman, ed., *The Antislavery Vanguard: New Essays on the Abolitionists* (Princeton: Princeton Univ. Press, 1965), 209–239.

jectory of development, along which the Constitution was forced toward an ever more proslavery character, and their judgment was validated in that *summa* of proslavery constitutionalism, the *Dred Scott* case. But this view was valid only looking backward in time; the trajectory was neither necessary nor inevitable. There is much to be said for the radical position, looking forward in time, which tried to discern what the constitution might be.

Four prominent abolitionists vaguely grasped this idea. Lewis Tappan explained to Charles Sumner his conversion from moderate to radical views: "You are right in saying that the abolitionists of 1830 to 40 'did not find any power in the Constitution to enter the Slave States' except with moral suasion. The power may have been there nevertheless." Tappan groped awkwardly for an explanation of how this power might be realized:

The democrats have interpreted the Constitution to be what a majority in Congress says it is. The Govt. has upheld slavery. The people have sanctioned it. [But] by the rule thus laid down, the Govt. can limit, nay abolish slavery, were there no other rule. 'No man shall be deprived of life, liberty or property without due process of law.' By what process of law are 3,000,000 of our fellow-beings held in slavery in this country? When public opinion is rectified there will be no difficulty, I apprehend, in bringing about the abolition of slavery in this country constitutionally.[3]

William Goodell approvingly quoted an unnamed lawyer who remarked to him that "the lawyers argue from the constitution, as it is now perverted. The present mis-interpretation of it they make their starting point." This perverted interpretation had become so canonical, admitted Edwin W. Clarke, that the radical abolitionist interpretation was "visionary." But then so had been the ideas of Granville Sharp when he launched his seemingly futile crusade against slavery in England in 1768, and if English courts could be brought around to Sharp's antislavery, so might American courts, once disenthralled of their subservience to the Slave Power.[4]

Samuel J. May, reflecting on intramural abolitionist conflicts, noted that Garrisonians maintained the American constitution was pro-

3. Lewis Tappan to Charles Sumner, 26 June 1860, Charles Sumner Papers, Houghton Library, Harvard University; quoted by permission of the Houghton Library.
4. William Goodell, "The Constitution and Slavery," *National Era*, 1 April 1847; E. W. C[larke], "The Constitution and Slavery," *ibid.*, 18 March 1847.

slavery, while the moderates and radicals insisted it was antislavery, but "it seemed to me that it might be whichever the people pleased to make it."⁵ May touched on the essential character of Everyman's Constitution: it was, and is, whatever the American people are pleased to make it, and they may alter it in modes other than formal amendment.

5. Samuel J. May, *Some Recollections of Our Antislavery Conflict* (Boston: Fields, Osgood, 1869), 143–144.

CHAPTER 1

The Ambiguous Beginnings of Antislavery Constitutionalism: *Somerset*

Americans, for better or worse, are a peculiarly legalistic people. Moral or ideological pressures alone, divorced from secular legal considerations, would not have accounted for the potency of antislavery in the United States. But slavery was, among other things, a legal institution, and attacks on its legitimacy were especially congenial to the American temperament. Abolitionists struck one of their most telling blows when they asserted that slavery had been established in America in violation of natural law, the common law, and the constitutional order of the British colonies.

The documentary bases of this legal attack were threefold: the Declaration of Independence, the constitutive documents of the American states and nation, and *Somerset* v. *Stewart* (1772), a decision handed down by William Murray, Lord Mansfield, Chief Justice of King's Bench, the highest common-law court in England.[1] Read strictly and technically, the holding of *Somerset* was limited to two points: a master could not seize a slave in England and detain him preparatory to sending him out of the realm to be sold; and habeas corpus was available to the slave to forestall such seizure, deportation, and sale. But Mansfield's decision, as reported by the young English lawyer Capel Lofft, contained utterances that imbued the holding with a much broader significance. As interpreted by American abolitionists and others, *Somerset* seemed to be a declaration that slavery was incompatible with natural law and that, in the

1. This chapter is adapted from William M. Wiecek, "*Somerset:* Lord Mansfield and the Legitimacy of Slavery in the Anglo-American World," *U. Chi. L. Rev.*, 42 (1975), 86–146. Cp. David Brion Davis, *The Problem of Slavery in the Age of Revolution, 1770–1823* (Ithaca: Cornell Univ. Press, 1975), ch. 10.

Anglo-American world, it could legitimately exist only if established by what Mansfield ambiguously termed "positive law."

Many contemporaries understood *Somerset* to have abolished slavery in England; a few thought it challenged slavery in the colonies as well. Mansfield's utterance had a plangent quality, suggesting that slavery was of dubious legitimacy everywhere. Though Mansfield later disavowed the broad implications imputed to *Somerset,* the decision took on a life of its own and entered the mainstream of American constitutional discourse. It furnished abolitionists with some of the most potent doctrinal weapons in their arsenal; even slave-state jurists at first accepted its antislavery premises and then later worked out a justification of slavery, as it were, around or in spite of *Somerset.* The case therefore became a cloud hanging over the legitimacy of slavery in America, a result that would have surprised Mansfield.

The long-continued existence of slavery anywhere in the world would sooner or later have presented problems to be resolved by English jurists, but the fact that Englishmen commanded slavers by the mid-sixteenth century and soon peopled English New World colonies with African slaves made the intrusion of such problems into English jurisprudence only a matter of time. When English courts did begin taking cognizance of slavery cases in the seventeenth century, they turned up an array of novel questions that had to be resolved by the familiar forms of the common law, with little guidance from Parliament or the Privy Council.

I. Could A "own" B as a slave in England?
   A. What did he own? The body of B? The right to B's services?
   B. How could the master enforce whatever rights he had?
   C. What was the legal source of A's claim? There were numerous possible theoretical bases: captivity in war; conviction of crime; voluntary self-sale; sale by the slave's parents or sovereign; status inherited from a slave parent; sale by the slave's owner; wrongful force (kidnaping, captivity in an unjust war, rapine, etc.); prescription; custom, either immemorial or recent; Mosaic law or Christianity; positive law, English, English colonial, or foreign, including statutes that regulated the incidents of slave status; the *jus gentium;* villeinage; implied quasi contract; Roman or civil law as expounded by the continental jurisprudents.

II. Could A "own" B as a slave in English colonies?
   A. What rights could A or B claim while either or both were in England?
   B. Could the metropolis establish, regulate, or abolish slavery in the colonies? What was the constitutional status of the colonies within the empire?
   C. Did colony slave laws have extraterritorial force? In England? In other English colonies? In non-English jurisdictions?
   D. Were the rights of slaves (or their masters) on English soil varied depending on whether they were: brought there by their master for permanent residence? Temporary residence (sojourners)? Runaways (fugitive slaves)? In transit?
III. How far would common-law courts recognize the legal incidents of slave status adhering to slaves in England?
   A. What were its essential incidents? Hereditable status? Lifetime slavery? Absolute dominion of the master, except as restrained by positive law? Could the common law accommodate the discipline necessary to slavery?
   B. Did slavery depend on racial distinction? Non-Christian religious status?
   C. Would English courts enforce a contract for the sale of a slave?
   D. Could a slave commit a tort or a criminal act? Could he be the victim of either? Who was responsible for his act or for injury to him, and to whom?
   E. Did the master have rights against third parties who interfered with his control over the slave (as, e.g., by impressment)?
IV. What rights did the slave have?
   A. Juridical capacity as witness or party? Right to own and dispose of property? To make contracts? To marry and control his children?
   B. Could a slave seek a writ of habeas corpus? Could he sue his master in *quantum meruit?*
V. Finally, was slavery delegitimated by:
   A. Natural law?
   B. The common law or the habeas corpus statutes?

   English precedents on slavery before 1772 suggested several different directions in which the law of slavery might evolve. The early

English decisions seemingly accommodated the peculiar legal characteristics of property in slaves to the forms of English law; yet their precedential weight was problematical. Ambiguity and equivocal authority characterized most of the principal English authorities on slavery.

Between 1677, the date of the first reliably reported English decision on slavery, and 1729, when Crown lawyers delivered an authoritative and comprehensive opinion on some of slavery's legal complications, the justices of King's Bench handed down seemingly contradictory opinions on slavery's status under common law. In *Butts* v. *Penny* (1677),[2] the court acknowledged the existence of property rights in slaves and suggested two possible legitimating origins for slavery: "infidel" status and sale by merchants. But then the court, through Chief Justice Sir John Holt, seemingly reversed *Butts* in three decisions between 1697 and 1706. Holt rejected the use of forms of action for the recovery of property as an appropriate means for recovering slaves in *Chamberlain* v. *Harvey* (1697),[3] recommending instead an old form of action used to recover for the loss of a servant's services. In *Smith* v. *Brown and Cooper* (1701),[4] Holt stated flatly that "as soon as a negro comes into England, he becomes free; one may be a villein in England, but not a slave." Yet Holt insisted that a seller might recover for the value of slaves sold. Mansfield later pointed out in *Somerset* that no English court questioned the validity of a contract for sale of slaves, thus suggesting that at least some features of the law of slavery would be hospitably received in English courts. Finally, in *Smith* v. *Gould* (1705–1706),[5] an ambivalent effort, the justices declared that *Butts* was "not law" and that humans cannot be "the subject of property," yet refurbished old procedural devices to protect the title to a slave acquired by purchase. The English bar was understandably confused by these conflicting holdings, and sought an authoritative resolution of them. They got it in 1729.

2. Lev. 201, 83 Eng. Rep. 518 (K.B. 1677).
3. Three reports of this case exist: Carthew 396, 90 Eng. Rep. 830; 1 Ld. Raym. 1274, 92 Eng. Rep. 338; and 5 Mod. 186, 87 Eng. Rep. 598 (*sub nom.* Chamberline v. Harvey) (K.B. 1697).
4. Salk. 666, 91 Eng. Rep. 566. Also reported Holt K.B. 495, 90 Eng. Rep. 1172.
5. This case was twice reported: 2 Salk. 666, 91 Eng. Rep. 567 (K.B. 1705), and 2 Ld. Raym. 1274, 92 Eng. Rep. 338 (K.B. 1706).

One evening over after-dinner wine at one of the Inns of Court, the members solicited Attorney General Philip Yorke and Solicitor General Charles Talbot for their opinions on the effect of baptizing Negro slaves in the plantations. Yorke and Talbot obliged with a joint opinion asserting the following points: (1) a slave coming to Great Britain from the West Indies, with or without his master, is not liberated; (2) the master's property right in such a slave in Great Britain is not "determined or varied"; (3) baptism does not liberate the slave or change his temporal condition; and (4) "the master may legally compel him to return again to the plantations."[6] Whatever else may be said of this opinion, it was at least unambiguous on the points to which it was addressed. One of its authors, Yorke, enjoyed a high reputation for legal acumen, and the opinion survived long enough to haunt Granville Sharp and provoke him to his first great effort on behalf of the slaves forty years later.

Then Chancery intervened to blur the clarity briefly induced by the Yorke-Talbot opinion. Sensing that the informal circumstances of the opinion's delivery made it something less than authoritative, Yorke, ennobled and elevated to the woolsack, tried to buttress it in *Pearne* v. *Lisle* (1749), a decision he rendered as Hardwicke, Lord Chancellor.[7] Sweeping away all Holt's handiwork through an insupportable construction of *Smith* v. *Brown and Cooper,* Hardwicke resurrected *Butts* v. *Penny,* saying trover will lie for a Negro slave: "It is as much property as any other thing." But Hardwicke's holding was reversed thirteen years later by his successor in Chancery, Lord Chancellor Henley (later Earl of Northington), in *Shanley* v. *Harvey* (1762),[8] who grandly declared that "as soon as a man sets foot on English ground he is free: a negro may maintain an action against his master for ill usage, and may have a habeas corpus if restrained of his liberty." These two Chancery decisions had the effect of canceling each other out. Though Hardwicke is esteemed a greater equity judge than Henley, it was the latter who had the later say.

In any event, the highest courts of both common law and equity had spoken on both sides of, and all around, the legal issues of slavery, and their opinions, reported sometimes poorly and always

6. The joint opinion is quoted in full in *Knight* v. *Wedderburn,* 8 Fac. Dec. 5, Mor. 14545 (Scotland Court of Sessions, 1778).
7. Ambl. 75, 27 Eng. Rep. 47 (Ch. 1749).
8. 2 Eden 126, 28 Eng. Rep. 844 (Ch. 1762).

long afterward, were more a matter of oral tradition than of cold print. The judges and counsel before them had canvassed some of the issues presented by the problem of incorporating ownership of man into a legal system that boasted its greatest glory as being in *favorem libertatis*, but the law of slavery was still unsettled when Granville Sharp challenged slavery in England.

By 1770, some fourteen to fifteen thousand slaves resided in the British isles. In addition to these, an unknown number of free blacks also lived in the realm, numerous enough to create a special group of London beggars known derisively as "St. Giles' blackbirds." Most of them were Africans or Creoles who had been brought to the metropolis via the island or mainland colonies as personal servants to West India planters.[9] Their presence had been visible throughout the eighteenth century, and by the 1770s they had attracted the attention of men who had been active in efforts to abolish the British slave trade. Thus crossed the paths of an obscure black, James Somerset, and Granville Sharp, the first great English abolitionist.

Sharp was an unusual person, even in eighteenth-century England. A grandson of the Archbishop of York, but son of a poor archdeacon, Sharp was self-educated, having been employed first as a cloth merchant's apprentice and later as a clerk in the Ordnance Department, a post he resigned in 1776 because he could not bring himself to make out orders for shipping munitions to the revolting colonies, whose cause he supported. Sharp became involved in antislavery activism by litigation in 1767 to free a slave named Jonathan Strong. Strong's master, David Lisle, brought countersuit against Sharp for detainer of the slave. Sharp urged his lawyer to defend on the grounds that no action could be brought for detainer because the master could not have a property right in a slave, but counsel rejected this suggestion on the basis of the 1729 Yorke-Talbot opinion. Thus frustrated, Sharp determined to reexamine from scratch the entire question of slavery, personal liberty, and the right to habeas corpus in England.[10]

Two years of research produced *A Representation of the Injustice . . . of Tolerating Slavery* (1769), in which Sharp condemned

9. James Walvin, *Black and White: The Negro and English Society 1555–1945* (London: Penguin, 1973), chs. 1–5.
10. See Davis, *Problem of Slavery in the Age of Revolution*, 386–402, on the influence of Sharp on English antislavery thought.

slavery as "a gross infringement of the common and natural rights of mankind" and as "plainly contrary to the laws and constitution of this kingdom" because no laws "countenance" it and others, according to his interpretation, made it actionable.[11] On this point, Sharp imaginatively cited statutes ranging from the mid-fourteenth century down to the Habeas Corpus Act (1679). From these provisions, Sharp argued that all persons in England, including black slaves, had a statutory right to contest their restraints in the courts through the writ of habeas corpus. He thus constituted a link in a chain of descent from Magna Charta through the mediaeval Parliaments to the nineteenth-century American antislavery movement and the origins of the due process and equal protection clauses of the Fourteenth Amendment.

Having relied on one group of parliamentary statutes in favor of liberty, Sharp could not avoid others recognizing or condoning slavery: those regulating the slave trade, granting concessions to slavers, and confirming masters' property rights in slaves.[12] In the face of these, he argued in an afterthought that statutes creating an injustice should be treated by the courts as being superseded by statutes favoring liberty, which are of superior obligation.[13]

Sharp unnecessarily suggested that a man might voluntarily enter into an agreement, for consideration, to become a slave, thereby conceding a contractual basis for slavery, but he denied any other source of legitimacy in the origins of slavery. "True justice makes no respect of persons," he insisted, "and can never deny to any one that blessing to which all mankind have an undoubted right, their natural liberty."[14]

11. Granville Sharp, *A Representation of the Injustice and Dangerous Tendency of Tolerating Slavery; or of Admitting the Least Claim of Private Property in the Persons of Men, in England* (London: Benjamin White and Robert Horsfield, 1769), 40–41.

12. 5 Geo. 2, c. 7 (1732); 23 Geo. 2, c. 31 (1750); 25 Geo. 2, c. 40 (1752); charter of the Royal African Company (1672), reprinted in W. Noel Sainsbury, ed., *Calendar of State Papers, Colonial Series: America and West Indies, 1669–1674* (London: HMSO, 1889), 409–412; Opinion of Solicitor General Sir Francis Winnington (1677), reprinted in W. Noel Sainsbury and J. Fortesque, eds., *Calendar of State Papers, Colonial Series: America and West Indies, 1677–1680* (London: HMSO, 1896), 120.

13. Granville Sharp, *An Appendix to the Representation, (Printed in the Year 1769,) of the Injustice and Dangerous Tendency of Tolerating Slavery, or of Admitting the Least Claim of Private Property in the Persons of Men in England* (London: Benjamin White, 1772), 24.

14. Sharp, *Representation*, 38.

He thus introduced two themes that pervaded later constitutional antislavery: the appeal to natural or higher law to override mere mundane and unjust ordinances, and the idea that a sweeping explicit declaration, such as the all-men-are-born-free-and-equal phrase of the Declaration of Independence, admits of no implicit racial exceptions.

In preparing the *Representation* and carrying forward the *Somerset* case, Sharp underwent the vexation of having William Blackstone, already recognized as an authoritative expositor of English law, modify his publicly and privately expressed opinions on slavery, thereby undercutting Sharp's reliance on him. In the first edition of his *Commentaries on the Law of England*, published in 1765, Blackstone declared that slavery "does not, nay cannot, subsist in England" and repudiated three origins of slavery that continental writers had recognized as legitimating slavery (captivity in war, self-sale, inherited status). Citing *Smith* v. *Brown and Cooper,* Blackstone ventured the opinion that as soon as a slave comes into England, he becomes free, just the doctrine Sharp was striving for. Like Sharp, though, he suggested that slavery might have a contractual basis, and that whatever rights an English master derived from this basis continued in force and were unaffected by baptism.[15]

However, troubled by the potential antislavery uses to which the libertarian part of his writings were being put by Sharp and others, Blackstone cautiously modified the relevant passages in his third edition to remove the implication that a slave enjoyed "liberty" under English law.[16] He stated that "whatever service the heathen negro owed to his American master, the same is he bound to render when brought to England and made a christian," and revised an earlier statement that a slave becomes free upon coming to England to read that he merely comes under the "protection of the laws, and so far becomes a freeman: though the master's right to his service may possibly still continue."[17] These were disastrous shifts of emphasis from Sharp's point of view.

Sharp distributed copies of the *Representation* gratis to attorneys

15. William Blackstone, *Commentaries on the Law of England* (Oxford: Clarendon, 1765–1769), I, 411–412.
16. Blackstone to Sharp, 20 Feb. 1769, copy in Granville Sharp transcripts, N-YHS; Blackstone, *Commentaries,* 3d ed. (Oxford: Clarendon Press, 1768–1769), I, 424–425.
17. On the last quoted statement, cp. the first edition, I, 123, with the fifth (Oxford: Clarendon Press, 1773), I, 127.

to propagate the doctrines he had worked out, and simultaneously sought an appropriate case in which they might be argued before some competent court. Several presented themselves between 1770 and 1772, and according to Thomas Clarkson's recollections in each the black secured his liberty, but none gave an authoritative answer to the question whether a slave is free upon being brought into England.[18] In one of these test cases promoted by Sharp, however, Mansfield made several tantalizing suggestions about the directions in which the law of slavery might be moving. In *Rex* ex rel. *Lewis* v. *Stapleton*,[19] the defendant was prosecuted for assault and false imprisonment for having seized the runaway Lewis for transport and sale outside the realm (the same factual situation as in *Somerset*). In the course of argument, Mansfield stated that being black did not prove that Lewis was a slave, and that whether masters "have this kind of property or not in England has never been solemnly determined." In colloquy with John Dunning, counsel for Lewis, Mansfield gave voice to his uneasiness at the prospect of having to pass on these larger legal issues: "You will find more in the question then [*sic*] you see at present. . . . It is no matter mooting it now but if you look into it there is more than by accident you are acquainted with. . . . Perhaps it is much better it never should be finally discussed or settled . . . for I would have all Masters think they were Free and all Negroes think they were not because they wo'd both behave better." The "more" that Mansfield so enigmatically referred to might have been only the value of slave property in England, which, at a conservative valuation, was worth £700,000, or it might have been the legitimacy of slavery itself. Whichever it was, Mansfield was loath to touch the question.

But finally in 1771–1772, Sharp came upon a case that provided the vehicle he needed to have Mansfield consider the arguments of the *Representation*. James Somerset, according to the return made by John Knowles, master of the vessel that was about to transport him to Jamaica, was born in Africa, brought to Virginia by a slaver in 1749, and bought there by Charles Stewart. Stewart then removed to Massachusetts, where he was stationed as a customs officer, and

18. Thomas Clarkson, *The History of the Rise, Progress, and Accomplishment of the Abolition of the African Slave-Trade by the British Parliament* (London: Longman, Hurst, Rees, and Orme, 1808), I, 75.
19. A transcript of arguments and other proceedings in this case is in Granville Sharp transcripts, N-YHS, from which all quotes in text are taken.

from thence went to England on business in 1769, taking Somerset along as a personal servant.[20] In October 1771, Somerset fled, but was recaptured by Stewart, who consigned him to Knowles to be sold in Jamaica. Through the intervention of Sharp and others, Mansfield issued a writ of habeas corpus on Somerset's behalf and referred the matter for a hearing by the full bench. To represent Somerset and the cause of antislavery, Sharp secured the services of some of the most eminent legal talent of the day: Serjeants William Davy and John Glynn, and barristers James Mansfield[21] and Francis Hargrave. The last of these, a young man in 1772, made his reputation with his arguments in this case. On the other side, representing Stewart, the West India Interest, and the cause of slavery, were the equally eminent barristers John Dunning, who had represented the slave Lewis the previous year, and William Wallace.

Mansfield deferred decision for a year, and ordered five separate hearings. He repeatedly urged Stewart to moot the matter by voluntarily liberating Somerset, but Stewart refused, causing Mansfield to remark in exasperation after the last argument, "If the parties will have judgment, *'fiat justitia, ruat coelum.'* " ["Let justice be done though the heavens fall."] Whatever Mansfield's feelings in the matter may have been, the stubbornness of Sharp and the West India Interest, who both saw the suit as a climacteric test case, left him little room to maneuver. Both tried to move the decision along by publishing legal arguments in the matter. Hargrave published *An Argument in the Case of James Somersett, A Negro* . . . (1772), a carefully drawn lawyer's brief arguing that slavery was antithetical to English laws and the constitution.[22] On the question of the imperial relation and slavery, Hargrave argued that the parliamentary statutes protecting the Royal African Company, even if construed most favorably to the interests of the slaveholders, only permitted slavery to be introduced into the colonies, not into the metropolis.

To counter Sharp and Hargrave, the West India Interest procured publication of several pamphlets defending the legitimacy of slavery

20. The Massachusetts residence of Somerset and Stewart, overlooked by many writers, is discussed in George H. Moore, *Notes on the History of Slavery in Massachusetts* (New York: Appleton, 1866), 117.

21. No relation, of course, to Lord Mansfield.

22. [Francis Hargrave], *An Argument in the Case of James Sommersett, a Negro. Wherein It Is Attempted to Demonstrate the Present Unlawfulness of Domestic Slavery in England. To Which Is Prefixed, a State of the Case. By Mr. Hargrave, One of the Counsel for the Negro* (London: For the Author, 1772).

in England. They appealed most forcefully to Mansfield in Samuel Estwick's *Considerations on the Negroe Cause* . . . (1772).[23] Relying heavily on the 1729 Yorke-Talbot opinion, Estwick insisted that the property relationship in slaves was recognized as legitimate by Parliament in the Royal African Company statutes. Even though this was a form of property "established by power and maintained by force," it was legitimate both in the metropolis and in the colonies. Thomas Thompson defended the slave trade and slavery against Sharp's natural-law arguments by admitting that all persons are free under natural law. "But absolute freedom is incompatible with civil establishments. Every man's liberty is restricted by national laws and natural privilege [*sic*] does rightly yield to legal constitutions."[24]

As 1772 wore on, it became apparent to Mansfield that he could not evade the dilemma thrust on him by Sharp and Hargrave on one hand, and the West India Interest on the other. Serjeant Davy in argument bluntly stated the first horn of the dilemma: "If the laws having attached upon him abroad are at all to affect him here it brings them all, either all the Laws of Virginia are to attach upon him here or none—for where will they draw the Line?"[25] Mansfield agreed: "The difficulty of adopting the relation, without adopting it in all its consequences, is indeed extreme; and yet, many of those consequences are absolutely contrary to the municipal law of England." He did not want to see the colonial tail wag the metropolitan dog in the matter of incorporating the law of slavery discipline into the English legal order. On the other hand, Mansfield continued, "the setting 14,000 or 15,000 men at once free loose by a solemn opinion, is much disagreeable in the effects it threatens." Not only would this racially alien mass of humanity be set free of their masters' discipline and support; the masters' property rights would be shaken—no light matter to a conservative jurist like Mansfield.[26]

23. "A West Indian" [Samuel Estwick], *Considerations on the Negroe Cause Commonly So Called, Addressed to the Right Honourable Lord Mansfield, Lord Chief Justice of the Court of King's Bench, Etc.* (London: J. Dodsley, 1772).

24. Tho. Thompson, *The African Trade for Negro Slaves, Shewn to Be Consistent with Principles of Humanity, and with the Laws of Revealed Religion* (Canterbury: Simmons and Kirkby, n.d. [1772?]), 23.

25. Transcript of Davy's argument in Granville Sharp transcripts, N-YHS.

26. The quotations from counsels' arguments and Mansfield's exchanges with them are from the report of *Somerset* v. *Stewart*, Lofft 1, 98 Eng. Rep. 499 (K.B. 1772), reprinted at 20 Howell's State Trials 2. There is some disagree-

Hence Mansfield settled on a dual strategy to dispose of the unwelcome case before him. First, he reaffirmed one point of English law concerning slaves that he thought was well settled—"Contract for slave of a slave is good here; the sale is a matter to which the law properly and readily attaches"—and threw out several hints that the West India Interest resort to Parliament (where they had considerable influence as well as a few members) to have other points of the law resolved by statute. (They did so, but without success.)[27] Second, he reduced the issue before him to the narrowest possible scope. The only question was whether any "coercion can be exercised in this country, on a slave according to the *American* laws"; and this was to be determined solely on the basis of the pleadings.

Yet the impact Mansfield so earnestly sought to restrict got out of bounds as soon as he tried to explain the result he reached, which was to discharge Somerset on the writ. He spoke to two points, one relating to conflict of laws, and the other to the opposition of natural and positive law, and on both his utterances gave the *Somerset* opinion its lasting and reverberating influence. On the conflicts question, Mansfield asserted that "so high an act of dominion [i.e. seizing a slave for sale abroad] must be recognized by the law of the country where it is used. The power of a master over his slave has been extremely different, in different countries." Inconclusive though this statement seems, standing alone and out of context, it nonetheless laid down a general rule that the *lex domicilii* by which a person is held in slavery does not of its own force determine the slave's status in England, even though the *lex fori* and the *lex domicilii* are based on the same general corpus of statutory and common law, as was true of the metropolis and the colonies in the British empire.[28] This complicated the workings of the American federal system.

Mansfield's statement on natural versus positive law had an even

---

ment as to just what Mansfield said. For a review of that controversy and a justification for relying on Lofft's report (which, it should be added, seems to have been the only report of *Somerset* known to American abolitionists), see appendix to Wiecek, "*Somerset:* Lord Mansfield and the Legitimacy of Slavery in the Anglo-American World."

27. Edward Fiddes, "Lord Mansfield and the Sommersett Case," *Law Q. Rev.,* 50 (1934), at 508–509.

28. Conflict of laws is a technical topic, and some use of its terms is unavoidable. *Lex domicilii* is the law of an individual's domicile; *lex fori* is a law of the jurisdiction in which the litigation takes place.

greater impact. "The state of slavery is of such a nature, that it is incapable of being introduced on any reasons, moral or political; but only [by] positive law, which preserves its force long after the reasons, occasion, and time itself from whence it was created, is erased from memory: It's so odious, that nothing can be suffered to support it but positive law." These forceful assertions raised more questions than they answered. Did "positive law" include custom? Did it require that the legislative or executive authority actually establish slavery, rather than merely recognize its existence in slave codes? If slavery was so contrary to natural law, could even positive law establish it? Mansfield concluded his brief opinion on a note of "I-told-you-so" to the planters: "Whatever inconveniences, therefore may follow from a decision, I cannot say this case is allowed or approved by the law of England; and therefore the black must be discharged."

Despite the sweep and implications of its language, this opinion did not abolish slavery even in England itself, as Mansfield and his contemporaries were at pains to point out.[29] *Somerset* notwithstanding, a qualified form of slavery continued to exist in England until final emancipation in 1833.[30] Far from abolishing slavery *in toto*, Mansfield merely held that, whatever else the master might do about or with his claimed slave, he could not forcibly send him out of the realm, and that habeas corpus was available to the black to forestall such a threatened deportation.

Mansfield's labored efforts to restrict the impact of his holding did not satisfy the West India Interest, however. One of their publicists, Edward Long, promptly published a diatribe refuting all of Sharp's contentions and criticizing Mansfield's judgment for its lack of supportive reasoning.[31] Long sarcastically predicted that "the name of **** M—— shall henceforth become more popular among the

29. Daines Barrington, *Observations on the More Ancient Statutes from Magna Charta to the Twenty-first of James I cap. XXVII* . . . (London: W. Bowyer & J. Nicholes, 1775), 312.

30. F. O. Shyllon, *Black Slaves in Britain* (London: Oxford Univ. Press, 1974), chs. 10–13; Walvin, *Black and White*, chs. 8–13.

31. "A Planter" [Edward Long], *Candid Reflections upon the Judgment Lately Awarded by the Court of King's Bench, on What Is Commonly Called "The Negroe Cause"* (London: T. Lowndes, 1772), iii. Quotations and arguments that follow are from pp. 3, 10, 55, 49, 58–59. The copy of this pamphlet in the Library of Yale University contains numerous indignant marginal annotations by Granville Sharp. See also the proslavery "A West Indian," "Considerations on a Late Determination in the Court of King's Bench on the Negroe Cause," *Gentleman's Magazine* (July 1772), 307–308.

Quacoes and Quashebas of America, than that of patriot Wilkes once was among the porter-swilling swains of St. Giles." He argued that slavery was a "species" of villeinage, supported explicitly by parliamentary statutes protecting the African trade, and that the laws concerning personal liberty from Magna Charta down through the Habeas Corpus Act were properly applicable only to free men. Long concluded with an exaggeration that, though unfounded in the substance of Mansfield's judgment, was strikingly predictive: all the West Indian colonial slave laws were nullified, implicitly, by Mansfield's holding.

In spite of the restricted scope of the holding, and the efforts of Mansfield and others to emphasize how narrow it was and to foreclose more liberating possibilities that appeared in the interstices of Mansfield's ideas, *Somerset* burst the confines of its author's judgment. This occurred chiefly for two reasons. First, the judgment itself, discharging a black alleged to be a slave by a writ of habeas corpus, struck a telling blow at slavery. The mere fact that habeas corpus was available to any black to test the legitimacy of his putative master's claim to him was in itself an extension of the scope of the Great Writ and a threat to the security of slavery in England. Second, Mansfield's statements justifying the result had implications for the imperial relation, for conflict of laws, and for the future of natural law that Mansfield probably did not foresee, and that the defenders of slavery later had cause to regret.

British courts began almost immediately to wrestle with the ambiguities and potentialities of Mansfield's opinion. Some English judges assumed that *Somerset* had worked an absolute abolition of slavery in England. In an unreported case, *Cay v. Crichton* (1773) [32] decided in the year after *Somerset*, the presiding judge held that the determination had retroactive effect, so that slavery had never had a legitimate existence in England. In a Scottish case, *Knight v. Wedderburn* (1778), counsel cited *Somerset* only for its narrow and technically correct holding, but the Court of Sessions went further, stating that a master's rights under Jamaican law were "unjust" in Scotland, so that a master could exercise no form of control whatever over a slave there. [33] A writer in the *Virginia Gazette* commented

---

32. A report of the decision in this case appears in the Granville Sharp transcripts, N-YHS.
33. 8 Fac. Dec. 5, Mor. 14545 (Scot. Court of Sessions, 1778).

on the proposal to have Parliament enact a statute regulating the master-slave relationship in England by asking "Can any human Law abrogate the divine? The Laws of Nature are the Laws of God. By those Laws, a Negro cannot be less free than a Man of any other Complexion."[34]

Such interpretations vexed Mansfield. In a private conversation with Thomas Hutchinson, the exiled American Loyalist, Mansfield insisted that "there had been no determination that [slaves] were free, the judgment (meaning the case of Somerset) went no further than to determine the master had no right to compel the slave to go into a foreign country."[35] Mansfield soon found an opportunity to lecture the English bar on the limits of the *Somerset* opinion in the case of *Rex* v. *Inhabitants of Thames Ditton* (1785), an action to determine whether a parish was responsible for the support of a pauper under the poor laws; the pauper was a black who had been brought to England a slave.[36] In the course of an involved argument concerning interpretation of the poor laws, counsel suggested that King's Bench had never decided that a slave brought into England was bound to serve his master. Mansfield interjected and corrected him reprovingly: "the determination got no further than that the master cannot by force compel him to go out of the kingdom," a precise construction of the holding of *Somerset*. Counsel tried again, suggesting that the slave relationship implied a hiring, and again Mansfield cut short that line of argument: "The case of *Somerset* is the only one on this subject. Where slaves have been brought here, and have commenced actions for their wages, I have always non-suited the plaintiff."

The potentialities of the *Somerset* opinion that Mansfield was trying to restrain quickly proved irrepressible. Aphorisms about slaves being liberated once they set foot on English ground or breathed English air fired the imagination of the poet William Cowper, who wrote, inaccurately, that

> Slaves cannot breathe in England, if their lungs
> Receive our air, that moment they are free
> They touch our country, and their shackles fall.[37]

34. Purdie & Dixon's *Virginia Gazette*, 20 Aug. 1772.
35. Peter O. Hutchinson, ed., *The Diary and Letters of . . . Thomas Hutchinson . . .* (London: Sampson Low et al., 1883–86), II, 277 (diary entry 29 Aug. 1779).
36. 4 Doug. 300, 99 Eng. Rep. 891 (K.B. 1785).
37. An unreported precedent, *Cartwright's Case* (1569), was said to have

Edward Christian, one of Blackstone's early American editors, observed with more accuracy that "it is not to the soil or to the air of England that negroes are indebted for their liberty, but to the efficacy of the writ of habeas corpus."[38]

Somerset had taken on a life of its own, independent of its factual circumstanes and of its author's later construction. Justices in both the Court of Common Pleas and King's Bench read it to mean that a black slave, at least while in England, was, in the words of Lord Chief Justice Alvanley, "as free as any one of us."[39] In *Forbes* v. *Cochrane & Cockburn* (1824)[40] Justice Holroyd stated that when a slave "puts his foot on the shores of this country, his slavery is at an end" simply because there is no positive law of England that sanctions slavery. His colleague, Justice Best, went further, construing *Somerset* to have held "on the high ground of natural right" that slavery is "inconsistent with the genius of the English constitution," and that human beings could not be the subject matter of property. Though Lord Chancellor Eldon disagreed, in the course of abolition debates in the House of Lords, and maintained that it was most unlikely that slavery was "contrary to the genius of the British constitution" in view of the Royal African Company statutes, William Holdsworth, premier historian of English law, considered Best's interpretation not only the "popular view," but also "substantially correct."[41]

Henry Pye, writing seventeen years after *Somerset*, went so far as to claim that slavery might be illegitimate in the islands as well as the metropolis because it was "not authorized by the common law of England" under which "every man is free" and entitled to an "equal distribution of justice." He advanced ideas later current among American abolitionists when he argued that every man in England, and in the islands as well, were "entitled to the full protection of the

---

held that "England was too pure an Air for Slaves to breath in"; quoted from *Rushworth's Historical Collections* in Helen T. Catterall, ed., *Judicial Cases concerning American Slavery and the Negro* (Washington: Carnegie Institution, 1926–1936), I, 9; Cowper, "The Task," Book II, in H. S. Milford, ed., *Cowper: Poetical Works* (London: Oxford Univ. Press, 1967), 147.

38. Blackstone, *Commentaries,* ed., Edward Christian (New York: Duyckinck, Long, Collins, 1822), editor's note p. 127.

39. *Williams* v. *Brown*, 3 Bos. & P. 69, 127 Eng. Rep. 39 (Common Pleas, 1802).

40. 2 Barn. & Cres. 448, 107 Eng. Rep. 450 (K.B., 1824).

41. XIV Hansard's *Parliamentary Debates*, 2d ser., col. 1156, (7 Mar. 1826); William S. Holdsworth, *A History of English Law* (London: Methuen, 1922–1938), XI, 247.

laws as to his life, his property, and his liberty. These are fundamental principles of the constitution, which any provincial, and subordinate legislature must be incompetent to repeal in any part of the British dominions."[42] This view, however, was atypical in its time. Whatever the theoretical impact of *Somerset* on slavery in England, it was the clear consensus among English authorities that the opinion, and the whole sweep of the metropolitan law of personal liberty, left slavery in the islands intact. The law clerk of a House of Commons committee investigating colonial slavery at the time Pye was writing expressed this consensus: "the Privileges of England are so universally extensive, as not to admit of the least Thing called Slavery," he conceded. But in the islands, "the Cases and Circumstances of Things were wonderfully altered," and slavery existed with metropolitan and colonial sanction, deriving its legitimacy from the original sale of slaves by African chieftains.[43]

Somerset's libertarian implications remained, nonetheless, as a shadow across the legality and security of colonial slavery. Conservative jurists felt a need to ground such interpretive flights as Pye's and Best's, and were cheered by an opinion from William Scott, Lord Stowell, who presided over the High Court of Admiralty. This decision, known variously as the case of *The Slave Grace* or as *Rex v. Allen* (1827), was considered by contemporaries, including so eminent an authority as Justice Joseph Story of the United States Supreme Court, to be the definitive reinterpretation of the real meaning of *Somerset*.[44] The circumstances of *Grace* were almost perfectly designed to test the implications of *Somerset*. Grace had been brought by her mistress from Antigua to England, where they resided for a year. They then went back to Antigua where the slave was seized by admiralty officials as illegally imported, the officials' assumption being that she became free in England and was thus a free person being brought into slavery. Stowell affirmed a judgment for the mistress, on the grounds that the slave, on her return to Antigua,

42. *Doubts concerning the Legality of Slavery in Any Part of the British Dominions* (London: John Stockdale, 1789), 11–13. The attribution to Pye is made on the copy in the Library of Yale University.
43. "General View of the Principles on Which This System of Laws Appears to Have Been Originally Founded," House of Commons *Accounts and Papers,* XXVI (1789), no. 646a, pt. iii (no pagination).
44. 2 Hag. Adm. 94, 166 Eng. Rep. 179 (1827); Story to Stowell, 22 Sept. 1828, in William W. Story, ed., *Life and Letters of Joseph Story* (Boston: Little and Brown, 1851), I, 558.

reassumed her status as a slave, which was only suspended, not terminated, during her stay in England. This has been called the "reattachment" doctrine. Most of Stowell's long and elaborate opinion was an effort to prune the luxuriant growth of antislavery interpretation stimulated by *Somerset.* He insisted that slavery had a legitimate origin in "ancient custom," which is "generally recognized as a just foundation of all law." Here Stowell drew on a tradition of western law extending back beyond Justinian, whose compilers wrote in the *Institutes* that "ancient customs, when approved by the consent of those who follow them, are like statute."[45] This was potentially a forceful legitimating basis for slavery. Though it did not exist in England, slavery did have a legal existence in the colonies; its incompatibility was only with English law, and even in England the incompatibility extended no further than to confer on the slave a "sort of limited liberty" that evaporated upon return to a slave jurisdiction.

There was a deeper connection between *Somerset* and *Grace,* however. Under both metropolitan and colonial law, the slave was considered in the eyes of the law as a thing, something capable of being owned. Hence Mansfield's emphasis on the validity of contracts for sale of a slave. But in order to maintain a system of slavery like that in the island and mainland colonies, more was needed, a superstructure of laws regulating the conduct of slaves and the rights of masters. Where that was lacking, as in England, a slave seeking to assert his personal liberty in the forum jurisdiction had a good chance of success, there simply being no law supporting the master's authority. In the islands, however, where such a superstructure already existed, jurists were not about to overthrow the legal and social order simply out of devotion to the ideal of human liberty.[46]

Stowell expressed the reattachment principle of *Grace* in a striking metaphor. For slaves coming into England, English laws had "put their liberty, as it were, into a sort of parenthesis." Parenthetical or not, the liberty that slaves enjoyed in England was extended to them in the colonies by Parliament in the Abolition Act of 1833.[47] Though colonial emancipation let loose a good deal of constitutional debate,

45. *The Institutes of Justinian,* trans. J. B. Moyle, 5th ed. (Oxford: Clarendon, 1913), lib. I, tit. 2.
46. Elsa V. Goveia, "The West Indian Slave Laws of the Eighteenth Century," *Revista de Ciencias Sociales,* 4 (1960), 75–105, at 82–83.
47. 3 & 4 Will. 4, c. 73.

few in the end doubted Parliament's power to bind the colonies.[48] But what was apparently a settled question by 1833 was not at all so before the American Revolution, and one of the most unsettling implications of Mansfield's opinion was the possibility that slavery, being incompatible with the English constitution, might somehow be illegitimate in the colonies.

Mansfield's premise that slavery was so contrary to natural law that it could be established only by positive law passed over into American constitutional development. In Robert Cover's judgment, the case "gave institutional recognition to antislavery morality, incorporating that view of natural law as a common law and conflict-of-law principle."[49] This tenet had profound implications. Where no positive law established slavery, it did not exist. To jurists who assumed with Blackstone that no positive law could override the dictates of natural law, slavery could not be legitimate anywhere, even where it did enjoy the sanction of positive law. Hence radical abolitionists drew from the doctrines of *Somerset* the basis for their contention that slavery was everywhere unconstitutional in America. Moderate abolitionists did not go so far. Admitting with Mansfield that positive law could establish slavery, they nevertheless indulged no presumptions in favor of the peculiar institution, and insisted that when a slave leaves the jurisdiction under whose laws he was enslaved, and entered into a free state, he became free and could not again be reenslaved. They discarded the *Grace* reattachment doctrine.

The misunderstandings of the *Somerset* opinion became even more important. Though Mansfield had not said, or even implied, that slavery was incompatible with the British constitution or that a slave became free the moment he came into England, some American abolitionists followed the lead of Justice Best and assumed that either of these ideas was a necessary inference from Mansfield's judgment. They thereby created a doctrine that we may call "neo-*Somerset*": that slavery, being incompatible with the common law, did not have a legal origin in the United States and was incompatible with the Constitution. This too led in both radical and moderate directions.

48. Robert L. Schuyler, *Parliament and the British Empire: Some Constitutional Controversies concerning Imperial Legislative Jurisdiction* (New York: Columbia Univ. Press, 1929), ch. 4.

49. Robert M. Cover, *Justice Accused: Antislavery and the Judicial Process* (New Haven: Yale Univ. Press, 1975), 98; see also pp. 87–88.

Radicals maintained that slavery was illegal in the states, and that therefore the power of the federal government should be used to extirpate it there. Moderates, rejecting that view as an insupportable departure from the premises of the American federal system, upheld a more narrow doctrine. They claimed that, under natural law, freedom was the normal condition of man, and that slavery, where established by positive law, was an anomaly and an exception to this natural state. They therefore insisted that the federal government be divorced from any support for slavery. This gave way to the more comprehensive doctrine "Freedom national, slavery sectional," which moderates used in their effort to keep slavery out of the western territories.

Somerset thus passed into the constitutional thought not only of radical abolitionists, but into that of the moderates who first controlled the Liberty party, and who later adopted Free Soil doctrines and went on to constitute one of the nuclei of the Republican party. A direct line of expanding doctrinal influence stretches from Mansfield's reluctant concession to the abolitionist fire of Granville Sharp and Francis Hargrave, through the early jurisprudence of both northern and southern state courts that absorbed *Somerset* into American case law, on to the abolitionists who founded the American Anti-Slavery Society, and then to the radicals who wished to use federal powers to abolish slavery through judicial or legislative action, and to the moderates who meant only to contain slavery within the southern states.

Few English judicial decisions have figured so prominently in the growth of American constitutional law. Cited innumerable times by opponents and defenders of slavery, *Somerset* long held sway over the thinking of Americans concerned about the relationship between slavery and law. *Somerset* was emblematic of Justice Oliver Wendell Holmes's ambition for jurists: to Mansfield unwittingly was due "the secret isolated joy of the thinker, who knows that, a hundred years after he is dead and forgotten, men who never heard of him will be moving to the measure of his thought."[50]

50. "The Profession of the Law," in Oliver Wendell Holmes, Jr., *Collected Legal Papers* (New York: Harcourt, Brace, 1920), 32.

CHAPTER 2

Antislavery during and after
the American Revolution

The doctrines of *Somerset* reinforced a secular tendency that began to emerge in American antislavery arguments during the Revolution. *Somerset* enriched the substantive content of Revolutionary ideology and in one province, Massachusetts, provided doctrinal support for freedom suits in the state courts. Several northern states either abolished slavery outright or began gradual emancipation. The Declaration of Independence and the republican constitutions of the new states formalized the dissonance between slavery and the ideals of the Revolution. Slavery eroded in the southern states because the upheaval of war enabled many blacks to seize freedom by running away or to earn it by service in the armies. The national government in its first constitutive document, the Articles of Confederation, and in its early laws took steps that inconsistently strengthened and weakened the prospects of slavery.

The *Somerset* decision and the arguments it spawned were promptly disseminated in the colonies. An extract of Estwick's *Considerations on the Negro Cause* appeared in the *Virginia Gazette* in November, 1772.[1] Sharp's *Representation* and Hargrave's *Argument* were reprinted in Boston in 1773 and 1774 respectively. The *Virginia Gazette*'s London correspondent followed the argument closely, and that paper published a variant version of Mansfield's opinion as well as erroneous summaries of the holding within two months of its delivery.[2] But the debate over *Somerset* did not by any means begin

1. Rind's *Virginia Gazette*, 12 Nov. 1772.
2. Purdie & Dixon's *Virginia Gazette*, 4 June, 23 July, 30 July, 20 August, 27 August, and 10 September 1772.

the controversy over slavery in America. Throughout the eighteenth century Americans either expressed reservations about slavery's consonance with divine law, or attacked it outright. New England Puritans like Judge Samuel Sewall of the Massachusetts Bay Colony and Quakers in the middle colonies, led by Benjamin Lay, John Woolman, and Anthony Benezet, condemned slavery. Benezet in particular, whom David Brion Davis has aptly termed "a middleman of ideas,"[3] played a pivotal role in acclimating the secular content of Sharp's *Representation* to the religio-moral orientation of previous American antislavery. His role is strikingly illustrated in the migration of ideas about the secular illegitimacy of slavery.

In *A Short Account of That Part of Africa, Inhabited by the Negroes* (1762) Benezet copied a passage from an obscure but influential Scottish legal treatise, George Wallace's *A System of the Principles of the Law of Scotland* (1760), in which Wallace flatly denied that any sort of legal title could be held in man, and that therefore any pretended sale of a slave must be "ipso jure Void."[4] Granville Sharp, poking around a London bookstall in 1767, came across a copy of Benezet's tract, had it reprinted, and distributed it widely. Sharp was soon to begin working on the *Representation,* and perhaps the Wallace-Benezet claim of the secular illegitimacy of slavery, which was the central thesis of the *Representation,* influenced his thought. In any event, the idea recrossed the Atlantic with Sharp's pamphlet, and found its way, in a form altered by rapidly changing circumstances, back into two tracts that Benezet brought out after the Declaration of Independence. In *Serious Considerations on Several Important Subjects* (1778),[5] Benezet claimed that "nothing can more

3. David Brion Davis, "New Sidelights on Early Antislavery Radicalism," *Wm. & M. Q.,* 28 (1971), 585–594 at 591.
4. [Anthony Benezet], *A Short Account of That Part of Africa, Inhabited by the Negroes* . . . , 2d ed. (Philadelphia: W. Dunlap, 1762), 30–32. Benezet misspelled the Scottish jurist's name thus: Wallis. The citation of Benezet's works is as appropriate a place as any to mention that I have taken only one liberty in transcribing all primary sources quoted in this study: I have rendered all italicizations into Roman, my reason for doing so being that early practice in the use of italics was so haphazard that keeping them would be distracting and misleading to a modern reader. Otherwise I have preserved original spelling and punctuation.
5. [Anthony Benezet], *Serious Considerations on Several Important Subjects;* . . . *Observations on Slavery* . . . (Philadelphia: Joseph Crukshank, 1778), 28.

clearly and positively militate against the slavery of the Negroes," than the libertarian ideals of the Declaration. More specifically, in *Notes on the Slave Trade* (1780),[6] Benezet modified Sharp's argument, saying "it cannot be, that either war, or contract, can give any man such a property in another as he has in his sheep and oxen. . . . Liberty is the right of every human creature, . . . and no human law can deprive him of the right, which he derives from the law of nature." Thus in a trans-Atlantic intellectual exchange, the idea of the inherent illegitimacy of slavery went back and forth, from the Scot Wallace to the American Benezet to the Englishman Sharp, and thence back to Benezet.

By the time *Somerset's* ideas flowed into the mainstream of policy debate during the Revolution, Americans had already begun exploring the relationship between slavery and the principles that underlay the American cause. In Massachusetts, James Otis, Nathaniel Appleton, the Reverend Samuel Webster, and John Allen condemned slavery's opposition to "the law of nature." They were echoed by Tom Paine and Benjamin Rush in Pennsylvania, and cheered on by English friends of the American cause, including Sharp and Thomas Day.[7] Boston slaves participated in this debate. A group of them, one of whom bore the peculiarly suggestive name of Sambo Freeman, petitioned the General Court for emancipation, arguing that "the efforts made by the Legislature of this province in their last sessions to free themselves from Slavery gave us, who are in that deplorable state, a high degree of satisfaction."[8] Another group of Boston blacks reminded the Massachusetts legislators that "every principle from which America has acted in the course of her unhappy difficulties with Great-Britain, pleads stronger than a thousand arguments in favour of your petitioners."[9] Samuel Hopkins, in the leading anti-

6. [Anthony Benezet], *Notes on the Slave Trade* (Philadelphia: n.p., 1780), 8.

7. For surveys of American Revolutionary antislavery ideas, see Davis, *Problem of Slavery in the Age of Revolution.* chs. 3–7; and Duncan J. MacLeod, *Slavery, Race and the American Revolution* (London: Cambridge University Press, 1974).

8. This memorial is reprinted in "A British Bostonian" [John Allen?], *An Oration on the Beauties of Liberty, or The Essential Rights of the Americans . . .* (Boston: E. Russell, 1773), 15.

9. The petition, dated 1777, is in Parish transcripts, N-YHS, Massachusetts, folder 202; see also others collected in Herbert Aptheker, ed., *A Documentary History of the Negro People in the United States* (New York: Citadel, 1959–), I, 6–12; and in "Negro Petitions for Freedom," Mass. Hist. Soc. *Collections,* 5th ser., III, 432–437.

slavery tract of the Revolution, *A Dialogue concerning the Slavery of the Africans* (1776), summed up the argument to date and anticipated later themes of American abolition when he equated the moral evil of slavery itself with that of the slave trade, classified both as sin, emphasized the link between slavery and racism, and, in an idea utterly atypical for his time, called on the Continental Congress to abolish slavery throughout the United States.[10]

Somerset was received by a legalistically inclined people familiar with the natural-law tradition. Though English abolitionists had used concepts of natural law to strike at slavery, natural law had become most readily acclimated in America through the Revolutionary debates. Thus the Massachusetts General Court considered bills declaring slavery to be "contrary to ye laws of Nature" and prohibiting the sale of two slaves in the Bay State on the grounds that such a sale would be "a direct violation of the Natural rights alike vested in all men."[11] The topic assigned for the formal debate that was then part of the Harvard College commencement exercises in 1773 was whether slavery was "agreable [*sic*] to the law of nature" even though sanctioned by positive law.[12]

During the Revolution, slaves in the Bay Colony had begun freedom suits in the colony courts. Though neither the bench nor the bar there seems to have been antislavery in outlook, counsel in such suits after 1768 regularly questioned the legitimacy of slavery. Such questions, when raised, had a way of answering themselves, as when a judge mused that "this is a Contest between Liberty and Property—both of great Consequence. But Liberty of most importance of the two."[13] Eclectically drawing on a variety of sources, including the *Institutes* of Justinian, Genesis, Voltaire, and metropolitan or colonial statutes, Massachusetts lawyers argued, echoing Lord Coke and James

10. Samuel Hopkins, *A Dialogue, concerning the Slavery of the Africans; Shewing It to Be the Duty and Interest of the American Colonies to Emancipate All Their African Slaves* . . . (Norwich: Judah P. Spooner, 1776). The *Dialogue* was reprinted in a second edition, 1785, with the word "Colonies" appropriately changed to "States."
11. Copies of the bills are in the Parish transcripts, N-YHS, Massachusetts, folder 202.
12. [Theodore Parsons and Eliphalet Pearson], *A Forensic Dispute on the Legality of Enslaving the Africans, Held at the Public Commencement in Cambridge* . . . (Boston: John Boyle, 1773). A similar disputation topic had been assigned at the College of Philadelphia (the modern University of Pennsylvania) in 1768: [Philadelphia] *Pennsylvania Chronicle*, 28 Nov. 1768.
13. Quoted in L. Kinvin Wroth and Hiller B. Zobel, eds., *The Legal Papers of John Adams* (Cambridge: Harvard Univ. Press, 1965), II, 54.

Otis, that "an act of parliament against natural Equity . . . is void."[14] When Boston-area blacks heard of the result of *Somerset,* they resorted to the courts more frequently, seeking not only freedom but even recovery in *quantum meruit.*[15]

Arguments in these cases took the radical ground that slavery was contrary to the common law, and the more moderate position that the petitioners could not be enslaved because there was no positive law of slavery in Massachusetts.[16] According to a contemporary account, such arguments, or at least the suits of the blacks, were invariably successful.[17] Thomas Hutchinson, erstwhile acting Governor of Massachusetts, recalled in 1779 that after *Somerset* became known in the colonies, "all the Americans who had bought Blacks, had, as far as I knew, relinquished their property in them, and rather agreed to give them wages, or suffered them to go free," a view concurred in by the contemporary historian of the Revolution, Jeremy Belknap.[18] The oral tradition of these arguments and suits later led Lemuel Shaw, antebellum Chief Justice of the Supreme Judicial Court, to speculate that possibly *Somerset,* of its own force, had abolished slavery in Massachusetts.[19]

The rudiments of an antislavery constitutional position emerged from these Massachusetts freedom suits and legislative memorials. One pamphleteer argued that slavery, or at least the slave trade, was "repugnant to the Charter of this Province, which must be deemed the great Bulwark and Support of our Liberty."[20] The provision referred

14. Ibid., 67.
15. [Jeremy Belknap], "Queries respecting the Slavery and Emancipation of Negroes in Massachusetts, Proposed by the Hon. Judge Tucker of Virginia, and Answered by the Rev. Dr. Belknap," Mass. Hist. Soc. *Collections,* 1st ser., IV, 202 (1795). *Quantum meruit* was a count in common-law pleading that demanded compensation for services on the grounds of implied contract.
16. E. A. Holyoke to Jeremy Belknap, quoted in [Jeremy Belknap], "Letters and Documents relating to Slavery in Massachusetts," Mass. Hist. Soc. *Collections,* 5th ser., III (1877), 400.
17. Samuel Dexter to Jeremy Belknap, 23 Feb. 1795, in [Belknap], "Letters and Documents relating to Slavery in Massachusetts," 386.
18. Hutchinson, ed., *Diary and Letters of Thomas Hutchinson,* II, 276–277 (diary entry 29 Aug. 1779); [Belknap], "Queries," 201.
19. *Commonwealth v. Aves,* 18 Pick. (35 Mass.) 193 (1836). Shaw was in error. The legal institution of slavery hung on in Massachusetts well after Somerset; Moore, *Notes on the History of Slavery in Massachusetts,* 124.
20. "A Lover of Constitutional Liberty," *The Appendix; or, Some Observations of the Expediency of the Petition of the Africans, . . . Lately Presented to the General Assembly of This Province* (Boston: E. Russell, [1773]), 5.

to (from the Massachusetts royal charter of 1691, which merely repeated phraseology found in the other colonial charters) provided that all American migrants or natives "shall have and enjoy all Liberties and Immunities of free and natural subjects within any of the Dominions of Us, . . . as if they . . . were born within this Our Realm of England." This provision, asserted an anonymous correspondent in the Boston *Massachusetts Spy,* of its own force nullified all provincial slave laws,[21] an argument amplified in the freedom suits to include the claim that under English law, "no man could be deprived of his liberty but by the judgment of his peers."[22] Thus even before the Declaration of Independence, two themes of later constitutional antislavery argument had been articulated in America: the appeal to the privileges and immunities of Americans, and resort to natural-law concepts incorporated into considerations of due process. As linked with *Somerset,* such arguments could be carried even further, to work a positive emancipation of every slave setting foot on American colonial jurisdictions. This point was suggested by the Philadelphian Richard Wells, who contended that "by the laws of the English constitution, and by our own declaration, the instant a Negro sets his foot in America, he is as free as if he had landed in England."[23]

Doctrinally, the Massachusetts freedom suits culminated in the Quock Walker cases. The institution of slavery slowly petered out there, as Belknap and his contemporaries noted, but a long tradition had it that the judges of the Supreme Judicial Court declared it unconstitutional and abolished it all at once. Theophilus Parsons, who was a young member of the bar at the time Quock Walker's cases were tried, later observed that up to 1780, slavery was "tolerated" in Massachusetts. Relying on the oral tradition of the bar so important to lawyers of his time, Parsons then claimed that "the judges [of the Supreme Judicial Court] declared, that, by virtue of the first article of the Declaration of Rights, slavery in this state was no more."[24] He thereby contributed to the almost mythic belief that Quock Walker's "case" had abolished slavery in Massachusetts by a declaration that all men really were born free and equal. In reality,

21. [Boston] *Massachusetts Spy,* 28 Jan. 1773.
22. [Belknap], "Queries," 202–203.
23. "A Citizen of Philadelphia" [Richard Wells], *A Few Political Reflections Submitted to the Consideration of the British Colonies* (Philadelphia: John Dunlap, 1774), 82.
24. *Winchendon* v. *Hatfield,* 4 Tyng (4 Mass.) 122 (1808).

the Quock Walker cases, like *Somerset,* were neither so decisive nor so clear. They and other freedom suits did play a role in ridding the Bay State of slavery, but Jeremy Belknap's contemporary evaluation, that slavery was destroyed in the 1790s by a change in public sentiment, comes closer to the truth.[25]

There were three Quock Walker cases, *Walker* v. *Jennison* (1781), *Jennison* v. *Caldwell* (1781), and *Commonwealth* v. *Jennison* (1783), all arising out of the following facts: Nathaniel Jennison acquired title to a young black named Quock Walker sometime after 1763 through marriage to the widow of Walker's former owner. In 1781 Walker left Jennison and went to work for John Caldwell and Seth Caldwell, whereupon Jennison pursued him, beat him with a whip handle or stick, and detained him.[26] Neither of the first two cases was important for the development of antislavery doctrine in the Bay State, though in *Jennison* v. *Caldwell,* one of the counsel, Levi Lincoln, used arguments similar to Hargrave's in *Somerset* to persuade the jury that "the air of America is too pure for a slave to breathe in."[27] But Chief Justice William Cushing's similar remarks in the third of the cases, *Commonwealth* v. *Jennison,* were more authoritative.

As the title of the case indicates, this was a criminal prosecution of Walker's master, who was indicted for beating Walker. The case was tried before a jury and the Supreme Judicial Court, with Chief Justice Cushing presiding. It was customary at that time for the sitting jus-

25. [Belknap], "Queries," 201; Charles Deane, "Judge Lowell and the Massachusetts Declaration of Rights," *Mass. Hist. Soc. Proceedings 1873–1875,* 1st ser., XIII, 304; Cover, *Justice Accused,* 44–46.

26. William O'Brien, "Did the Jennison Case Outlaw Slavery in Massachusetts?" *Wm. & M. Q.,* 17 (1960), 217–241; John D. Cushing, "The Cushing Court and the Abolition of Slavery in Massachusetts: More Notes on the 'Quock Walker Case'," *Am. J. Legal Hist.,* 5 (1961), 118–144; Arthur Zilversmit, *The First Emancipation: The Abolition of Slavery in the North* (Chicago: Univ. of Chicago Press, 1967), 113–115; Zilversmit, "Quok Walker, Mumbet, and the Abolition of Slavery in Massachusetts," *Wm. & M. Q.,* 25 (1968), 614–624; Moore, *Notes on the History of Slavery in Massachusetts,* 204–223; Robert M. Spector, "The Quock Walker Cases (1781–83)—Slavery, Its Abolition, and Negro Citizenship in Early Massachusetts," *J. Negro Hist.,* 53 (1968), 12–32.

27. A literal transcription of Lincoln's notes of argument is in [Belknap], "Letters and Documents Relating to Slavery in Massachusetts," 438–442; an embroidered version of the argument is in Emory Washburn, "The Extinction of Slavery in Massachusetts," *Mass. Hist. Soc. Collections,* 4th ser., IV, 333–346 at 337.

tices to address the jury on points of law and fact. In the *Jennison* case, Cushing kept minutes of the evidence and his charge to the jury. It is here that we come as close as possible to historical proof of what Quock Walker's case "held."[28]

Cushing charged the jury that, though the province long recognized the presence of slaves and slavery, "nowhere do we find it [slavery] expressly established"; it had merely been a "usage" acknowledged by the statutes, something that "slid in upon us." Since the Revolution, however, "sentiments more favorable to the natural rights of mankind, and to that innate desire for liberty which heaven, without regard to complexion or shape, has planted in the human breast— have prevailed since the glorious struggle for our rights began." These sentiments led the framers of the 1780 Massachusetts constitution to adopt Article I of the Declaration of Rights, which provided that "All men are born free and equal, and have certain natural, essential, and unalienable rights; among which may be reckoned the rights of enjoying and defending their lives and liberties; that of acquiring, possessing, and protecting property; in fine, that of seeking their safety and happiness."[29] "In short," Cushing concluded, "without resorting to implication in constructing [*sic*] the constitution, slavery is in my judgment as effectively abolished as it can be by the granting of rights and privileges wholly incompatible and repugnant to its existence . . . perpetual servitude can no longer be tolerated in our government."

Jennison was convicted and fined 40 shillings, though we do not know whether this was a result of Cushing's instructions, or whether the jury went off on some other ground. Because of the ambiguity of the cases, it cannot be said that any one of them held slavery unconstitutional. At most, Walker's was the most famous of a number of freedom suits brought in Massachusetts after 1769. Together with the general desuetude of slavery in Massachusetts, manumissions, running away, conversion to term servitude, payment of wages, antislavery petitions and bills in the General Court, and antislavery pamphleteering, the freedom suits of the period 1760 to 1790 molded

28. Cushing's charge is in Cushing, "Cushing Court." The version in [Horace Gray], "The Commonwealth v. Nathaniel Jennison," *Mass. Hist. Soc. Proceedings 1873–75,* 1st ser., XIII, 292–304, transcribed by Chief Justice Cushing's historically-minded remote successor on the bench, Chief Justice Gray, is from a draft in the handwriting of someone other than Cushing.

29. Francis N. Thorpe, comp., *The Federal and State Constitutions . . .* (Washington, D.C.: GPO, 1909), III, 1889.

public opinion in a consensus that slavery should wither away in the Bay State.

Slavery was abolished elsewhere by constitutional or statutory provisions. The simplest way to abolish slavery was to do so by constitutional declaration, the method eventually adopted in 1865 by the states and by the nation to destroy slavery everywhere. In the eighteenth century, only one state—or rather republic, for Vermont was independent at the time—chose this method. One other state, Delaware, in its constitution forbade the importation of slaves. The free states admitted to the Union in the nineteenth century inserted a prohibition of slavery in their new constitutions, though for all of them in the territorial stage (except Oregon) slavery had already been excluded by the terms of the Northwest Ordinance or the Missouri Compromise.

In the first article of its Declaration of Rights, the Vermont constitutional convention of 1777 adapted the phrasing of the 1776 Virginia Declaration of Rights, adding to it an extrapolation following the word "therefore":

That all men are born equally free and independent, and have certain natural, inherent and unalienable rights; among which are the enjoying and defending life and liberty; acquiring, possessing and protecting property; and pursuing and obtaining happiness and safety. Therefore, no male person, born in this country, or brought from over sea, ought to be holden by law to serve any person, as a servant, slave, or apprentice, after he arrives to the age of twenty-one years; nor female in like manner, after she arrives to the age of eighteen years; unless they are bound by their own consent after they arrive to such age, or bound by law for the payment of debts, damages, fines, costs or the like.[30]

This provision was implemented by a 1786 statute forbidding the sale or transportation of blacks out of the state, which stated that, by the Vermont Constitution, "the idea of slavery is expressly and totally exploded from our free government."[31] Slavery had never begun to take hold as an economic system in Vermont. In such a social climate, the libertarian ideals of the American revolution had the field to themselves. This meant only that Vermont did not have to deal with

30. Ibid., VI, 3739–3740.
31. "An Act to prevent the sale and transportation of Negroes and Molattoes out of this State," 30 Oct. 1786, in *Acts and Laws . . . of Vermont . . . 1786* (n.p., n.d.).

the problem of blacks in a white man's republic, rather than that it grappled with the problem successfully. It was not a dilemma resolved, but rather one never encountered, in the Green Mountains.

Rhode Island, Connecticut, New York, New Jersey, and Pennsylvania rid themselves of slavery by gradual abolition statutes. The Pennsylvania law of 1780, after a long preamble drafted by Tom Paine that mixed sentiments of revolutionary idealism with fulsome self-congratulations, liberated all *post-nati,* but bound them to service until the age of twenty-eight on the same terms as indentured servants.[32] It required the registration of all extant slaves, somewhat in the way that titles to real property were recorded by a registrar of deeds, to prevent the sale of slaves out-of-state in evasion of the act's spirit. Any slave not so registered by November following passage of the act was declared free. British abolitionists sought enactment of similar registration provisions forty years afterward in the struggle for colonial emancipation.

Though the statute explicity preserved some portions of the colonial black code, such as the reward for capture of runaways, the procedures for valuing condemned slaves, and the prohibition against slaves testifying against free men, it dismantled the remainder, particularly the criminal codes for blacks. To make doubly sure that its objectives were attained, the legislature limited all indentures for nonwhites to seven years (or age twenty-eight, in the case of minors) and provided that "no man or woman of any nation or colour, except the Negroes or Mulattoes who shall be registered as aforesaid, shall, at any time hereafter, be deemed, adjudged or holden, but as free men and free women." This was a forward-looking provision since it reversed the presumption that blacks were slaves. It not only placed the burden on the master to prove that a black was a slave, but also put him to the additional trouble and expense of registering anyone to whom he wanted to claim title.

There were still a considerable number of slaves in Philadelphia at the time of the statute's enactment, despite earlier Quaker disavowal of slaveholding, and there existed the possibility of more

32. "An Act for the Gradual Abolition of Slavery," ch. 881, in Alexander J. Dallas, comp., *Laws of the Commonwealth of Pennsylvania* (Philadelphia: Hall & Sellers, 1792–1801), I, 838–842. A *post-nati* ("after-born") statute was one that freed slaves born after passage of the act or after some specified future date.

coming in for temporary residence as servants to congressmen, federal officials, and diplomats, since Philadelphia at the time entertained hopes of becoming the new national capital. Hence the statute contained a "sojourner's" provision, permitting slaveowners temporarily resident in the state with the slaves to retain title for a definite term. This may have indirectly reflected the doctrines of *Somerset,* implying as it did that a sojourning slaveowner might otherwise be divested of his human property.

Eight years later Pennsylvania strengthened the abolition act by a statute freeing the slaves of persons who entered the state with an intention to reside there, forbidding slaves to be removed out of the state except with their consent, punishing the sale of slaves out of the state, providing that vessels fitted out in Pennsylvania ports for the slave trade would be forfeited to the state, prohibiting the separation of wives from husbands and children from parents, and heavily penalizing the kidnaping of blacks.[33] The 1780 and the 1788 acts continued to be the most forceful antislavery statutes in the United States until the 1840s; they effectively destroyed all but vestiges of slavery in Pennsylvania by the Jacksonian period, if not sooner.

Rhode Island and Connecticut also succeeded in passing *post-nati* gradual abolition statutes before 1790. Rhode Island's invoked the Declaration of Independence by declaring that "all men are entitled to life, liberty, and the pursuit of happiness, and the holding mankind in a state of slavery, as private property, which has gradually obtained by unrestrained custom and the permission of the laws, is repugnant to this principle." It freed all children born after 1 March 1784 and relieved the masters of their mother of the expense of raising them by binding them out, as with paupers, till the ages of twenty-one and eighteen for men and women respectively.[34] Any traces of slavery in Rhode Island remaining in the Jacksonian period were finally wiped out in the aftermath of the Dorr Rebellion (1842) by adoption of the 1843 constitution, which stated, with elemental simplicity, "Slavery will not be permitted in this state."[35]

Connecticut adopted a *post-nati* emancipation act in 1784 and supplemented it with statutes in 1788 and 1792 prohibiting citizens

33. Act of 1788 in Dallas, comp., *Laws of Pennsylvania,* II, 586–590.
34. Act of 1784 in John Russell Bartlett, ed., *Records of the Colony of Rhode Island and Providence Plantations, in New England* (Providence: A. Crawford Greene, 1856–1865), X, 7–8.
35. Art. I, §4, in Thorpe, *Federal and State Constitutions,* VI, 3223.

of the Nutmeg State from participating in the slave trade and from kidnaping blacks for sale into slavery elsewhere.[36] New York and New Jersey did not succeed in passing abolition acts till well after the Revolutionary period, when the statutes were enacted in response to a more advanced level of antislavery activity. Constitutional developments in Massachusetts settled the status of slavery in the territory of Maine, which did not separate from the mother state until 1820. In New Hampshire, slavery just seems to have faded away by inanition.

The New England aversion to slavery had its counterpart southwards, but the social context of southern Revolutionary-era antislavery made the application of antislavery doctrine more complex and difficult than it was in areas where slaves were nearly nonexistent. Southern opponents of slavery saw the consequences of emancipation more vividly than they felt the evils of continuing enslavement. Where the good of the whole society clashed with considerations of equity to blacks, Duncan MacLeod has concluded, "justice ceased to be an abstraction and became a calculation."[37] This is revealed in the southern interpretation of the Declaration of Independence and the 1776 Virginia Declaration of Rights, the predecessor of most other bills of rights in the state constitutions of the eighteenth and early nineteenth century. Thomas Jefferson's opening paragraph of the Declaration of Independence contained the pith of the case against slavery: "We hold these truths to be self-evident, that all men are created equal, that they are endowed by their Creator with certain unalienable Rights, that among these are Life, Liberty and the pursuit of Happiness." But did Jefferson's self-evident truths contain an implicit racial exception? Did the lines, properly read in the light of American social conditions of 1776, contain the word "white" before the word "men"? Contemporaneous and later events in Jefferson's state suggested that they did.

Less than a month before Jefferson wrote the Declaration, the Virginia Provincial Convention adopted the Virginia Declaration of Rights. George Mason, its author, had drafted Article I to read: "That all men are by nature equally free and independent, and have

36. *Acts and Laws of the State of Connecticut in America* (New London: Timothy Green, 1784), 233–235.
37. MacLeod, *Slavery, Race and the American Revolution,* 29 (quotation) and *passim.*

certain inherent rights, of which [   ] they cannot by any compact deprive or divest their posterity; namely, the enjoyment of life
and liberty, with the means of acquiring and possessing property, and
pursuing and obtaining happiness and safety." Despite its monoton-
ously rhythmic pairings, so congenial to lawyers, the Virginia Declaration was widely imitated in subsequent state bills of rights, including
the Massachusetts Declaration of 1780. But the Virginians who contemplated it on 12 June 1776 saw acutely what would be obvious to
others only over time: "all men" meant just that, and might have
included slaves. Rather than scrap an otherwise appealing restatement of Revolutionary ideals, the Convention amended Mason's
draft by inserting into the space indicated above by brackets the
phrase "when they enter into a state of society." Though this qualification appears ambiguous to a modern eye, the Virginians adopted it
specifically to exclude blacks from the benefits of the Declaration.[38]

The delegates' circumlocution nearly failed. Thirty years later,
Virginia's Chancellor George Wythe, who had been Jefferson's law
teacher, was quoted as having interpreted the Article to mean that
"freedom is the birthright of every human being [including blacks],
which sentiment is strongly inculcated by the first article of our 'political catechism,' the bill of rights." Virginia's Supreme Court of
Appeals found it necessary to remind Wythe of what the framers of
1776 well knew: blacks were an exception to the sonorous Declaration. The appellate court rebuked the Chancellor's indiscretion.[39]

But however ambivalent southern antislavery may have been, it
did produce one solid achievement: abolition of the foreign slave
trade. Throughout the eighteenth century, most of the colonies had
levied duties on the importation of slaves in order to stanch capital
outflow, limit rising indebtedness, and control the makeup of the
labor force and the aggregate black population.[40] The Privy Council
disallowed many of these, and the Board of Trade instructed gov-

38. A. E. Dick Howard, *Commentaries on the Constitution of Virginia*
(Charlottesville: Univ. Press of Virginia, 1974), I, 61–62.
39. *Hudgins* v. *Wrights,* 1 Hen. & M. 134 (Va. 1806).
40. The colonial legislation is conveniently summarized and excerpted in
W. E. B. DuBois, *The Suppression of the African Slave-Trade to the United
States of America, 1638–1870* (1896; rpt. New York: Schocken, 1969), app.
A. See Darold D. Wax, "Negro Import Duties in Colonial Virginia: A Study of
British Commercial Policy and Local Public Policy," *Virginia Mag. Hist. &
Biog.,* 79 (1971), 29–44.

ernors-designate to veto them, which provoked Jefferson to his condemnation of the slave trade in the passage deleted from the Declaration of Independence. In 1774, as part of its boycott-embargo-non-importation program, the First Continental Congress comprehensively withdrew American participation from the international slave trade, a ban reaffirmed just before independence.[41] Though adopted for self-serving rather than altruistic purposes, and often dishonored or ineffectually enforced, these resolutions were an important constitutional milestone. What then served as a national government had, after debate, formally adopted an official policy based on the premise that the importation of slaves was, for whatever reason, wrong. The resolutions set a precedent for the later workings of American federalism. They were the forerunner of constitutional provisions that empowered the federal government to abolish the foreign slave trade by statute. They also suggested to later abolitionists that the federal government might derive comparable powers over the internal slave trade from the commerce clause.

The national resolutions were supplemented by various state statutes, constitutional provisions, and resolves that abolished the foreign slave trade for individual states. The 1774 Continental Association and the April 1776 resolves were merely precatory, whereas the state statutes were legally binding. Rhode Island, of all the northern provinces the one most heavily involved in slaving, was the first to adopt an anti-importations act, a suggestive statute that indicated that blacks were no more welcome than slavery. After a preamble that could have been lifted out of contemporary antislavery polemics, the statute prohibited the importation of all Negro slaves, not just those brought in from Africa and the islands, and freed any imported in violation of the act.

But much of what the Rhode Island General Assembly gave with the right hand it took away with the left. The statute included the first sojourner's law to be enacted in what was to be the United States. It exempted from its coverage slaves aboard Rhode Island vessels who could not be sold in the West Indies, and required that such slaves be "exported" out of Rhode Island within a year. It also levied a £100 fine on persons who brought slaves into Rhode Island "clandestinely . . . in order that they may be free" and required the slave so

41. Worthington C. Ford, ed., *Journals of the Continental Congress 1774–1789* (Washington, D.C.: GPO, 1904–1936), I, 77; IV, 258.

brought in to be "sent out" of the province in the manner of non-resident paupers.[42] This statute, which might be considered the first antislavery act of the American nation, with its mixture of revolutionary idealism, negrophobia, and cautious respect for the master's title as a property right, was a paradigm of later efforts to abolish slavery by force of law.

After Rhode Island's action, all the new states prohibited the foreign trade by 1794.[43] New Jersey's act of 1786 was revealing on the motivation of its legislators: "the Principles of Justice and Humanity require, that the barbarous Custom of bringing the unoffending Africans from their native Country and Connections into a state of Slavery ought to be discountenanced"; but, of equal importance, "sound Policy also requires, in order to afford ample Support to such of the Community as depend upon their Labour for their daily Subsistence" that the state not increase the unfree black labor pool.[44]

State statutory abolition of the slave trade was neither comprehensive nor successful. To do the job adequately, the states would have had to prohibit their citizens and vessels from participating in the trade elsewhere, forbidden slavers from being fitted out in ports within their jurisdictions, prohibited taking slaves out of the state for sale, and penalized kidnaping. Not all states enacted such provisions. Even had they done so, their effectiveness would have remained problematical. As many Africans were imported into the United States, legally and illegally, between 1780 and 1810 as had been brought in during the entire previous 160 years that Americans had participated in the traffic, and illegal smuggling remained brisk until the Civil War.[45]

Where slavery died away in northern New England by desuetude and in New York by changing economic conditions, in the southern states slavery was weakened by the upheaval that accompanied the War for Independence. Black soldiering and running away presented difficult policy problems for southern legislators. When blacks volunteered for the state lines in the early days of the war, southern

42. Bartlett, comp., *Records of the Colony of Rhode Island,* VII, 251–253.
43. The statutes are summarized in DuBois, *Suppression of the Slave Trade,* apps. A and B.
44. Act of 2 March 1786, ch. 119, in *Acts of . . . New-Jersey* [1786] (Trenton: Isaac Collins, 1786).
45. Robert W. Fogel and Stanley L. Engerman, *Time on the Cross: The Economics of American Negro Slavery* (Boston: Little, Brown, 1974), 24 and figure 6, p. 25.

leaders in the state legislatures and the Continental Congress opposed their enlistment as "inconsistent with the [Revolutionary] principles."[46] But when the Loyalist Governor of Virginia, Lord Dunmore, offered freedom to black slaves and servants of either race who would take up arms for his majesty, Whigs reversed themselves and accepted enlistments by free blacks and slaves. Eventually about five thousand served with the patriot forces. Individual blacks distinguished themselves in action in various ways, a point not lost on later abolitionists.[47] Some served in integrated units, but by and large most blacks were relegated to more menial military functions: pioneers, drummers and fifers on land, messmen and powder monkeys at sea, a degraded status perpetuated in all later American wars until Korea. In smaller numbers, blacks also served as Loyalist troops.

Blacks who were not soldiers also presented problems and opportunities. Their massive presence in the South made them a potential fifth column, or, as the Loyalist Joseph Galloway opportunistically described them, "so many intestine enemies, being all slaves and desirous of freedom."[48] White manpower was diverted into slave constabulary duties, to such an extent that in March 1779, a time of heavy British pressure in the South, Daniel Huger of South Carolina had to admit that his state could not defend itself "by reason of the great proportion of citizens necessary to remain at home to prevent insurrection among the Negroes, and to prevent the desertion of them to the enemy."[49] But a problem could be transmuted into an opportunity. Virginia and South Carolina offered slaves as enlistment bounties, a practice that troubled James Madison, who unsuccessfully proposed liberating the slave and embodying him instead, an alternative that would "certainly be more consonant to the principles of liberty."[50]

46. Quoted in George H. Moore, *Historical Notes on the Employment of Negroes in the American Army of the Revolution* (New York: Charles T. Evans, 1862), 5; *Journals of the Continental Congress,* III, 263.

47. George Livermore, *An Historical Research respecting the Opinions of the Founders of the Republic on Negroes as Slaves, as Citizens, and as Soldiers* (Boston: John Wilson, 1862); William C. Nell, *The Colored Patriots of the American Revolution* (1855; rpt. New York: Arno, 1968).

48. Galloway to Lord Dartmouth, 23 Jan. 1778, in Benjamin F. Stevens, ed., *Facsimiles of Manuscripts in European Archives relating to America 1773–1783* (London: Malby, 1889–95), XXIV, no. 2079.

49. *Journals of the Continental Congress,* XIII, 386.

50. James Madison to Joseph Jones, 28 Nov. 1780, in William T. Hutchinson and William M. E. Rachal, eds., *The Papers of James Madison* (Chicago: Univ. of Chicago Press, 1962–), II, 209.

The greatest practical blow to slavery during the war was the opportunity that wartime dislocations gave to voluntary and involuntary emancipation. It is impossible to estimate how many blacks became free because of the war; no one kept even an informal count, and the official American claims for slaves appropriated by the British, which might have served as a crude index, are suspect for obvious reasons. The foremost scholar of black history in the Revolutionary period, Benjamin Quarles, could conclude only that the number of slaves who ran away to the British was in "the tens of thousands."[51] And this vague figure does not take into account those slaves who decamped but did not end up with the British, who went instead into the cities, to sea, to the Spanish, to distant states, to East Florida, or into the woods and swamps.

These varying pressures on slavery—its manifest opposition to the ideals of the Revolution, as well as the hemorrhaging of the system brought on by slaves soldiering and decamping—weakened its institutional power, at least in the states above South Carolina, but it did not slow the absolute quantitative growth of the slave population. In 1760, there had been 325,000 slaves in the British mainland colonies. Thirty years later, the first census (1790) found 698,000 slaves in the United States, plus 60,000 free blacks.[52] If these figures

51. Benjamin Quarles, *The Negro in the American Revolution* (Chapel Hill: Univ. of North Carolina Press, 1961), 119.

52. The computation of ratios of slave to free in the American black population for 1760 and 1790 is imprecise, particularly for the earlier date, due, among other things, to the fact that many blacks escaped enumeration because they were fugitives or for some other reason. I have arbitrarily used figures rounded off from those in Peter M. Bergman, *The Chronological History of the Negro in America* (New York: Harper & Row, 1969), 40, 68. Figures for the later date correspond roughly with those in United States Bureau of the Census, *Negro Population in the United States, 1790–1915* (Washington, D.C.: GPO, 1918), 57. Karl E. Taueber and Alma F. Taueber estimate that in 1790, 8 percent of the total black population was free; "The Negro Population in the United States," in John P. Davis, *American Negro Reference Book* (Englewood Cliffs: Prentice-Hall, 1966), 100. If the 325,000 figure for slaves cited in text is correct, then the proportion of free blacks in the mainland colonies' population of 1760 must have been statistically insignificant; the figure for the total black population given in Bureau of the Census, *Historical Statistics of the United States: Colonial Times to 1957* (Washington, D.C.: GPO, 1965), p. 756, ser. Z 1–19, being 325,806. This conclusion is supported by Robert V. Wells, *The Population of the British Colonies in America before 1776: A Survey of Census Data* (Princeton: Princeton Univ. Press, 1975), 39, 291. For other studies of the colonial population that provide data respecting blacks, see Stella H. Sutherland, *Population Distribution in Colonial America* (New

are even remotely accurate, the slave population in the new nation roughly doubled during the Revolutionary and Confederation periods, indicating that the antislavery tendencies of the Revolution did little to stem the growth of the American slave population, which was due to importations and natural increase.

Aside from Samuel Hopkins' unique suggestion that the Continental Congress abolish slavery, no one in 1776 proposed that the new national government should have any authority to abolish or control slavery in the states. The federal consensus was a universal working assumption at Independence. Nonetheless, the Continental Congresses discovered that the involvement of the national government with slavery was inescapable and the consensus steadily eroded after that. Slavery issues began troubling Congress less than a month after Independence. The Second Congress had to deal with the problem of allocating the benefits and burdens to the states, and, more specifically, the means by which the wealth of the states was to be measured so as to allot financial requisitions equitably. In debates over apportioning taxes on a per capita basis, several southern spokesmen vigorously objected to including Negroes in the count. Though their economic and political self-interest was obvious, they also had other considerations on their minds. To count black heads as well as white in the per capita valuation would perhaps challenge the slave's status as a chattel by emphasizing his status as a human. On 30 July 1776, Thomas Lynch of South Carolina insisted bluntly: "If it is debated, whether their slaves are their property, there is an end of the confederation. Our slaves being our property, why should they be taxed more than the land, sheep, cattle, horses, &c?" To this first southern threat of disunion, Benjamin Franklin, then representing Pennsylvania, acidly replied that there was one important difference: "Sheep will never make any insurrections."[53]

A congressional committee tried seven years later to finesse this persistent issue by a compromise that, though not adopted, was to

---

York: Columbia Univ. Press, 1936), and Evarts B. Greene and Virginia D. Harrington, *American Population before the Federal Census of 1790* (New York: Columbia Univ. Press, 1932). The precise accuracy of the figures is not important for our purposes here, though. Even allowing for a colossal margin of error in the 1760 data, it is certain that the total slave population increased substantially in the succeeding thirty years. What is not clear is the increase, if any, in the ratio of free blacks to slaves.

53. *Journals of the Continental Congress,* VI, 1080.

have enormous long-run significance. It recommended an amendment to the Articles of Confederation changing the basis of apportionment from land to population. In enumerating people, all free persons (excluding untaxed Indians) were to be counted, "and three-fifths of all other persons not comprehended in the foregoing description."[54] The black had for the first time been specifically denominated three-fifths of a human and the principle, though rejected at the time, carried over as the basis for the "federal number" clause of the Constitution.

Other slavery-related matters demanded the attention of the national government. Should troop quotas be apportioned on the basis of all inhabitants, or just whites (whites); should black troops be raised for the defence of South Carolina and Georgia (absolutely not, insisted those two states); were slaves aboard captured vessels to be treated in prize proceedings like any other kind of property (yes); what can be done to stop the British from carrying off slaves and getting restitution for slaves who were carried off (not much); what can be done to recover runaways from the southern Indians and from the Spanish in Florida (nothing). Two Quaker petitions, one in 1783 and one in 1785, demanded the abolition of the slave trade and of slavery, with no success.[55] The cause of black rights did secure one token victory, though. In voting on the substance of the Articles of Confederation before they went out for ratification, South Carolinian delegates moved to restrict the privileges and immunities clause of Article IV to whites.[56] The motion lost, thus keeping free blacks within the ambit of the clause's protection, for whatever good it may have done them.[57]

The Articles themselves, though they did not mention slavery, and alluded to the racial or free status of persons only twice, contained several clauses that, had national government gone on longer under the first Constitution, would have regulated the relationship between

54. *Journals of the Continental Congress,* XXIV, 260.
55. The addresses from Philadelphia Quakers, dated 4th day, 10th month, 1783, and 26th day, 1st month, 1785, are in *Papers of the Continental Congress,* U.S. National Archives, R.G. 11, microform no. 247, roll 57.
56. "The better to secure and perpetuate mutual friendship and intercourse among the people of the different states in this union, the free inhabitants of each of these states, paupers, vagabonds and fugitives from Justice excepted, shall be entitled to all privileges and immunities of free citizens in the several states. . . ." The South Carolina motion was to insert the word "white" between "free" and "inhabitants."
57. *Journals of the Continental Congress,* XI, 652.

Confederation and states in the control of slavery. The federal consensus was secure under the Articles. Article I denominated the union a "confederacy" and Article III referred to it as a "league of friendship," both descriptions underscoring the sovereign status of the constituent states. As a consequence of this, the states had complete control over domestic institutions like marriage and divorce, the established churches, and slavery. The Confederation's lack of authority over these institutions was emphasized by the "expressly" clause of Article II: "Each state retains its sovereignty, freedom and independence, and every Power, Jurisdiction and right, which is not by this confederation expressly delegated to the United States, in Congress assembled." After 1781 (date of the adoption of the Articles), slavery remained what it had always been: the creature of the colonies-become-states. The central authority—the Continental and Confederation Congresses—succeeded to no more authority over it than the imperial government had exercised.

Clearly the consensus could not settle all problems related to slavery in the Confederation, because some of the incidents of slavery transcended the boundaries of a single state's jurisdiction. The Articles implicitly regulated some of these suprastate aspects of slavery. The Confederation Congress was disabled from making commercial treaties that would have prohibited the states from abolishing, regulating, or taxing the international slave trade.[58] A provision in Article IV might have been construed to restrain the states from interfering with a sojourning or in-transit master's rights in his slave.[59] Congress could requisition troops from the states in proportion to their "white inhabitants" (Article IX). The privileges and immunities clause (Article IV) pertained to all "free inhabitants" of the states, without distinction of color. Congress might also have derived some vaguely

58. "Art. IX. The united states in congress assembled, shall have the sole and exclusive right and power of . . . entering into treaties and alliances, provided that no treaty of commerce shall be made whereby the legislative power of the respective states shall be restrained from . . . prohibiting the exportation or importation of any species of goods or commodities whatsoever. . . ."

59. "Art IV. . . . the people of each state shall have free ingress and regress to and from any other state, and shall enjoy therein all the privileges of trade and commerce, subject to the same duties, impositions and restrictions as the inhabitants thereof respectively, provided that such restriction shall not extend so far as to prevent the removal of property imported into any state, to any other state of which the Owner is an inhabitant. . . ."

bounded power over the international and interstate slave trade from its jurisdiction over piracy, military maritime, admiralty, and Indian trade granted by Article IX. And perhaps other powers might have been found in the interstices of the Articles had the Confederation government lasted longer.

The Articles were indefinite on the problem of controlling the western territories to which the United States succeeded by the Treaty of Paris (1783). When the states having claims to this territory agreed to cede them to the Confederation, it became necessary to provide for their government. When Congress did so, it enacted the first national exclusion of slavery and thereby tentatively established a tier of free states in the west.

Though individuals in and out of Congress had been gestating plans for the western territories since 1776, the first appearance of a clause explicitly dealing with slavery in them was in Jefferson's draft of the 1784 report of the three-man committee chaired by him that was to prepare a plan of government for all the western territories. Jefferson's draft provided that "after the year 1800, of the Christian era, there shall be neither slavery nor involuntary servitude in any of the said states, otherwise than in punishment of crimes whereof the party shall have been convicted to have been personally guilty."[60] This provision was stricken and the 1784 ordinance adopted without it. Whether this was any great loss must remain conjectural, but two surmises may be safely made. Had the clause been embodied in the ordinance, it might not have been possible to secure adoption of the preferable antislavery clause of the 1787 ordinance. Further, Jefferson's clause was, in effect, a permission to the western territories and states to establish slavery and retain it to the year 1800. Whether it would have been possible for the new states and territories to disestablish slavery once it gained a foothold is doubtful. The difficulties of eradicating the crypto-slavery in Indiana and Illinois that slunk in under the much stronger 1787 provisions suggest that a complete ban, rather than Jefferson's *in futuro* version, was necessary.[61]

Slavery was finally excluded, but only from the Northwest Territories, by the famous provision of the 1787 ordinance, "There shall

60. Julian P. Boyd, ed., *The Papers of Thomas Jefferson* (Princeton: Princeton Univ. Press, 1950–), VI, 607–609.
61. For a differing estimate of the 1784 clause, much more favorable to Jefferson, see MacLeod, *Slavery, Race and the American Revolution,* 47–49.

be neither slavery nor involuntary servitude in the said territory, otherwise than in the punishment of crimes, where of the party shall have been duly convicted."[62] This was an improvement on earlier versions in two respects: slavery was excluded from the territorial stage, and this provision, along with all the other remarkable parts of what might be called the "bill of rights" of the 1787 ordinance were expressly to "forever remain unalterable, unless by common consent" and to constitute "articles of compact" not only between the states, but between the people of the territory and the original states.

Tacked onto Article 6, however, was an undesirable feature of an exclusionary clause proposed by Massachusetts delegate Rufus King in 1785, a fugitive slave provision: "Provided always, that any person escaping into the same, from whom labor or service is lawfully claimed in any one of the original States, such fugitive may be lawfully reclaimed and conveyed to the person claiming his or her labor or service as aforesaid." This clause was a proximate ancestor of the fugitive slave clause of the Constitution, but unlike the later clause, it explicitly restricted the reclamation privilege to masters deriving their claim from the laws of one of the original thirteen states. Abolitionists later tried unsuccessfully to extrapolate this limitation of the Articles into the constitutional provision.

Slavery had been considerably buffeted by the ideas and the events of the American Revolution. Five of the original thirteen states had begun or concluded its abolition, and Congress had excluded it from the Northwest Territory. A movement for its gradual abolition had been begun in the middle states. The antislavery tradition of the pre-Revolutionary era had been carried forward and expanded. Above all, the great sonorous phrases of the Declaration of Independence had been announced by Jefferson and adopted by his countrymen. A nation that staked its existence on the proposition that all men are created equal would sooner or later have to square that grand declaration with slavery. The history of the century following the Declaration could be written as the account of that struggle.

62. Art. 6 of the Northwest Ordinance of 1787 in Thorpe, *Federal and State Constitutions*, II, 962.

CHAPTER 3

Slavery in the Making
of the Constitution

The Confederation Congresses had demonstrated that decisions concerning slavery could be incorporated into national policy making without disturbing the federal consensus. But the inadequacies of national authority under the Articles led nationalists to work for a change in the constitutional basis of the American federation, and this provided an opportunity for some slave-state representatives to establish slavery more securely under national authority. As a result of their efforts, the Philadelphia Convention inserted no less than ten clauses in the Constitution that directly or indirectly accommodated the peculiar institution. They were:

1. Article I, section 2: representatives in the House were apportioned among the states on the basis of population, computed by counting all free persons and three-fifths of the slaves (the "federal number" or "three-fifths" clause);
2. Article I, section 2 and Article I, section 9: two clauses requiring, redundantly, that direct taxes (including capitations) be apportioned among the states on the foregoing basis, the purpose being to prevent Congress from laying a head tax on slaves to encourage their emancipation;
3. Article I, section 9: Congress was prohibited from abolishing the international slave trade to the United States before 1808;
4. Article IV, section 2: the states were prohibited from emancipating fugitive slaves, who were to be returned on demand of the master;
5. Article I, section 8: Congress was empowered to provide for

calling up the states' militias to suppress insurrections, including slave uprisings;

6. Article IV, section 4: the federal government was obliged to protect the states against domestic violence, again including slave insurrections;

7. Article V: the provisions of Article I, section 9, clauses 1 and 4 (pertaining to the slave trade and direct taxes) were made unamendable;

8. Article I, section 9 and Article I, section 10: these two clauses prohibited the federal government and the states from taxing exports, one purpose being to prevent them from taxing slavery indirectly by taxing the exported products of slave labor.

Later opponents and supporters of slavery found other clauses relevant in ways not foreseen by the framers, among them the clauses requiring the federal government to guarantee to the states republican forms of government (Article IV, section 4), giving Congress full legislative power over the federal district (Article I, section 8), and giving Congress power to admit new states and make "Regulations" for the territories (Article IV, section 3, clauses 1 and 2.)

The presence of these proslavery provisions was due principally to the efforts of one of the four regional blocs at the convention, the deep-South bloc comprising the South Carolina and Georgia delegates.[1] Not only was this bloc a numerical minority at Philadelphia; its aims ran counter to the mildly antislavery views of most of the influential delegates, who considered slavery obsolescent and expected its eventual disappearance. Yet slavery was more clearly and explicitly established under the Constitution than it had been under the Articles.[2] Fifty years later, abolitionists adopted malign conspiracy theories to explain slavery's gains under the new constitutive document, but there are more obvious explanations for the change. For one thing, slavery was too important an interest to ignore. It was one element that differentiated the regions of the new nation, and the economic interests of those regions had to be accommodated in the

---

1. On regional blocs at Philadelphia as a determinant of voting patterns, see S. Sidney Ulmer, "Subgroup Formation in the Constitutional Convention," *Midwest J. Pol. Sci.,* 10 (1966), 288–303.

2. See Staughton Lynd, "The Abolitionist Critique of the United States Constitution," in his *Class Conflict, Slavery, and the United States Constitution* (Indianapolis: Bobbs-Merrill, 1967), 153–183.

structure and functioning of the new government. James Madison noted that "the real difference of interest lay, not between the large & small but between the N[orthern] & Southn. States. The institution of slavery & its consequences formed the line of discrimination." Hence "the most material [of differentiating interests among the states] resulted partly from climate, but principally from the effects of their having or not having slaves. These two causes concurred in forming the great division of interests in the U. States."[3] The Constitution embodied a mediation of sectional differences that were based chiefly on slavery.

In this mediation, the most determined parties to the bargaining, the deep-South bloc, were able to secure more for their position than the other groups because they were demanding where their opponents were tepid and ambivalent, and because they knew just what they wanted, where their opponents had no particular program concerning slavery. Madison pointed out the first quality to Jefferson: the Carolinians were "inflexible on the point of the slaves."[4] They were untroubled by doubts about the policy and morality of slavery and the slave trade. In the South Carolina ratification debates, Rawlins Lowndes, a native West Indian, defended his region's position: "Negroes were our wealth, our only natural resource." "While there remained one acre of swampland uncleared of South Carolina," Charles Cotesworth Pinckney added in support, "I would raise my voice against restricting the importation of negroes."[5]

In contrast to the clearheaded drive and purpose of the Carolinians, upper-South delegates were torn between antislavery ideals and the practical difficulties of abolition. James Iredell at the North Carolina ratification convention condemned the slave trade and said that abolition "will be an event which must be pleasing to every generous

3. Max Farrand, ed., *The Records of the Federal Convention of 1787*, rev. ed. (New Haven: Yale Univ. Press, 1937), II, 10 (14 July); I, 486 (30 June). Unless otherwise noted, all citations to Farrand are to Madison's notes of debates.

4. Madison to Jefferson, 24 Oct. 1787, in Gaillard Hunt, ed., *The Writings of James Madison* (New York: Putnam, 1900–1910), V, 32.

5. Jonathan Elliot, comp., *The Debates in the Several State Conventions, on the Adoption of the Federal Constitution . . .* , 2nd ed., rev. (Philadelphia: Lippincott, 1901), IV, 272, 285. Regrettably, Merrill Jensen, ed., *The Documentary History of the Ratification of the Constitution* (Madison: State Historical Society of Wisconsin, 1976), vols. I and II, became available to me only after I had completed final substantive revisions.

mind, and every friend of human nature; but we often wish for things which are not attainable."[6] He urged the necessity of accommodating the deep-South's intransigence on the subject. In Virginia, he was echoed by Patrick Henry: "As much as I deplore slavery, I see that prudence forbids its abolition. . . . [Is] it practicable, by any human means, to liberate [the slaves] without producing the most dreadful and ruinous consequences[?]" Even George Mason, who was among the Virginians the most determined foe of slavery, reluctantly admitted that "it will involve us in great difficulties and infelicity to be now deprived of" slaves.[7]

Spokesmen for the New England bloc displayed the same feckless attitude. Thomas Dawes in the Massachusetts convention reminded his colleagues that "the members of the Southern States, like ourselves, have their prejudices. It would not do to abolish slavery, by an act of congress, in a moment, and so destroy what our southern brethren consider as property." He then made his often-quoted and sadly wrong prediction, that "although slavery is not smitten by an apoplexy, it has received a mortal wound, and will die of a consumption."[8] This concilatory posture, adopted in more extreme form by Connecticut delegates Roger Sherman and Oliver Ellsworth at Philadelphia, produced the New England-Deep South axis at the convention that made the slavery compromises possible, leading George Mason to lament that "under this coalition the great principles of the Const were changed in the last days of the Convention."[9]

Slavery made its influence felt at the Convention as soon as the delegates convened. Most delegates assumed the one state–one vote apportionment under the Articles would be scrapped, so they had to determine what new method of representation in the national legislature would take its place. This problem nearly destroyed all hopes for a new Constitution, in part because it immediately became entangled with one slavery issue: whether slaves were to be counted as part of a state's population for purposes of apportionment, assuming voting strength in the legislature would somehow reflect population.[10]

6. Elliot, *Debates*, IV, 100.
7. Elliot, *Debates*, III, 590–591, 269–270.
8. Elliot, *Debates*, II, 41.
9. Mason is quoted in a memorandum of a conversation between him and Jefferson in 1792, reprinted as "ex relatione G. Mason" in Farrand, *Records*, III, 367.
10. See Donald L. Robinson, *Slavery in the Structure of American Politics*,

The Virginia Plan, as presented by Virginia's Governor Edmund Randolph on Tuesday, 29 May 1787, provided for a bicameral national legislature, a popularly elected "first branch" and a "second branch" to be elected by the first. Representation in both was to "proportioned to the Quotas of contribution, or to the number of free inhabitants, as the one or the other rule may seem best in different cases."[11]

On Monday, 11 June, James Wilson, a Pennsylvanian abstractly opposed to slavery, introduced a refinement to the Virginia Plan's apportionment formula by proposing that voting in the popular branch be apportioned by population, counting all free inhabitants "of every age, sex and condition" (including indentured servants), "and three-fifths of all other persons not comprehended in the foregoing description."[12] This was the 1783 Confederation formula for apportioning taxes. Thus, the "subject of such awful importance," as William Davie was to call it in the North Carolina ratification convention, was broached.[13]

The so-called "small state" or "landless state" bloc—Maryland, Delaware, New Jersey, and Connecticut—quickly attacked the principle of popular representation in either house, demanding that voting in both houses be by state, so as to preserve the equal voting weight with the larger or "landed" states that they enjoyed under the Articles' one state–one vote mechanism. But this challenge to the Virginia Plan soon shifted subtly to reflect more substantial divisions than the artificial small versus large, landed versus landless split. Delegates defended their interests in this division on the bases of three considerations: republican theory, the clash of economic interests, and sectional logrolling. (1) Should the calibration of voting power reflect people, wealth, state sovereignty in a federation, or other criteria? How immediately should the people control their representatives to the national government? (2) Would the shipping and commercial interests concentrated on the seaboard and along the major rivers

---

1765–1820 (New York: Harcourt Brace Jovanovich, 1971), ch. 5; and Howard A. Ohline, "Republicanism and Slavery: Origins of the Three-Fifths Clause in the United States Constitution," *Wm. & M. Q.*, 28 (1971), 563–584. For an interpretation of the work of the Convention as a whole differing from that presented here, see Ohline, "Politics and Slavery: The Issue of Slavery in National Politics, 1787–1815," Ph.D. diss., University of Missouri, 1969.

11. Farrand, *Records,* I, 20 (29 May).
12. Farrand, *Records,* I, 193 (11 June; Journal).
13. Elliot, *Debates,* IV, 30.

have anything to fear from a shift of political power inland, which would presumably reflect an increase in "agrarian" interests? Would the commerce, shipping, and fisheries of New England and the Middle Atlantic states be jeopardized by the expected shift of population toward the planting south? (3) Sectional differences, as Madison noted, were based primarily on slavery, and this, in turn, made the enumeration of slaves a vital question. According to a modern calculation,[14] the percentage of voting power exercised by the five principal slave states of Maryland, Virginia, North Carolina, South Carolina, and Georgia under different apportionment formulae would have been: one state–one vote, 38 percent; all inhabitants (counting slaves and blacks equally with whites), 50 percent; free inhabitants (not counting slaves at all), 41 percent; and federal number, 47 percent.

Reflecting these theoretical and practical considerations rather than any principled opposition to slavery as such, northern delegates led by the voluble Gouverneur Morris attacked the Wilson formula of fractional representation for slaves.[15] Wilson himself was having second thoughts about his proposal. He "did not well see on what principle the admission of blacks in the proportion of three-fifths could be explained. Are they admitted as Citizens? Then why are they not admitted on an equality with White Citizens? Are they admitted as property? Then why is not other property admitted into the computation?"[16] The northern delegates were perplexed by the dilemma inherent in the slave's legal status: was he a person or a chattel? William Paterson of New Jersey, objecting to any slave representation, insisted on the latter: "They are no free agents, have no personal liberty, no faculty of acquiring property, but on the contrary are themselves property." If the South counted this sort of property for apportionment, then Massachusetts' Elbridge Gerry demanded to know why New Englanders should not count their cattle.[17]

14. The figures, which I have rounded off, are from a table in Robinson, *Slavery in the Structure of American Politics,* 180. Ohline, "Republicanism and Slavery," 574, denies that the controversy over fractional slave representation had a sectional basis.

15. Farrand, *Records,* I, 581–582 (11 July) and 604 (13 July). All references in this chapter to "Morris" will be to Gouverneur Morris. Robert Morris, also a delegate from Pennsylvania, seldom spoke in debate and played little part in the convention.

16. Farrand, *Records,* I, 587 (11 July).

17. Farrand, *Records,* I, 561 (9 July); I, 201 (11 June, Yates). See Luther Martin's recapitulation of the northerners' theoretical objections in his "Genuine Information," ibid., III, 172–232 at 197–198.

As the debates over slave representation wore on, the delegates became first testy, then intransigent. Morris "was compelled to declare himself reduced to the dilemma of doing injustice to the Southern States or to human nature, and he must therefore do it to the former."[18] William Davie of North Carolina responded to this with an ultimatum, demanding the federal number as the price of his state's accession to the union. "If the Eastern States meant therefore to exclude them altogether the business was at an end."[19] Pierce Butler of South Carolina felt it was time to speak some blunt truths to the northern delegates: "The security the Southn. States want is that their negroes may not be taken from them which some gentlemen within or without doors, have a very good mind to do."[20] If Butler seriously thought that any of his colleagues contemplated emancipation, he was hallucinating. But he had expressed an elemental slave-state response to real or imagined exogenous pressures on slavery that would characterize southern constitutionalism until the Civil War. Unnerved by such threats, Randolph of Virginia begged for concessions from the north. "He lamented that such a species of property [slaves] existed. But as it did exist the holders of it would require this security [i.e. the federal number]."[21]

Morris meanwhile was reconsidering his reaction to Madison's observation that the true line of division at the Convention was between slave and free states. He at first thought the idea "heretical." But the intransigence of the Carolinians had almost persuaded him otherwise. "Either this distinction is fictitious or real: if fictitious let it be dismissed & let us proceed with due confidence. If it be real, instead of attempting to blend incompatible things, let us at once take a friendly leave of each other."[22] Thus the delegates arrived at the first impasse of the Convention.

This was resolved three days later by the so-called "Connecticut Compromise," by which one house was to be based on popular representation computed by the federal number. The slaveholding states thereby got a double security for their property: additional weight in the House based on counting sixty percent of their slave population,

18. Farrand, *Records,* I, 588 (11 July).
19. Farrand, *Records,* I, 593 (12 July).
20. Farrand, *Records,* I, 605 (13 July).
21. Farrand, *Records,* I, 594 (12 July).
22. Farrand, *Records,* I, 604 (13 July).

together with a guarantee that any sort of direct taxation, including a head tax on slaves, would be based on the federal number. The compromise did, in a peculiar way, reflect some realities. The legal status of the black slave was something less than that of the free white, and perhaps three-fifths was, as Nathaniel Gorham of Massachusetts remarked, "pretty near the just proportion."[23]

Madison, writing for a northern audience in *Federalist* Number 54, expanded on this point. He reviewed the basic northern argument against fractional slave representation: because the southern states considered the slaves property, they should be included in the enumeration for tax purposes at one hundred percent, and excluded altogether for apportionment purposes. To this, he replied, "the true state of the case is, that they partake of both these qualities; being considered by our laws, in some respects as persons, and in other respects, as property." Therefore, "let the compromising expedient of the Constitution be mutually adopted, which regards them as inhabitants, but as debased by servitude below the equal level of free inhabitants, which regards the slave as divested of two-fifths of the man." This was an odd, yet not altogether illogical way of putting it, though Madison admitted that some of these arguments were "a little strained in some points."[24]

The federal number clause provoked surprisingly little debate in the ratifying conventions. In the South, Federalists touted its advantages, arguing that it was at the least "the only practicable rule or criterion of representation," and at best "an immense concession in our favour."[25] In the North, Federalists faintly apologized for it along the lines of Madison's *Federalist 54*.[26]

Carefully wrought as the compromise over fractional slave repre-

23. Farrand, *Records*, I, 580 (11 July).
24. All citations to the *Federalist Papers* are from the edition of Jacob E. Cooke, *The Federalist* (Middletown: Wesleyan Univ. Press, 1961). Number 54 is one of the papers of disputed authorship, but the probabilities lie with Madison rather than Hamilton. See Cooke's comments, xix–xxx.
25. Edward Rutledge in the South Carolina legislature, Elliot, *Debates*, IV, 277; George Nicholas and Madison, Virginia Convention, ibid., III, 457–459; William Davie in the North Carolina Convention, ibid., IV, 31; [David Ramsay], *An Address to the Freemen of South Carolina on the Subject of the Federal Constitution* . . . (1788) in Paul L. Ford, ed., *Pamphlets on the Constitution of the United States, Published during Its Discussion by the People, 1787–1788* (Brooklyn: n.p., 1888), 378.
26. See Alexander Hamilton in the New York Convention, in Elliot, *Debates*, II, 226–227, 237.

sentation was, it was almost undone by the overreaching of the deep-South bloc in the matter of the foreign slave trade. The Carolinians' inflexibility in this matter brought on the second crisis of the Convention. The slave trade was a sensitive topic.[27] Spokesmen of the upper South considered it an "inhuman traffic," and George Mason played Cassandra when he warned that "the Western people are already calling out for slaves for their new lands; and will fill that Country with slaves if they can be got thro' S. Carolina & Georgia."[28] Yet the South Carolinians unapologetically insisted on its necessity for their state and Georgia. They needed the trade if they were to expand their slave population significantly by any means other than natural increase. Between 1735 and 1775, six out of seven slaves imported into South Carolina came from Africa, one from the islands, and only a statistically insignificant number from other mainland colonies.[29] Carolinians argued that the New Englanders and Virginians, who were the most vocal critics of the trade, were estopped from condemning them for wanting to keep it open, the Virginians because of their obvious self-interest—with the trade closed, the prices of Virginia's slaves would rise—and the New Englanders because so much of the trade had been, and still was, carried in New England bottoms. Indeed, if men like John Brown, a merchant of Providence, Rhode Island, and brother of the Quaker abolitionist Moses Brown, had their way, New England slavers would ply their trade as long as the New World provided a vent for it: "This Trade has been permitted by the Supreame Govenour of all things for time Immemmoriel and . . . allowed by all the Nations of Europe. . . . I cannot thinke this State ought to Decline the Trade."[30]

The question of the trade did not come before the Convention until the Committee of Detail, which sat from 26 July till 6 August, began preparing a working draft constitution that was used in the prepa-

27. To avoid awkwardly long phrases, in this chapter the phrase "slave trade" will refer only to the maritime importation of slaves from non-American areas. For a good background discussion of the slave trade clause at the Convention, see Davis, *Problem of Slavery in the Age of Revolution,* 119–131.

28. James Iredell in the North Carolina ratifying convention, Elliot, *Debates,* IV, 178; Mason at Philadelphia, Farrand, *Records,* II, 370 (22 Aug.).

29. W. Robert Higgins, "The Geographical Origins of Negro Slaves in Colonial South Carolina," *South Atlantic Q.,* 70 (1971), 34–47.

30. John Brown to Moses Brown, 27 Nov. 1786, reprinted in Forrest McDonald and Ellen Shapiro McDonald, eds., *Confederation and Constitution, 1781–1789* (New York: Harper & Row, 1968), 89–92.

ration of later drafts. One of the committee's members, Randolph, inserted into this draft a double restraint on Congress' power to meddle with the trade: "no prohibition on ye Importations of such inhabitants of People as the sevl. States think proper to admit" and "no duties by way of such prohibition."[31] The committee reported this out as an absolute denial of Congress' power to prohibit or tax the "emigration or Importation of such persons as the several States shall think proper to admit."[32]

Back on the floor, on Wednesday 8 August, this draft provision provoked Morris and Rufus King of Massachusetts to an attack on slavery and on the Connecticut Compromise. King demanded that either slaves be excluded from representation or Congress have power to tax exports, so as to derive a revenue from the products of slave labor that might be used to defend the slave states weakened by their internal black menace. Morris went well beyond King, denouncing slavery itself as "a nefarious institution—It was the curse of heaven on the States where it prevailed." In support of a motion to undo the Connecticut Compromise and to limit representation to freemen, Morris said the Compromise, "when fairly explained, comes to this: that the inhabitant of Georgia and S. C. who goes to the Coast of Africa, and in defiance of the most sacred laws of humanity tears away his fellow creatures from their dearest connections & damns them to the most cruel bondages, shall have more votes in a Govt. instituted for protection of the rights of mankind, than the Citizen of Pa. or N. Jersey who views with a laudable horror, so nefarious a practice." For this sacrifice of principle, he sarcastically added, the northern states were to be rewarded by having to march their militias southward to put down slave insurrections. Meanwhile the southern states would be encouraged to continue importations by increased representation and by the exemption of their slaves and their slaves' products from taxation. Morris insisted that he "would sooner submit himself to a tax for paying for all the Negroes in the U. States than saddle posterity with such a Constitution."[33] The repealer motion was killed overwhelmingly, but the issue of slave imports was far from dead.

31. Farrand, *Records*, IV, 44 (papers of the Committee of Detail). The quotations are from the original draft as amended by John Rutledge of South Carolina.
32. Farrand, *Records*, II, 169 (papers of Committee of Detail).
33. Farrand, *Records*, II, 220–223 (8 Aug.).

On Tuesday 21 August, Luther Martin, himself a slave-state delegate (from Maryland), supported Morris, urging that the slave trade clause be amended to allow a tax or prohibition on imported slaves. In addition to Morris' points, Martin urged that "it was inconsistent with the principle of the revolution and dishonorable to the American character to have such a feature in the Constitution." John Rutledge and Charles Pinckney of South Carolina, together with Oliver Ellsworth of Connecticut, rose in turn to condemn Martin's proposal. "Religion & humanity had nothing to do with this question," Rutledge coldly retorted. "Interest alone is the governing principle with Nations"; and on that basis, the northern states should support the slave trade because it would increase the exports to be carried in northern vessels. Ellsworth agreed, chiding his colleagues that "the morality or wisdom of slavery are considerations belonging to the States themselves." Pinckney warned that South Carolina would never accept the Constitution with Martin's proposed restriction. "In every proposed extension of the powers of Congress, [South Carolina] has expressly & watchfully excepted that of meddling with the importation of negroes." His stubborn warning that "the true question at present is whether the Southn. States shall or shall not be parties to the Union" hung in the air as the Convention adjourned for the day.[34]

When the debate resumed the next day, sectional recriminations threatened to undo all that had been accomplished so far. Though the Connecticut delegates Ellsworth and Roger Sherman strove to moderate attacks on slavery and the trade, and to restore the conciliatory mood that had prevailed at the time of the mid-July compromise, Virginian George Mason attacked the trade by cataloguing the ill effects of slavery on whites. This goaded Charles Pinckney, his older cousin Charles Cotesworth Pinckney, and Yankee-born Abraham Baldwin of Georgia to a freewheeling defense of slavery. The younger Pinckney argued that "if slavery be wrong, it is justified by the example of all the world," while the elder appealed to the commercial self-interest of the north to encourage the export of slave-produced rice and indigo. He also "thought himself bound to declare candidly that he did not think S. Carolina would stop them occasionally as she now does." Both Pinckneys threatened disunion again, while Wilson, Nathaniel Gorham of Massachusetts, and John Dickinson of Delaware tried to call their bluff.

34. Farrand, *Records,* II, 364–365 (21 Aug.).

To the elder Pinckney's warning that the clause's rejection would mean "an exclusion of S. Carola from the Union," Gorham retorted that "the Eastern States [i.e. New England] had no motive to Union but a commercial one. They were able to protect themselves. They were not afraid of external danger, and did not need the aid of the Southn. States." This sort of talk alarmed compromise-minded delegates like Ellsworth, Sherman, and Randolph, threatening as it did to disrupt the laboriously knitted compromise of July. Ellsworth feared that the debates "had a threatening aspect. If we do not agree on this middle & moderate ground he was afraid we should lose two States, with such others as may be disposed to stand aloof, should fly into a variety of shapes & directions, and most probably into several confederations and not without bloodshed."[35]

The convention therefore gladly seized on another compromise suggestion, this time from Morris, who was no longer as forward as he had been earlier in condemning slavery. It referred to a special committee composed of one delegate from each state the related questions of slave importations, export taxes, capitations, and navigation acts. From this committee emerged a complex proposal that, as amended, constituted the second major and essential compromise of the Convention.[36] It contained the following elements: Congress could, but need not, prohibit the importation of slaves in 1808 or thereafter; slaves thus imported might be taxed, up to ten dollars a head; all capitations or other direct taxes could be laid only proportionately to the ratio between a state's population and the total national population; navigation acts needed only a majority for passage, rather than two-thirds; Congress and the states were forbidden to lay export taxes. Capping all this was a provision that ultimately ended up in Article V prohibiting amendment of the slave import and capitation clauses before 1808, adopted at the eleventh hour to allay the suspicions of Rutledge that states "prejudiced against" slavery might use the amendment power to strike at the trade prematurely.[37]

The slave trade compromise demonstrated that, for the framers, the highest good was national union. For this, they sacrificed all other considerations, including the well-being of black Americans. Though Madison and Sherman objected to the ten-dollar tax provision be-

35. The 22 August debates are in Farrand, *Records,* II, 369–375.
36. Farrand, *Records,* II, 400 (24 Aug.), 414–417 (25 Aug.).
37. Farrand, *Records,* II, 559 (10 Sept.).

cause, in Madison's words, it was "wrong to admit in the Constitution the idea that there could be property in men,"[38] their objections were overridden. The Constitution acknowledged slavery, and in differing ways protected it. George Mason wrote Jefferson that the New Englanders humored the desires of South Carolina and Georgia to import slaves, "a more favourite Object with them than the Liberty and Happiness of the People," and thus secured the second vital compromise of the Convention.[39]

The slave importation clause did have one possible antislavery catch to it, however, that sheds light on the anticipations—not the intentions—of the framers. Only "the states now existing" were to be allowed to import slaves; Congress had an implicit power to forbid importations by states other than the original thirteen. It exercised this power in 1798 by prohibiting the importation of slaves from outside the United States into Mississippi Territory, and again by a similar prohibition for the southern portion of the Louisiana Purchase territory in 1804.[40] The framers meant to prevent the spread of slavery into new states via the international slave trade. Acceding to this was no great concession for the deep-South bloc, who were not then concerned with extending slavery elsewhere. They were determined only to open up and exploit their own lands as fully as possible with slave labor. This would, however, have carried slavery potentially to the Mississippi River, because North Carolina did not cede its western claims (the area now Tennessee) until 1790, and Georgia did not cede its claims (most of modern Alabama and Mississippi) until 1802. The vision of a great inland slave empire was a development of later times. Hence James Wilson was led to make his erroneous prediction in the Pennsylvania ratifying Convention that, until 1808, "the new States which are to be formed will be under the control of Congress in this particular, and slaves will never be introduced amongst them."[41]

38. Farrand, *Records,* II, 417 (25 Aug.).
39. Mason to Jefferson, 26 May 1788, in Robert A. Rutland, ed., *The Papers of George Mason* (Chapel Hill: Univ. of North Carolina Press, 1970), III, 1044–1046.
40. Act of 7 April 1798, ch. 28, §7, 1 Stat. 549; Act of 26 March 1804, ch. 38, §10, 2 Stat. 283.
41. John Bach McMaster and Frederick D. Stone, eds., *Pennsylvania and the Federal Constitution, 1787–1788* (Lancaster: Historical Society of Pennsylvania, 1888), 312.

The delegates' habitual use of euphemisms when referring to slavery resulted in a major ambiguity in the slave importation clause: it applied to "the Migration or Importation of such Persons." Later controversy demonstrated that this phrase could be construed in two ways. The first, potentially a weapon in the hands of moderate abolitionists, would have defined "such Persons" as referring exclusively to slaves, and "Migration" to their movement in interstate commerce (as opposed to international commerce).[42] The second, which became canonical for the defenders of slavery, was first suggested by Thomas Jefferson in the Kentucky Resolutions of 1798.[43] It interpreted "such Persons" to mean both slaves and white immigrants, "Importation" to refer exclusively to bringing slaves in through international commerce, and "Migration" to refer exclusively to the more or less voluntary immigration of more or less free whites.[44] (It conceivably applied not only to entirely free whites, but to convicts and indentured servants as well.) If the antislavery interpretation were accepted, Congress would have power to regulate and abolish the interstate slave trade as an aspect of its general power over interstate commerce derived from the commerce clause (Article I, section 8), with the slave importation clause being a specific and temporary exception to the general commerce power.[45]

This later debate raises the general question of why the delegates resorted to circumlocutions when they meant to speak of slavery. To evade introducing the words "slave" or "slavery" into the document, they chose ambiguous and inelegant phrases that clouded their meaning. Many of them were competent lawyers who presumably could detect poor legal draftsmanship. Repeatedly in the ratifying conventions they stated that "in plain English" the euphemisms referred to slaves.[46] Seventeen years later, United States Senator Abraham Ven-

---

42. William A. Duer, *A Course of Lectures on the Constitutional Jurisprudence of the United States* . . . (New York: Harper, 1856), 209.

43. Paul L. Ford, ed., *The Writings of Thomas Jefferson* (New York: G. P. Putnam's, 1892–1899), VII, 288–289 (resolution V).

44. See James Iredell in North Carolina ratifying convention, Elliot, *Debates*, IV, 102.

45. Walter Berns, "The Constitution and the Migration of Slaves," *Yale L. J.*, 78 (1968), 198–228.

46. King and Melancthon Smith in New York, Iredell in North Carolina, and Randolph in Virginia, in Elliot, *Debates*, II, 36, 226–227; IV, 102; III, 599; Wilson in Pennsylvania, in McMaster and Stone, eds., *Pennsylvania and the Federal Constitution*, 311–312.

able pointed out what his contemporaries well knew: "The Constitution does not contain the word slave—but it admits the thing and protects it."[47] Why then the muddy language if everyone knew what was meant?

James Iredell, who, though not a delegate, kept in touch with acquaintances in Philadelphia, explained that the euphemisms were the South's verbal concessions to the "particular scruples" and the "religious and political prejudices of the Eastern and Middle States."[48] Luther Martin thought no one should be deceived by appearances. He explained that the framers avoided "expressions which might be odious in the ears of Americans, although they were willing to admit into their system those things which the expressions signified."[49] This may have palliated northern opposition to the slavery clauses, but, like all examples of lawyers' poor phrasing, it created problems later.

No slavery-related clause provoked as much debate in the ratifying conventions as the slave importation one. The debate reflected moral indignation at the slave trade, nearly universal above the Carolinas. Luther Martin's position indicated how the antitrade arguments could become an argument against slavery itself: "Slavery is inconsistent with the genius of republicanism, and has a tendency to destroy those principles on which it is supported, as it lessens the sense of the equal rights of mankind, and habituates us to tyranny and oppression." The trade itself, Martin thought, was morally repugnant, increased the possibility of slave insurrections, and expanded the power of the slave states.[50] Martin was echoed in the conventions of New Hampshire, Massachusetts, Pennsylvania, Virginia, and North Carolina.[51] Rhode Island, which at first refused to ratify the Constitution, recommended an amendment eliminating the slave trade clause.[52]

47. Quoted in Everett S. Brown, ed., *William Plumer's Memorandum of Proceedings in the United States Senate 1803–1807* (New York: Macmillan, 1923), 130 (31 Jan. 1804).

48. Elliot, *Debates*, IV, 176, 285.

49. Farrand, *Records*, III, 210.

50. "Genuine Information," in Farrand, *Records*, III, 210–213; see also Charles Cotesworth Pinckney's summary of arguments he had to combat: Elliot, *Debates*, IV, 285.

51. Massachusetts: Elliot, *Debates*, II, 149–150; New Hampshire: ibid., II, 203–204; Virginia: ibid., III, 452; North Carolina: ibid., IV, 100–102; Pennsylvania: McMaster and Stone, *Pennsylvania and the Federal Constitution*, 311–313; letter no. 3 of "Centinel" series in Pennsylvania *Independent Gazeteer*, reprinted in ibid., 599.

52. DuBois, *Suppression of the African Slave Trade*, 68.

To such objections, Federalists could only reply, following the lead of Madison in *Federalist* Numbers 38 and 42, that the 1808 clause was at least an improvement over the Articles, which might have been interpreted to prohibit Congress from ever interfering with the trade. The Constitution's twenty-year-deferred power "ought to be considered a great point gained in favor of humanity."[53] Tench Coxe and Noah Webster, pamphleteering pseudonymously outside the conventions, both hinted that the clause might somehow encourage the abolition of slavery, though both admitted the necessity of compromise to accommodate "the peculiar situation of our southern fellow-citizens."[54]

In the slave states, the Federalists' argument necessarily took another form. James Iredell, responding to Mason's objections to the clause, argued that the upper slave states "could not with decency" have insisted on refusing to let South Carolina and Georgia recoup the losses of slaves occasioned by military operations in those states during the late war. Hence, Iredell resignedly concluded, "our situation makes it necessary to bear the evil as it is." He went beyond this, however, in stating that striking at the injustice of the slave trade was none of the other states' business anyhow; "this is a matter between God and [the slavers'] own consciences."[55] In the South Carolina ratification debates, Robert Barnwell boasted that "without we ourselves put a stop to [slave imports], the traffic for negroes will continue forever." He then reversed the arguments of apologists for the 1808 clause by saying that South Carolina would benefit from having the federal government prohibited from interfering with the trade for twenty years.[56] His fellow Federalist David Ramsay sug-

---

53. *Federalist*, 381, and, to the same effect, James Wilson in the Pennsylvania ratifying convention, McMaster and Stone, eds., *Pennsylvania and the Federal Constitution*, 312.

54. "An American Citizen" [Tench Coxe], *An Examination of the Constitution for the United States of America* . . . (1788), in Ford, ed., *Pamphlets*, 146; "A Citizen of America" [Noah Webster], *An Examination into the Leading Principles of the Federal Constitution Proposed by the Late Convention Held at Philadelphia* . . . (1787), in ibid., 54.

55. "The Objections of the Hon. George Mason, to the Proposed Federal Constitution, Addressed to the Citizens of Virginia," (1788 broadside), in Ford, ed., *Pamphlets*, 331; James Iredell, "Answer to Mason's Objections," ibid., 367; Oliver Ellsworth made the same point in Connecticut: "The Landholder" [Oliver Ellsworth], in the *Connecticut Courant*, 10 Dec. 1787, reprinted in Paul L. Ford, comp., *Essays on the Constitution of the United States* (Brooklyn: Historical Printing Club, 1892), 163–164.

56. Elliot, *Debates*, IV, 296.

gested that since it would be to the carrying states' interest to encourage South Carolina's staple exports (rice, chiefly), they would probably not insist on abolishing the trade in 1808, and that even if they did, South Carolina would have filled its needs by then through importations, natural increase, and surplus slaves sent down from the upper South.[57] As it turned out, Ramsay overestimated the venality of the carrying states. Charles Pinckney complacently summed up the Carolinians' achievements: "Considering all circumstances, we have made the best terms for the security of this species of property it was in our power to make. We would have made better if we could, but, on the whole, I do not think them bad."[58]

The federal consensus posed one difficulty for the proslavery bloc: the status of fugitive slaves. The interstate rendition of fugitive slaves among the American states was a well-established constitutional tradition by 1787. It originated in intercolonial efforts to prohibit the absconding of white servants, and never lost its association with the problem of controlling elopement by those in limited-term servitude.[59] The New England Confederation in 1643 had provided that "if any servant run away from his master into any other of these confederated Jurisdictions, that in such case, upon the certificate of one magistrate in the Jurisdiction out of which the said servant fled, or upon other due proof; the said servant shall be delivered, either to his master, or any other that pursues and brings such certificate or proof."[60] This early provision parallelled the later fugitive slave clause of the Constitution, especially in its association with a fugitives-from-justice clause and in its mechanism for reclaiming the runaway.

Before 1787, rendition was exclusively a matter of comity between states. In the absence of a constitutionally superior authority having competence in the matter, the states dealt with the fugitive problem as sovereign entities. The Articles of Confederation contained no provisions for the rendition of fugitive slaves, so the slave states depended on the good will of the other states in fugitive recaptures. Madison claimed in the Virginia ratifying convention that "if any

57. [Ramsay], *Address to the Freemen of South Carolina*, in Ford, ed., *Pamphlets*, 378.

58. Elliot, *Debates*, IV, 286.

59. Marion G. McDougall, *Fugitive Slaves, 1619–1865* (1891; rpt. New York: Bergman, 1967), 8–10.

60. Articles of Confederation [of the New England Confederation], §8, in Thorpe, *Federal and State Constitutions*, I, 80.

slave elopes to any of those states where slaves are free, he becomes emancipated by their laws. For the laws of the states are uncharitable to one another in this respect."[61] No evidence exists, however, that northern states placed obstacles in the way of masters trying to exercise their common-law right of recaption,[62] or that they were deliberately remiss in meeting their obligation, if any, to return fugitives on demand. But the slave states seem to have been vaguely disturbed by the lack of a positive constitutional obligation to return fugitives.

Dissatisfied though they may have been, they did not raise the issue at any point during early Convention debates. Perhaps encouraged by the success of their colleagues in New York, who had just succeeded in getting a fugitive slave provision written into the Northwest Ordinance, on Tuesday, 28 August, Pierce Butler and Charles Cotesworth Pinckney demanded that something pertaining to slaves be inserted into a fugitive criminal rendition clause that would "require fugitive slaves and servants to be delivered up like criminals." Sherman and Wilson immediately objected, not so much to the idea that the northern states must connive at slave catching, as to the cost involved, and Butler temporarily withdrew his proposition.[63]

On the following day, Butler offered a fugitive slave clause in substantially the form it finally assumed in Article IV, section 2. The easy acceptance of the clause can be explained by the fact that Butler opportunistically offered his motion on the heels of one of the Convention's most successful horse-trades, the abandonment of the requirement for a two-thirds majority for navigation acts. The convention at that point seemed suffused with an aura of goodwill and conciliation toward the deep South.

The clause thus incorporated into the Constitution was full of ambiguities. There was no doubt that it referred to slaves as well as servants; Butler's comments on 28 and 29 August demonstrate unequivocally that his colleagues knew they were dealing with slaves. Yet here again the draftsmen resorted to a circumlocution: "Person held to Service or Labour in one State." Perhaps Butler chose this

61. Elliot, *Debates,* III, 453.
62. This was a right that an owner of goods (like a horse) or a person in a relationship of superiority to another (like a parent, husband, or master) could exercise to recover a runaway, the only limitation on it being that the retaking could not be attended by a breach of the peace. See Blackstone, *Commentaries,* III, *4.
63. Farrand, *Records,* II, 443 (28 Aug.).

euphemism so as not to shatter the conciliatory spirit that prevailed, since his original proposal contained the naked word "slaves." Yet a floor amendment offered by Randolph on 13 September made the fugitive slave provision even more ambiguous. Referring to the indentured servants mentioned in the federal number clause, Randolph asked that the word "servitude" in the draft then on the floor be deleted in favor of "service" because the latter word referred to the status of freemen, while "servitude" connoted slaves. This amendment was accepted, but no parallel change was made in the fugitive clause, despite the fact that "service" there was clearly meant to refer to slaves.[64]

The phrase "under the Laws thereof" also embodied a curious compromise. The version reported out by the Committee of Style spoke of a "person legally held." On Saturday 15 September, the word "legally" was stricken "in compliance with the wish of some who thought the term equivocal, and favoring the idea that slavery was legal in a moral view."[65] Presumably, these were the Carolinians. The amended phrasing of the clause was apparently adopted to recognize implicitly the moral legitimacy of slavery.

In contrast with the federal number and slave trade clauses, those giving the federal government power to suppress insurrections in the states provoked little convention debate, due principally to the fact that the delegates were almost unanimous on the desirability of the nation having the power to suppress at least one kind of uprising, that of white men typified by the Shays Rebellion in Massachusetts during the winter of 1786–1787. Thus any insurrections clause should have been noncontroversial; however, the Carolinians' ethical obtuseness on the question of the slave trade provoked explosions from King and Morris on the federal insurrections power.

"Shall all the States then be bound to defend each [other]; & shall each be at Liberty to introduce a weakness [imported slaves] which will render defence more difficult?" King asked. "There was so much inequality and unreasonableness in all this, that the people of the N. States could never be reconciled." Morris complained that the northern states "are to bind themselves to march their militia for the defence of the S. States; for their defence agst. those very slaves of

64. Farrand, *Records,* II, 590, 607 (13 Sept.).
65. Farrand, *Records,* II, 628 (15 Sept.).

whom they complain."[66] These objections were immediately subsumed in debates over the slave trade, but the issue rankled for two weeks in the minds of some northern delegates. But because the argument against northern militias suppressing black uprisings was merely a makeweight for more important objections, northern criticism subsided, and both the insurrections clause of Article I, section 8, and the domestic violence clause of Article IV, section 4, were adopted with little further opposition.[67]

Madison, oddly, in *Federalist* Number 13 suggested a use for the domestic violence clause of Article IV that had not even been broached in the Philadelphia or ratification debates: it could be used not only to suppress insurrections, but to repress nonviolent, extralegal attempts by blacks to secure political power for themselves. "May it not happen," he warned, "that the minority of CITIZENS may become a majority of PERSONS, by the accession of . . . those whom the Constitution of the State has not admitted to the rights of suffrage?" such as "an unhappy species of population abounding in some of the States, who during the calm of regular government are sunk below the level of men; but who in the tempestuous scenes of civil violence may emerge into the human character, and give a superiority of strength to any party with which they may associate themselves."[68] This never happened, and northern militiamen were never called to put down black uprisings, but regular federal forces were available and often used for the same end, from Jefferson's contemplated Franco-American expedition to overthrow Toussaint L'Ouverture in Santo Domingo (1801) to the use of United States Marines to suppress John Brown in 1859.

Fifty years after the Philadelphia Convention, sparked by the posthumous publication of Madison's notes of the debates, a lively debate flared among abolitionists and others about the framers' true intentions concerning slavery. The debate smolders on among scholars today. Three things may be said with assurance about the framers' intent. First, the Philadelphia Convention knowingly and deliberately inserted into the Constitution several provisions, distributed among ten clauses, that were intended to enhance the internal security of slavery in the states and to protect two of its extrajurisdictional

66. Farrand, *Records,* II, 220, 222 (8 Aug.).
67. Farrand, *Records,* II, 390 (23 Aug.) and 467 (30 Aug.).
68. *Federalist,* 294 (capitalization in original).

effects (fugitive slaves and the slave trade). Second, despite somewhat vague and tepid antislavery sentiments of many of the delegates from the states above North Carolina, these proslavery provisions were inserted due to the determination and bluff of the deep-South regional bloc, supported by pleas for compromise from Connecticut and Virginia delegates.

Third, and most importantly, the delegates did not intend to disturb the federal consensus. Both Federalist and Antifederalist delegates to the ratifying conventions, as well as the members of the Philadelphia Convention, emphasized their dedication to the consensus. James Madison, in the Virginia convention, assured his colleagues that "no power is given to the general government to interpose with respect to the property in slaves now held by the states." Any effort by the federal government in that direction "would be a usurpation of power. There is no power to warrant it in [the Constitution]. . . . I believe such an idea never entered into any American breast."[69] Nonetheless, Patrick Henry, leading Antifederalist opposition in the Old Dominion, conjured up the bugbear that somewhere in the Constitution a power might be found to meddle with slavery, which he insisted was "a local matter, and I can see no propriety in subjecting it to Congress." This provoked Edmund Randolph to rebuke him; Randolph denied that any part of the Constitution "has a tendency to the abolition of slavery." He reassured the Virginians that "the southern states, even South-Carolina herself, conceived this property [i.e. slaves] to be secure by these words [the slave importation clause]. . . . There was not a member of the Virginia delegation who had the smallest suspicion of the abolition of slavery."[70] Charles Cotesworth Pinckney in the South Carolina debates concurred: "We have a security that the general government can never emancipate [South Carolina's slaves], for no such authority is granted."[71]

Delegates in free-state Massachusetts agreed. Thomas Dawes noted that each state was left to control the introduction of slaves within its own borders. "What could the convention do more?" he asked rhetorically. Nor could the separate states compel emancipation outside their jurisdiction. "It is not in our power," said William Heath,

69. Elliot, *Debates,* III, 453, 622.
70. Elliot, *Debates,* III, 591, 598–599.
71. Elliot, *Debates,* IV, 286.

"to do anything for or against those who are in slavery in the Southern States." Abolition might be desirable, "but to this we have no right to compel them." Heath concluded with a precise articulation of the consensus: "Each state is sovereign and independent to a certain degree, and the states have a right, and they will regulate their own internal affairs as to themselves seems proper . . . the federal Convention went as far as they could."[72]

As Gouverneur Morris indistinctly suspected, the compromises of the Constitution tried "to blend incompatible things," and were therefore inherently unstable, containing tensions whose resolution could be procrastinated but not indefinitely evaded. The Constitution was built on the principles of the Declaration of Independence and on the objectives outlined in its own preamble, but these were incompatible with the system of slavery ensconced in the document. Unlike the Virginia provincial congress that accepted Mason's 1776 Declaration of Rights, neither the Second Continental Congress nor the Philadelphia Convention voiced an understanding that black slaves were an understood, if not express, exception to those principles and objectives. In this area, as in others, the framers passed on to posterity a document embodying open-ended possibilities, leaving it to them to work out a resolution of new problems as they came up. These problems were not slow in arising. The First Congress, in fact, had some of them thrown into its lap as early as 1790, and the period between the ratification of the Constitution and the appearance of the second crisis of the union was marked by a constant recurrence of a sectional malady that seemed more and more to be endemic—as in fact it was.

72. Elliot, *Debates*, II, 40, 115.

CHAPTER 4

Antislavery in
the New Nation

In the thirty years that separated the first two crises of the union (1788–1819), the efforts of the antislavery movement produced mixed results. Antislavery activists organized societies that encouraged manumission and protected free blacks. The Abolition Societies, as they were collectively called, united in a loose national federation, the American Convention, which coordinated a campaign of memorials to Congress calling for national antislavery action within the limits of the federal consensus. The states responded to problems of slavery in differing ways. In the north, the process of gradual emancipation continued. In the south, the state legislatures consolidated the legal system of slavery, and South Carolina reopened the slave trade. Slavery expanded into the new states of the southwest. Congress reaffirmed the federal consensus, abolished the international slave trade, enacted the first national fugitive slave legislation, and ratified the existence of slavery in the territories, including the District of Columbia.

Abolitionists in the Middle Atlantic States, especially New York and Pennsylvania, where slavery was waning and free blacks were often seized by slave catchers, organized societies whose names tell a good deal about the goals of early antislavery: the Pennsylvania Society for Promoting the Abolition of Slavery, the Relief of Free Negroes Unlawfully Held in Bondage, and for Improving the Condition of the African Race; the Providence [Rhode Island] Society for Abolishing the Slave Trade; the Delaware Society, for Promoting the Abolition of Slavery, for Superintending the Cultivation of Young Free Negroes, and for the Relief of Those Who May Be Unlawfully Held in Bondage; the New-York Society, for Promoting the Manumission of Slaves and Protecting Such of Them as Have Been or May Be Liberated; the Kentucky Abolition Society; the Manumission Society of Tennessee.

The Abolition Societies were distinguished by three characteristics that contrasted with the antislavery movement of the 1830s. First, their members were strongly oriented toward state action. Though they petitioned Congress several times and sought goals, like abolition of the foreign slave trade, that required some national action, they devoted the bulk of their efforts to action at the state level. The later movement reversed these emphases. Second, early abolition was gradualistic, impeded by a sober and realistic calculation of the practical difficulties that stood in the way of universal emancipation. Later antislavery was immediatist, impatient of its predecessor's caution. Third, the early effort relied principally on legal, as opposed to political action. They did lobby, and were actually adept and successful at it, but they subordinated this and other forms of political action to more conventional, lawyer-like activities such as litigating, counseling, keeping an eye on slave registries, and compiling statutes. By contrast, the antislavery organizations of the 1830s went in for comparatively little litigation and considerably more politicking. These were all differences of degree rather than kind, but they set off the two phases of the organized movement and made the latter seem more radical than its relatively staid predecessor.

The individual societies, led by Pennsylvania's, sent petitions to the state legislatures and to the Confederation Congress and national Congress from the 1780s on. At the first national convention (1794), the delegates memorialized Congress for passage of statutes that would restrain American citizens from engaging in the slave trade by sending slaves to non-American nations and to prohibit aliens from fitting out ships in the United States to engage in the trade.[1] They urged Secretary of State Timothy Pickering to prevent Americans from engaging in slaving under Danish and other foreign flags, and asked Secretary of the Treasury Alexander Hamilton—himself a member of the New-York Society—to have his collectors stringently enforce federal legislation inhibiting peripheral incidents of the slave trade.[2]

1. *Minutes of the Proceedings of a Convention of Delegates from the Abolition Societies* . . . [1794] (Philadelphia: Zacharaiah Poulson, 1794), 8–9.
2. *Minutes of the Proceedings of the Fourth Convention of Delegates from the Abolition Societies* . . . [1797] (Philadelphia: Zachariah Poulson, 1797), 9.

The Abolition Societies enjoyed some gratifying successes in lobby-ing. The Pennsylvania Society, assisted by Anthony Benezet, secured enactment of Pennsylvania's 1780 gradual abolition act, regarded by contemporaries as a model statute. The federal slave trade act of 1794, prohibiting all persons from fitting out in, or sailing from, American ports for the slave trade to foreign countries,[3] was enacted in response to the American Convention's 1794 memorial. Their lobbying may have had some indirect influence in getting the New York and New Jersey legislatures to begin gradual emancipation.

The Societies petitioned state legislatures as vigorously as they ap-proached Congress, requesting the states to prohibit the importation of slaves into their ports; to annihilate all other aspects of the slave trade, as, for example, by prohibiting their citizens from engaging in the slave trade to foreign areas, "to promote such plans as may tend to diminish the number of slaves . . . meliorate their situation, and eventually eradicate [the] evil," and to pass laws making private manumissions easier.[4] In 1821, the American Convention even sug-gested that its constituent societies demand that blacks in felony trials be tried only by a "jury selected from among the most respectable of his black associates or neighbors."[5] They lobbied antiemancipation bills to death, and sought stiff antikidnaping statutes.

The Societies were intensely litigious, so much so that they some-times skirted the edges of barratry and maintenance.[6] The Societies assumed that slavery was a creature of state statutes and judicial precedent and attacked it by seeking to overturn those bases. The older Societies had officers known as "Counsellors" whose functions included providing counsel to blacks in freedom suits; explaining and publicizing state laws and constitutional provisions pertaining to emancipation, the slave trade, kidnaping, and the rights of free blacks; giving legal advice to indigent blacks; and in states like Pennsylvania, whose gradual emancipation statute provided for manu-

3. Act of 22 March 1794, ch. 11, 1 Stat. 347.
4. *Minutes of a Convention of the Abolition Societies* [1794], 13–16.
5. *Minutes of the Seventeenth Session of the American Convention . . . 1821* (Philadelphia: Atkinson & Alexander, 1821), 7.
6. Barratry is the common-law offense of stirring up litigation. Maintenance is "an unauthorized and officious interference in a suit in which the offender has no interest, to assist one of the parties to it, against the other, with money or advice to prosecute or defend the action" (*Black's Law Dictionary,* 4th ed., "maintenance")

mission registers, of seeing to it that manumissions were properly recorded.[7]

The counsellors of the Pennsylvania Society, led by William Lewis, Jared Ingersoll, and William Rawle,[8] mounted an all-out assault on slavery in the Keystone State, hoping that its Supreme Court would declare slavery unconstitutional as they believed the Massachusetts Supreme Judicial Court had done in Quock Walker's cases. In this effort, they met with repeated failure. In *Pirate* (*alias Belt*) v. *Dalby* (1786), Chief Justice Thomas McKean instructed the jury that slavery in Pennsylvania had a legitimate origin in the principle of *partus sequitur ventrem*,[9] which he held to be "authorized by the civil law," "consistent with the precepts of nature," and "the law of the land." The jury, not surprisingly, found for the alleged slave's owner.[10]

In arguments in *Respublica* v. *Blackmore* (1797),[11] Hugh Henry Brackenridge, counsel for the owner of slaves unregistered under the 1780 act, conceded that under the Pennsylvania constitution's "all men are born equally free and independent" clause, slavery was "questionable," thus suggesting that the Abolition Society's efforts were not wholly quixotic. But in an unreported case, *Negro Flora* v. *Graisberry* (1802), the Pennsylvania High Court of Errors and Ap-

7. On these various activities, see "Minutes of the Standing Committee" and "Register of Manumission of Slaves New York City 1816–1818," Papers of the New-York Manumission Society, N-YHS; Edgar McManus, *A History of Negro Slavery in New York* (Syracuse: Syracuse Univ. Press, 1966), 169–170. [New-York Manumission Society], *Selections from the Revised Statutes of the State of New York; Containing All the Laws of the State relative to Slaves, and the Law relative to the Offence of Kidnapping* . . . (New York: Vanderpool & Cole, 1830); [New-Jersey Abolition Society], *Cases Adjudged in the Supreme Court of New-Jersey; relative to the Manumission of Negroes* . . . (Burlington: Isaac Neale, 1794); *Constitution of the Providence Society for Abolishing the Slave Trade. With Several Acts of the Legislatures of the States of Massachusetts, Connecticut, and Rhode-Island, for That Purpose* (Providence: John Carter, 1789).

8. Ingersoll had been a member of the Constitutional Convention of 1787 and was at the time Attorney General of Pennsylvania; Rawle was then United States Attorney for Pennsylvania and later author of *A View of the Constitution of the United States* (1825), a distinguished constitutional treatise second only to Story's *Commentaries on the Constitution.*

9. "The [status of the] offspring follows the [condition of the] mother," a rule exogenous to the common law but adopted in Anglo-American jurisdictions to determine the status of children born of one or both slave parents. It was essential to the hereditability of slave status.

10. 1 Dall. 167 (Pa. 1786).

11. 2 Yeates 234 (Pa. 1797).

peals was reported to have held that slavery had had a legal existence in the state prior to the constitution, and that the 1780 gradual emancipation act had not totally abolished it.[12]

The Societies had more success in freedom suits, where they sought merely to secure the freedom of individual blacks without establishing a more encompassing principle. The Maryland Society was said to be so successful in these actions that it was useless to defend a suit sponsored by it.[13] The counsellors of the Societies were especially vigilant to prevent kidnaping. In states close to the planting areas, and in those having large ports, kidnaping was extensive, especially when prices of slaves were high. Slave catchers frequently decoyed and shanghaied free blacks. Antislavery lawyers therefore formed committees to keep an eye on suspected slave catchers in port. They ran down reports and rumors of kidnapings, in an effort both to free the black and to get the kidnaper punished. The New-York, Pennsylvania, Maryland, and Virginia Societies checked registers of manumission and saw to it that private manumissions were properly recorded under law, so as to preserve evidence in antikidnaping actions.

The Abolition Societies had neither the impact nor the notoriety of the later antislavery societies, but their achievements were considerable in their time. They constituted the first organizational vehicle for the development and transmission of the antislavery afflatus of the Revolution, and in their formal discourses and memorials kept that tradition vital. Their members had the satisfaction of knowing that thousands of black men and women secured or preserved their freedom thanks to their efforts. They could take credit for some early antislavery legislation, both state and national. They were the first to use laws and the legal process against slavery. They thereby converted what had been principally a religio-moral impulse into a secular legal activity. They never lost sight of their goal, "the ultimate and entire abolition of slavery in our land," and passed it on to their successors.[14]

During the first generation of political and constitutional antislav-

12. Edward R. Turner, "The Abolition of Slavery in Pennsylvania," *Pa. Mag. Hist. & Biog.,* 36 (1912), 129–142.

13. Jeffrey R. Brackett, *The Negro in Maryland: A Study of the Institution of Slavery* (Baltimore: Johns Hopkins University, 1889), 54; this was the opinion of a legislative committee, and may have been exaggerated.

14. *Minutes of the Proceedings of the Fifteenth American Convention . . . 1817 . . .* (Philadelphia: Merritt, 1817), 36.

ery, the states took steps that solidified the sectional division of the country. In the North, gradual abolition went on apace, with the usual scrupulous regard being paid to property relationships and legally established social norms. In the South, slavery was entrenched in the new states of Kentucky, Tennessee, Louisiana, Alabama, and Mississippi; the states where it had been long established tinkered with their slave codes to make the control of blacks more secure; and Georgia and South Carolina insulted the consciences of Americans elsewhere by continuing and reopening the high seas slave trade.

In the late eighteenth century, gradual or total emancipation had occurred only in the New England states and Pennsylvania. New York and New Jersey resisted this trend. Both states enacted legislation prohibiting the importation of slaves and in other ways easing the lot of enslaved blacks in their jurisdictions.[15] Finally, however, after a decade of political maneuvering and because the state's need for a servile labor force was dwindling, New York in 1799 passed a *post-natl* gradual emancipation act, placing the children thus freed in servitude to age twenty-eight (males) and twenty-five (females).[16] It left their owners the option of turning over these children to the overseers of the poor, possibly as a means of compensating owners circuitously by having these children bound back to them with compensation for raising them as apprentices.[17] New Jersey followed suit in 1804 with a more liberal *post-nati* statute.[18]

With gradual abolition set in motion in five northern states, the legislatures had only to tie up several loose ends left in the dismantling

15. Act of 12 April 1785, ch. 68, in *Laws of the State of New-York . . .* (New York: Samuel Loudon, 1785), misleadingly captioned "An Act Granting a Bounty on Hemp . . ."; Laws of 1786, ch. 58, and Laws of 1788, ch. 40, in *Laws of the State of New-York . . . from the First to the Fifteenth Session, Inclusive* (New York: Thomas Greenleaf, 1792), I, 278, and II, 85–88; *Acts of the Tenth General Assembly of the State of New-Jersey . . .* (Trenton: Isaac Collins, 1786), ch. 119; *Acts of the Thirteenth General Assembly of the State of New-Jersey . . .* (Trenton: Isaac Collins, 1788), ch. 244.

16. Laws of 1799, ch. 62, in *Laws of the State of New-York . . . 1799* (Albany: Loring Andrews, 1799); McManus, *Negro Slavery in New York,* 194.

17. Arthur Zilversmit, *The First Emancipation: The Abolition of Slavery in the North* (Chicago: Univ. of Chicago Press, 1967), 182.

18. *Acts of the Twenty-Eighth General Assembly of the State of New-Jersey . . .* (Trenton: Wilson and Blackwell, 1804), ch. 103. See Arthur Zilversmit, "Liberty and Property: New Jersey and the Abolition of Slavery," *New Jersey Hist.,* 88 (1970), 215–226.

of slavery. New York in 1809 and 1813 extended certain civil rights to slaves, including the power to contract marriages indissoluble by the master, the power to own property, the right to testify in court, and a right to jury trial in all felony prosecutions.[19] These statutes, placing slaves on a plane close to that of free blacks, were a certain sign that slavery in the Empire State was virtually extinct. Recognizing this, the legislature in 1817 administered the *coup de grâce* to slavery by converting the status of the *ante-nati* not liberated by the 1799 statute to limited-term servitude.[20] Connecticut passed a *post-nati* emancipation act in 1797 and abolished slavery completely in 1848.[21] Despite a lingering conviction in Pennsylvania that the remaining slavery was unconstitutional under the 1780 gradual abolition act,[22] a belief not shaken by the failure of the Abolition Society's test cases, the state legislature never formally abolished the vestiges of slavery, leaving the institution to die out with the diminishing number of elderly slaves. In New Jersey, following Alvan Stewart's unsuccessful assault on the constitutionality of slavery in that state's Supreme Court in 1845, the legislature in 1847 converted extant slavery to apprenticeship, a modified form of involuntary servitude.[23] Slowly, by desuetude rather than dramatic action, slavery's legal bases in the states above Maryland dwindled.

In the southern states, the debates over slavery induced by the Revolution reaffirmed a commitment to the maintenance of race control. During the War for Independence hostility to manumission surfaced in North Carolina legislation and in popular memorials to the Virginia legislature.[24] Maryland, Virginia, and Georgia consolidated

19. *Public Laws of the State of New York. Passed at the Thirty-Second Session* . . . (Albany: S. Southwick, 1809), ch. 44; *Public Laws of* . . . *New York* . . . [1813], ch. 88.

20. *Public Laws of* . . . *New York* . . . [1817], ch. 137.

21. *Acts and Laws* . . . *of Connecticut* . . . 1797, (n.p., n.d.), p. 462; *Public Acts of* . . . *Connecticut* . . . *1848*, ch. 79.

22. A committee of the Pennsylvania house averred in 1792 that slavery was "contrary to the laws of nature, the dictates of justice, and the Constitution of this state"; *Journal of the* . . . *Third House of Representatives* . . . [1792] (Philadelphia: Bailey and Lang, 1792), 55.

23. *New Jersey Revised Statutes* . . . (1847), tit. 11, ch. 6.

24. Laws of 1777, ch. 6, in James Iredell, comp., *Laws of the State of North-Carolina* (Edenton: Hodge & Wills, 1791), 288; Walter Clark, ed., *The State Records of North Carolina* (Winston and Goldsborough: [publisher varies], 1895–1906), XIII, 659–660, 686; Frederika T. Schmidt and Barbara R. Wilhelm, "Early Proslavery Petitions in Virginia," *Wm. & M. Q.*, 30 (1973), 133–146.

and reenacted their colonial slave codes, though with their harsher features softened.[25] (On the other hand, Kentucky, Maryland, and Virginia eased the process of manumission, and the Old Dominion went so far as to extend the "rights, privileges and advantages of citizens" to free blacks.)[26] Slavery proved its staying power in the repeated failure of constitutional and legislative efforts at emancipation in Virginia and Maryland. Thomas Jefferson claimed to have drawn up a *post-nati* emancipation bill that was coupled with provisions for mandatory expatriation of freed blacks. Nothing came of it because, in its author's words, "the public mind would not yet bear the proposition."[27] Despite the efforts of William Pinkney, a rising star in Maryland politics, the Maryland legislature regularly rejected gradual emancipation bills between 1785 and 1790. The hopelessness of emancipation efforts in the upper South was best revealed when Governor James Monroe expressed his hopes for emancipation to President Jefferson in 1802: "It would certainly be a very fortunate attainment if we could make [blacks] instrumental to their own emancipation, by a process gradual and certain, on principles consistent with humanity, without expense or inconvenience to ourselves."[28] By making emancipation turn on unlikely, not to say fantastic, conditions, Virginians committed themselves to maintaining slavery indefinitely.

The Kentucky constitutional convention of 1790 turned back a vigorous attack on slavery and, like its mother state Virginia, accepted slavery with few misgivings. This set a precedent for the new states of the southwest, Tennessee, Mississippi, and Alabama. Louisiana (purchased 1803) and East Florida (ceded 1819) came into Ameri-

25. Laws of 1796, ch. 67 in *Laws of Maryland.* . . . (Annapolis: Frederick Green, n.d. [1797?]); the Georgia and Virginia statutes are summarized in John Codman Hurd, *The Law of Freedom and Bondage in the United States*, 2d ed. (Boston: Little, Brown, 1862), 102, 5–7.
26. Laws of 1782, ch. 21, and Laws of 1783, ch. 16, in William W. Hening, ed., *The Statutes at Large: Being a Collection of All the Laws of Virginia* . . . (Richmond, New York, and Philadelphia: [publisher varies], 1809–23), XI, 39–40, and 322–324; Laws of 1796, ch. 67, in Thomas Herty, ed., *A Digest of the Laws of Maryland* (Baltimore: for the editor, 1799), 349–350; Laws of 1799, ch. 54, in *Laws of Kentucky* . . . (Lexington: John Bradford, 1799).
27. The draft bill is reprinted in Julian P. Boyd, ed., *The Papers of Thomas Jefferson* (Princeton: Princeton Univ. Press, 1950–), II, 470–472. Jefferson, "Autobiography," in Ford, ed., *Writings of Jefferson*, I, 68.
28. Monroe to Jefferson, 11 June 1802, in Stanislaus M. Hamilton, ed., *The Writings of James Monroe* (New York: Putnam's Sons, 1898–1903), III, 353.

can possession with slavery already established there. Thus by 1819, not only was most of the cis-Mississippi United States slave states or territory, but slavery had a foothold in the vast domains of the Louisiana Purchase.

In the upper South and the border areas, slavery was at least open to challenge. In the deep-South states of the Carolinas and Georgia, even that was impossible. The three states made manumissions more difficult in the postwar period. South Carolina in 1800 required an examination of the slave by a magistrate and five freeholders before a manumission could legally be valid, though this seems to have been aimed at preventing the emancipation of the aged and infirm slaves. But in 1820, the Palmetto State forbade emancipation without the approval of the legislature.[29] Georgia's 1798 constitution prohibited the legislature from emancipating slaves without consent of the owners, an effective bar to general abolition. In 1801, the legislature also forbade individual emancipation without the permission of the legislature.[30] North Carolina went even further, requiring in an 1801 statute a prohibitive £100 maintenance bond for individual emancipation.[31]

To cap the deep-South commitment to slavery, South Carolina reopened the high seas slave trade in 1803. (Georgia had permitted importation, except from the West Indies and Florida, until 1798). South Carolina had banned the importation of slaves in 1787, not for humanitarian reasons, but to get out from under postwar indebtedness. Because they left off the practice from economic motives, the Carolinians could resume it when the dictates of self-interest overcame the need to economize. These dictates became imperious as the region beyond the Low Country was settled, and the state reopened the trade in 1803.

The Carolinians' act immediately brought down on them the denunciation of everyone northward, especially in Congress, where shocked congressmen could not at first believe that the Carolinians

29. Thomas Cooper and David J. McCord, comps., *The Statutes at Large of South Carolina* (Columbia: A. S. Johnston, 1836–1841), VII, 442–443, 459. (Hereinafter cited: Cooper & McCord, by volume and page.)

30. Georgia Constitution of 1798, Art. IV, §11, in Thorpe, *Federal and State Constitutions* . . . II, 801; Act of 5 Dec. 1801, in *Acts of the General Assembly of the State of Georgia* . . . *1801* (Louisville; Day and Helt, 1802), 71–72.

31. Laws of 1801, ch. 20, in *Laws of North-Carolina* . . . [1801].

were serious in wanting to resume what was everywhere regarded as a crime and what would in six years be outlawed as piracy.[32] The reopened trade was not a minor venture. Though modern estimates vary widely as to the number of slaves imported into the United States after the Revolution,[33] it is a safe assumption that the number of slaves brought in under the legal trade in the period of 1803 to 1807 numbered in the tens of thousands. For their part, the Carolinians, who had anticipated this denunciation, did not attempt to defend the morality of their venture, but only its necessity.[34] American attitudes about the legality and morality of the trade had peculiar geographic perimeters. By 1810, federal laws would hang a man who carried a slave from Guinea to New Orleans, yet protect a similar voyage, with American naval power if necessary, if the port of origin was Charleston, South Carolina, rather than some slave factory on the West African coast. Moreover, southern laws provided that blacks illegally imported were to be disposed of, not by being handed over to federal authorities for transportation back to the point of origin, but rather by being sold into slavery, with the proceeds accruing to the benefit of the state.[35]

Though these varying trends at the state level were important for the constitutional status of slavery in America, significant precedents were being set at the federal level too. This seems odd at first view, since the federal consensus assumed only an incidental role, if any at all, for the federal government in the regulation of slavery. This assumption proved wrong from the outset, as slavery's opponents regularly sought congressional action to inhibit slavery and as slavery's defenders tried to promote its expansion.

32. Elizabeth Donnan, ed., *Documents Illustrative of the History of the Slave Trade* (1930–35; rpt. New York: Octagon, 1965), IV, 503, 518.

33. Philip D. Curtin, *The Atlantic Slave Trade: A Census* (Madison: Univ. Wisconsin Press, 1969), 72 (70,000 slaves imported 1791–1807); Fogel and Engerman, *Time on the Cross*, 24, and Robert W. Fogel and Stanley L. Engerman, *Time on the Cross: Evidence and Methods* (Boston: Little, Brown, 1974), 30–31 (raising Curtin's estimates considerably); Davis, *Problem of Slavery in the Age of Revolution*, 121 (40,000 during the period of the legal trade).

34. *Annals of Congress*, 8 Cong. 1 sess. 991, 1006 (14 Feb. 1804).

35. Laws of 1816, ch. 12, in *Laws of the State of North-Carolina . . . 1816 . . .* (Raleigh: Thomas Henderson 1817); Act of 19 Dec. 1817 in *Acts . . . of the State of Georgia . . . 1817* (Milledgeville: S. & P. Crestland, 1817), 78–79; Act of 8 Dec. 1815 in *Acts . . . of the Mississippi Territory . . .* (Natchez: Peter Isler, 1815), 19–20.

Quakers in Philadelphia and New York began this struggle in 1790 with petitions urging Congress to do all it constitutionally could to impede the international slave trade. An accompanying memorial from the Pennsylvania Abolition Society, signed by its president, Benjamin Franklin, in studiedly vague language asked Congress to use "all justifiable endeavors to loosen the bands of slavery," and to promote "the restoration of liberty to those unhappy men."[36] This provoked southern representatives to responses ranging along a spectrum of vehemence. At the extreme were Senator William Loughton Smith of South Carolina and Representatives James Jackson of Georgia and Thomas Tudor Tucker of South Carolina, who defended slavery as the southern "palladium" sanctioned by the Bible and threatened "civil war" if Congress moved against slavery. James Madison, then representing Virginia in the House, took a more centrist position, soothing the deep-South bloc by assuring them that it was "not contemplated by any gentleman" that Congress could "abolish slavery in all the states," yet at the same time hinting to northern colleagues that there were "a variety of ways by which [Congress] could countenance the abolition [of the slave trade] and regulations might be made in relation to the introduction of [slaves] into the new States to be formed out of the Western Territory." (The Father of the Constitution would change his mind on the latter point in the Missouri debates of 1820.) On the antislavery side of the debate, Representative Thomas Scott of Pennsylvania, perhaps with an eye on the Massachusetts freedom cases and the Abolition Society's challenge to the constitutionality of slavery in his own state, mused that "I do not know how far I might go, if I was one of the Judges of the United States, and those people were to come before me and claim their emancipation; but I am sure I would go as far as I could." Jackson retorted that such a judge would be lynched in Georgia.[37]

Back in the Senate Smith reiterated the federal consensus—"the toleration of slavery in the several States was a matter of internal regulation and policy, in which each State had a right to do as she pleases, and no other State had any right to intermeddle with her

36. *Annals*, 1 Cong. 2 sess. 1182–1183 (11 Feb. 1790), 1197–1198 (12 Feb. 1790).
37. The debate provoked by the memorials is at *Annals*, 1 Cong. 2 sess. 1189 (11 Feb. 1790), 1198–1204 (12 Feb. 1790), 1466–1471 (22 March 1790); [Edgar S. Maclay, ed.], *The Journal of William Maclay, United States Senator from Pennsylvania, 1789–1791* (New York: Boni, 1927), 192.

policy or laws"—but he recognized that the consensus alone would prove inadequate in the defense of slavery. He therefore went beyond it and asserted that "there was an implied compact between the Northern and Southern people that no step should be taken to injure the property of the latter, or to disturb their tranquillity," an early example of proslavery willingness to read into the Constitution guarantees for slavery that were not there.[38]

To rid themselves of the whole business, which had proved more ominous and wearisome than anyone anticipated, the House adopted a final report that affirmed its inability to end the high seas slave trade before 1808 but that recognized ways in which Congress might restrict American participation in the trade to foreign ports. The report also reaffirmed the federal consensus: "Congress have no authority to interfere in the emancipation of slaves, or in the treatment of them within any of the States; it remaining with the several states alone to provide any regulations therein, which humanity and true policy may require."[39]

This compromise resolution may have been a disappointment to the Pennsylvania Abolition Society, but its president had the last laugh. Disgusted with Representative Jackson's proslavery sentiments, Franklin composed a letter to the Philadelphia *Gazette of the United States* that was published only twenty-four days before his death. Franklin quoted from a fictive American consul's report of debates in the Divan of Algiers on abolishing slavery of whites by the Algerians.[40] An Algerian minister, Sidi Mehemet Ibrahim (*sc.* James Jackson) denounced the sect of Erika (*sc.* Quakers) for their "whimsical" proposal to abolish slavery. To justify enslaving whites, Sidi Mehemet used the same arguments Jackson had to justify enslaving blacks: they were indolent and would not work without compulsion; they could not intermarry because they would pollute the blood of the master race; slavery was good for them because it exposed them to the true religion; slaves were necessary to cultivate the Algerian lands because their masters would not stoop to servile labor to do it; manumission would encourage insurrections; and the Koran explicitly

38. *Annals,* 1 Cong. 2 sess. 1450–1464 (17 March 1790).
39. Reprinted in *Annals,* 1 Cong. 2 sess. 1473–1474.
40. Reprinted in Albert H. Smyth, ed., *The Writings of Benjamin Franklin* (New York: Macmillan, 1905–1907), X, 87–91. This parody created a bibliographic ghost: for some time afterward, persons asked booksellers for "Martin's Account of His Consulship, anno 1787."

sanctioned slavery. It was a virtuoso performance, with the satire being just subtle enough to fool many into thinking that the account was genuine, only to be brought up sharply when they realized they had been hoaxed. The satire was lost on Jackson, but there must have been some guffawing at the next meeting of the Pennsylvania Abolition Society.

Notwithstanding the contumely heaped on them by Jackson and Smith, antislavery petitioners had some positive results to show for their efforts after 1790. Their greatest success came in efforts to curtail the high seas slave trade. The Abolition Societies took the hint tendered in the 1790 House resolution and requested Congress to restrict the trade from American ports to foreign areas. Twice rebuffed, the Societies in 1794 organized their national federation, the American Convention, which had better luck, securing passage of the 1794 federal anti–slave trade act noted earlier.

In debates on strengthening the statute in 1800 to prohibit the kidnaping of free blacks, defenders of slavery briefly extended their theoretical position. As John Rutledge of South Carolina was laboriously reiterating the federal consensus in an effort to have some antislavery petitions tabled or rejected, it occurred to Henry Lee of Virginia that the consensus would not sufficiently protect the South's long-term interests. He therefore proposed a different position: Congress "had no authority but to protect [slavery], and not take measures to deprive citizens of it."[41] There was no occasion for Lee to elaborate this idea at the time, and it lapsed temporarily, only to resurface in the Missouri debates and later enter the mainstream of proslavery constitutional thought in the late 1840s. In 1804, when the House debated South Carolina's reopening of the high seas trade, the innovation in constitutional argument appeared on the antislavery side. Representative John Baptiste Lucas of Pennsylvania claimed that "wherever [slaves] go, the poor white man need not fix himself; for his labor and relative importance in society will be as nothing."[42] This proto–Free Soil idea was born out of its time and languished, but it too would be resurrected in the Missouri debates, and a generation later take on irresistible force as the *raison d'être* of the Republican party.

As the time approached when Congress could constitutionally

41. *Annals,* 6 Cong. 1 sess. 231 (2 Jan. 1800).
42. *Annals,* 8 Cong. 1 sess. 1010 (13 Feb. 1804).

move against the trade, President Jefferson called for action at the earliest possible moment. Yet even then, with no major substantive question open, Congress managed heated disagreement, particularly over penalties for violation of the ban. In a day of almost riotous debate in the House (31 December 1806), Representative Joseph Stanton of Rhode Island suggested that if slavers were to be hanged for violation of the law, consistency required that their customers stretch a rope, too, since it took two, seller and buyer, to create a market for illegally imported slaves. The reporter discreetly omitted mention of southern reaction to that engaging suggestion.[43] The act was passed, making the slave trade to American ports piracy.[44]

As with all other kinds of federal legislation, enforcement of the statute was as important as its passage. The American navy did make an effort to stop slave smuggling, but it was ineffectual to the extent that a modern authority estimates that about fifty-four thousand slaves were illegally brought into the United States after 1807, an average of nearly a thousand a year.[45] Despite this, and notwithstanding later abolitionist charges that abolition of the trade was accomplished solely to augment the prices of slaves on the domestic market and to encourage slave breeding,[46] the antitrade acts represented a serious effort to strike at what nearly all Americans above Carolina were agreed was a moral evil.

Congress' concession to antislavery sentiment in the slave trade statutes was more than offset by its actions protecting slavery in other ways. Though the federal consensus may have impeded action hostile to slavery, it was no bar to slavery's expansion into free states and territories. Congress institutionalized a double standard concerning federal power over extrajurisdictional slaves: it could be used to recover but not to protect them.[47]

Congress did not get around to resolving the ambiguities of the fugitive slave clause of the Constitution for four years. When it did

43. *Annals,* 9 Cong. 2 sess. 240 (31 Dec. 1806); see pp. 167–190 *passim* for the debates.

44. Act of 2 March 1807, ch. 22, 2 Stat. 426.

45. Curtin, *Atlantic Slave Trade,* 74–75; the author states that his figure is a "shot in the dark" guess.

46. Henry C. Wright, *The Dissolution of the American Union, Demanded by Justice and Humanity as the Incurable Enemy of Liberty* . . . (London: Chapman, Brothers, 1846), 9.

47. Davis, *Problem of Slavery in the Age of Revolution,* 133.

do so in 1793, Congress was attempting to break a deadlock between Virginia and Pennsylvania over the rendition by the former of three men, two of whom were wanted for the murder of four Indians, and two of whom were wanted for the kidnaping of a black out of Pennsylvania. An involved triangular legal dispute between Governor Thomas Mifflin of Pennsylvania, United States Attorney General Edmund Randolph, and Virginia Attorney General James Innes over the obligation of Virginia to comply with Pennsylvania's extradition request prompted President Washington to submit the controversy to Congress.[48] After considerable debate, none of it, unfortunately, reported in the *Annals,* Congress enacted the Fugitive Slave Act of 1793.[49] Because this act was supplemented, not replaced, by the 1850 Fugitive Slave Act, and hence was the governing statute until the abolition of slavery, it should be examined with care.

The act was remarkably simple, containing only four sections, the first two of which dealt with the interstate rendition of fugitives from justice. Section 3, following closely the wording of the constitutional clause, provided that when "a person held to labor" escaped into any states or territories of the United States, "the person to whom such labor or service may be due" or his "agent or attorney" could seize the runaway, hale him before a judge of the federal courts in the state or before "any magistrate of a county, city or town corporate," and by affidavit or oral testimony prove title, whereupon the judge or magistrate had to provide a certificate entitling the petitioner to remove the slave. The act contained no provisions for the alleged slave to offer evidence of his own behalf, though this did not mean he was disbarred from doing so if the presiding judge or magistrate chose to let him. Section 4 provided criminal penalties, in addition to any civil action the owner might have under state law, for obstructing the capture and for rescuing, harboring, aiding, or hiding the fugitive. Congress rejected an amendment to the bill that would have allowed the black to prove that he was a native of the forum state or had resided there an unspecified number of years, a provision that would have moderated considerably the harsh procedures of the act.[50]

48. William R. Leslie, "A Study in the Origins of Interstate Rendition: The Big Beaver Creek Murders," *Am. Hist. Rev.,* 57 (1951), 63–76. Most of the relevant documents of the legal dispute can be found in *American State Papers,* Misc. I (Washington: Gales and Seaton, 1834), 38–43.
49. Act of 12 Feb. 1793, ch. 7, 1 Stat. 302.
50. This provision and the legislative history of the act are ably discussed

Though eminent jurists repeatedly held the act to be constitutional,[51] abolitionists after 1830 had little trouble proving to themselves that the statute was invalid. (The debate continues in the twentieth century.)[52] Their universe of discourse was one much different from that of 1793, but they did make three points that were probably valid in 1793. First, that part of section 3 empowering state judicial and executive officials to enforce the federal statute may have been unconstitutional if it were construed to force those officials to do so. This point was implicitly recognized in Justice Joseph Story's opinion in *Prigg v. Pennsylvania* (1842), in which he claimed that such state officials were not obliged to assist in the enforcement of the act. The states could, however, permit their officials to do so. The abolitionist argument was indirectly supported in *Kentucky v. Dennison* (1861), holding that the fugitive-from-justice procedures in the companion sections 1 and 2 of the 1793 act were a binding obligation on a state's governor, but were not enforceable by federal authority.[53]

Second, since the fugitive slave clause refers only to slaves "in one State . . . escaping into another," the application of section 3 of the 1793 statute to territories was an improper extension of Congress' authority. Though this had a precedent in the Northwest Ordinance's fugitive slave provision, the Ordinance was enacted under the authority of a different constitutive document, by a body distinct from the Constitutional Convention and later Congresses, and thus was not pertinent on this point.

---

in Thomas D. Morris, *Free Men All: The Personal Liberty Laws of the North, 1780–1861* (Baltimore: Johns Hopkins Univ. Press, 1974), 19–21.

51. Explicitly in *Prigg v. Pennsylvania*, 16 Pet. (41 U.S.) 608 (1842); implicitly in *Ableman v. Booth*, 21 How. (62 U.S.) 506 (1859), which in dictum upheld the constitutionality of the supplementary and derivative 1850 act. Other significant assertions of the act's constitutionality are Story, *Commentaries on the Constitution of the United States*, §1812; Tilghman, C.J., in *Wright v. Deacon*, 5 Serg. & R. 62 (Pa. 1819); Parker, C.J., in *Commonwealth v. Griffin*, 2 Pick. 11 (Mass. 1823).

52. For modern arguments, see Leslie, "Origins of Interstate Rendition," who argues that Congress adhered to the intention of the framers of the fugitive slave clause; Allen Johnson, "The Constitutionality of the Fugitive Slave Acts," *Yale L.J.*, 31 (1921), 161–182, who argues unpersuasively for the act's constitutionality by *post hoc* reasoning; and Dwight L. Dumond, *Antislavery: The Crusade for Freedom in America* (Ann Arbor: Univ. Michigan Press, 1961), 58 ("the most flagrantly unconstitutional act of Congress ever enforced by the courts").

53. 24 How. (65 U.S.) 66 (1861).

Third, the 1793 act did impinge on the powers of the states to protect their free residents from kidnaping. The *Prigg* decision of 1842 construed it and the fugitive slave clause as voiding state statutes, like the personal liberty laws, that interfered with rights the master enjoyed under the federal Constitution and laws. Yet the fugitive slave clause and the 1793 act refer, euphemistically but unmistakably, only to slaves. This raised the vital question of which state, the forum jurisdiction or the master's domicile, was to determine the status of the alleged fugitive. If the 1793 act were construed to exclude the forum jurisdiction from making that determination, it would have been an unconstitutional invasion of the states' police powers.

Congress also promoted the extension of slavery by establishing and protecting it in all federal territories, districts, and properties outside the free states and the Northwest Territory. At the time President Washington chose a ten-mile-square site on the Potomac River for the location of the federal city that was to be named after him, slaves already resided in the area. Ten years later, when the federal establishment moved to the District of Columbia, there were some 3,200 slaves and 800 free blacks living there, out of a total population of only 14,000.[54] Much of Washington's physical plant, including the White House and the Capitol, was rebuilt by gangs of leased slaves after being fired by the British in 1814. That the Capitol of the United States should have been built by the labor of black slaves had a great, though usually overlooked, symbolic significance for the place of slavery in American life.

The District's slaves needed laws for their governance and, under the *Somerset* precedent, for their very status as slaves. Rather than go to the trouble of drawing up a slave code for the District from scratch, Congress simply adopted the extant state laws, by declaring that the statutes of Maryland and Virginia relating to slavery in force on 1 December 1800 should remain in force.[55] These congressionally adopted state laws were supplemented with municipal ordinances drafted by the Corporation of the City of Washington, including an 1827 code, that were designed principally as police regulations governing the immigration and behavior of free blacks.[56]

54. Constance M. Green, *The Secret City: A History of Race Relations in the Nation's Capital* (Princeton: Princeton Univ. Press, 1967), ch. 2.
55. Act of 27 Feb. 1801, ch. 15, 2 Stat. 103.
56. The Corporation's ordinances were reprinted in "A Member of the

This tripartite derivation of the positive law of slavery for the District was more expedient than sensible. The Virginia and Maryland laws differed between themselves, and the District was governed by their inconsistent provisions until the retrocession of the Virginia portion of the District in 1846.[57] Apart from their multifariousness, the statutes contained provisions, some dating back to eighteenth-century codes, that all regarded as inhumane in the antebellum era. Technically, for example, a slave in Washington could have had his ears cropped for striking a white, though no instance is known of this punishment actually being carried out. Maryland repealed its cropping law in 1821, yet it hung on in a grisly afterlife in the District.[58]

Even more offensive was a provision derived from a 1719 Maryland statute providing that blacks seized as runaways and held in District jails could be sold for jail costs and other expenses of capture if unclaimed after public advertisement of their seizure. Because nothing in the statute exempted free blacks who were seized by mistake, free persons were sometimes taken up, imprisoned, and sold into slavery because no master would claim them, for the obvious reason that they were free.[59] Maryland rid itself of this feature of its laws shortly after cession, but the jailor's sale provision continued with undiminished vitality in the District.

This law produced the 1826 *cause célèbre* of Gilbert Horton, a free black citizen of New York, who was seized as a runaway in the District and advertised for sale. He was rescued by the timely intervention of William Jay and other New York abolitionists, who prevailed on New York Governor DeWitt Clinton to secure his release.[60] The Horton incident and the jailor's sale law displayed the legal system of slavery in its most oppressive light. If a humane jailor became

---

Washington Bar," *The Slavery Code of the District of Columbia* (Washington: L. Towers, 1862), an unofficial compilation, rearranged topically, of congressional, state (Maryland only), and local components of the District slave code as of 1862, with footnote citations to decisions of the Maryland and District courts construing these laws; a useful compilation.

57. Mary Tremain, *Slavery in the District of Columbia: The Policy of Congress and the Struggle for Abolition* (New York: Putnam's, 1892), 36–37.

58. Tremain, *Slavery in the District of Columbia*, 38.

59. For one example, see Washington *Daily National Intelligencer*, 3 March 1825, advertising John Brown, Henry Hanson, and William Brown for sale. All of them, the ad noted, claimed to have been born free.

60. Bayard Tuckerman, *William Jay and the Constitutional Movement for the Abolition of Slavery* (1893; rpt. New York: Franklin, 1969), 29–34.

persuaded that one of his black charges was in reality a freeman, he faced the difficult choice of nonetheless selling him into slavery to recoup his costs, for which, under the southern fee system of the time, he was personally responsible, or bearing the expenses of the black's unjustified detention out of his own pocket.

Congress' moral and legal responsibility for slavery in the Capital heightened after 1808 with the rise of a thriving slave trade in Washington and Alexandria. Alexandria residents and Virginia Representative John Randolph denounced the trade. Abolitionists emphasized the spectacle of slave coffles shuffling by the Capitol on their way south.[61] Virginians of Jefferson's time, even when defending slavery, condemned slave traders as "the *feculum* of society," so the thought of a brisk trade in humans going on in the environs of the Capitol was uncomfortable to everyone, and was responsible for the prohibition of the District trade as part of the Compromise of 1850. But until then the federal city contained barracoons and slave pens; traders auctioned slaves and advertised in the city's papers; slave catchers and kidnapers—and the two were often indistinguishable—plied their trade through the city under the aegis of congressionally adopted laws.

If slavery in the District of Columbia had a largely symbolic significance, the expansion of slavery into other federal territories was a different matter. Fast becoming an anomaly in western civilization as the nineteenth century progressed, slavery possibly might not have maintained its dynamism, and perhaps could not even have long survived as a significant form of labor organization in the United States, without spreading into new slave territory, which in turn led to the dream of a continental or hemispheric slave empire, and to the need to subvert the policies of nonslaveholding states and communities. This expansionist thrust was connived at by the policy of the federal government, which either established slavery in the western territories or protected it by federal law.

That the history of the southwestern territories turned out so differently from that of the Northwest Territory was due in some measure to the action of North Carolina, which, in its 1790 cession of its western land claims that formed a part of "The Territory South of the

61. Jesse Torrey, *A Portraiture of Domestic Slavery, in the United States: . . . including Memoirs of Facts on the Interior Traffic in Slaves, and on Kidnapping* (Philadelphia: John Bioren, 1817).

River Ohio," stipulated that the benefits of the Northwest Ordinance should be made available to the settlers, "provided always that no regulations made or to be made by Congress shall tend to emancipate slaves."[62] Congress respected this proviso, admitting as slave states Kentucky (part of the Virginia cession) in 1792, Tennessee (including the aborted State of Franklin and part of the North Carolina cession) in 1796, Mississippi in 1817 and Alabama in 1819 (both carved out of the Georgia and South Carolina cessions, plus portions of West Florida annexed between 1810 and 1812). This policy was extended to East Florida, ceded by Spain in 1819 and admitted as a state in 1845.

Congress did not write, or even adopt, a slave code for these areas while they were in the territorial stage. This was the function of the territorial government which, during the first stage of its existence, was empowered to adopt the constitution and laws of any of the original states for its territorial code. Congress then accepted the laws, including slave codes, thus adopted, but it did not do so without opposition. In 1798, when Congress tried to create Mississippi Territory (encompassing roughly the southern third of modern Mississippi and Alabama less West Florida), northern congressmen tried unsuccessfully to block the extension of slavery there.[63]

An even more significant leap of slavery westward took place in 1803 with the Louisiana Purchase. Under the Spanish and French regimes, the white settlers of Louisiana[64] had held slaves and participated in the international slave trade. At the time of Napoleon's cession, there were about thirteen thousand slaves in Louisiana, more than the number of whites, according to the information furnished President Jefferson.[65] The French residents were determined not only to hold onto these, but to acquire more by keeping open the interna-

62. Clarence E. Carter, comp., *The Territorial Papers of the United States* (Washington, D.C.: GPO, 1933–), IV, 7.
63. *Annals*, 5 Cong. 2 sess. 1306–1311 (23 March 1798).
64. These included residents of settlements not only around the mouth of the Mississippi River near modern New Orleans, but also those in distant trading outposts up the river, including Kaskaskia and Cahokia in present-day Illinois, Vincennes in modern Indiana, Cape Girardeau, Ste. Genevieve, St. Charles, and St. Louis in modern Missouri.
65. See Jefferson's "An Account of Louisiana," *American State Papers*, Misc., I, 348.

tional trade.[66] The Treaty of Cession provided that the Louisiana inhabitants should "as soon as possible" enjoy "the rights, advantages and immunities of citizens of the United States; and in the mean time they shall be maintained and protected in the free enjoyment of their liberty, property, and the Religion which they profess."[67] Opponents of the international trade included those opposed to slavery on principle, as well as upper-South representatives who feared the influx of black rebels from Santo Domingo.[68] On the other side, a proslavery coalition insisting on unlimited imports revealed the dynamism of slavery's expansionist tendency. To the argument that republican America should support freedom, not further enslavement, Senator Jackson of Georgia responded, "you cannot prevent slavery—neither laws moral or human can do it—men will be governed by their interest, not the law." Senator David Stone of North Carolina insisted that slaves were merely property, whose owners had the same right to carry them into the territories as they had to bring in any other sort of property, a dim anticipation of Chief Justice Taney's position in *Dred Scott.*[69]

In the end, a compromise prevailed. Extant slavery was secured; immigrating slaveowners were permitted to bring in their human chattels; but the inhabitants of the territory were prohibited from importing slaves from ports outside the United States, and from bringing slaves in by the interstate trade who had been imported into the United States since 1 May 1798, and indirect slap at South Carolina's reopening of the trade.[70]

66. "Remonstrance of the People of Louisiana," reprinted in *Annals,* 8 Cong. 2 sess. 1597–1608 at 1606; see George Dargo, *Jefferson's Louisiana: Politics and the Clash of Legal Traditions* (Cambridge: Harvard Univ. Press, 1975), 7, 30.

67. Art. III, Treaty of 30 April 1803, in Hunter Miller, ed., *Treaties and Other International Acts of the United States of America* (Washington, D.C.: GPO, 1931–48), II, 501.

68. Memorials from the American Convention and Philadelphia Quakers, reprinted in *Annals,* 8 Cong. 2 sess. 1569, 39, 996; David Humphrey's, *A Valedictory Discourse, Delivered before the Cincinnati of Connecticut . . . 1804 . . .* (Boston: Gilbert and Dean, 1804), 26–33; Davis, *Problem of Slavery in the Age of Revolution,* 157; for a survey of constitutional issues generally, see Everett S. Brown, *The Constitutional History of the Louisiana Purchase, 1803–1812* (Berkeley: Univ. of California Press, 1920).

69. Everett S. Brown, ed., *William Plumer's Memorandum of Proceedings in the United States Senate, 1803–1807* (New York: MacMillan, 1923), 116, 125; debates generally on Louisiana are at 111–122, 125–129.

70. Act of 26 March 1804, ch. 38, §10, 2 Stat. 283.

The actions of the federal government during the first generation of antislavery were decisive on several issues. The federal consensus was, after repeated and protracted debate, elevated to the status of a constitutional principle—though some proslavery political leaders had begun to sense its inadequacy, and had urged a more positive role of the national government in the protection and promotion of slavery. Slavery expanded smoothly into the southwest territories, and, in the acquisition of Louisiana, established a trans-Mississippi beachhead. The free states were obliged to extend a measure of hospitality to slave catchers on their soil. With a suddenness that took observers by surprise, these potentially disruptive tendencies erupted in 1819, when a salient of slave expansion in Illinois was attacked by a bold flanking movement of antislavery forces onto Missouri territory. The years from 1789 to 1819 had set the stage for the second crisis of the Union.

CHAPTER 5

Missouri Statehood: The Second Crisis of the Union

The first generation of America's national existence had revealed that slavery was a politically sensitive issue, yet not one threatening to disrupt the union. The federal consensus, together with the de facto apportionment of the western territories to slavery and freedom, seemed to enable the sections to get along. These arrangements were thrown into disarray by America's acquisition of the Louisiana Purchase in 1803, which doubled America's landed area and which intensified two ongoing disruptive tendencies. Both were caught up in the political vortex of the Missouri crises from 1819 to 1821.

The first was a persistent free-state discontent with the constitutional compromise whose core was the three-fifths clause.[1] The representation of sixty percent of the slaves gave the southern states from 1792 to 1802 twelve congressmen they would not have had had slaves been entirely excluded from the basis of representation, fifteen from 1802 to 1811, and eighteen from 1811 to 1822.[2] As early as 1791, Elias Boudinot, a New Jersey congressman, complained of this bargain in the House.[3] He was echoed by his fellow Jerseyman William Paterson from an unusual forum, the United States Supreme Court,

1. James M. Banner, *To the Hartford Convention: The Federalists and the Origins of Party Politics in Massachusetts, 1789–1815* (New York: Knopf, 1970), 100–109; Shaw Livermore, *The Twilight of Federalism: The Disintegration of the Federalist Party 1815–1830* (Princeton: Princeton Univ. Press, 1962), 88–95; and Linda K. Kerber, *Federalists in Dissent: Imagery and Ideology in Jeffersonian America* (Ithaca: Cornell Univ. Press, 1970), ch. 11.

2. Albert F. Simpson, "The Political Significance of Slave Representation, 1787–1821," *J. Southern Hist.*, 7 (1941), 315–342 at 325, n. 40.

3. *Annals*, 2 Cong. 1 sess. 203 (21 Nov. 1791), 244 (12 Dec. 1791).

who denounced the apportionment rule as "radically wrong."[4] But though discontent in New Jersey persisted through 1819 (the legislature of that state complaining in that year of its loss of equal representation)[5] hostility to the clause was strongest among New England Federalists.

New England's indignation at having been outmaneuvered in the sectional bargain intensified after Jefferson's election to the presidency by the House of Representatives in 1801. With that supposed demonstration of power by what northern Federalists called the "negro votes," opposition to the federal number became linked with hostility to the Virginia Dynasty and the Republican Ascendancy. Even their political doggerel reflected this:

> A southern negro is, you see, man,
> Already three-fifths of a freeman.
> And when Virginia gets the staff,
> He'll be a freeman and a half.[6]

Their fears were confirmed by the Louisiana Purchase, which the Federalist Hartford *Connecticut Courant* in 1804 denounced as leading to the creation of more "negro boroughs" comparable to the rotten boroughs of England.[7] "Boreas" predicted that "when state has been added to state for centuries, the region [i.e. the Purchase area] will not be exhausted; but enough will always be left to furnish another, and another, and yet another; as often as the supremacy of the Slave Country shall demand additional support."[8] John Quincy Adams summed up New England's grievances in a biblical metaphor: "Slave representation has governed the union. Benjamin portioned above his brethren has ravined as a wolf."[9]

This Federalist malaise produced disunion sentiment, privately

4. *Hylton* v. *United States*, 3 Dall. (3 U.S.) 177 (1796).
5. New Jersey resolutions, in *Journal* of the U.S. Senate, 16 Cong. 1 sess. 114 (24 Jan. 1820).
6. Quoted in David H. Fischer, *The Revolution of American Conservatism: The Federalist Party in the Era of Jeffersonian Democracy* (New York: Harper & Row, 1965), 160.
7. Quoted in Simpson, "Political Significance of Slave Representation," 324.
8. "Boreas," *Slave Representation. Awake! O Spirit of the North* (n.p., 1812), 3, 6.
9. Charles Francis Adams, ed., *Memoirs of John Quincy Adams, Comprising Portions of His Diary from 1795 to 1848* (Philadelphia: J. B. Lippincott, 1874–1877), V, 11 (entry of 3 March 1820); Genesis 49:27.

expressed as early as 1803 (the year of the Louisiana Purchase),[10] and openly voiced after the Republicans enacted the sectionally discriminatory, ruinous, yet ineffective Embargo of 1807. The War of 1812 stimulated secessionist ideas.[11] The Hartford Convention (1814) demanded abrogation of the three-fifths clause.[12] With peace in 1815, northern disunionism abated, but dislike of slave representation did not.

The second tendency that produced the Missouri crises was slavery's westward expansion, not only into the new southwestern states, but into the Northwest Territory as well. A proposal to admit slavery into Ohio was only narrowly defeated by a committee of the Ohio constitutional convention of 1802,[13] and the new state legislature, as a sop to proslavery sentiment, immediately began constructing the harshest black code of the free states.[14] Slavery was already entrenched in Indiana Territory[15] among the French settlers around Vincennes and among southern Americans who had migrated along the Ohio River valley with their slaves.[16] These slaveholders claimed that their rights in slaves were secured by the guarantee of

10. See Timothy Pickering to Stephen Higginson, 24 Dec. 1803; Pickering to Theodore Lyman, 11 Feb. 1804; Pickering to Rufus King, 4 March 1804; and Higginson to Pickering, 17 March 1804; quoted in Henry Cabot Lodge, *Life and Letters of George Cabot* (Boston: Little, Brown, 1877), 441–453.

11. Rep. Josiah Quincy of Massachusetts in *Annals*, 11 Cong. 3 sess. 525 (14 Jan. 1811); "Massachusetts," *The New States or a Comparison of the Wealth, Strength, and Population of the Northern and Southern States; as Also of Their Respective Powers in Congress; with a View to Expose the Injustice of Erecting New States at the South* (Boston: J. Belcher, 1813); Gouverneur Morris, diary entry of 3 May 1812 recording a conversation with DeWitt Clinton, in Anne C. Morris, ed., *The Diary and Letters of Gouverneur Morris* (New York: Scribner's, 1888), II, 541.

12. Resolves of the convention are reprinted in Theodore Dwight, *History of the Hartford Convention* . . . (New York: N. & J. White, 1833), 352–379 at 377.

13. Beverley W. Bond, ed., "Memoirs of Benjamin Van Cleve," *Quarterly Publications of the Historical and Philosophical Society of Ohio*, 17 (1922), 70–71.

14. "An Act, to regulate black and mulatto persons," ch. 4, *Acts of the State of Ohio* . . . [1803] (Chillicothe: N. Willis [1803]).

15. Indiana Territory comprised modern Indiana, Illinois, Michigan, and Wisconsin, 1803–1805. In 1805, Michigan Territory was set off from it. In 1809, modern Indiana was set off from the remainder, and was admitted as a state in 1816.

16. Morton M. Rosenberg and Dennis V. McClurg, *The Politics of Pro-Slavery Sentiment in Indiana, 1816–1861* (Muncie: Ball State Univ., 1968), 1–10.

extant property rights in the Virginia cession of 1783. They were supported by Arthur St. Clair, governor of the Northwest Territory, who claimed that the Northwest Ordinance was only prospective in its impact, and did not liberate any existing slaves.[17] St. Clair's interpretation was probably in accord with the intention of the framers of the ordinance.[18] Abetted by William Henry Harrison, then governor of Indiana Territory and later President of the United States, Indiana slave interests secured passage of a territorial statute in 1805 that permitted slaves to be brought into the territory under an indenture and held there indefinitely as "indentured" servants. Their children born in the territory would be held as slaves to a certain age.[19]

The Indiana indenture law was carried over into Illinois Territory when that area was set off in 1809.[20] The hold of slavery was more tenacious in Illinois because of the demand for slave labor at the Shawneetown saline and the Galena lead mines. Slavery therefore persisted in Illinois, either as the holdover of French slavery in Kaskaskia, or as indentured servitude at Shawneetown, throughout the territorial period. The new state constitution, adopted in 1818, secured indentured slavery and protected the Shawneetown slave enclave until 1825. It proved to be the spark that touched off the Missouri controversy. Only an intensive abolitionist effort, emphasizing the interests of white farmers rather than the wrongs to black slaves, prevented the people of Illinois from amending their constitution in 1823 to sanction slavery formally.[21]

17. St. Clair to President Washington, 1 May 1790, in Clarence E. Carter, comp., *The Territorial Papers of the United States* (Washington, D.C.: GPO, 1934–), II, 244–246; Bartholomew Tardiveau to St. Clair, 30 June 1789, in William Henry Smith, ed., *The St. Clair Papers: The Life and Public Services of Arthur St. Clair* (Cincinnati: Robert Clarke, 1882), II, 117–119. See Francis S. Philbrick, ed., *The Laws of Illinois Territory, 1809–1818* (Springfield: Illinois State Historical Library, 1950), ccxxiii–ccxlviii.

18. See report of a committee consisting of James Madison, Hugh Williamson, and Abraham Clark, 25 Sept. 1788, *Journals of the Continental Congress*, XXXIV, 540–542.

19. Eugene H. Berwanger, *The Frontier against Slavery: Western Anti-Negro Prejudice and the Slavery Extension Controversy* (Urbana: Univ. of Illinois Press, 1967), 8–9; Francis S. Philbrick, ed., *The Laws of Indiana Territory, 1801–1809* (Springfield: Illinois State Historical Library, 1930), xx–xliii; the 1805 statute is at 136–139.

20. The adoption statute is at Philbrick, ed., *Laws of Illinois Territory*, 5–6.

21. [Morris Birkbeck], *An Appeal to the People of Illinois, on the Question of a Convention* (Shawneetown: C. Jones, 1823); [Roberts Vaux or Morris Birkbeck?], *An Impartial Appeal to the Reason, Interest and Patriotism, of the*

Four related items of business before the Fifteenth Congress (1818–1819) drew these two tendencies together. Illinois, Alabama, and Missouri Territories sought admission as states, and the residents of what would soon be Arkansas Territory sought a territorial government.[22] An informal pattern of balanced state admissions had already been established: Ohio (free) 1803 and Louisiana (slave) 1812, Indiana (free) 1816 and Mississippi (slave) 1817. Northern congressmen therefore expected Illinois to come in free, and Alabama as a slave state. A few of them were dismayed to discover in the Illinois constitution the provisions that recognized indentured servitude, required registration and servitude for the children of indentured crypto-slaves, and allowed the annual employment of slaves in the Shawneetown salt works until 1825. Representative James Tallmadge of New York objected to these provisions.[23] His opposition failed to keep Illinois out, but he and other northern congressmen— thirty-four voted against Illinois' admission—had been alerted to the expansive character of slavery.

At almost the same time, the Alabama, Arkansas, and Missouri problems came up. On Saturday, 13 February 1819, Tallmadge introduced a *post-nati* amendment to the Missouri enabling bill, prohibiting "the further introduction of slavery" and providing that "all children of slaves, born within the said state, after the admission thereof into the Union, shall be free, but may be held to service until the age of twenty five years."[24] Tallmadge's proposal marked the formal beginning of the Missouri controversies.[25]

People of Illinois, on the Injurious Effects of Slave Labour (n.p., 1824); [Edward Coles?], *Remarks Addressed to the Citizens of Illinois, on the Proposed Introduction of Slavery* (n.p., n.d., [1823?]); Berwanger, *Frontier against Slavery*, 14–18.

22. Arkansas Territory (1819–1824) embraced modern Arkansas and most of modern Oklahoma, which became the unorganized Indian Territory after Arkansas was set off from it. Arkansas was admitted as a state in 1836.

23. *Annals*, 15 Cong. 2 sess. 306–307 (23 Nov. 1819).

24. *Journal* of the House of Representatives, 15 Cong. 2 sess. 272 (13 Feb. 1819). The wording of the amendment as reported in the *Annals*, 15 Cong. 2 sess. 1170 (15 Feb. 1819) varied slightly.

25. For surveys, see Glover Moore, *The Missouri Controversy 1818–1821* (Lexington: Univ. of Kentucky Press, 1953); George Dangerfield, *The Era of Good Feelings* (New York: Harcourt, Brace & World, 1952), 199–248; Dangerfield, *The Awakening of American Nationalism, 1815–1828* (New York: Harper & Row, 1965), ch. 4; Ronald F. Banks, *Maine Becomes a State: The Movement to Separate Maine from Massachusetts, 1785–1820*

Missouri Statehood   111

In a long but moderate Senate speech on 26 and 27 February 1819, Rufus King first set forth the position of "restrictionists," those who would restrict the spread of slavery into Missouri.[26] Under the clauses empowering Congress to make "all needful Rules and Regulations respecting the Territory or other Property belonging to the United States" (Article IV, section 3, clause 2) and permitting it to admit new states (clause 1), Congress could require the territory or new state to exclude slavery as a condition of admission. King's speech created a sensation, partly because he was one of the few surviving framers still active. Slavery's defenders came to regard it as the debut of constitutional antislavery. Thirty years later, Virginia Senator Robert M. T. Hunter recalled King's speeches vividly as "the declaration of that war upon slavery, which, with some intermissions, has been waged ever since by the North against the South."[27]

The House passed Tallmadge's amendment, but the Senate killed it, and the matter lay over to the new Congress. At the same time, both houses defeated efforts to impose comparable restrictions on Arkansas Territory, and, at the beginning of the next session, admitted Alabama without restriction. During the ensuing summer and autumn (1819), opponents of slavery throughout the northern states drummed up an astonishing amount of support in favor of restriction. Every major northern city, and even Baltimore in the slave states, witnessed a large crowd adopting restrictionist resolutions. John Jay, the elderly former Chief Justice of the United States, staggered antirestrictionists with a public letter in which he supported Congress' power to restrict slavery on the basis of the migration or importation clause of Article 1, section 9.[28] Because Jay had been one of the coauthors of the Federalist Papers, no one alive in 1820 except James

(Middletown: Wesleyan Univ. Press, 1970), ch. 9; and Charles S. Sydnor, *The Development of Southern Sectionalism, 1819–1848* (Baton Rouge: Louisiana State Univ. Press, 1948), 120–133. On Missouri's role in the controversy, see Harrison A. Trexler, *Slavery in Missouri, 1804–1865* (Baltimore: Johns Hopkins Univ. Press, 1914), 100–112; and Floyd C. Shoemaker, *Missouri's Struggle for Statehood, 1804–1821* (Jefferson City: Stephens, 1916).
  26. This speech, unreported in the *Annals,* is reprinted in Charles R. King, ed., *The Life and Correspondence of Rufus King . . .* (New York: Putnam's, 1894–1900), VI, 690–703.
  27. *Congressional Globe,* 31 Cong. 1 sess., app. 375–376 (25 March 1850).
  28. Jay to Elias Boudinot, 17 Nov. 1819, in Henry P. Johnston, ed., *The Correspondence and Public Papers of John Jay* (New York: Putnam's, 1890–1893), IV, 430–431.

Madison spoke with more authority about the meaning of the Constitution, and Madison was being careful to keep his expressions of opinion on the Missouri matter private.

When the first session of the Sixteenth Congress met in December 1819, enabling bills for Missouri were introduced in both Houses. Southerners promptly gave notice of their intention to hold Maine, a territory of Massachusetts seeking admission as a free state, as hostage for the admission of Missouri, thereby practicing a bit of legislative extortion on the less firm restrictionists. Opponents of Missouri's admission as a slave state outlined the premises that underlay their arguments. Slavery "was an evil of so much magnitude that it became necessary to provide for it in the constitution; but, being an evil, the provisions of the Constitution never meant to foster and cherish it in the Government."[29] "The Constitution was universally considered as leading to the gradual abolition of slavery even in the old states," thought Senator William Plumer of New Hampshire, "and as furnishing no excuse for its extension to the new."[30] Therefore the ambiguities of the document had to be resolved by reading them in the light furnished by principles derived from the egalitarian phrases of the Declaration of Independence and Article VI of the Northwest Ordinance.

Given these assumptions, it was axiomatic that the Constitution permitted and possibly required Congress to prevent the further extension of slavery. Restrictionists accepted the burden of proof resting on them to show the constitutionality of restriction, and found no difficulty sustaining it. Three clauses—new states, territories, and slave importation—were directly germane. A fourth, the guarantee of republican government, was also pertinent, but unsettling.

Article IV, section 3, provides that "New States may be admitted by the Congress into this Union. . . ." To restrictionists, the key word was *may,* which implied a power that was discretionary rather than mandatory. Because Congress' power was "full, perfect, and complete," it could impose any condition it wished on a state's admission, and deny admission because of some fundamental defect in a state's constitution.[31] Congress had imposed conditions on the admission of every state, beginning with Northwest Ordinance and the

29. William Hendricks of Indiana, *Annals,* 16 Cong. 1 sess. 1350 (15 Feb. 1820).
30. *Annals,* 16 Cong. 1 sess. 1437 (21 Feb. 1820).
31. Benjamin Ruggles of Ohio, Prentiss Mellen of Massachusetts (Maine),

admission of the fourteenth state, Vermont, and these conditions cut close to the essential attributes of sovereignty, such as the power to alienate the lands of the state or the power to tax.[32] Thus Congress was justified by precedent in requiring Missouri, as a condition of admission, to provide for emancipation of *post-nati* and the nonintroduction of slavery, and to keep Missouri out until it did so.

Southern congressmen claimed that, under the new states clause, Congress was restricted to deciding only whether to admit a state or not. The clause implied no power to impose conditions, because such a power would impose on the new state a status inferior to the extant or original states. Some Missourians even maintained that their admission did not depend on congressional consent at all.[33] Antirestrictionists' rebuttal arguments under the new states clause ranged from Madison's reasonable and modest suggestion that if a congressional power to exclude existed at all, it was only inferential, and that the framers probably did not have any clear ideas at all about the relationship of slavery to the new states clause,[34] to extremist arguments *ad horrendum*. Some southerners argued that if Congress could exclude slavery, it would "sound the tocsin of freedom to every negro of the South" and ultimately lead to communism—called by John Scott of Missouri in those innocent early days "the Agrarian principle."[35]

It may seem perverse that both sides could read the same words and derive contradictory, mutually exclusive conclusions from them.

Hendricks, and Timothy Fuller of Massachusetts, in *Annals,* 16 Cong. 1 sess. 280 (27 Jan. 1820), 181 (19 Jan. 1820), 1350 (15 Feb. 1820), 1468 (24 Feb. 1820).

32. David Morril of New Hampshire in *Annals,* 16 Cong. 1 sess. 143 (17 Jan. 1820).

33. Delegate John Scott of Missouri, *Annals,* 15 Cong. 2 sess. 1196 (15 Feb. 1819); Nathaniel Macon of North Carolina, Nicholas Van Dyke of Delaware, James Barbour of Virginia, Robert W. Reid of Georgia in *Annals,* 16 Cong. 1 sess. 230 (20 Jan. 1820), 307 (28 Jan. 1820), 321 (1 Feb. 1820), 1028 (1 Feb. 1820); Mark Hill, "Fellow Citizens of the State of Maine," (1820), reprinted in Banks, *Maine Becomes a State,* 361–365; resolutions of Kentucky legislature in *Journal* of the U.S. Senate, 16 Cong. 1 sess. 115–116, (24 Jan. 1820); preamble to resolutions of Virginia legislature, reprinted in Richmond *Enquirer,* 5 Feb. 1820. Resolves of St. Louis mass meeting are quoted in Shoemaker, *Missouri's Struggle for Statehood,* 85.

34. Madison to Robert Walsh, 27 Nov. 1819, in Gaillard Hunt, ed., *The Writings of James Madison* (New York: Putnam's, 1900–1910), IX, 6–8.

35. "An American," "Missouri Question . . . No. 1," Richmond *Enquirer,* 29 Dec. 1819; Linn Banks to James Barbour, 20 Feb. 1820, reprinted in [Lyon G. Tyler, ed.], "Missouri Compromise. Letters to James Barbour . . . ," *William and Mary College Q.,* [1st ser.], 10 (1902), 5–24; *Annals,* 15 Cong. 2 sess. 1201 (15 Feb. 1819).

Two things, both inherent in the processes of American constitutionalism, resolve the puzzle. The first is the ambiguity of the words found in the Constitution. None of the important phrases of the clauses central to the Missouri debates—"may be admitted," "all needful Rules and Regulations respecting the Territory," "The Migration or Importation of such Persons," "Commerce . . . among the several States," "Republican Form of Government"—furnished imperative and unambiguous answers to the questions put to the Constitution by the extension of slavery into the western empire. Take the first phrase as an example: all conceded that it was discretionary with Congress whether or not to admit a new state. But the critical point still lay beyond this. Could Congress stipulate conditions and make the admission of the state contingent on acceptance of these conditions? In order to answer such a question, or comparable ones relating to other phrases, men had to cantilever an answer, as it were, using the phrase as a fulcrum, supporting their view by an extension of principles not inherent in the constitutional formula. This process was not singular to the Missouri debates.

The second explanation for the puzzle of men reading the same words and deriving antithetical answers is related to the first. In drafting the phrases, the framers did not anticipate the precise problem facing later generations and, a fortiori, did not attempt to answer it. Again, take the new states clause: the men who penned and ratified it were citizens of a cis-Mississippi nation, the principal new-state problem of which would be to carve new states out of territories claimed by the original states. They entertained only the mistiest aspirations, if any at all, about a trans-Mississippi empire. Thus the Missouri antagonists, when faced with the question "What answer does the Constitution give to our problem?" would have had to answer "None," if they had been frank. They were rescued by their resort to fundamental principles anterior to the Constitution.

Restrictionists found a second source of authority in the territories clause of Article IV, section 3: "The Congress shall have Power to dispose of and make all needful Rules and Regulations respecting the Territory or other Property belonging to the United States. . . ." This clause was, as Madison observed in one of his understatements, "of a ductile character."[36] Restrictionists read it to confer "complete

36. Madison to Robert Walsh, 27 Nov. 1819, in Hunt, ed., *Writings of Madison,* IX, 6.

and universal" congressional power over the territories, comparable to the powers a state has over the land and people within its jurisdiction, and far broader than federal power over the states.[37] Until Congress accepted its constitution, Missouri was a territory subject to this plenary federal power.[38] "Needful Rules and Regulations" meant legislation; "Power," especially power "to dispose of," was unrestricted in its terms. Hence there was no limit in the text of the Constitution that would suggest anything less than unlimited police power, and the restrictionists assumed momentarily the strict-constructionist posture, as to the territories clause, that their opponents had taken up for the new states clause. In a general way, the restrictionist reading of congressional power was countenanced by the United States Supreme Court eight years later in *American Insurance Co.* v. *Canter* (1828).[39] When President James Monroe received the first Missouri bill for his signature, he referred it to his cabinet and to some outside consultants for opinions on its constitutionality. The cabinet was unanimously of the opinion that Congress had power to exclude slavery in the territories under the territories clause, which was surprising because the cabinet included such slave-state spokesmen as John C. Calhoun, William H. Crawford of Georgia, and William Wirt of Maryland.[40]

Slavery's defenders rebutted arguments based on the territories

37. *A Memorial to the Congress of the United States, on the Subject of Restraining the Increase of Slavery in New States to Be Admitted into the Union* (Boston: Sewell Phelps, 1819), 4. This memorial, which may have been drawn up by Daniel Webster, was adopted at a mass meeting in Boston in December 1819, and will henceforth be referred to as the *Boston Memorial*.

38. John Taylor of New York in *Annals*, 15 Cong. 2 sess. 1173 (15 Feb. 1819); New York and Delaware resolutions in *Journal* of U.S. Senate, 16 Cong. 1 sess. 130, 124 (17 Jan. 1820). Delaware was the only slave state to maintain the restrictionist position.

39. 1 Pet. (26 U.S.) 511 (1828); see generally Robert R. Russel, "Constitutional Doctrines with Regard to Slavery in Territories," *J. Southern Hist.*, 32 (1966), 466–486.

40. The written cabinet opinions that Monroe requested had disappeared by the 1840s when a search was made for them. The only records surviving of individuals' opinions is the diary entry of Secretary of State John Quincy Adams of 3 March 1820 in Adams, ed., *Memoirs of John Quincy Adams*, V, 5. Madison, one of Monroe's consultants, denied congressional restrictionist powers under the territories clause, the only one who did so; Madison to Monroe, 23 Feb. 1820, Hunt, ed., *Writings of Madison*, IX, 23–26. See Harry Ammon, *James Monroe: The Quest for National Identity* (New York: McGraw-Hill, 1971), ch. 25.

clause by defining "Territory" to mean land. They argued that Congress could legislate only concerning landholding, not the people, government, or social order of the territories. Congress consequently derived no power from the clause over the persons of slaves in the territories or the rights of their masters. Some Missourians went even further, and denied all congressional power over a territory, except the power to see to it that the territorial government was republican in form.[41]

Because Missouri's admission seemed imminent, arguments based on the territories clause were, if not a makeweight, then little more than a supplement to new-states-clause arguments. But the debates over federal power in the territories had a deeper significance, only dimly perceived by the Missouri antagonists. On the one side, restrictionists stood for an expansive reading of federal power to control slavery, carrying their arguments right up to the outer limits of the federal consensus. There was also the possibility, underscored by the Adams-Onis treaty of 1819, that the Louisiana Purchase might not be America's last major territorial acquisition, so the territorial arguments had a practical pertinence, even apart from the status of Missouri and Arkansas.

Southern writers and politicians worked out a "trustee theory" of congressional power over the territories, under which Congress administers the territory as the trustee for all the states, and may not act inimically to the interests of any of them, as by excluding slavery or by depriving the people of any of the states of the right to migrate to the territories with their human property.[42] This trustee theory was adopted by Chief Justice Roger B. Taney in *Dred Scott*. Missouri territorial delegate John Scott and Representative Alexander Smyth of Virginia anticipated another of Taney's *Dred Scott* points when they claimed that the Tallmadge Amendment's provisions liberating *post-nati* would violate the Fifth Amendment by taking property without due process of law or just compensation.[43]

41. Walter Leake of Mississippi, Macon, William Smith of South Carolina, Alexander Smyth of Virginia, in *Annals,* 16 Cong. 1 sess. 199 (19 Jan. 1820), 230 (20 Jan. 1820), 262–263 (26 Jan. 1820), 1003 (27 Jan. 1820); resolve of Ste. Genevieve, Missouri, county meeting, reprinted in *Niles Weekly Register,* 2 Oct. 1819.
42. "An American," "Missouri Question . . . No. 4," Richmond *Enquirer,* 8 Jan. 1820.
43. *Annals,* 16 Cong. 1 sess. 1521 (25 Feb. 1820), 998 (27 Jan. 1820).

The third clause providing a textual foundation for restrictionist arguments was the slave trade clause of Article I, section 9, restricting Congress' power to prohibit the international slave trade until 1808. But restrictionists were agreed on only one point of interpretation of the 1808 clause: the word *migration* referred to slaves.[44] Beyond that, they drew varying inferences from the clause. Most agreed with Representative John W. Taylor of New York that it empowered Congress to prohibit the interstate slave trade, and as such "was intended to protect non-slave holding States, against the intrusion of slaves, and to restrict them within the States where the evil was tolerated."[45] Some restrictionists agreed further with Justice Joseph Story and Senator Benjamin Ruggles of Ohio that the slave trade clause was merely a specific exception from Congress' power over all aspects of the slave trade, both domestic and foreign, that was derived from the commerce clause.[46] But whatever the source of congressional power, restrictionists agreed that the slave trade clause was what lawyers and logicians call a "negative pregnant." By saying Congress shall not exercise a certain power for a stated period of time as to particular objects, the framers implied that it had the power fully, since it was necessary to make this explicit reservation of it.[47]

All of this was bad enough from a proslavery viewpoint, but a few restrictionists made it worse by drawing a logical conclusion from the negative pregnant argument. If the purpose of the clause was, as Senator James Burrill of Rhode Island claimed, to "restrain and circumscribe slavery," then perhaps it was a power Congress could use to pen up slavery in the states where it existed in 1789 or 1808 by the simple expedient of prohibiting the trade out of those states,

44. Walter Lowrie of Pennsylvania, *Annals*, 16 Cong. 1 sess. 203 (20 Jan. 1820).

45. Taylor, *Annals*, 16 Cong. 1 sess. 959 (27 Jan. 1820); Fuller, *Annals*, 15 Cong. 2 sess. 1183 (15 Feb. 1819); Clifton Claggett of New Hampshire, *Annals*, 16 Cong. 1 sess. 1039 (1 Feb. 1820); *Boston Memorial*, 9; [Lemuel Shaw], "Slavery and the Missouri Question," *North American Rev.*, 10 (1820), 137–168 at 152–153; report of the Delaware Abolition Society to the American Convention, 5 Oct. 1819, in *Niles Weekly Register*, 6 Nov. 1819; "A Philadelphian" [Robert Walsh], *Free Remarks on the Spirit of the Federal Constitution, the Practice of the Federal Government, and the Obligations of the Union, respecting the Exclusion of Slavery from the Territories and New States* (Philadelphia: A. Finley, 1819), 14–21.

46. *Annals*, 16 Cong. 1 sess. 281 (27 Jan. 1820); Joseph Story, *Slavery and the Slave Trade* (n.p., n.d. [1820]), 2–4.

47. Daniel P. Cook of Illinois, *Annals*, 16 Cong. 1 sess. 1094 (4 Feb. 1820).

or at least prohibiting it into the new states.[48] This idea was reinforced by the language of the clause itself, which speaks of slavery only in "the States now existing." On purely syntactical grounds, the restrictionist negative pregnant argument was persuasive. But another inference by Representative Daniel Cook of Illinois went further: Congress might abolish slavery even in the extant states by the simple expedient of abolishing the interstate slave trade entirely and thus choking slavery's internal population adjustments.[49]

In rebuttal, antirestrictionists argued that "Migration" in the 1808 clause referred only to the movement of free white aliens, denying Congress power to control the interstate movement of enslaved blacks.[50] Charles Pinckney, one of the few surviving framers and, with King, the only one in Congress at the time, accepted this interpretation. But Pinckney raised the argument several notches in importance by insisting that

it was an agreed point, a solemnly understood compact, that, on the southern States consenting to shut their ports against the importation of Africans, no power was to be delegated to Congress, nor were they ever to be authorized to touch the question of slavery; that the property of the Southern States in slaves was to be as sacredly preserved, and protected to them, as that of land, or any other kind of property in the Eastern States were to be to their citizens.[51]

Pinckney's claim, as well as restrictionists' arguments derived from the 1808 and new states clauses, revealed that both sides in the slavery debates were diverging over the future development of the federal consensus. Pinckney saw it as assuring an attitude of benevolent neutrality toward slavery on the part of the federal government, while opponents of slavery advanced from viewing it as a means of coexistence by free and slave states in the union to interpreting it as a principle of containment. The consensus was already proving inadequate as a determinant of federal relations.

48. Burrill and Morril, *Annals,* 16 Cong. 1 sess. 212 (20 Jan. 1820), 139 (17 Jan. 1820).
49. *Annals,* 16 Cong. 1 sess. 1104 (4 Feb. 1820).
50. Elliott, Smith, Macon, Barbour, Leake, Scott, in *Annals,* 16 Cong. 1 sess. 130–131 (17 Jan. 1820), 261–262 (26 Jan. 1820), 231 (20 Jan. 1820), 318 (1 Feb. 1820), 198 (19 Jan. 1820), 1501 (25 Feb. 1820).
51. *Annals,* 16 Cong. 1 sess. 1316 (14 Feb. 1820).

Restrictionist arguments based on the new states, territories, and migration clauses, being tied to specific and definable textual provisions, were narrowly focused. Occasionally, though, restrictionists in and out of Congress cut loose from textual analysis and allowed themselves some free speculation on the relationship between slavery and republican government. When they did this, the scope of argument widened, and considerations of policy were overtaken by considerations of legitimacy.

It seemed axiomatic to restrictionists that slavery was incompatible with a republican government, or at least an anomaly in a republic.[52] This assumption led in two directions. Broadly developed, it suggested slavery's illegitimacy under the Declaration of Independence, the bills of rights in the state constitutions, and the Preamble to the Constitution. In this way, antislavery ideology was absorbed into the Missouri political debates.[53] Narrowly developed, it suggested that slavery was seemed somehow inconsistent with that clause of Article IV, section 4, that provides: "The United States shall guarantee to every State in this Union a Republican Form of Government. . . ."[54]

The related Declaration-of-Independence and guarantee-clause arguments were raised early in the Missouri debates by Timothy Fuller of Massachusetts, who maintained that the Declaration was a

52. Plumer, Charles Rich of Vermont, Morril, Ezra Gross of New York, and Taylor in *Annals*, 16 Cong. 1 sess. 1426 (21 Feb. 1820), 1395 (17 Feb. 1820), 150 (17 Jan. 1820), 1251 (11 Feb. 1820), 959 (27 Jan. 1820); Josephus Wheaton, *The Equality of Mankind and the Evils of Slavery, Illustrated: A Sermon . . . 1820* (Boston: Crocker & Brewster, 1820).

53. *Minutes of the Seventeenth Session of the American Convention for Promoting the Abolition of Slavery . . . 1821* (Philadelphia: Atkinson & Alexander, 1821), 3; [William Hillhouse], *The Crisis, No. 1. or, Thoughts on Slavery, Occasioned by the Missouri Question* (New Haven: A. H. Maltby, 1820), 8; [Hillhouse], *The Crisis, No. 2 . . .* (New Haven: A. H. Maltby, 1820), 16; [Walsh], *Free Remarks*, 4; Report of the Delaware Abolition Society in *Niles Weekly Register*, 6 Nov. 1819; Story, *Slavery and the Slave Trade*, 4; Report of a Philadelphia mass meeting, 23 Nov. 1819, in *Niles Weekly Register*, 11 Dec. 1819; John Wright, *A Refutation of the Sophisms, Gross Misrepresentations, and Erroneous Quotations . . .* (Washington, D.C.: for the author, 1820), 50; resolution of the Pennsylvania legislature, 22 Dec. 1819, in Herman V. Ames, *State Documents on Federal Relations: The States and the United States* (Philadelphia: Univ. of Pennsylvania, 1906), 197–199; George Bourne, *The Book and Slavery Irreconcilable* (Philadelphia: J. M. Sanderson, 1816), 35–36.

54. Claggett and Morril, *Annals*, 16 Cong. 1 sess. 1039 (1 Feb. 1820), 150 (17 Jan. 1820).

key to understanding the principles of republican government, providing substantive content to the vague textual phrase "Republican Form of Government."[55] Fuller's suggestion produced a commotion in the House, with slaveholding members warning him that his principles would challenge slavery in the old states, a possibility that Fuller firmly denied.

If Fuller backed away from his implicit challenge to the federal consensus, other New Englanders did not. Charles Rich of Vermont a year later argued that "the legality [of slavery] must be determined by a reference to the laws of nature and natural rights, and not to the Constitution," thereby relying on a touchstone of legitimacy superior to the written guarantees for slavery in the Constitution.[56] Lemuel Shaw, future Chief Justice of the Massachusetts Supreme Judicial Court, wrote in the *North American Review* that slaveholding never shook off its criminal origin, so that a claim to own a slave or the child of a slave is "a continuance of such criminality."[57] In the Senate, Rufus King went well beyond his original attack on slavery expansion. In 1819, King had hewed closely to specific clauses (migration, new states); now he moved on to the dangerous higher ground of natural law: "All men being by natural law free and equal, . . . one man could not rightfully make another his slave, so in their social state, they could not confer on others a right to do what they themselves could not do—hence it follows that no prince or government can make and hold slaves."[58] Paraphrasing King's ideas, Alabama Senator John W. Walker claimed that King

has emancipated the whole of our slaves by one potent ipse dixit. By the Declaration of Independence all men are created equal! The law of nature—that is the law of God—that is the Christian dispensation—forbids slavery. The law of God is supreme to the law of man. Therefore no

55. *Annals,* 15 Cong. 2 sess. 1180–1182 (15 Feb. 1819); see generally Philip F. Detweiler, "Congressional Debate on Slavery and the Declaration of Independence, 1819–1821," *Am. Hist. Rev.,* 63 (1958), 598–616.
56. *Annals,* 16 Cong. 1 sess. 1396 (17 Feb. 1820).
57. Shaw, "Slavery and the Missouri Question," 142.
58. This speech of 11 Feb. 1820 unfortunately went unreported in the *Annals.* Robert Ernst has reconstructed its substance in *Rufus King: American Federalist* (Chapel Hill: Univ. of North Carolina Press, 1968), 372, from draft fragments, King's correspondence, and paraphrases by others responding to him. The quoted portion is from a draft fragment in the King Papers, N-YHS.

human law, compact or compromise can establish or continue slavery. They are all null and void, being contrary to the law of God. No man can rightfully enslave his fellows. Therefore slavery cannot exist.[59]

Restrictionists in Congress insisted that they did not mean to go so far. Fuller, who had broached the subject, reflected somberly yet realistically that "our Declaration of Independence, our Revolution, our State institutions, and above all, the great principles of our Federal Constitution, are arrayed on one side, and our legislative acts and national measures, the practical specification of our real principles and character, on the other." He resolved his difficulty by suggesting that the existence of slavery in the old states was settled by the compromises of 1787, and was an evil that simply had to be borne, but that Congress should assert principles of justice by forbidding further extension of the evil.[60] Harrison Gray Otis, a Massachusetts Federalist, "disavowed entirely the right of Congress to interpose its authority in relation to slavery in the old States, and protested against the wish or design to promote a general emancipation of their slaves."[61]

Slavery's defenders capitalized on their opponents' discomfiture by trying to show them that their implications were dangerous because their premises were false. The true theory of republican government was that "rights, political and civil, may be qualified by the fundamental law, upon such inducements as the freemen of the country deem sufficient."[62] Antirestrictionists also began the gradual disavowal of the Declaration of Independence that ended with their repudiation of it fifteen years later. Being merely a statement of "abstract theoretical principles, in a national manifesto in 1776," the Declaration was not part of the American Constitution and liberated no slaves. It was not even correct; "the self-evident truths announced in the Declaration of Independence are not truths at all, if taken literally."[63]

59. Walker to Charles Tait, 11 Feb. 1820, quoted in William S. Jenkins, *Pro-Slavery Thought in the Old South* (Chapel Hill: Univ. of North Carolina Press, 1935), 68–69.
60. *Annals*, 16 Cong. 1 sess. 1467 (24 Feb. 1820).
61. *Annals*, 16 Cong. 1 sess. 251 (25 Jan. 1820).
62. Pinkney, *Annals*, 16 Cong. 1 sess. 412 (15 Feb. 1820); "A Southron," "Missouri Question," Richmond *Enquirer*, 6 Jan. 1820; "On the Slave Trade and Slavery," [Washington] *National Intelligencer*, 4 Dec. 1819.
63. Van Dyke, Smyth, Pinkney in *Annals*, 16 Cong. 1 sess. 301 (27 Jan. 1820), 1004 (27 Jan. 1820), 405 (15 Feb. 1820).

Southerners demanded that the restrictionists accept the logical outcome of their principles. If slavery and republicanism are incompatible in Missouri, how can they be reconciled in Alabama or Virginia? William Pinkney, among the ablest of the southern spokesmen, asked, "Is it denied that those [existing slave] states possess a republican form of government? If it is, why does our power of correction sleep? Why is the constitutional guaranty suffered to be inactive? Do gentlemen perceive the consequences to which their arguments must lead, if they are of any value? Do they reflect that they lead to emancipation in the old United States?"[64] The idea that slavery and republicanism were incompatible "goes directly to the emancipation of slavery [*sic*] throughout the whole United States," insisted the Virginian Philip Pendleton Barbour.[65]

A final resolution of the first Missouri crisis began to take shape in the Senate on 17 February 1820 when Senator Jesse Thomas of Illinois introduced an amendment that would admit Maine and Missouri without restriction, and that would prohibit slavery in all the Purchase territory north of 36° 30′ (Missouri's southern border), excepting Missouri. The House rejected this and passed its own enabling bill with a restrictionist amendment. The Senate insisted on the Thomas formula, the House rejected it again, and a select committee was appointed to find some way out of the deadlock. This it did by recommending the substance of the Thomas bill to the House, which accepted it by voting on it not as a whole, but on its separate features separately. Thus Maine came in free, Missouri was permitted to come in any way it wished—which meant as a slave state—and slavery was excluded from the areas north and west of Missouri, while being permitted in Arkansas Territory.

The Missouri constitutional convention of 1820 precipitated the second crisis a year later by engrafting into the new state constitution two provisions concerning slavery and free blacks. The first, modeled on the 1798 Georgia constitution, prohibited the state legislature from emancipating slaves without their owners' consent and without paying the full value of the slave. This amounted to a constitutional guarantee of slavery's perpetuity in Missouri. The second provision required the legislature to "pass such laws as may be necessary . . . to prevent free negroes and mulattoes from coming to and settling in

64. *Annals*, 16 Cong. 1 sess. 411 (15 Feb. 1820).
65. *Annals*, 16 Cong. 1 sess. 1240 (10 Feb. 1820).

this State, under any pretext whatsoever."[66] Both provisions rekindled restrictionists' hostility and Congress, to everyone's dismay, found itself in a replay of the previous two sessions' arguments. The second session of the Sixteenth Congress rehashed many of the issues it had gone through before, but one important new element appeared: what was the place in America for the black person who was not a slave? This question forced Americans to confront issues of racism and egalitarianism.

Debates in the second crisis centered on the clause of Article IV, section 2, that provides: "The Citizens of each State shall be entitled to all Privileges and Immunities of Citizens in the several States." Free-state representatives claimed that free blacks were citizens of their states, even though they were under disabilities, such as being disfranchised, excluded from militia duty, or subjected to attenuated remnants of the colonial black codes. Hence a black New Yorker should enjoy the same right to enter Missouri as a white one.[67] Though some southerners conceded the validity of the northern interpretation of the clause,[68] few would admit it publically, and in Congress they launched into a redundant attack on the restrictionist position. Charles Pinckney, still representing South Carolina in the House, tried to silence the restrictionists by insisting incorrectly that he had been the author of the privileges and immunities clause at the federal convention, and that in his mind the clause comprehended only whites. "There did not then exist such a thing in the Union as a black or colored citizen, nor could I then have conceived it possible such a thing could ever have existed in it; nor, notwithstanding all that is said on the subject, do I now believe one does exist in it."[69] Philip Pendleton Barbour voiced the fear that lay in white southern hearts: free blacks are "the most dangerous [class] to the community that can possibly be conceived. They are just enough elevated to have some sense of liberty, and yet not the capacity to estimate or enjoy all its rights, if they had them—and being between two societies, above

66. Art. III, §26 in Thorpe, *Federal and State Constitutions,* IV, 2154.
67. Otis in *Annals,* 16 Cong. 2 sess. 96 (9 Dec. 1820); see also resolution of Vermont legislature, *ibid.,* 78–79; Burrill, James Strong of New York, Morril in *ibid.,* 47 (7 Dec. 1820), 570 (9 Dec. 1820), 111–112 (11 Dec. 1820).
68. John Quincy Adams claimed that John C. Calhoun admitted to him in private conversation that the Missouri clause was unconstitutional; Adams, ed., *Memoirs of John Quincy Adams,* V, 199 (12 Nov. 1820).
69. *Annals,* 16 Cong. 2 sess. 1134–1136 (13 Feb. 1821).

one and below the other, they are in a most dissatisfied state . . . firebrands to the other class of their own color."[70]

In the end the second crisis was compromised, and its issues swept under the rug, by a resolution of admission drafted by Henry Clay, which admitted Missouri on the "fundamental condition" that the free Negro clause "shall never be construed to authorize the passage of any law" that would deny a citizen of any of the states a privilege or immunity to which he is entitled.[71] In George Dangerfield's words, "It became a 'fundamental condition' of the admission of Missouri that her unamended Constitution should require the General Assembly to pass laws excluding free Negroes . . . but that no law, so passed, should ever be interpreted as meaning what it did mean."[72] Missouri's response was no more than such a measure deserved: it first stated that Congress lacked power to impose the condition; then in 1825 passed a statute permitting the entry of free blacks only if they were citizens of some other state, and then only if they could produce naturalization papers (an impossible condition to fulfill, since no state naturalized its natives); and finally in 1847 flouted the "fundamental condition" altogether by prohibiting all free blacks from entering the state.[73] Missouri's action was justified both before and after 1821 by the policy of Congress, which in 1790 had limited naturalization to "free white person[s]," and which in 1837 violated the first Missouri Compromise by authorizing the "Platte Purchase" of 1837, by which a small area of modern northwest Missouri was transferred from the Louisiana Purchase territory (where slavery was prohibited) to Missouri, where it augmented the acreage of a slave state.[74]

The Missouri compromises worked well in their time. They laid to rest an issue that had distracted Congress for two years, and were based on a simple line-drawing expedient that made the federal consensus workable for another generation. Over the objections of south-

70. *Annals,* 16 Cong. 2 sess. 549 (8 Dec. 1820).
71. *Annals,* 16 Cong. 2 sess. 1228 (26 Feb. 1821).
72. Dangerfield, *Awakening of American Nationalism,* 136.
73. "An Act Concerning Negroes and Mulattoes," 7 Jan. 1825, §4, in *Laws of the State of Missouri, Revised* . . . (St. Louis: E. Charless, 1825), II, 600; "An Act Respecting Slaves, Free Negroes, and Mulattoes," 16 Feb. 1847, §4, in *Laws of the State of Missouri* . . . [1847], (Jefferson City: James Lusk, 1847).
74. Act of 26 March 1790, ch. 3, §1, 1 Stat. 103; Perry McCandless, *A History of Missouri: 1820 to 1860* (Columbia: Univ. of Missouri Press, 1972), 117.

ern spokesmen, Congress affirmed the power of the federal government to exclude slavery from the territories, a concession to the antislavery position that became weightier over time.

But the longer-run effects of the compromises showed that the constitutional confrontation between slavery and abolition had only been procrastinated, not averted. The first consequence was purely political: the Republican Ascendancy or Virginia Dynasty rapidly evolved into a new and different party. The Jacksonian Democracy adopted the federal consensus as its central ideological tenet, insisting that slavery issues be resolved by the states, not the federal government. To enforce this doctrine, southerners used the party as a vehicle to assure proslavery dominance of the national government. They maintained this control by electing as president either a southerner posing as a westerner (e.g. Andrew Jackson) or a northern man with southern principles (e.g. Martin Van Buren). The process of admitting new states in free state–slave state pairs assured southern control of the Senate, because some free-state Democrats could always be found to vote with their southern brethren for the sake of party unity on any issue affecting the vital interests of the south.[75]

A second effect of the compromises was glimpsed by Thomas Jefferson, who wrote in a famous passage that "a geographical line, coinciding with a marked principle, moral and political, once conceived and held up to the angry passions of men, will never be obliterated."[76] The Missouri crises foreshadowed the overlapipng geographic, moral, and political division that was to destroy the Union. That was not obvious to Jefferson's contemporaries as the second crises of the Union subsided, but the 1820s, like the period that preceded the Missouri controversy, witnessed a persistent, low-level eruption of controversies over slavery.

75. This is an extension of the thesis of Richard H. Brown, "The Missouri Crisis, Slavery, and the Politics of Jacksonianism," *South Atlantic Q.*, 65 (1966), 55–72.
76. Jefferson to John Holmes, 22 April 1820, in Andrew A. Lipscomb and Albert E. Bergh, eds., *The Writings of Thomas Jefferson* (Washington, D.C.: Thomas Jefferson Memorial Assn., 1905), XV, 248–250.

CHAPTER 6

The Southern Counteroffensive

Thoughtful southern leaders recognized that they had suffered at least a partial defeat in the Missouri controversy. The restriction of slavery north of 36° 30′ might not have been so threatening had Secretary of State John Quincy Adams not ceded American claims to Texas. But after the Adams-Onis treaty of 1819, slavery's westward expansion within the extant United States was confined to Louisiana, Missouri, and Arkansas Territory. Thomas Ritchie warned in the Richmond *Enquirer* that "if we are cooped up on the north [i.e. north of Missouri], we must have elbow room to the west," and urged continued southern interest in Texas despite the treaty.[1] But suddenly southern attention was diverted from the external expansion of slavery into the territories to the protection of its internal security in the extant states. In meeting this new threat, the defenders of slavery mounted a counteroffensive against what they regarded as officious northern meddling with their internal affairs. This effort produced a reinterpretation of the federal consensus that made it an aegis of slavery, and a well-argued reformulation of constitutional premises that provided a foundation for all subsequent proslavery constitutionalism.

The first threat to slavery's internal security came from a most unlikely source: the movement for expulsion of free black people headed by the American Colonization Society. Founded in 1816, the ACS enjoyed the patronage of America's national political elite, including Chief Justice John Marshall of the United States Supreme Court and Associate Justice Bushrod Washington, a nephew of George Washington and long-time honorary ACS president who in 1821 embarrassed

1. Richmond *Enquirer*, 7 March 1820.

some colonizationists by selling off fifty of his own slaves southward for insolence and insubordination. Others included Henry Clay, William Crawford, Charles Carroll, James Madison, James Monroe, John Randolph of Roanoke, John Taylor of Caroline, Daniel Webster, Horace Binney, Richard Rush, Francis Scott Key, Charles F. Mercer, and Robert Goodloe Harper.[2] Despite this support, the ACS had difficulty getting financial aid from Congress, and its efforts provoked Carolinians' hostility.

Though some colonizationists, especially in the early years of the movement, were opposed to slavery, the ACS came to be dominated by defenders of slavery. Southern colonizationists emphasized that Article II of the ACS charter confined its activities "exclusively" to "colonizing (with their consent) the free people of colour, residing in our country." They denounced free blacks as useless, pernicious, ignorant, degraded, insane, hopeless, "an anomalous race of beings, the most debased upon earth . . . a vile excrescence upon society."[3] Colonizationists boasted of their respect for the "sacred" property rights of slaveholders, pointing to the large number of slaveowners in their own ranks.[4] Henry Clay, an ACS charter member, went so far as to admit ingenuously that slaveowners would benefit by colonization through an increase in the value of their slaves due to the removal of free black economic competition.[5] Perceiving such attitudes, black leaders and organizations, including the American Society of Free Persons of Colour and its presidents James Forten and Hezekiah Grice, condemned colonization as "the direct road to perpetuate slavery."[6]

2. On the Society generally, see P. J. Staudenraus, *The African Colonization Movement 1816–1865* (New York: Columbia Univ. Press, 1961).

3. Henry Clay's speech at the founding of the ACS, in Washington *National Intelligencer*, 24 Dec. 1816.

4. Speech of James S. Green to the Colonization Society of New Jersey, *African Repository*, 1 (1825), 283; Cyrus Edwards, "An Address . . . ," ibid., 7 (1831), 97–100.

5. *African Repository*, 2 (1827), 344.

6. "Conventional Address," *Minutes and Proceedings of the First Annual Convention of the People of Colour* . . . (Philadelphia: for the committee, 1831), 15; "Address of the Free People of Colour," (1817), reprinted in *Minutes of the Proceedings of a Special Meeting of the Fifteenth American Convention for Promoting the Abolition of Slavery . . . 1818* . . . (Philadelphia: Hall & Atkinson, 1818), 15. "Conventional Address," *Minutes of the Proceedings of the Third Annual Convention, For the Improvement of the Free People of Colour in the United States* . . . (New York: for the Convention, 1833), 35.

Despite the decided proslavery drift of the supporters of colonization, Carolinians regarded it as covert abolitionism. This seems perverse, to say the least, unless seen in the perspective of Denmark Vesey's insurrection, which supposedly was to occur in Charleston in 1822. Vesey, the Missouri debates, and colonization convinced Carolinians that slavery as a system of race control was threatened from within and without. Individuals, organizations, the free states, and even foreign nations seemed to be taking an unwelcome interest in the future of slavery—possibly a prelude to an antislavery challenge to the federal consensus. The blacks themselves, slave and free, seemed to become restless. The day-to-day disciplinary problems of slavery—insubordination, shirking, running away—increased and were compounded by a heightened tempo of real or imagined acts of petty treason and individual or group rebellion. All this was made worse by the endemic problem of lax enforcement of the black codes. Nothing less than a perfect police state might have kept the blacks in unchallenged subjection, and South Carolina was not a police state. Slaveholders and nonslaveholders, especially in the upper South, seemed to be faltering in their determination to maintain slavery rigidly, just at the time when such maintenance was more needed than ever before. All around them alarmed Carolinians thought they saw an unraveling of the fabric of institutions that kept black men in subjection to whites.

The great irony of Vesey's insurrection was that momentous constitutional consequences flowed from what may have been a pseudo-event. Contemporaries and recent historians have divided sharply on whether there actually was an incipient black insurrection in Charleston in 1822. There may have been nothing more than the usual amount of slave and black restiveness, magnified out of proportion by rumor and panic; or a small number of blacks may have actually laid plans for an uprising, doomed to failure by insufficient slave support; or perhaps a well-planned and extensively supported rebellion was aborted at the last minute.[7] The significance of the Vesey insur-

7. Those historians who insist on the reality of a massive incipient rebellion include Robert Starobin, ed., *Denmark Vesey: The Slave Conspiracy of 1882* (Englewood Cliffs: Prentice-Hall, 1970), 1–9, 178–180, and John Oliver Killens, ed., *The Trial Record of Denmark Vesey* (Boston: Beacon, 1970), vii–xxi. Somewhere in the middle, accepting the reality of the rebellion but discounting its size, are William W. Freehling, *Prelude to Civil War: The Nullification Controversy in South Carolina, 1816–1836* (New York: Harper

rection for the development of American constitutionalism lay not in the uprising itself, though, but in the reaction of white Carolinians.

During the winter of 1821–1822, Vesey, a free black of Charleston who had bought his way out of slavery with a lucky draw in a lottery, gathered a group of subordinates who in turn recruited others—how many, no one knows. Estimates ran from eighty to nine thousand. The uprising was aborted twice by blacks who warned city authorities. Nothing ever happened; the whole plot, insofar as it exists in evidence, consists of testimony about what the blacks intended to do. They had actually done nothing; none were caught with weapons; none were taken under incriminating circumstances. Nonetheless the white community reacted massively. Charleston Intendant (mayor) James Hamilton and Governor Thomas Bennett called out militia and watch units. Authorities and vigilantes began rounding up suspected blacks and interrogating them.

Vesey and other alleged conspirators were tried by two special slave courts, which included some of South Carolina's political elite: Joel R. Poinsett, Robert Y. Hayne, and William Drayton. Ultimately thirty-five men, including Vesey and his lieutenants, were hanged; thirty-two were deported; twenty-six were acquitted; and thirty-eight discharged. The courts' proceedings were promptly published to convince doubters about the reality of the insurrection, as well as for their *in terrorem* effect on slaves.[8]

Feeling themselves beset from within and without, Carolinians erected a comprehensive defense of slavery's legitimacy and worked out a constitutional theory to complement that defense. The Bible, both in the Old and New Testaments, sanctioned slavery and contained God's virtual command that superior races maintain inferior ones in subjection.[9] Slavery was based on two primal facts of the hu-

---

& Row, 1966), 53–63; and John Lofton, *Insurrection in South Carolina: The Turbulent World of Denmark Vesey* (Yellow Springs: Antioch Press, 1964). At the other extreme is Richard C. Wade, who in "The Vesey Plot: A Reconsideration," *J. Southern Hist.*, 30 (1964), 143–161, regards the evidence of an insurrection as being so insufficient that he concludes that there was either no conspiracy at all or merely a "vague and unformulated plan" (p. 150).

8. [James Hamilton], *An Account of the Late Intended Insurrection among a Portion of the Blacks of This City* (Charleston: A. E. Miller, 1822).

9. *Rev. Dr. Richard Furman's Exposition of the Views of the Baptists, Relative to the Coloured Population of the United States . . .* (Charleston: A. E. Miller, 1823); "A South-Carolinian" [Frederick Dalcho], *Practical Considerations Founded on the Scriptures, Relative to the Slave Population of South-Carolina* (Charleston: A. E. Miller, 1823).

man condition: most men had to be compelled to labor, and the human race was obviously differentiated into ranks. Putting these two together, Carolinians concluded that since the superior must command the inferior to labor, slavery was "the step-ladder by which civilized countries have passed from barbarism to civilization."[10] Though Chancellor Henry Desaussure still admitted slavery to be an evil, others repudiated that concession, arguing that slavery was a blessing to blacks and a necessity to whites. Charles Cotesworth Pinckney and Edwin Holland maintained that Carolina's slaves were better off than the laboring class anywhere else in the world, particularly those areas hospitable to antislavery sentiment. Northern criticism of slavery was merely the effusion of a "whining, canting, sickly kind of humanity."[11]

Given this justification of slavery, Carolinians revised their constitutional attitudes in order to protect it from tendencies toward what Thomas Cooper called "Consolidation." Cooper denied that a national government had been created by the Constitution and insisted that the states remained independent sovereigns, relinquishing only those powers expressly delegated to Congress.[12] Robert Turnbull adopted a slightly less extreme position. He viewed the Colonization Society as a "nest egg" that would hatch into abolition under the warm feathers of congressional support, and as being just one other aspect of consolidationist tendencies that also included the Bank of the United States, federal aid for internal improvements, the tariff, and Henry Clay's "American System." Turnbull recurred to the Virginia and Kentucky Resolutions, seeing them as the embodiment of a constitutional theory that could throttle consolidationist tendencies. Under their doctrine, the federal government could exercise no power over any matter within the authority of the states; its proper sphere was limited to international commerce and defense. The federal Con-

10. [Edward Brown], *Notes on the Origin and Necessity of Slavery* (Charleston: A. E. Miller, 1826), 6.
11. "A Columbian" [Henry W. Desaussure], *A Series of Numbers Addressed to the Public, on the Subject of the Slaves and Free People of Colour . . .* (Columbia: State Gazette Office, 1822), 5; "A South-Carolinian" [Edwin C. Holland], *A Refutation of the Calumnies Circulated against the Southern & Western States, respecting the Institution and Existence of Slavery Among Them . . .* (Charleston: A. E. Miller, 1822), 13, 47; Charles Cotesworth Pinckney, *An Address Delivered in Charleston before the Agricultural Society of South-Carolina . . .* (Charleston: A. E. Miller, 1829).
12. [Thomas Cooper], *Consolidation. An Account of Parties in the United States, from the Convention of 1787, to the Present Period* (Columbia: Black & Sweeney, 1824).

stitution was the product, not of all the American people *en masse,* but of the people of the sovereign and independent states. The federal government was capable of exercising only those powers that the people of the states had delegated to it.[13]

Whitemarsh Seabrook approached the problem of congressional meddling on a less theoretical plane than Cooper or Turnbull. He demanded that Congress avoid discussion of any "subject, in which the question of slavery may be directly or incidentally introduced," and recommended popular censorship of the press, both of which objectives Carolinians were to achieve within a decade. Seabrook claimed that even a duly ratified constitutional amendment adversely affecting slavery would be "unconstitutional" because slavery in South Carolina enjoyed a status based on "inherent principles of the national compact" and thus was immune from any sort of interference by Congress or the state legislatures. In this sense, slavery enjoyed a status higher than the Constitution itself.[14] This position was echoed forty years later by a few die-hards who insisted that the Thirteenth Amendment was unconstitutional.

Carolinians saw that their erstwhile nationalism was becoming dysfunctional. The assumptions underlying interstate relations in the American union would have to be reconsidered. Holland warned the free states that they would have to respect a "proper equilibrium" in the political relations among the states, meaning that they would have to do more than they had in the way of honoring the sovereign power of the states to regulate slavery. "Established constitutional rights and privileges of slave owners" could be adequately respected only if northerners refrained from criticism of slavery, of which they were in any event ignorant.[15] The restrictionist position in the Missouri debates was a "violation of the federal compact" because it transmitted an "indiscreet zeal in favor of Universal liberty" to the slaves.[16] Any northern effort to restrict the spread of slavery or its

13. "Brutus" [Robert J. Turnbull], *The Crisis: or, Essays on the Usurpations of the Federal Government* (Charleston: A. E. Miller, 1827), 7, 81, 104, 121–126, 133.

14. Whitemarsh B. Seabrook, *A Concise View of the Critical Situation, and Future Prospects of the Slave-Holding States, in relation to Their Coloured Population* . . . (Charleston: A. E. Miller, 1825), 5, 11–12, 14–15, 16.

15. [Holland], *Refutation of the Calumnies,* 8–11.

16. "Achates" [Thomas Pinckney], *Reflections, Occasioned by the Late Disturbances in Charleston* (Charleston: A. E. Miller, 1822), 6–8; [Hamilton], *Account of the Late Intended Insurrection,* 30.

political power in the national government would be a violation of the rights of the southern states.

This extreme sensitivity accounts for that peculiar quality of Carolinian constitutional discourse that baffled contemporaries: their ability to speak about one issue explicitly (such as the tariff or internal improvements) while in reality but only implicitly talking about another—slavery. Their instinctive resort to the *argumentum ad horrendum* and their disposition to inflate trifles into impending calamities were annoying and appeared hallucinatory, but they may have been perspicuous. James Hamilton explained that the constitutional quarrel over tariffs and internal improvements (the vehicles used by Cooper in his attact on consolidation) was actually "a battle at the out-posts, by which, if we succeed in repulsing the enemy, the citadel would be safe."[17] It was unnecessary for Hamilton to add that the "citadel" was slavery, though this would have prevented northerners and historians from confusing tactical skirmishing with strategic defense.

Even before the Vesey plot, the South Carolina legislature, responding to the restrictionist and neorestrictionist positions in the Missouri debates, had tightened up the black code by forbidding private manumissions, prohibiting the ingress of free blacks, and making distribution of "incendiary" publications a felony.[18] After the plot was suppressed, legislators noted that Vesey had once been a slave seaman and that his lieutenants Peter Poyas and Gullah Jack were slaves of shipyard owners. They concluded that free black seamen coming into Charleston on shore leave who mingled with free and enslaved blacks contaminated Carolina's slaves. Hence the Negro Seamen's Act of 1822,[19] which provided that any free black seaman debarking from a vessel in any port of the state was to be jailed immediately and held until his vessel cleared. The master was liable for the costs of incarceration. If the master of the vessel failed to redeem his sailor on departure he (the master) was to be fined at least $1,000 and jailed two months, and the black was to be sold into slavery by the sheriff.

17. Hamilton to John Taylor, 14 Sept. 1830, excerpted in William W. Freehling, ed., *The Nullification Era: A Documentary Record* (New York: Harper & Row, 1967), 100–101.
18. Cooper & McCord, *Statutes at Large,* VII, 459–460.
19. Ch. 3, *Acts and Resolutions of . . . South-Carolina . . . 1822* (Columbia: Daniel Faust, 1823), 11–14.

Carolinians might have anticipated a hostile reception by foreign and northern shippers, but they were unpleasantly surprised to find that the most forceful challenge to the constitutionality of the statute came from two southerners, Associate Justice William Johnson of the United States Supreme Court, a native Charlestonian, and United States Attorney General William Wirt of Maryland. As Charlestonians began to split into "militant" and moderate factions over the severity of reaction to the plot, the militants organized themselves as the "South Carolina Association" and clamored for drastic action against free blacks in the state. Johnson, his brother-in-law the outgoing Governor Bennett, and Joel R. Poinsett tried to cushion the impact of the Seamen's Act, but the frisky Association could not long be restrained. So Johnson, in his capacity as Chief Judge of the United States Circuit Court for the District of South Carolina, took the opportunity to strike directly at the statute from the bench.

His opportunity came when the Charleston sheriff arrested a free black British seaman, Henry Elkison, and the sailor challenged the constitutionality of the statute in Johnson's court. Though the state did not appear, the South Carolina Association, determined to get a heavy-handed enforcement of the black codes, hired prominent attorneys to defend the statute. Benjamin F. Hunt, for the Association, groped toward a state sovereignty theory in his arguments. Insisting that no state could be presumed to have surrendered to the federal government any vital power over internal police, Hunt concluded that in any clash between federal and state authority, state power must override federal if such an area of police was involved, and that only the state can be the judge of whether it was or not.[20]

Johnson indignantly rejected this argument in an opinion that he himself characterized as unusually severe in its language.[21] The statute, "passed hastily and without due consideration," "leads to dissolution of the Union, and implies a direct attack upon the sovereignty of the United States." He held the statute unconstitutional on two grounds: it interfered with the "paramount and exclusive" federal power to regulate foreign commerce; and it violated a treaty, the commercial convention of 1815 with Great Britain, which Johnson

20. Hunt's argument is quoted and paraphrased in Donald G. Morgan, "Justice William Johnson on the Treaty-Making Power," *Geo. Wash. L. Rev.,* 22 (1953), 187–215 at 192.
21. *Elkison* v. *Deliesseline,* 8 Fed. Cas. 493 (No. 4366) (C.C.D.S.C. 1823).

considered to be the supreme law of the land under the supremacy clause of Article VI. Johnson held that so egregious a state interference with foreign and interstate navigation "is in effect a repeal of the laws of the United States, *pro tanto.*" He concluded with a direct refutation of Hunt's police power argument: "Where is this to land us? Is it not asserting the right in each state to throw off the federal constitution at its will and pleasure? If it can be done as to any particular article, it may be done as to all; and like the old confederation, the Union becomes a mere rope of sand." Johnson, however, denied effective relief, holding that under section 14 of the 1789 Judiciary Act,[22] habeas corpus would not lie from a federal court to a state official.

Johnson's holding was a tactically clever maneuver worthy of Marshall in *Marbury* v. *Madison,* since it denied Johnson's adversaries the opportunity to flout his judicial order. Elkison was left to secure his freedom through informal diplomatic and political pressures, which he did. Johnson condemned his state's action at great personal cost and had to remove to Pennsylvania where he spent his remaining years in virtual exile from his native state.

The Seamen's Act controversy continued to reverberate until the constitutional, diplomatic, and political issues it raised were subsumed in the furor over the Wilmot Proviso. It immediately provoked rancorous newspaper debate.[23] Writing under an assortment of bastard-classical pseudonyms, led by the unknown "Zeno" and by Robert J. Turnbull and Isaac E. Holmes as "Caroliniensis," Johnson's critics blasted his constitutional reasoning and political savoir-faire. Turnbull and Holmes claimed that the state's police power to exclude blacks was so much superior to the federal treaty-making power that a treaty interfering with it was void, insisting that treaties must conform to the limitations on federal power in the Constitution. Emphasizing the Tenth Amendment and the "inherent rights" of the states, they claimed that the states were "still free, sovereign, and independent, as to every object of internal polity and government." On the commerce-clause issue, they agrued that exclusion of free blacks was analogous to a health quarantine, and hence not an interference with

22. Act of 24 Sept. 1789, ch. 20, §14, 1 Stat. 73.
23. On the constitutional issues of this debate, see Donald G. Morgan, *Justice William Johnson: The First Dissenter* (Columbia: Univ. of South Carolina Press, 1954), 196–202.

the federal commerce power, a position later endorsed by Chief Justice Taney.[24]

Being a dogged controversialist, Johnson had his opinion distributed in pamphlet format, wrote several public letters in the press over his signature, and rebutted his attackers under the pen name "Philonimus" in the *Charleston Mercury*. The "Philonimus" series was an extension of Johnson's *Elkison* opinion.[25] Johnson seized on another of Hunt's points, that the only proper subjects of the federal treaty power were those matters expressly delegated to the federal government under Article I, section 8, and turned the argument around, insisting that the states surrendered all powers that might be the subject matter of treaties to the federal government, thus touching off a dispute over limitations of the treaty-making power and the impact of treaties on the internal politics of the states that echoed through *Missouri* v. *Holland* (1920) and the 1952–1954 Senate controversies over the Bricker Amendment.

Even then Johnson was not done. The newspaper exchange had not yet sated either his appetite for controversy or his compulsive need to assert absolute federal supremacy over the states. He had his last word on the subject the following year when the United States Supreme Court delivered its judgment in the landmark case of *Gibbons* v. *Ogden* (1824).[26] Chief Justice John Marshall, for the court, there held unconstitutional a New York steamboat monopoly grant on the grounds that it conflicted with federal authority to regulate interstate and foreign commerce.[27] In a strongly nationalistic opinion, Marshall went close to holding federal power over such commerce exclusive of any concurrent power in the states, but left the point vaguely unresolved. He struck down the New York statute on the

24. *Caroliniensis*, a pamphlet having no title page, date, or place of publication. The copy in the South Caroliniana collection of the Library of the University of South Carolina, a microfilm of which I used, is listed under the title *A Series of Articles Discussing a Pamphlet Entitled "The Opinion of the Honorable William Johnson . . ."* and suggests a publication date of 1824. It is a reprint of articles originally appearing in the Charleston *Mercury*.

25. "Philonimus" is quoted in Morgan, "Justice William Johnson on the Treaty-Making Power," 202–203. He was in turn answered by "Philo-Caroliniensis," reprinted with *Caroliniensis*.

26. Wheat. (22 U.S.) 1 (1824); Johnson, J., concurring at 27–33.

27. On the ramifications of Gibbons and its relationship to the Seamen's Act controversy, see Maurice G. Baxter, *The Steamboat Monopoly: Gibbons v. Ogden, 1824* (New York: Knopf, 1972), 57–60.

grounds that it conflicted with a federal coastal-licensing act, which he construed as an explicit regulation of the commerce in question, and with which the state statute clashed. Johnson found both points in Marshall's reasoning insufficient, and, despite the Chief Justice's disapproval of concurrences, wrote a concurrence going well beyond the substance of Marshall's reasoning.

Just as the "Philonimus" letters gave Johnson a chance at refining his treaty-powers reasoning, the *Gibbons* concurrence gave him another shot at the commerce-clause rationale. In an ultranationalistic opinion, Johnson insisted that federal commerce regulatory power is not only plenary but exclusive of all state regulatory power. On this question, neither Marshall nor Johnson was to have the final word. The problem of federal versus state authority in commerce regulation continued to bedevil the Court well beyond the Civil war. Subsequent judicial opinions rejected Johnson's extreme position of plenary and exclusive federal commerce power and squeezed concessions to state sovereignty out of the one narrow area of vagueness in Marshall's otherwise clear and explicit *Gibbons* opinion. In cases where slavery was involved or where the regulatory problem suggested a close parallel with federal-state authority over slavery, the Court rejected entirely the Marshall-Johnson nationalist position in favor of a state sovereignty theory, formulated by Taney, that exalted the state's police power as superior to any federal commerce power as far as the control of ingress and egress of persons into the state was concerned.

The federal courts were not the only branch of the federal government embroiled in disputes stirred up by the Seamen's Act. British and northern shippers remonstrated with Secretary of State John Quincy Adams over South Carolina's imprisonment of black seamen on their vessels. Adams found himself in a difficult position. Though he had little respect for the pretensions of the slaveowners and was sympathetic to the shippers' complaints, Adams nevertheless respected the state of feeling in Charleston and the barrier to national authority posed by the American federal system.[28] At first he hoped that the shippers would get informal redress through South Carolina moderates like Johnson and Poinsett. The state legislature did in fact modify the statute a year after its original enactment by abolishing the enslavement provisions and exempting both American and foreign

28. Adams, ed., *Memoirs of John Quincy Adams,* VI, 307 (entry 24 April 1824), 376 (entry 7 June 1824).

naval vessels from its provisions.[29] But the enforcement of the statute was erratic, with Charleston authorities oscillating between lenience and vigilance. After a second wave of British complaints, Adams and President James Monroe decided to bring federal pressure on the state.[30] But Monroe's preferred mode, bringing a test case before the United States Supreme Court, never succeeded because appropriate cases became mooted in one way or another before reaching the Court. Even had a case reached the high court, it is doubtful that John Marshall would have held the act unconstitutional. Writing to Joseph Story in September 1823, Marshall mentioned a case before him on circuit, *Wilson* v. *United States* (1820),[31] that raised questions comparable to those in *Elkison,* and explained his evasion of those issues by noting that "fuel is continually adding to the fire at which the exaltees are about to roast the judicial department. . . . a case has been brought before me in which I might have considered [a Virginia statute's] constitutionality had I chosen to do so, but it was not absolutely necessary, and, as I am not fond of butting against a wall in sport, I escaped on the construction of the act."[32]

Perhaps sensing Marshall's reluctance to take on the Carolinians judicially, Adams turned to another device, an opinion by the United States Attorney General. Adams' colleague in this post happened to be another southern nationalist and constitutional authority, William Wirt, native Marylander, Virginia attorney, and a leader of the Supreme Court bar. In an opinion of 8 May 1824, two months after Marshall handed down his *Gibbons* opinion, Wirt held the South Carolina statute unconstitutional, even as amended, because it interfered with the "exclusive" federal power to regulate commerce. Using what lawyers call the "silence of Congress" argument, Wirt said that since Congress had passed no statute forbidding blacks to enter American ports as seamen, free blacks had a right to do so, and that a state statute interfering with such a right was void.[33]

29. Ch. 20 in *Acts and Resolutions of . . . South-Carolina . . . 1823* (Columbia: D. & J. M. Faust, 1824), 59–63.

30. Philip M. Hamer, "Great Britain, the United States, and the Negro Seamen's Acts, 1822–1848," *J. Southern Hist.,* 1 (1935), 3–28.

31. 30 Fed. Cas. 239 (No. 17846) (C.C.D.Va. 1820).

32. Marshall to Story, 26 Sept. 1823, in Joseph Story Papers, Massachusetts Historical Society. The date and most recent editorial revisions of this letter were supplied through the courtesy of Charles T. Cullen, Associate Editor of the Papers of John Marshall, for which I express my gratitude.

33. Wirt's opinion is reprinted in "Free Colored Seamen—Majority and Minority Reports," *H. R. Report,* 27 Cong. 3 sess., ser. 426, doc. 80 (1843).

South Carolina's response to Wirt's opinion was explosive. Governor John L. Wilson transmitted the opinion to the state legislature with a message claiming that "the crisis seems to have arrived when we are called upon to protect ourselves." Dismissing Wirt's effort as "sophistry and error," Wilson in a fire-eating peroration claimed that "there would be more glory in forming a rampart with our bodies on the confines of our territory, than to be the victims of a successful rebellion, or the slaves of a great consolidated government."[34] Responding in kind, the state senate (in resolutions that were not approved by the lower house) staked out several important constitutional positions that were to dominate the mind of Carolina political leaders for the next generation. The Wirt-Adams meddling was an "unconstitutional interference" with slavery, an institution "distinctly guaranteed" by the federal number clause of Article I, section 2. Then, carrying Hunt's 1823 argument a step forward, the Carolina senators resolved that the "duty" of the state to guard against black uprisings was "paramount to all laws, all treaties, *all* constitutions. [Emphasis supplied.] It arises from the supreme and permanent law of nature, the law of self-preservation; and will never, by this state, be renounced, compromised, controlled or participated with any power whatever" [*sic*]. Thus Carolina politicians projected the federal consensus as something superior to all constitutions and federal relations.

With the South Carolina house concurrently resolving that slavery had by 1824 become "inseparably connected with their social and political existence," the Senators concluded by reemphasizing the consensus: they rejected

any claims of right, of the United States, to interfere in any manner whatever, with the domestic regulations and preservatory measures in respect to that part of their property which forms the colored population of the state, and which property they will not permit to be meddled with, or tampered with, or in and [*sic; sc.* "any"] manner ordered, regulated, or controlled by any other power, foreign or domestic, than this legislature.

In this formulation, the proslavery reinterpretation of the consensus began to take on a double aspect. On the one hand, as in the Senate's conclusion just quoted, it was a prophylactic barrier against any federal intrusion hostile to slavery. On the other, as had been antici-

34. This message and the following legislative reports are reprinted in Ames, ed., *State Documents on Federal Relations,* 205–208.

pated in the pre-Missouri congressional debates, other southern leaders saw the consensus as guaranteeing a benevolent, protective, promotive posture of the federal government toward slavery in the states and especially toward slavery's expansion into the territories.

Unfortunately for the peace of mind of white Carolinians, the issue would not die. In 1829, 1830, and 1832 respectively, Georgia, North Carolina, and Florida enacted black-seaman-quarantine statutes. These acts, plus the irregular enforcement of the South Carolina statute, vexed the British, and they again mounted a major protest, but a different set of men now dominated the national executive. President Andrew Jackson referred the British protests to his Attorney General, the Georgian John Macpherson Berrien, who reversed Wirt's earlier opinion.[35] Adopting reasoning soon to be embraced by Taney in cases involving a state's power to exclude goods or persons that endanger its social climate, Berrien held that the state's power of "internal police," supported by the reservation of authority in the Tenth Amendment, overrode inconsistent federal regulation under the commerce power. Congress was in fact required to pass commerce legislation supporting state laws like the seamen's quarantine statutes because of the primacy of the reserved rights of the states. Berrien was seconded by his successor as Attorney General, Roger B. Taney, a year later in an opinion never officially published. Taney adopted the substance of Hunt's arguments, claiming that a state's police powers overrode any treaty, especially one going beyond the limits of the federal government's treaty-making power. He gratuitously went further and insisted, as he would in his *Dred Scott* opinion twenty-five years later, that free blacks could not be citizens of the United States and hence could not claim, as of right, the protection of the federal Constitution.[36]

The Berrien-Taney opinions were no more effective in squelching the Seamen's Act controversy than Wirt's earlier effort had been. In 1843, John Quincy Adams, then a Massachusetts congressman, reentered the fray. The twenty years between his first involvement with the acts and his last had not sweetened his opinions about slavery

35. 2 *Official Opinions of the Attorneys-General of the United States . . .* (1852), 427–442.
36. The corrected drafts of Taney's unprinted opinion are excerpted in Carl B. Swisher, "Mr. Chief Justice Taney," in Allison Dunham and Philip B. Kurland, eds., *Mr. Justice* (Chicago: Univ. of Chicago Press, 1964), 43–45.

and slavocrats. Adams reopened agitation by introducing a memorial of Boston merchants condemning the Seamen's Acts and vaguely calling upon Congress to enforce the privileges and immunities clause of Article IV, section 2. The select committee of the House, to which the memorial was referred, was chaired by the Boston Whig, Robert C. Winthrop, who wrote the report for the seven-man majority condemning the acts as a violation both of the privileges and immunities and the supremacy clauses. He urged Congress to so resolve, but suggested that the petitioners would have to seek redress from the federal courts and from the states. The two-man minority report written by North Carolina Whig Kenneth Rayner reiterated the police power arguments of the Berrien-Taney opinions and insisted that the states could restrict the privileges and immunities that they were obliged to accord under Article IV to such classes of persons as they chose.[37]

The House took no action on the report, so Massachusetts fell back on state authority. The state sent Samuel Hoar to South Carolina and Henry Hubbard to Louisiana as commissioners to procure the repeal of the Seamen's Acts of those two states, and to litigate their constitutionality if necessary. Both men were rudely treated at their destinations, Hubbard being threatened with a lynching and the elderly Hoar condemned as a dangerous incendiary. Both were forced to flee the states promptly for their safety, Hoar being hurried on his way by a resolution of the South Carolina legislature asserting its right to exclude any persons dangerous to its peace and insisting that free Negroes were not citizens of the United States.[38] Northern and southern states then engaged in recriminations, condemning each other's actions. Further British protests to Secretary of State James Buchanan proved useless, given his ardent proslavery sympathies. The Seamen's Act controversy, which had sputtered on and off for a quarter of a century, dwindled, overtaken by more momentous slavery issues.

Carolinian constitutional thought was further stimulated by another incident in the complex and interrelated tangle of events surrounding the colonization movement, the Vesey plot, and the Negro Seamen's Acts. Apparently as a gesture of sympathy for the plight of white Carolinians, the Ohio legislature in 1823 recommended to Congress

37. "Free colored seamen," ser. 426, doc. 80.
38. Ames, ed., *State Documents on Federal Relations,* 45–46.

and other state legislatures that they adopt "a system providing for the gradual emancipation of the people of color" and "a system of foreign colonization, with correspondent measures . . . that would in due time effect the entire emancipation of the slaves in our country." The Ohioans carefully specified that they did not intend "any violation of the national compact, or infringement of the rights of individuals" and helpfully assured the southern states that "the evil of slavery is a national one, and that the people and the states of this Union ought mutually to participate in the duties and burthens of removing it.[39] Between 1816 and 1818, the Virginia, Georgia, Maryland, and Tennessee legislatures had endorsed colonization; after 1823, Pennsylvania, Massachusetts, New Jersey, Illinois, Delaware, Connecticut, Vermont, and Indiana passed resolutions comparable to Ohio's.[40]

The South Carolina legislature responded immediately to the unwelcome Ohio Resolutions, the senate dismissing them as "a very strange and ill-advised communication" and the house insisting that the Palmetto State intended to "adhere to a system, descended to them from their ancestors, and now inseparably connected with their social and political existence."[41] Undaunted by such intransigence, supporters of colonization tried again the next year, but this time the proposals came from what was, to Carolinians, a sinister quarter. New York Senator Rufus King had been a bogey to South Carolina since 1820 for his prominent role among Missouri restrictionists. One of Vesey's condemned fellow conspirators, Jack, stated that Vesey had induced him to join the uprising on the grounds that King was a voice against slavery in the Senate, and the Columbia *State Gazette* had darkly hinted that King's restrictionist speeches "were calculated to promote Insurrection."[42] In February 1825, King reopened these old wounds by offering a resolution in the Senate urging use of proceeds from the sale of public lands to pay for the emancipation of slaves.

Robert Y. Hayne, one of the militant faction of 1822, who was now a senatorial colleague of King's, denounced the measure as "un-

39. Ames, ed., *State Documents on Federal Relations,* 203–204.
40. These resolutions are collected in "Slave Trade," *H. R. Reports,* 21 Cong. 1 sess., doc. 348, ser. 201 (1830).
41. Ames, ed., *State Documents on Federal Relations,* 207–208.
42. Killens, ed., *Trial Record of Denmark Vesey,* 88; Starobin, ed., *Denmark Vesey,* 90.

constitutional . . . and dangerous."[43] Governor George M. Troup of Georgia, one of the South's foremost state sovereignty exponents, sent a special message to his state's legislature denouncing such "impertinent intermeddlings with our domestic concerns." He predicted that the federal government might "openly lend itself to a combination of fanatics for the destruction of everything valuable in the Southern country" and he threatened secession if Congress tampered with the "sacred guaranty" of slavery in the United States Constitution. Next, Troup edged toward a positive-good defense of slavery: if slavery "be an evil, it is our own—if it be a sin, we can implore the forgiveness of it: it may be our physical weakness—it is our moral strength."[44] As southern political leaders and polemicists moved toward the positive-good rationale of slavery, the southern judiciary followed, though more slowly. Southern jurists adapted their legal and constitutional thought to the defense of slavery against intrusion from outside and insurrection within, adding another element to the proslavery counteroffensive of the twenties.

The judges of southern state courts in the early nineteenth century had sometimes displayed a surprising animosity toward slavery, and had gone out of their way to uphold the freedom of one-time slaves who had been taken by their masters out of slave jurisdictions to reside in free states. In 1796, the Supreme Court of South Carolina, which at the time included two of the most illustrious jurists of that state's history, Aedanus Burke and John Faucheraud Grimké, stated that slavery had been established only in derogation of the common law, or as an exception to it, as something "inconsistent with the particular constitutions, customs, and laws of this (then) province, which left an opening for this part of the provincial constitution and custom of tolerating slavery, and everything relative to the government of slaves in Carolina."[45] Virginia's Chancellor George Wythe declared sweepingly that "freedom is the birth-right of every human being, which sentiment is strongly inculcated by the first article of our 'political catechism,' the bill of rights."[46] The Mississippi Supreme

---

43. *Register of Debates,* 18 Cong. 2 sess. 623 (18 Feb. 1825), 696 (28 Feb. 1825).

44. Ames, ed., *State Documents on Federal Relations,* 208–209.

45. *White* v. *Chambers,* 2 Bay 70 (S.C. 1796).

46. *Hudgins* v. *Wrights,* 1 Hen. & M. 134 (Va. 1806), a doctrine disapproved on appeal insofar as it pertained to blacks.

Court, in freeing slaves taken to reside in the territory or state of Indiana, stated that their owners "say, you take from us a vested right arising from the municipal law. The petitioners [slaves] say you would deprive us of a natural right guaranteed by the [Northwest] Ordinance and the [Indiana] Constitution. How should the court decide, if construction was really to determine it? I presume it would be in favour of liberty."[47] The Kentucky Court of Appeals carried this impulse even further, and adopted an American extrapolation of the principles of *Somerset* to hold that "freedom is the natural right of man" and that slavery is "without foundation in the law of nature, or the unwritten and common law."[48] The Louisiana Supreme Court held, under similar principles, that a slave free anywhere, for no matter how brief a period of time, can never be reenslaved.[49] Though none of these cases challenged the legitimacy of slavery in the slave states, their libertarian spirit was not compatible with the deep South's need for unquestioning support of slavery after the Vesey Rebellion.

Southern jurists responded to the shifting intellectual climate around them after Vesey. The clarion of this new proslavery jurisprudence was a saturnine meditation on slavery by the South's greatest antebellum state judge, Thomas Ruffin of the North Carolina Supreme Court. In a decision holding that a master or his bailee cannot be convicted for unnecessarily cruel assaults on a slave, Ruffin composed these somber musings:

The end [of slavery] is the profit of the master, his security, and the public safety; the subject is one doomed in his own person and his posterity, to live without knowledge and without the capacity to make anything his own, and to toil that another may reap the fruits. . . . Such services can only be expected from one who has no will of his own; who surrenders his will in implicit obedience to that of another. Such obedience is the consequence only of uncontrolled authority over the body. There is nothing else which can operate to produce the effect. The power of the master must be absolute to render the submission of the slave perfect. I most freely confess my sense of the harshness of this proposition; I feel it as deeply as any man can; and as a principal [*sic*] of moral right, every

47. *Harry* v. *Decker & Hopkins,* Walker (1 Miss.) 36 (1818).
48. *Rankin* v. *Lydia,* 2 A. K. Marshall 468 (Ky. 1820).
49. *Lunsford* v. *Coquillon,* 14 Martin 465 (La. 1824).

person in his retirement must repudiate it. In the actual condition of things it must be so. There is no remedy.[50]

Judge D. L. Wardlaw of the South Carolina Court of Appeals later repudiated the spirit that had informed the jurisprudence of his predecessors Grimké and Burke a generation earlier: "A slave can invoke neither magna charta nor common law. . . . Every endeavour to extend to [a slave] positive rights, is an attempt to reconcile inherent contradictions. In the very nature of things, he is subject to despotism."[51] That despotism, as southerners realized after Vesey's plot, required a stern legal order. "Our laws to regulate slaves," admitted a relatively benign Floridian, "are entirely founded on terror."[52] The juridical world of Wythe and the other early slave-state judges did not survive the 1820s.

The proslavery insecurity that produced these constitutional innovations was concentrated in the lower South. In the upper tier of the slave states, colonization found its natural home, and even gradual emancipation was tolerated in the twenties and beyond. Virginia, the bellwether among these states, was relatively free of the constraints and ambitions that rigidified slavery in the deep South. Between 1829 and 1832 Virginia's political leaders debated the future of slavery, not only for their state, but as surrogates for the entire upper South. In the end, the Virginia emancipationist-colonizationist effort failed by a slim margin and Virginia unenthusiastically threw in her lot with the deep-South states, a decision ratified by one of the most influential proslavery rationales ever composed, Thomas R. Dew's *Review of the Debates* (1832).

The slavery issue in Virginia was first raised indirectly. Like many of the original states at the time, Virginia's legislature was badly malapportioned and about half the adult white males of the state were voteless. In Merrill Peterson's fine phrase, "the Jeffersonian idea of a freeholders' republic became a shield of aristocracy rather than a sword of democracy."[53] Over conservative opposition, a constitutional

50. *State* v. *Mann*, 2 Dev. 263 (N.C. 1829).
51. Ex parte *Boylston*, 2 Strob. 41 (S.C. 1846).
52. "An Inhabitant of Florida" [Zephaniah Kingsley], *A Treatise on the Patriarchal, or Co-operative System of Society* . . . *under the Name of Slavery, with Its Necessity and Advantages* (n.p., 1829), 12.
53. Merrill D. Peterson, ed., *Democracy, Liberty, and Property: The State Constitutional Conventions of the 1820s* (Indianapolis: Bobbs-Merrill, 1966), 280–281.

convention met in 1829 and 1830 to take up these and other reform issues. Venerable figures from the early republic—James Madison, James Monroe, John Marshall, John Randolph—joined younger men whose political leadership was in the ascendant: Philip Pendleton Barbour, Abel Parker Upshur, Benjamin Watkins Leigh, John Tyler, all the latter being conservatives and defenders of slavery. Though not called to consider slavery and emancipation, the convention found those issues inextricably mixed with problems of reapportionment and franchise extension because conservatives opposed both on the grounds that they would weaken the security of slavery in the Tidewater.

Conservatives bludgeoned proposals for white manhood suffrage and reapportionment based on white population, in favor of only a modest extension of freehold suffrage and a complex system of reapportionment based on the four natural geographic sections of the state. Eastern conservatives feared that equalizing the political power of the western counties, where slaves were scarce and where the economy did not depend on the export of slave-produced staples, would enable the west to raise taxes for internal improvements, which would fall on lands and slaves, and thus be borne disproportionately by eastern slaveholders. Upshur insisted to the reformers that "property is entitled to protection, and . . . our property [slaves] imperiously demands that kind of protection which flows from the possession of power." Leigh presented the convention with a false choice, between democratization and "states' rights," and warned westerners that equality in representation for the state would disable Virginia from objecting to equality of representation in Congress.[54]

The frustrated western democrats recognized black slavery as an obstacle to full political equality for whites. Charles S. Morgan, voicing the grievances of disfranchised state militiamen who were obliged to perform duty on the slave patrols, predicted the necessity of a police state to achieve white equalization: "Make all the free white men as free and independent, as Government could make them," he counseled, because "all the slave holding States are fast approaching a crisis truly alarming: a time when freemen will be needed . . . when not only Virginia, but all the Southern States

54. Ibid., 328 (Upshur), 351 (Leigh).

must be essentially military; and will have military Governments!"[55]

The victory of the conservatives in the 1829–1830 convention left slavery not only intact but even strengthened. But the peace of mind of white Virginians was soon shattered by the bloodiest slave insurrection in American history, Nat Turner's in Southampton County of southern Virginia (1831). It shocked white Virginians into another reconsideration of the future of slavery in the Old Dominion. Before the rebellion, vigorous emancipationist sentiment had been discouraged in the complacent climate of Virginia; after it, a slaveholder remarked, "a few months have wrought a great change in public sentiment concerning this subject."[56]

Stimulated by emancipationist memorials,[57] the General Assembly that convened in the winter of 1831–1832 appointed a select committee to consider them and a portion of Governor John Lloyd's message recommending colonization. This provoked an uninhibited debate on slavery and emancipation between January and March 1832 that was fully reported to the public in Richmond newspapers. The legislature ultimately did nothing except tighten up the black code, but before that it provided the Old Dominion with an amazingly free discussion of the evils of slavery.

Virginia legislators who harbored antislavery sentiments capitalized on the trauma of Turner's Rebellion. William B. Preston said that the slaveowners "are ready to accuse me with attacking their Constitutional rights. I do attack them openly, boldly, and if they ask me by what right I attack them, I answer by the right which is given me by that great law of necessity—self-preservation." Samuel Moore echoed the Virginia Declaration of Rights when he designated "the right to the enjoyment of liberty" as "one of those perfect, inherent and inalienable rights, which pertain to the whole human race, and of which they can never be divested, except by an act of gross injustice." James McDowell had the final word for slavery's opponents when he pointed out that the hysterical white reaction to Turner's uprising, even in regions distant from Southampton County, was based on

55. Ibid., 408–409.
56. Quoted in Joseph C. Robert, *The Road from Monticello: A Study of the Virginia Slavery Debate of 1832* (Durham: Duke Univ. Press, 1941), 14.
57. J. H. Johnson, "Antislavery Petitions Presented to the Virginia Legislature by Citizens of Various Counties." *J. Negro Hist.*, 12 (1927), 670–691.

"the suspicion eternally attached to the slave himself, the suspicion that a Nat Turner might be in every family, that the same bloody deed could be acted over at any time in any place."[58]

These bold ideas provoked a rebuttal so intense that it pushed the development of proslavery ideology even further than the Carolinians and Georgians had developed it hitherto. James Gholson demanded that northern states repress abolitionists and threatened civil war if they did not. William Roane claimed that "history, experience, observation, and reason, have taught me, that the torch of liberty has ever burnt brightest when surrounded by the dark and filthy, yet nutritious atmosphere of slavery. Nor do I believe in that Fan-faronade about the natural equality of man." Not content with merely repudiating the Declaration of Rights, Alexander Knox claimed that slavery gave Virginia "the high and elevated character which she has heretofore sustained" and concluded that it was "indispensably requisite in order to preserve the forms of a Republican Government."[59]

In the end, it was neither the colonizationist-emancipators nor the militantly proslavery men (whose numbers were about evenly balanced), but the moderates in the General Assembly who determined that emancipation and colonization were inexpedient. The matter was dropped, never again to be taken up. But outside the General Assembly, a young professor of political economy at William and Mary College had followed the debates with great interest and apprehension. Putting his thoughts into an essay republished several times, Thomas R. Dew drafted a systematic and definitive defense of slavery and rebuttal of both colonizationist and emancipationist beliefs.[60] Though it only glancingly discussed constitutional points, Dew's *Review of the Debates* (1832) provided an ideological basis for proslavery constitutionalism and was definitive to later constitutional theorists on issues of political economy, racial inferiority, the legiti-

58. Robert, *Road from Monticello*, 83 (Preston), 64 (Moore), 104 (McDowell).

59. Robert, *Road from Monticello*, 81 (Roane), 94 (Knox).

60. *Review of the Debate in the Virginia Legislature, 1831–32*, first published in the Philadelphia *American Quarterly Review*, then (1832) as a pamphlet, reprinted as *An Essay on Slavery*, and finally incorporated into one of the four sections of *The Pro-Slavery Argument, as Maintained by the Most Distinguished Writers of the Southern States* . . . (Philadelphia: Lippincott, Grambo, 1853). All citations that follow are to the pagination in the last source, which was the most widely-read and influential edition of the essay.

macy of slavery, political theory, and the fallacy of Jeffersonian egalitarianism.[61]

Dew assumed that blacks were hopelessly inferior to whites, yet in America were inseparable from them. Slavery existed at all times and in all places; was legitimated by the *jus gentium* as expounded by Vattel and Grotius; and was a normal property relationship and form of labor discipline in advanced societies. The Old and New Testaments condoned it; perhaps it was "intended by our Creator for some useful purposes."

Colonization was a fatuous project because it would deprive Virginia of a third of its total wealth: the capitalized value of the slaves—not counting depreciation in land values, crop-export losses, and the annual value of slaves sold out of Virginia. Dew adopted some points made by his friend Leigh, who had argued that the government of a society must "conform to" the property of a state, rather than destroy it. But emancipation without colonization would be even worse. Blacks in freedom were inherently shiftless and idle, prone to criminality, and incapable of improvement in anything short of geologic eons.

Any form of abolition would have worse consequences than slavery's continuance. Moreover, much could be said positively of slavery. Slaves were happy and docile—this only a year after Nat Turner's uprising—and Virginia was in 1832 one of the most secure places in the world for whites. The depressed state of Virginia's economy was attributable to federal "oppressions" (the tariff and internal improvements) rather to the supposed unproductivity of slave labor. Dew ended conclusively: slavery was a justifiable, divinely ordained, natural ordering of the races and work relationships in society. Hence the subject should not be further agitated lest it induce an unnatural discontent among the slaves with what was, after all, part of the natural order of things.[62]

South Carolina's sensitivity about internal and external threats to slavery, together with the constitutional skirmishing over colonization and the Negro Seamen's Acts, indicated that the Missouri compromises had not really laid sectional animosity to rest. But these disputes need not have flared into outright confrontation, as they did

61. Kenneth M. Stampp, "An Analysis of T. R. Dew's *Review of the Debate in the Virginia Legislature*," *J. Negro Hist.*, 27 (1942), 380–387.
62. Dew, *Review of the Debate*, 288, 359, 387, and *passim*.

by the 1840s. White Americans had compromised their differences before by letting black people bear the burden of adjustment, and they might have done so again, had it not been for several developments in the northern states. Immediatism had begun to spread among abolitionists by the time of Nat Turner's uprising. Two northern states took steps to repel the intrusion of slavery into their jurisdictions. The status of free blacks continued to agitate white northerners. And, above all, as the lights of the old Abolition Societies winked out, new immediatist antislavery societies sprang up throughout the north. The southern counteroffensive proved not to be misguided after all.

CHAPTER 7

Antislavery Renascent

Despite the influence of antislavery ideas during the Missouri debates, the organized abolition movement slumped into quiescence in the 1820s to such an extent that the southern counteroffensive seemed directed at a chimera. This lull was interrupted by two widely separated events of the twenties that were to have far-reaching impacts on later constitutional efforts to abolish slavery. In 1824 Elizabeth Heyrick published the manifesto of immediatism in London, England; and in 1826, members of the only active Abolition Society left in the field secured passage of the first northern personal liberty act. As the doctrines of immediatism and the example of the British antislavery movement became widely known among American opponents of slavery, an antislavery revival occurred. In place of the defunct Abolition Societies, new antislavery societies formed in the northern states, and were quickly subsumed as state auxiliaries to a united national organization, the American Anti-Slavery Society. With the debut of the AA-SS, the movement took on not only a reinvigorated militancy, but a new emphasis on constitutional action as well.

Immediatism was not unknown to the American antislavery movement before 1824. It had always been implicit in the unequivocal religious or ideological condemnations of slavery of the Revolutionary era. Samuel Hopkins' *Dialogue concerning the Slavery of the Africans* (1776) hinted at immediatism in a religious context. John Cooper of New Jersey in 1780 made a secular plea for immediatism, based on Revolutionary ideology.[1] George Bourne in 1816 and John Ken-

---

1. [Burlington] *New-Jersey Gazette,* 20 Sept. 1780.

rick in 1817 both called for immediate abolition.[2] But in its early appearances, immediatism was rhetorical rather than programmatic, addressed to the conscience of individuals rather than offered as a concrete plan for eradicating a political evil. Thus early American immediatists seemed sometimes equivocal. Reverend David Rice condemned slavery comprehensively at the 1792 Kentucky constitutional convention and urged his colleagues to "resolve unconditionally to put an end to slavery in this state," but he disavowed radical programs and merely proposed a gradualist *post-nati* emancipation effort.[3] The Abolition Societies also seemed to speak equivocally on immediatism. The Pennsylvania Society in 1819 called for an immediate abandonment of holding and selling slaves,[4] while the New Jersey Society warned in 1804 it could not "be wished . . . that sudden and general emancipation should take place. A century may and probably will elapse . . . before it can be eradicated from our country."[5]

Immediatism was a complex, or perhaps compound, idea, having different connotations. Looked at in the long view, it signalized a romantic rebellion against the cool, rational formalism that nurtured the gradualistic approach of the *post-nati* emancipation statutes in the late eighteenth and early nineteenth centuries.[6] Immediatism of this sort did not appear in American antislavery thought until after the War of 1812, and only later was it translated into a practical call to action by which various schemes of emancipation might be measured and by which individual activist commitment could be asserted. But until its appearance, the antislavery effort was based on gradualistic assumptions, which accounted for its moderate, meliorist, and paternalistic character.

2. George Bourne, *The Book and Slavery Irreconcilable* . . . (Philadelphia: J. M. Sanderson, 1816), 7–8; John Kenrick, *Horrors of Slavery . . . Demonstrating that Slavery Is Impolitic, Antirepublican, Unchristian, and Highly Criminal; and Proposing Measures for Its Complete Abolition through the United States* (Cambridge: Hilliard and Metcalf, 1817), 38–39, 58–59.
3. "Philanthropos" [David Rice], *Slavery Inconsistent with Justice and Good Policy* (Lexington: J. Bradford, 1792).
4. *Minutes of the Sixteenth American Convention for Promoting the Abolition of Slavery . . . 1819* (Philadelphia: William Fry, 1819), 6–8.
5. *Address of the President of the New-Jersey Society, for Promoting the Abolition of Slavery, to the General Meeting . . . 1804* (Trenton: Sherman and Mershon, 1804), 7.
6. David Brion Davis, "The Emergence of Immediatism in British and American Antislavery Thought," *Miss. Valley Hist. Rev.*, 49 (1962), 209–230.

The hold of gradualism was weakening in America in the twenties, and scattered, obscure abolitionists began exploring immediatist ideas again. An Indiana minister, James Duncan, the Virginia exile John Rankin in Ohio, and Samuel Melancthon Worcester in Massachusetts, groped toward the idea of abolishing slavery totally and quickly.[7] But it was an English abolitionist, Elizabeth Heyrick, who first presented immediatism as a coherent doctrine in her 1824 pamphlet, *Immediate, not Gradual Abolition*.[8] Heyrick approached immediatism indirectly, by linking the slave trade with slavery itself, showing that the one was as iniquitous as the other, and that both survived only so long as it was in the interest of the metropolis to sustain them. Gradualism therefore was "the grand marplot of human virtue and happiness;—the very masterpiece of satanic policy." Heyrick also made three other points which were adopted by American antislavery in the thirties. First, every individual bore a personal responsibility for slavery; no one could avoid taking a position on slavery, for inaction was in effect a decision to support it. "The perpetuation of slavery in our West India colonies, is not an abstract question, to be settled between the Government and the Planters,—it is a question in which we are all implicated;—we are all guilty,— (with shame and compunction let us admit the opprobrious truth) of supporting and perpetuating slavery." Second, Heyrick insisted that the only "right" involved in the controversy was the slave's, to his individual liberty; the planter had no right that the government need respect. Third, she insisted that immediate emancipation would not free the slaves into a great orgy of massacre and loafing, but rather into the protection and control of the law. *Immediate, not Gradual Abolition* was reprinted in New York in 1825, and Benjamin Lundy published it serially in the *Genius of Universal Emancipation*. William Lloyd Garrison read it, together with Bourne's proto-immediatist *Book and*

7. James Duncan, *A Treatise on Slavery. In Which Is Shown Forth the Evil of Slaveholding both from the Light of Nature and Divine Revelation* (1824; rpt. New York: American Anti-Slavery Society, 1840); John Rankin, *Letters on American Slavery, Addressed to Mr. Thomas Rankin . . .* (1826; rpt. Boston: Garrison & Knapp, 1833); [Samuel M. Worcester], *Essays on Slavery . . . 1825* (Amherst: M. H. Newman, 1826).

8. [Elizabeth Heyrick], *Immediate, not Gradual Abolition; or, An Inquiry into the Shortest, Safest, and Most Effectual Means of Getting Rid of West Indian Slavery* (London: n.p., 1824). Quotations in text below are from pp. 9, 4.

Slavery Irreconcilable, and by the end of the decade became a convert to immediatism.[9]

Abolitionists who espoused immediatist doctrine quickly came into conflict with colonizationists, who were the heirs of gradualism, to the extent that they supported abolition of any sort. On the New England lecture circuit, immediatists like Arnold Buffum, Simeon S. Jocelyn, and George Bourne clashed with the Colonization Society's agents, the Reverends R. R. Gurley and Joshua Danforth. This struggle for the northern conscience brought three giants of the antislavery movement into prominence for the first time. Garrison, who had begun publishing the *Liberator* in Boston on New Years Day 1831, soon filled its columns with denunciations of colonization and lectured against it. He culled the pages of the ACS's national organ, the *African Repository,* as well as other colonizationist publications, and in June 1832 brought out his influential polemic, *Thoughts on African Colonization.*[10] This was followed by two equally important anti-colonization tracts, James Gillespie Birney's *Letter on Colonization* (1834) and William Jay's *Inquiry into the Character and Tendency of the American Colonization, and American Anti-Slavery, Societies* (1835).

Birney's *Letter*[11] was scarcely a triumph of propaganda. It owed its influence not to its pallid rhetoric but to the experiences and immense personal integrity of its author. Birney, a former slaveowner who had freed all his slaves, was a Princeton graduate and had read law in the Philadelphia office of Alexander J. Dallas. He had been elected to the legislature of his native Kentucky, and then to the Alabama legislature after his remove to Huntsville in 1817. After undergoing a religious conversion, Birney gave up his political career and lucrative law practice to become one of the American Colonization Society's most prominent field agents, in charge of its Southwestern District, which comprised Alabama, Mississippi, Louisiana, and

9. For a good survey of the early spread of immediatist thought in America, see the editors' introduction to John W. Christie and Dwight L. Dumond, eds., *George Bourne and the Book and Slavery Irreconcilable* (Wilmington: Historical Society of Delaware, 1969).

10. William Lloyd Garrison, *Thoughts on African Colonization: or, An Impartial Exhibition of the Doctrines, Principles, and Purposes of the American Colonization Society* . . . (Boston: Garrison and Knapp, 1832).

11. James Gillespie Birney, *Letter on Colonization, Addressed to the Rev. Thornton J. Mills* . . . (New York: Anti-Slavery Reporter, 1834).

Arkansas Territory.[12] Nothing in such a background portended immediatist radicalism, which made the impact of the *Letter,* with its heartfelt renunciation of gradualism and colonization, all the greater.

William Jay was, if anything, a less likely candidate for radicalism than Birney. Son of John Jay, the former Chief Justice of the United States, and judge of a Westchester County, New York magistrate's court, Jay was a self-described Federalist "of the old Washington school."[13] A devout Episcopal layman but an evangelical, Jay wrote prolifically on reform causes like temperance, bible societies, peace, the sabbatarian movement, and dueling. Propelled to an ever more radical antislavery stance because of slavery's expansionist pressures, Jay became a disunionist after the Mexican War, epitomizing in his career the travail of a principled conservative forced to radical positions despite his emotional and personal inclinations. Jay's *Inquiry*[14] marked the beginning of its author's personal development in that direction.

Immediatism was the parricide of colonization. By destroying their intellectual parent, colonization, immediatists found themselves and eliminated their principal rival for the allegiance of slavery's enemies. Every major figure of the abolitionist movement who became prominent in the 1830s had been a colonizationist. The roll of this ex-colonizationist cohort is astonishing: Garrison, Birney, Jay; Arthur and Lewis Tappan, Amos A. Phelps, Sarah Grimké, Nathaniel P. Rogers, Elizur Wright, Salmon P. Chase, Alvan Stewart, Gerrit Smith, Simeon S. Jocelyn, Theodore Dwight Weld, Benjamin Lundy, Samuel J. May, Joshua Leavitt, William Goodell, Samuel Fessenden, Beriah Green, Oliver Johnson.[15] Though their attachment and contribution to colonization varied from slight to substantial, all found it necessary to repudiate the source of their first antislavery impetus.

Colonizationists and other antiabolitionists accused their im-

12. Betty Fladeland, *James Gillespie Birney: Slaveholder to Abolitionist* (Ithaca: Cornell Univ. Press, 1955), ch. 5.

13. Quoted in Bayard Tuckerman, *William Jay and the Constitutional Movement for the Abolition of Slavery* (New York: Dodd, Mead, 1894), 123.

14. *Inquiry into the Character and Tendency of the American Colonization, and American Anti-Slavery, Societies* (1835), reprinted in William Jay, *Miscellaneous Writings on Slavery* (Boston: John P. Jewett, 1853).

15. The colonizationist beliefs of these men and women are noted in Wendell P. Garrison and Francis J. Garrison, *William Lloyd Garrison, 1805–1879: The Story of His Life Told by His Children* (Boston: Houghton Mifflin, 1885–1889), I, 273, 299–300.

mediatist adversaries of wanting to free all slaves instantly, whatever the social cost. In rebutting this misconception, abolitionists redefined immediatism in a conservative way, emphasizing that the slaves would not be freed out of legal restraint, but rather into the discipline and protection of law. Immediatism does not "mean that the shackles of slavery shall be instantly severed, and the slaves cast out upon the country without the restrictions of wholesome laws," Edwin P. Atlee, a Philadelphia moderate, reassured his critics.[16] Elizur Wright insisted that immediate emancipation would merely extend to blacks "the full protection of the law, as well as its control."[17] "Shall we set loose 2,000,000 of vagabonds to ravage the land and cut our throats?" asked Samuel J. May. "No, by no means. This is not emancipation. We would have them placed under the protection and the restraints of law, instead of being removed from either."[18]

This view of the law as a system of restraint and protection led abolitionists to the earliest formulations of ideas that eventually became embodied in the due process and equal protection clauses of section 1 of the Fourteenth Amendment. Abolition required, in Amos A. Phelps's view, "wise and equitable enactments, suited to the various circumstances of the various classes of [society's] members . . . as subjects of equal law, under its, and only its control, to be deprived of 'life, liberty, and the pursuit of happiness,' on no account but that of crime, and then, by due and equitable process of law."[19] The Boston *Abolitionist* declared that immediatism "simply [means] that the slaves who are without the protection of law shall have that protection."[20] These concepts of equal protection of laws and deprivation of liberty without due process of law spread rapidly throughout the

16. Edwin P. Atlee, *An Address to the Citizens of Philadelphia, on the Subject of Slavery. Delivered . . . 1833* (Philadelphia: W. P. Gibbons, 1833), 10; see also "What Is Meant by Immediate Emancipation?" *Emancipator,* 15 June 1833.

17. Elizur Wright, *The Sin of Slavery, and Its Remedy; Containing Some Reflections on the Moral Influence of African Colonization* (New York: for the author, 1833), 40; see also James A. Thome in *Emancipator,* 15 June 1833 and Illinois State Anti-Slavery Society, Minute Book, 1837–1844, in Chicago Historical Society.

18. Speech of May, quoted in *First Annual Report of the American Anti-Slavery Society; With the Speeches Delivered at the Anniversary Meeting . . . 1834 . . .* (New York: Dorr & Butterfield, 1834), 21.

19. Amos A. Phelps, *Lectures on Slavery and Its Remedy* (Boston: New-England Anti-Slavery Society, 1834), 178.

20. *Abolitionist,* Jan. 1833, 5.

movement and became central to the constitutional thought of radicals.

Abolitionists made a distinction between civil rights, in the nineteenth-century sense of that phrase, and political rights. They insisted that immediatism required that blacks be given civil rights as part of emancipation, but they were indifferent about voting power for freedmen. William Jay provided a catalogue of those civil rights that were included in immediatist demands, and at the same time indicated how conservative the doctrine of immediatism could be:

Immediate emancipation does not necessarily contemplate any relaxation of the restraints of government or morality; any admission to political rights, or improper exemption from compulsory labor. What then, does such emancipation imply? It implies, that black men, being no longer property, will be capable of entering into the marriage state, and of exercising the rights and enjoying the blessings of the conjugal and parental relations; it implies, that they will be entitled to the fruits of their honest industry, to the protection of the laws of the land, and to the privilege of securing a happy immortality, by learning and obeying the will of their Creator.[21]

Jay was a conservative immediatist, but more radical brethren agreed with him. Garrison maintained that "immediate abolition does not mean that the slave shall immediately exercise the right of suffrage, or be free from the benevolent restraints of guardianship."[22] One abolitionist, the authority on West Indian emancipation, James A. Thome, even envisioned special black codes to control the freedmen.[23]

While the ferment of immediatism was altering the contours of the rejuvenated antislavery movement, its older predecessor, the Pennsylvania Abolition Society was working in traditional ways to protect free blacks in the Keystone State. Before 1820, seven northern states had enacted laws that in one way or another might have proved serviceable to free blacks seeking to avoid rendition as slaves under the 1793 federal Fugitive Slave Act. Vermont, New York, New Jersey, and Ohio prohibited the kidnaping of blacks, and Maine,

---

21. Jay, "Inquiry," in *Miscellaneous Writings on Slavery,* 168.
22. *Liberator,* 7 Jan. 1832.
23. Thome to Theodore Weld, 9 Feb. 1836, in Gilbert H. Barnes and Dwight L. Dumond, eds., *Letters of Theodore Dwight Weld, Angelina Grimké Weld, and Sara Grimké, 1822–1844* (1934; rpt. Gloucester: Peter Smith, 1965), I, 257. Hereinafter cited: *Weld-Grimké Letters.*

Massachusetts, Pennsylvania, and Ohio explicitly or inferentially provided the writs of habeas corpus or homine replegiando to alleged fugitives.[24] These might be considered proto–personal liberty laws. In 1824, Indiana enacted a statute regulating fugitive recapture procedures, though this does not seem to have been a true personal liberty law.[25] In 1820 and 1826, Pennsylvania passed the first personal liberty laws aimed specifically at providing some measure of state protection to supposed fugitive slaves. These caused friction with neighboring Maryland and provided the basis for the United States Supreme Court's 1842 decision, *Prigg* v. *Pennsylvania,* that tried to delineate state and federal responsibilities for enforcement of the Constitution's fugitive slave clause.

Section 11 of Pennsylvania's 1790 gradual abolition statute provided claimants of fugitives with the right of recaption.[26] It is not clear whether this created a new statutory right or merely recognized a preexisting common law right. Neither section 11 nor the 1793 federal act caused any particular controversy in Pennsylvania, though the Pennsylvania Abolition Society and its predecessor, the Society for the Relief of Free Negroes Unlawfully Held in Bondage, had worked manfully since 1775 to prohibit black kidnaping. The fugitive slave controversy in the Keystone State began with an 1819 opinion of Chief Justice William Tilghman of the Pennsylvania Supreme Court, *Wright* v. *Deacon.*[27] Tilghman held that the writ of homine replegiando was not available to an alleged runaway seeking a jury trial to determine his putative master's claim to him if the claimant held a certificate under the 1793 federal act. Tilghman left

24. The writ of habeas corpus is the single most important procedural device for protecting individual liberty in the Anglo-American legal tradition. In the antebellum United States, it permitted judges to inquire into the legality of confinement of an individual by the executive branch of the government. Homine replegiando, sometimes called the writ of personal replevin, was a lately revived mediaeval writ used to recover possession of an individual out of the hands of someone who detained him. Unlike habeas corpus, issues of fact raised by the writ of homine replegiando were triable by a jury, making it an increasingly valuable procedural device to northern abolitionists seeking to wrest blacks out of the hands of slave catchers and kidnapers.

25. William R. Leslie, "The Constitutional Significance of Indiana's Statute of 1824 on Fugitives from Labor," *J. Southern Hist.,* 13 (1947), 338–353.

26. Recaption was a common-law right enjoyed by an owner or a master to recover an escaped horse, servant, etc., provided he could do it without a breach of the peace.

27. 5 Serg. & R. 62 (Pa. 1819).

the slave to try his remedies in the state of the claimant's domicile, cold comfort indeed. In response to *Wright* v. *Deacon,* Pennsylvania abolitionists secured passage of the 1820 personal liberty law, which made the kidnaping of blacks a stiffly punished felony and prohibited minor quasi-judicial officers of the state (aldermen and justices of the peace) from participating in enforcement of the federal act.[28]

Southern congressmen and the Maryland legislature protested the 1820 statute, but to no avail. The Maryland legislature then appointed three commissioners, one of them a prominent colonizationist, Robert H. Goldsborough, to approach both the Delaware and Pennsylvania legislatures to secure statutes providing for easier retrieval of Maryland fugitives who made it into either of those states. They were successful in slave-state Delaware, getting a stiff fugitive act that also permitted free Negroes to be sold into slavery if found without a freedom pass and unable to give a good account of themselves.[29] At first the Maryland commissioners found a cordial reception in Pennsylvania, and the 1820 act seemed in danger of repeal. Alarmed, the Pennsylvania Abolition Society sent three men to lobby in Harrisburg, led by the Philadelphian Thomas Shipley. The abolitionists were so successful in their counterlobbying that Goldsborough called the bill they sponsored, which in substance became the 1826 statute, "a bill to prevent runaway slaves from being recovered."[30] The 1826 statute[31] modified extant recapture procedures two significant ways. First, it repealed section 11 of the 1780 statute (the right of recaption provision), thus depriving masters of the do-it-yourself method of recapture. Under the 1826 statute, only state judicial officials could authorize seizure of an alleged fugitive; if an individual tried to seize a black, he would be liable to prosecution under the kidnaping statute. Second, it prohibited judges from acting solely on an agent's

28. "An Act to Prevent Kidnaping," ch. 53, in *Acts of . . . Pennsylvania . . .* [1819] (Harrisburg: C. Gleim, 1820); William R. Leslie, "The Pennsylvania Fugitive Slave Act of 1826," *J. Southern Hist.,* 13 (1952), 429–445; Morris, *Free Men All,* 42–53.

29. "An Act Relating to Fugitives from Labour," ch. 316, in *Laws of the State of Delaware . . .* [1826] (Dover: J. Robertson, 1826).

30. Thomas Shipley to Isaac Barton, 15 Feb. 1825, in MSS. Papers of the Pennsylvania Abolition Society, Historical Society of Pennsylvania (microfilm).

31. "An Act to Give Effect to the Provisions of the Constitution of the United States, Relative to Fugitives from Labor, for the Protection of Free People of Color, and to Prevent Kidnaping," ch. 50, in *Acts of . . . Pennsylvania . . .* [1825] (Harrisburg: Cameron & Krause, 1826).

(i.e. slave catcher's) oath when authorizing seizure; the agent had to produce a detailed oath of ownership from the claimant-owner in this statutory hearing, thus forcing claimants to resort to costlier and more difficult modes of proof. Moreover, the oath of ownership was not admissible in proof in the requisite subsequent hearing to determine whether the black could be removed.

The upshot of the 1826 statute seemed to accord with the views of the Pennsylvania Abolition Society, which claimed that although "the constitution of the United States may perhaps be construed by some to recognize the existence of slavery," the state need not do anything to make it easier to recapture alleged runaways.[32] The 1826 statute was a compromise designed to meet Pennsylvania's obligations under the fugitive slave clause, yet at the same time provide some security, through the mechanism of a thorough judicial hearing and the writ of habeas corpus, to free blacks in danger of being deliberately or inadvertently kidnaped.[33] Even if seen as a compromise, the Pennsylvania statutes represented an advanced position, and encouraged later northern resistance to fugitive recaptures.

At the same time, New York enacted a somewhat similar measure, though without the conflicting pressures of abolitionists and slave-state representatives. As part of the 1828 revision of its laws, New York made habeas corpus available to an owner-claimant to secure arrest of an alleged fugitive. After an elaborate hearing, at which apparently the black was permitted to offer evidence, the court could either authorize removal of the fugitive as a slave or find him not to be the slave of the claimant, in which case the claimant was subject to a forfeiture penalty, costs, and damages in a civil action. The statute further provided for homine replegiando, thus securing to the black a right of jury trial, and apparently denied masters the common-law right of recaption.[34]

Independently of these developments in the states, American abolitionists, already agitated by immediatist ideas, were beginning to consider revitalized antislavery organizations that would enhance their impact. Here again, they looked to Great Britain for example. After

32. "Remonstrance" of the Pennsylvania Abolition Society, 11 Feb. 1826, in Minutes of the Society, Historical Society of Pennsylvania (microfilm).
33. Morris, *Free Men All,* 53; cp. Leslie, "Pennsylvania Fugitive Slave Act of 1826," who maintains that the statute was enacted in a spirit of hostility to fugitive recaptures, rather than as a compromise.
34. Morris, *Free Men All,* 53–57.

British abolition of the slave trade in 1807, opponents of slavery founded the Society for the Mitigation and Gradual Abolition of Slavery throughout the British Dominions, which created an agency system that carried on lecturing and fund raising throughout the realm, assisted auxiliaries, and brought out serial and occasional publications. Despite these organizational innovations, the British movement met with continual frustration chiefly from obstruction by the West Indian legislatures. This in turn converted the gradualists in the movement to immediatism.[35]

Garrison sympathized with these developments across the ocean. He called for creation of a national society, founded on an immediatist program, that would sponsor a petition campaign, distribute tracts, publish antislavery periodicals, and send out lecturers under the agency system.[36] He soon changed his mind, though, deciding that a "concentration of moral strength" organized on a regional rather than national basis would be more effective. He gathered a dozen New Englanders as the nucleus of the society, including Connecticut Unitarian minister Samuel J. May; Oliver Johnson, editor and later historian of the Garrisonian wing of the antislavery movement; Arnold Buffum, Rhode Island Quaker hatter; David Lee Child, Boston editor and lawyer; Ellis Gray Loring and Samuel Sewall, Boston lawyers; and Amos A. Phelps, clergyman and editor.[37] On 6 January 1832, these men formed the New-England Anti-Slavery Society. The N-EA-SS adopted two tenets that influenced the constitutional thought of organized antislavery in its first decade. It first reaffirmed the federal consensus: "The People of New England cannot legislate for the southern States."[38] Second, it adopted an uncompromising egalitarianism: "A mere difference of complexion is no reason why any man should be deprived of any of his natural rights, or subjected to any political disability."[39]

35. Betty Fladeland, *Men and Brothers: Anglo-American Antislavery Cooperation* (Urbana: Univ. of Illinois Press, 1972).

36. "What Shall Be Done?" *Liberator,* 30 July 1831.

37. Oliver Johnson, *William Lloyd Garrison and His Times; or, Sketches of the Anti-Slavery Movement in America, and of the Man Who was Its Founder, and Moral Leader* (Boston: Houghton Mifflin, 1881), 82–95.

38. Excerpts from *First Annual Report* of the N-EA-SS, reprinted in the *Abolitionist,* March 1833, 35.

39. *Constitution of the New-England Anti-Slavery Society: With an Address to the Public* (Boston: Garrison & Knapp, 1832), Preamble, 3.

Shortly thereafter, a second major node of antislavery activity began to form in the New York City area. A loose association of men in benevolent and reform causes produced several individuals with a growing interest in antislavery: Arthur and Lewis Tappan, successful merchants and evangelicals; William Jay; and three editors, Joshua Leavitt, William Goodell, and, later, Elizur Wright.[40] In June 1831, Arthur Tappan accompanied Garrison to the first annual convention of free blacks in Philadelphia, where he met Connecticut abolitionist Simeon S. Jocelyn, Benjamin Lundy, and the black leaders James Forten and Samuel Cornish. With Jocelyn, Tappan conceived a scheme of establishing a black manual labor college near Yale in New Haven, which fell through when New Haven residents and lawyers, abetted by Yale faculty and students, vociferously denounced the project. Seeing the hand of colonizationists in the near mobbing in New Haven, the Yorkers cut their ties to colonization.[41]

Having moved some distance toward immediatism, the Yorkers decided to found their own organization, the New York City Anti-Slavery Society.[42] At their inaugural meeting, a mob forced them to move from a public hall to Chatham Street Chapel, where they hurriedly prayed, organized, drew up a constitution, adjourned, and fled. Under these inauspicious circumstances, the second major immediatist society came into existence. It, in turn, provided valuable links to other centers of abolitionist sentiment. One was Philadelphia, where the Quaker-dominated Pennsylvania Abolition Society remained active. Wooing Quaker leaders like Edwin Atlee and Thomas Shipley proved delicate because the Philadelphians believed that immediatism was too radical a doctrine to have much popular appeal.[43]

40. See Leavitt's reminiscences in the *National Anti-Slavery Standard,* 24 Oct. 1844; Bertram Wyatt-Brown, *Lewis Tappan and the Evangelical War against Slavery* (Cleveland: Press of Case Western Reserve Univ., 1969), chs. 5–7; Gerald Sorin, *The New York Abolitionists: A Case Study of Political Radicalism* (Westport: Greenwood, 1971).
41. Elizur Wright to Theodore Weld, 1 Feb. 1833, *Weld-Grimké Letters,* I, 103; [Lewis Tappan], *The Life of Arthur Tappan* (New York: Hurd and Houghton, 1870), 148–152.
42. The NYCA-SS should be distinguished from the New York State Anti-Slavery Society, fl. 1835–1845, which was a center of political-action, third-party sentiment, and the New York Anti-Slavery Society, fl. 1854–1855, a group of radical constitutionalist abolitionists.
43. Atlee, Shipley, and others to Arthur Tappan, 7 tenth month 1833, in MSS. of the Pennsylvania Abolition Society, Historical Society of Pennsylvania (microfilm).

Nonetheless, reassured by the relative moderation and respectability of the New Yorkers, and impressed with the suggestion of Philadelphia as the site where a new national antislavery organization should be founded, the Pennsylvania Quakers supported the Boston and New York groups.

Other centers of antislavery activity in the Burned-Over District of western New York and in the Western Reserve of Ohio supplied more recruits.[44] Lewis Tappan had sent his sons to the Oneida, New York Manual Labor Institute, where they came under the influence of Theodore Dwight Weld, who was teaching there briefly. Weld put Tappan in touch with Beriah Green and Elizur Wright at Western Reserve College near present-day Cleveland, Ohio, then went west and was himself converted to immediatism by Green and Wright while at Western Reserve. He matriculated at Lane Theological Seminary in Cincinnati, and in 1834 organized a debate with colonizationists there. After two weeks of intense dispute, nearly the entire student body was converted to abolition. A heavy-handed effort by the trustees to squelch the progress of abolitionist thought, and to discourage the students from working as missionaries among the black population of the city, forced about fifty students to withdraw from the seminary and remove to Oberlin in northern Ohio, which thereafter was an outpost of immediatist activism. Weld became a full-time agent for the AA-SS, and in the summer of 1834 converted Birney, whom he had met earlier, from colonization to immediatism.

By late 1833 all these northern centers of antislavery agitation were linked by ties of friendship and influence. Two regional immediatist societies were operating and were supporting weekly newspapers. An embryonic agency system had begun, and immediatists had drawn blood in debates with colonizationists. But Garrison and others saw that a national organization was needed to exert maximum organizational control over the sprawling abolitionist effort, as well as to provide a national propaganda forum.

Before they could achieve this goal, however, a dramatic incident occurred in Connecticut that promoted constitutional issues to the fore of abolitionists' thinking, gave the coalescing movement an egali-

44. On the former, see Whitney R. Cross's classic *The Burned-over District: The Social and Intellectual History of Enthusiastic Religion in Western New York, 1800–1850* (1950; rpt. New York: Harper & Row, 1965); for the latter, Gilbert H. Barnes, *The Antislavery Impulse 1830–1844* (1933; rpt. New York: Harcourt, Brace & World, 1964).

tarian impetus, stoked colonizationist-abolitionist animosity, and re-kindled issues raised in the second Missouri debates. A Quaker lady, Prudence Crandall, who ran a dame school in Canterbury, created a local sensation when she first admitted a black girl to her school and then, after some parents objected, announced that she would run her school exclusively as a "High School for young colored Ladies and Misses."[45] Canterbury's political elite, led by colonizationist Andrew T. Judson, brought both legal and illegal pressure to close the school down.[46] Samuel J. May, George W. Benson (a future brother-in-law of Garrison), and Arnold Buffum worked with Crandall to keep the school going, and prevented the townsfolk from having the selectmen whip the girls out of town under provisions of an old Connecticut pauper and vagrancy statute. Frustrated in their resort to the old law, Judson and his coworkers got a new one passed that prohibited any-one from operating a private school for nonresident blacks without first obtaining the permission of the selectmen and a majority of the "civil authority" of the town. This was known among abolitionists as the "Connecticut Black Law."[47]

Crandall was first tried for violation of this statute in a county court, with Judson acting as prosecuting attorney, but was not con-victed because of a hung jury.[48] Judson then secured a second trial before Chief Judge David Daggett of the Connecticut Supreme Court of Errors. Daggett, who was a vice-president of the New Haven Colonization Society, charged the jury that the Black Law was con-stitutional on the grounds that free blacks were not citizens of a state within the meaning of the privileges and immunities clause.[49] Crandall

45. Quoted in Garrisons, *William Lloyd Garrison*, I, 319.
46. Good secondary treatments are: Edmund Fuller, *Prudence Crandall: An Incident of Racism in Nineteenth-Century Connecticut* (Middletown: Wesleyan Univ. Press, 1971); Edwin Small and Miriam Small, "Prudence Crandall: Champion of Negro Education," *New Eng. Q.*, 17 (1944), 506–529; and Lawrence J. Friedman, "Racism and Sexism in Ante-bellum America: The Prudence Crandall Episode Reconsidered," *Societas*, 4 (1974), 211–277.
47. Act of 24 May 1833, ch. 9, in *The Public Statute Laws of . . . Con-necticut . . . 1833* (Hartford: John Russell, 1833).
48. *A Statement of Facts, Respecting the School for Colored Females, in Canterbury, Ct., Together with a Report of the Late Trial of Miss Prudence Crandall* (Brooklyn: Advertiser Press, 1833); *Report of the Trial of Miss Prudence Crandall before the County Court for Windham County, August Term, 1833 . . .* (Brooklyn: Unionist, 1833).
49. Daggett's jury charge is reprinted in *Andrew T. Judson's Remarks, to the Jury, on the Trial of the Case, State v. P. Crandall . . .* (Hartford: John Russell, [1833]) and in 10 Conn. 341–348.

was convicted, but on appeal the conviction was reversed on a technicality of pleading not related to the substantive issues raised by Daggett's charge.[50] According to the recollection of one of its surviving members a generation later, the entire court, with the exception of Daggett, disagreed with the charge's opinion that blacks could not be citizens.[51]

Unsuccessful in the courts, the people of Canterbury reverted to extrajudicial modes of persuasion. They tried to burn the house down with the girls inside, and, that failing, mobbed the house, breaking its windows and terrorizing the girls. Discouraged, Crandall and her supporters finally gave up. She dismissed the girls, married a Baptist minister, and spent the rest of her days teaching black children in northern Illinois and southern Kansas. In 1886, near the end of her life, the state of Connecticut officially extended an apology and indemnity to her for her persecution.

The Prudence Crandall episode was one of the first acts of antiabolitionist mobbing that hardened antislavery commitment and discredited colonization. But its enduring significance lay in the impetus it gave to antislavery constitutional thought. Because the case raised issues concerning the rights of free blacks in northern states, not slaves in the South, it conceptually leapfrogged difficult constitutional questions about slavery that were not yet ripe for resolution, and instead impelled abolitionists further along the road toward a legal egalitarian theory that matured fully in the revised privileges and immunities clause of the Fourteenth Amendment's first section.

The Crandall arguments swirled around the privileges and immunities clause of Article IV, section 2. The Missouri debates had not resolved the meaning of that clause as it pertained to free blacks removing from one state to another, despite Charles Cotesworth Pinckney's *ex cathedra* and historically wrong claim that he was draftsman of the clause and that it did not comprehend blacks within the category of citizens. In 1821, United States Attorney General William Wirt contributed his misleading bit to the debate over black citizenship and the privileges and immunities clause when he held that free blacks could not be licensed as masters of vessels under federal coastal licensing laws.[52] He did so, however, by construing the phrase

50. *Crandall* v. *State*, 10 Conn. 339 (1834).
51. Judge Williams to Judge Bissell, 1865, in 32 Conn. 565 (app.) (1865).
52. Opinion of 7 Nov. 1821 in 1 *Official Opinions of the Attorneys General* . . . 506–509.

"citizen of the United States" which appears nowhere in the federal Constitution, except in the nonpertinent clauses describing the qualifications for congressmen and the president. It was a statutory phrase,[53] and hence not determinative of the meaning of the clause.

The next benchmark in this debate was Justice Bushrod Washington's U.S. Circuit Court opinion of 1823, *Corfield* v. *Coryell*,[54] which provided the first judicial construction of the clause. Washington enumerated the privileges of state citizenship as those:

which are, in their nature, fundamental; which belong, of right, to the citizens of all free governments; and which have, at all times, been enjoyed by the citizens of the several States which compose this Union, from the time of their becoming free, independent, and sovereign. What these fundamental principles are, it would be more tedious than difficult to enumerate. They may, however, be all comprehended under the following general heads: Protection by the government; the enjoyment of life and liberty, with the right to acquire and possess property of every kind, and to pursue and obtain happiness and safety; subject nevertheless to such restraints as the government may justly prescribe for the general good of the whole. The right of a citizen of one State to pass through, or to reside in any other State, for purposes of trade, agriculture, professional pursuits, or otherwise; to claim the benefit of the writ of habeas corpus; to institute and maintain actions of any kind in the courts of the State; to take, hold and dispose of property, either real or personal; and an exemption from higher taxes or impositions than are paid by the other citizens of the State; may be mentioned as some of the particular privileges and immunities of citizens, which are clearly embraced by the general description of privileges deemed to be fundamental; to which may be added, the elective franchise.

By his close paraphrase of Article I of the Virginia Declaration of Rights, Washington incorporated into the privileges and immunities clause the whole range of substantive liberties that Mason, in drafting the Declaration, assumed were derived from natural law. Further, he construed the clause to mean that a citizen of state *A*, removing to state *B*, enjoyed the same rights in *B* as other citizens of *B*—as opposed to a different construction, which surfaced briefly during the Missouri debates, that suggested that a citizen of *A* removing to *B* carried with him all rights that he enjoyed in *A*, whether or not state

53. See, e.g., Act of 3 March 1813, ch. 42, §1, 2 Stat. 809, distinguishing between "citizens of the United States" and "persons of colour, natives of the United States."
54. *Corfield* v. *Coryell*, 6 Fed. Cas. 546 (No. 3230) (C.C.E.D.Pa. 1823).

B granted these to its own citizens. Washington also held that a state need not extend to nonresidents all the privileges it accorded to residents.

Washington did not even suggest that there could be such a thing as national citizenship, under which a person could be a citizen of the United States, as well as of a state. Both William Rawle in 1825, and then, though more ambiguously, Joseph Story in 1833, suggested that the qualifications of congressmen clause and the privileges and immunities clause created a national, or what Story called, "if one may say so, a general citizenship."[55] But this concept of a national citizenship was not endorsed by a prominent court until 1844, when the New York Court of Chancery held that under the privileges and immunities clause a citizen of a state was also a "citizen of the United States" as a "national right or condition."[56] This was therefore an unresolved question in 1833. The controversies over the Negro Seamen's Acts had contributed much heat but little light to the question, so the Connecticut courts had an open field when they were asked to determine whether Connecticut could prohibit one of its citizens from schooling nonresidents who happened to be black.

Both Judson in argument and Judge Daggett in his opinion had stated or assumed that the privileges and immunities clause was inadequate to sustain Crandall's and her pupils' rights because free blacks were not citizens and therefore could not claim the privileges secured by Article IV, whatever those might be. To combat this contention, Crandall's counsel, Calvin Goddard and William W. Ellsworth, maintained that blacks were citizens of the state of their nativity or residence and hence came within the phrase "Citizens of each State." Ellsworth carried this further, arguing that as such, they were citizens of every other state in the Union, which, though it sounds peculiar today, was not an unnatural conclusion in an era before the possibility of national citizenship was accepted. Ellsworth also voiced an argument later popular with radical abolitionists when he claimed that since blacks owe allegiance and support to their state, the state

55. William Rawle, *A View of the Constitution of the United States of America,* 2d ed. (Philadelphia, Philip H. Nicklin, 1829), 86 (1st ed. 1825); Story, *Commentaries on the Constitution of the United States,* II, §1806 (1st ed. 1833).
56. *Lynch* v. *Clarke,* 1 Sandf. Ch. 583 (New York Court of Chancery 1844) at 641–642; *accord,* U.S. Attorney General Edward Bates, 29 Nov. 1862, in 10 *Official Opinions of the Attorneys General* 382, reversing Wirt's 1821 opinion.

owes them the correlative, protection of its laws. Neither extrajurisdictional citizenship nor race provided valid grounds for excluding nonresident blacks from an education in Connecticut, and so the Black Law was invalid as a violation of the clause. Goddard, differing from his colleague, found the black girls' protection in their status as citizens of the United States, a status derivative from their state citizenship.[57]

As the Crandall affair dragged on from trial through appeal, officers of the NYCA-SS issued a call for a constitutive meeting of a new national antislavery organization to be held in Philadelphia on 4 December 1833. The convention gathered most abolitionists then prominently active in the United States. Among the New Englanders were May, Phelps, Buffum, and Jocelyn. Three black abolitionists attended: James G. Barbadoes, Robert Purvis, and James McCrummell of Philadelphia, who was Garrison's host and at whose house Garrison composed the Declaration of Sentiments. The New York group was represented by Lewis Tappan (the absent Arthur was elected first President of the Society), George Bourne, the evangelical merchants William Green and John Rankin,[58] Charles W. Dennison, James Miller McKim, Goodell, and Wright. Thomas Shipley, Evan Lewis, Edwin Atlee, and Lucretia Mott, one of four women present, represented the Philadelphia ganglion. Beriah Green led the western delegates and was chosen to preside over the convention after Philadelphian Roberts Vaux declined the honor. Ten states were represented in the persons of some fifty to sixty delegates.

In its constitution and Declaration of Sentiments the newly formed American Anti-Slavery Society presented the ideas and plans of the immediatist movement as of 1833. These constitutive documents were the source of later Garrisonian, radical, and moderate constitutionalist developments, and outlined the early constitutional theory of the antislavery movement. Hence they should be examined in detail.

Most of the constitution[59] was given over to structural details not

57. "A Member of the Bar" [Chauncey F. Cleveland], *Report of the Arguments of Counsel in the Case of Prudence Crandall, Plff. in Error, v. State of Connecticut, before the Supreme Court of Errors, at Their Session at Brooklyn, July Term, 1834* (Boston: Garrison & Knapp, 1834), 8, 6, 9, 28, 31; see also "The Canterbury Law," *Emancipator,* 22 June 1833.

58. To be distinguished from the Ohio abolitionist of the same name, who was the author of *Letters on American Slavery* (1826).

59. Printed in *Proceedings of the Anti-Slavery Convention, Assembled at*

significant for constitutional thought, but it did contain an unusually long statement of principles, embracing the following elements:

I. Slavery as a moral and political evil.
   A. God's laws: slavery violated the command of Jesus Christ: "Thou shalt love thy neighbor as thyself," and frustrated the purpose of the Creator, who "hath made of one blood all nations of men for to dwell on all the face of the earth."[60]
   B. Natural law: slavery was "contrary to the principles of natural justice," which were antecedent and superior to the American Constitution.
   C. The ideology of the American republic: slavery was contrary to the Declaration of Independence's assertions that "all men are created equal, that they are endowed by their Creator with certain unalienable Rights, that among these are Life, Liberty, and the pursuit of Happiness;" and also inimical to "the principles of . . . our republican form of government."
II. Immediatism.
   A. "The objects of this society are the entire abolition of slavery in the United States" [*sic*].
   B. It is "the duty and the interest of the masters, immediately to emancipate their slaves."
   C. Anticolonization: "no scheme of expatriation, either voluntary or by compulsion, can remove this great and increasing evil."
III. Egalitarianism.
   A. Blacks should "according to their intellectual and moral worth, share an equality with the whites, of civil and religious privileges."
   B. Whites must "encourag[e] their intellectual, moral and religious improvement, and . . . remove public prejudice."
IV. The *modus operandi* of the AA-SS.
   A. It would "convince all our fellow-citizens, by arguments addressed to their understandings and consciences."

Philadelphia, Dec. 4, 5, and 6, 1833 (New-York: Dorr & Butterfield, 1833), 5–8; reprinted with the Declaration of Sentiments and with some hints about the early constitutional speculations of the unified AA-SS in *The Declaration of Sentiments and Constitution of the American Anti-Slavery Society; Together with Those Parts of the Constitution of the United States, Which Are Supposed to Have Any Relation to Slavery* (New York: AA-SS, 1835).
   60. Matthew 19:19; Acts 17:26.

B. The AA-SS "will never, in any way, countenance the oppressed in vindicating their rights by resorting to physical
force."

C. The AA-SS's only weapons were "appeals to the consciences,
hearts, and interests of the people, to awaken a public sentiment throughout the nation."

V. Political action: the AA-SS "will endeavour, in a constitutional
way to influence Congress" to

A. abolish the interstate slave trade;

B. abolish slavery in the District of Columbia;

C. abolish slavery in the territories; and

D. prevent the extension of slavery into new states.

VI. The federal consensus: the AA-SS "admits that each State, in
which slavery exists, has, by the Constitution of the United
States, the exclusive right to legislate in regard to its abolition in
said State."

The federal consensus thereby became dogma for the AA-SS for
about five years, and was interwoven with its other doctrinal positions. An abolitionist minister in Ohio thus summed up immediatist
doctrine in 1837, near the end of the period when the consensus
would go unchallenged in the AA-SS: "The doctrine of immediate
emancipation, is not that Congress should immediately abolish slavery throughout the Union, but that it is the duty of each slaveholder,
immediately to relinquish his unrighteous claim to his slaves as
property."[61] This position discouraged political action in favor of an
ineffectual and counterproductive reliance on moral suasion directed
at the consciences of those who would have most to lose and least to
gain by emancipation.

The Declaration of Sentiments, which was drafted by Garrison,
served different purposes than the constitution; it breathed life into
the organization that the latter had formed.[62] Acutely conscious of the
historical echoes around him, Garrison pronounced the achievement
of 1776 incomplete; the 1833 convention "for its magnitude, solem-
nity, and probable results upon the destiny of the world, as far trans-
cends theirs, as moral truth does physical force." He demanded that

61. Hezekiah Johnson, *The Unity and Purity of the Morality Contained in
the Two Testaments* (Circleville: Religious Telescope Office, 1837), 50.
62. The Declaration of Sentiments was technically titled the "Declaration
of the Anti-Slavery Convention, Assembled in Philadelphia, Dec. 4, 1833" and
was printed in *Proceedings of the Anti-Slavery Convention,* 12–16.

emancipated slaves be "brought under the protection of law" and be given equal privileges conditioned only on their personal qualifications, not their race. Then, in phrases that would return to haunt him, he called for political action on four constitutional issues. The people of the free states must: urge Congress to abolish slavery in the territories; refuse to use physical force to put down slave insurrections; abrogate the federal number clause; and ignore the fugitive slave clause. Going beyond that, though neither he nor any other delegate seems to have thought out the implications of the words, Garrison declared that "all those laws which are now in force, admitting the right of slavery, are therefore before God utterly null and void." This agenda, with its latter formula, made up much of the platform of Garrison's later radical opponents when the antislavery movement split.

After the drama of the Philadelphia convention, the history of the society it created was a dull anticlimax. The leadership of the AA-SS passed into the hands of colorless philanthropists like the Tappans and William Green, or of professional reformers like Wright, Leavitt, and Goodell, all of whom lacked the flamboyance of Garrison. But their lack of flair should not obscure their great contribution in keeping alive an administrative vehicle for the antislavery movement that might otherwise have dissipated geographically and ideologically.

Under the aegis of the AA-SS, state and local immediatist societies rapidly formed throughout the North, and some of these, like the Illinois and Ohio societies, published their own papers and tracts, organized state conventions, and helped runaways and free blacks. At the time of the schism, the AA-SS claimed that 1,350 auxiliaries had formed, with a membership of around 250,000.[63] This figure may have been inflated, and doubtless some of the auxiliaries were little more than a village dissenter and his family, but the numbers are at least a gross index of the extent to which the AA-SS disseminated its principles. Its agents carried the immediatist message into mission territory where no constituted society functioned, and Weld raised an apostolic group, The Seventy, in 1836, who labored in the western fields with Pauline success. A pariah among the benevolent societies, a Joseph cast into the pit by his brothers, the AA-SS became in time

---

63. Louis Filler, *The Crusade against Slavery, 1830–1860* (New York: Harper, 1960), 67.

the most influential, and the blessings of Jacob fell on "the head of him that was separate from his brethren."[64]

The year 1833 marked the debut of American antislavery constitutionalism. With the founding of the AA-SS, abolition moved into a more vigorous, contentious, and effective phase. The characteristics that had dominated antislavery movements before 1830—gradualism, state and local organization loosely federated through a series of annual national conventions, the predominance of the Middle Atlantic and upper-South states, and an emphasis on legal action in the courts and legislatures of the states—gave way to different assumptions and a new form of organization. For the five years that the AA-SS served as the voice of a united antislavery movement, it articulated constitutional theories that represented a temporary agreement among abolitionists. When this unity fell apart, the constitutive ideas of the AA-SS served as the baseline for radical extrapolations that forced the course of American constitutionalism into new channels.

64. Genesis 49:26.

CHAPTER 8

Constitutional Sparring

For five years after its founding, the AA-SS enjoyed a spirit of internal amity, and was able to begin the important business of propagating immediatist doctrine. In this period, abolitionists needed all the cohesion they could muster, for they immediately found themselves plunged into constitutional controversy. But it was not the controversy they had anticipated at Philadelphia; rather than arguing over the rights of black slaves in the south, abolitionists found themselves defending the rights of free whites and allegedly free blacks in the north. Throughout the thirties, both abolitionists and defenders of slavery saw themselves as parrying the thrusts of the other. Abolitionists, from a southern viewpoint, carried their hateful doctrines into areas where they should have recognized that they were constitutionally impotent: the southern states and Congress. Defenders of slavery therefore fended off these unconstitutional attacks. From the abolitionists' vantage, slavery, in the form of pursuers of runaways, seemed to be thrusting at the liberties of northern blacks and whites. The antislavery movement spent much of its energy warding off these intrusions. The period closed when abolitionists' attention was diverted by two unexpected developments: Texas annexation and schisms within the antislavery church.

The first abolitionist thrust was "the great postal campaign," an effort to circulate antislavery publications by mail throughout the United States. The New York managers of the AA-SS planned to bring out four monthly publications for mass distribution, one to be issued each week of the month, so as to insure a steady flow of abolitionist propaganda. They were taking advantage of a technological revolution in printing, which enabled publishers to circulate tracts at greatly diminished cost, and which permitted them to use woodcuts and other illustrative material on a scale thitherto financially prohibitive.[1]

Southerners found this propaganda unwelcome in the extreme. In 1829, when the Missouri debates, the Vesey plot, and the Negro Seamen's Act controversy were still recent events, David Walker, a Boston black, published his *Appeal to the Colored Citizens of the World,* calling on blacks to kill in self-defense if necessary and threatening whites with insurrection.[2] Soon thereafter, Garrison began publishing the *Liberator.* Southerners warned that such publications would incite slave uprisings. As if to confirm their fears, in 1832 Nat Turner fulfilled the prophecy of Ezekiel: "Go through the midst of the city, through the midst of Jerusalem . . . and smite: Let not your eye spare, neither have ye pity: Slay utterly old and young, both maids, and little children, and women."[3]

The Virginians had reacted cooly toward the Vesey uprising nine years earlier, but Nat Turner convinced them that the Carolinians were correct in their analysis of the causes of slave unrest. Virginia Governor John Floyd wrote James Hamilton, who had been mayor of Charleston in 1822 and was now governor of South Carolina, that Turner and other black preachers had imbibed ideas about religious equality originating "from the Yankee population" including peddlers, preachers, and authors of tracts. "Often from the pulpits these pamphlets and papers were read—followed by the incendiary publications of Walker, Garrison and Knapp of Boston, these too with songs and hymns of a similar character were circulated, read and commented upon."[4] Southerners linked Garrison and Walker as

1. Leonard L. Richards, *"Gentlemen of Property and Standing": Anti-Abolition Mobs in Jacksonian America* (New York: Oxford Univ. Press, 1970), 56–58, 71–73; Bertram Wyatt-Brown, "The Abolitionists' Postal Campaign of 1835," *J. Negro Hist.,* 50 (1965), 227–238.
2. The third edition (Boston: David Walker, 1830) is reprinted in Herbert Aptheker, ed., *One Continual Cry: David Walker's Appeal to the Colored Citizens of the World (1829–1830)* (New York: Humanities, 1965); on Southern reaction to it, see Clement Eaton, "A Dangerous Pamphlet in the Old South," *J. Southern Hist.,* 2 (1936), 323–334.
3. Ezekiel 9:4–6. The metropolis of Southampton County, Virginia, where Turner's uprising took place, was a town named Jerusalem.
4. Floyd to Hamilton, 19 Nov. 1831, in Henry I. Tragle, comp., *The Southampton Slave Revolt of 1831* (1971; rpt. New York: Vintage, 1973). Isaac Knapp was Garrison's partner.

instigators of slave revolts. The Vigilance Association of Columbia, South Carolina offered a $1,500 reward for the conviction of any white distributing the *Liberator* in South Carolina.

Given such attitudes, it need not have surprised the AA-SS managers that southern postmasters would be reluctant to deliver abolitionist propaganda. The most volatile destination for such mail was Charleston, South Carolina. The postmaster there, Alfred Huger, wrote his superior officer, Postmaster General Amos Kendall, requesting instructions. The same evening, a mob relieved him of his difficulty and his mail by seizing the mailsacks containing AA-SS literature and burning them. Huger then notified Kendall that "nothing short of a regular army" could protect the safety of the mails in Charleston.[5] Kendall faced a predicament. Having adopted Kentucky as his home, and being a national leader of the proslavery Democracy, he sympathized with the views of southern communities. But no federal statute authorized refusal to deliver mail; in fact, the postal statutes required postmasters to deliver mail to willing and identifiable recipients. He therefore passed the buck back to Huger. "We owe an obligation to the laws," he instructed the Charlestonian, "but a higher one to the communities in which we live, and if the former be perverted to destroy the latter, it is patriotism to disregard them." He told Huger to decide whether or not to deliver antislavery mail on the basis of "the character of the papers detained and the circumstances by which you are surrounded."[6]

The mails dispute was then quickly shunted from political channels into constitutional ones, where it played out in two odd and ironic denouements. Kendall began the constitutional dialogue by arguing that the states as sovereigns at the time of Independence had full power to control the inflow of harmful propaganda, a power they did not surrender by the adoption of the Constitution.[7] Hence whatever the extent of congressional power under the post office clause,[8] it did not supercede the fundamental police power of the sovereign

5. Huger to Kendall, 29 July 1835 and 10 Aug. 1835, both reprinted in Richmond *Enquirer,* 25 Aug. 1835.

6. Kendall to Huger, 4 Aug. 1835, quoted in Richmond *Enquirer,* 25 Aug. 1835.

7. Kendall to Samuel Gouverneur, postmaster of New York City, Aug. 1835, reprinted in *Niles Weekly Register,* 5 Sept. 1835.

8. Art. I, section 8: "The Congress shall have Power . . . To Establish Post Offices and post Roads."

states. Whatever the abolitionists' rights of speech and press—and
Kendall seemed doubtful that they had any—they could not use the
mails to disseminate propaganda in states where such propaganda
was illegal. Missouri Senator Thomas Hart Benton put it more col-
loquially: the post office need not be made "a pack-horse for the
abolitionists."[9]

Kendall added a second point a few months later in his annual
departmental report, and kept alive privileges and immunities clause
arguments. He claimed that under the clause, citizens of free-state *A*
had no greater rights, either under the First Amendment or under the
post office clause, to mail antislavery materials into slave-state *B*
than the citizens of *B* had. Moreover, since the federal government
had an obligation to protect the states against domestic violence under
Article IV, section 4, it could not permit the mails to be used to promote internal unrest.[10] Kendall then asked President Andrew Jackson
for his opinion on the propriety of his (Kendall's) actions, and suggested that Congress should set legislative guidelines for his department.[11] Jackson at first impulsively suggested that postmaster publish
the names of recipients of abolitionist literature, so as to "put them in
Coventry," but on more mature reflection recommended to Congress
that they prohibit circulation "in southern states, through the mail,
of incendiary publications intended to instigate the slaves to
insurrection."[12]

Jackson's recommendation stirred John C. Calhoun to a counter-
proposal of his own in the Senate. Calhoun and Jackson loathed each
other and the Carolinian wanted to thwart the President partly out of
personal animus, but also because he considered Jackson's constitutional premises mischievously wrong. He secured appointment of a
special committee stacked heavily with southern Democrats to consider Jackson's recommendation, and on 4 February 1836 he reported

9. *Globe,* 24 Cong. 1 sess. 301 (13 April 1836).
10. "Report of the Postmaster General," *H. Ex. Docs.* 24 Cong. 1 sess.,
ser. 286, doc. 2, (1835), 396–398.
11. Kendall to Jackson, 7 Aug. 1835, in John Spencer Bassett, ed., *Correspondence of Andrew Jackson* (Washington, D.C.: Carnegie Institution,
1926–35), V, 359–360; "Report of the Postmaster General," ser. 286, doc. 2.
12. Jackson to Kendall, 9 Aug. 1835, in Bassett, ed., *Correspondence of
Jackson,* V, 360–361; Seventh Annual Message, 7 Dec. 1835, in James D.
Richardson, comp., *A Compilation of the Messages and Papers of the Presidents* (Washington, D.C.: Bureau of National Literature, 1897–1914), IV,
1395.

out a recommendation, but only for a minority of the committee.[13] Calhoun recommended rejection of Jackson's proposed bill on the grounds that it was doubly unconstitutional.[14] First, the guarantee of freedom of the press in the First Amendment was of superior obligation to the delegated congressional post office power. Second, Jackson's measure invaded the "reserved rights of the states." If Congress could determine what is incendiary, it could also decide what is not, and force such material into the states despite statutes forbidding its circulation. Calhoun nevertheless insisted that the slave states had a right, and the free states a correlative duty, to have antislavery efforts repressed. Neither the First Amendment nor equivalent guarantees in the state constitutions protected antislavery efforts because slavery in the southern states was not just a property relationship, but also a regulation of the "social and political relations" of two diverse races. To disturb this system would destroy the union and plunge it into a civil war.

Calhoun recommended a bill that would prohibit postmasters from putting into the mails any publication "touching on the subject of slavery" addressed to anyone in a slave state that prohibited its circulation. Responding to criticism of this measure, he warned that if it failed to pass, the southern states would resort to interposition because their laws concerning slavery were paramount to all federal powers, including those over commerce and the mails.[15] Proposing an idea that Roger B. Taney would shortly endorse as Chief Justice of the United States, Calhoun claimed that the right of the slave states to erect an intellectual *cordon sanitaire* that was proof to anti-

13. After objecting to referral of Jackson's recommendation to the Senate Post Offices and Post Roads Committee because it contained only one slave-state Senator, Calhoun ensured that the special committee of five had men from four slave states. But by an irony, Calhoun in his report could carry only Willie Mangum of North Carolina with him. On the make-up of the committee, see *Globe,* 24 Cong. 1 sess. 36 (21 Dec. 1835), 151 (3 Feb. 1836).

14. Calhoun's report is in an untitled *S. Rep.,* 24 Cong. 1 sess., ser. 280, doc. 118 (1836).

15. [Thomas Hart Benton], *Abridgment of the Debates of Congress, from 1789 to 1850* (New York: D. Appleton, 1859), XII, 758 (12 April 1836); this speech went unreported in the *Globe.* For the Twenty-fourth Congress, three reporting systems preserved parts of congressional debates: Benton's *Abridgment;* Gales & Seaton's *Register of Debates,* which up till then had been the principal source of congressional reportage after the *Annals of Congress* had expired; and the *Congressional Globe,* which soon came to have semiofficial status.

slavery propaganda was analogous to their quarantine and immigrant exclusion powers, and was derived from their inherent sovereignty.[16]

Unimpressed with Calhoun's appeal to free-state conservatism, Massachusetts Whigs Daniel Webster and John Davis opposed his bill, not only on First Amendment grounds, but also because they violated the Fourth Amendment's guarantee against searches and seizures.[17] John P. King of Georgia, speaking for southern Democrats, raised a different objection: freedom of the press was a state right, merely recognized and protected from federal intrusion by the First Amendment. It was necessarily subordinated to more exigent matters like preservation of internal peace and could not control an "expressly delegated power [i.e. congressional post office authority] for purposes inconsistent with . . . the general purposes of the national compact," one of which was maintenance of domestic tranquility.[18] Outside Congress, William Plumer, former senator from New Hampshire, outlined a position closest to modern libertarian concepts. Calhoun had failed, Plumer wrote, in his attempt to "invent a north west passage to get around the obstacle" of the First Amendment. Freedom of speech and press were reserved to the people from both federal and state interference.[19]

Because of these divergences of viewpoint, Calhoun's bill was lost. Hence the first of the ironies: Jackson's effort to suppress abolitionist propaganda was killed by the South's foremost spokesman, aided by an odd coalition of free- and slave-state representatives. The second irony soon followed from the other side of the Capitol. The House had not acted on Jackson's recommendation, but had complied with another suggestion of Kendall that Congress reorganize the Post Office Department. Seemingly oblivious of the constitutional struggles across the way, the House passed a reorganization bill that included a provision making it a federal misdemeanor for postmasters to detain or delay delivery of letters, pamphlets, and newspapers.[20] In what seems to have been a fit of legislative absence of mind and not from

16. *Register of Debates,* 24 Cong. 1 sess. cols. 1140–1141 (12 April 1836).
17. *Globe,* 24 Cong. 1 sess. 288 (7 April 1836; Davis), app. 437 (8 June 1836; Webster).
18. *Globe,* 24 Cong. 1 sess. app. 285 (11 April 1836).
19. "Cincinnatus" [William Plumer], *Freedom's Defence; or, A Candid Examination of Mr. Calhoun's Report on the Freedom of the Press . . .* (Worcester: Dorr, Howland, 1836), 11, 19.
20. It became Act of 2 July 1836, ch. 43, §32, 5 Stat. 80.

any endorsement of abolitionists' right of access to the mails, Congress guaranteed that abolitionists could mail their incendiary material. The law was a dead letter in the South, partly because southern postmasters ignored it, and partly because the AA-SS abandoned its postal campaign by 1837.

Defenders of slavery did not rely solely on federal action to suppress abolitionist mailings, however; their efforts to work through interstate cooperation provided another battleground for constitutional skirmishing. Public meetings and newspapers through the South first tried to scare abolitionists by crude physical threats. The Charleston *Courier,* after noting with satisfaction that Garrison and Arthur Tappan had been burnt in effigy in New York City, warned them they would be actually burnt at the stake "could they only be brought within catching distance."[21] Its competitor, the *Mercury,* warned that any AA-SS agent coming into South Carolina "would assuredly expiate his offense upon the gallows."[22] When the New York AA-SS leaders met these threats with indifference and staid humor, southerners realized that their threats were mere bluster if they did not have their bird in hand. So they demanded legal or extralegal delivery of abolitionists.

A Tuscaloosa, Alabama, grand jury indicted Ransom G. Williams, then editor of the *Emancipator,* for violation of an Alabama slave incitement statute because he had published a statement in his paper that God condemned slavery. Governor John Gayle wrote to his New York counterpart, William Marcy, demanding Williams' extradition as a fugitive from justice under the extradition clause of Article IV, section 2.[23] Admitting that Williams had not "fled" Alabama "according to the strict literal import of that term," Gayle nevertheless demanded that he be surrendered on the grounds that the verb "flee" did not necessarily denote physical flight across a boundary, but meant rather any evasion of justice.[24] Gayle justified this bizarre

21. Quoted in *Niles Weekly Register,* 30 Oct. 1835.
22. Charleston *Mercury,* 30 July 1835.
23. "A Person charged in any State with Treason, Felony, or other Crime, who shall flee from Justice, and be found in another State, shall on Demand of the executive Authority of the State from which he fled, be delivered up, to be removed to the State having Jurisdiction of the Crime." Williams was a resident of New York, and the *Emancipator* was published there.
24. Gayle to "Marcey," 14 Nov. 1835, and gubernatorial message to the

reasoning by claiming that "strict construction" was appropriate only for clauses granting powers to the federal government, not to those reserving powers to the states. Defending the substance of Gayle's demand, but not his reasoning, Richard Yeadon, Whig editor of the *Courier,* argued that South Carolina's right to Williams' extradition was derived from principles of international law.[25] Marcy, despite his adhesion to the proslavery bent of the national Democracy, politely refused Gayle's request.

The failure of Gayle's demand led southern state legislatures to try a different mode of appeal for the cooperation of the North. An extralegal ad hoc group calling itself the "Committee of 21" had effectively displaced regular municipal government in Charleston during the furor over AA-SS mailings in August 1835. This committee outlined an agenda for northern state action that was widely endorsed elsewhere in the South. They insisted that "the people of no other state have any right to interfere [with slavery] in any manner whatsoever." Therefore nonabolitionists in the North must "manifest that disapprobation, not merely by the expression of their opinions, but by the most active, zealous, and perservering efforts to put down [antislavery] associations"; that is, northerners should mob the AA-SS out of existence.[26] Though southern legislatures had begun making such demands as early as 1831,[27] after 1835 they outdid each other in their calls for repression. Tennessee, Maryland, Missouri, and Mississippi banned publications that were, in the words of the Tennessee statute, "calculated to excite discontent . . . amongst the slaves or free persons of color."[28] South Carolina, Georgia, Virginia, and

Alabama legislature, both reprinted in Thomas M. Owen, "An Alabama Protest against Abolitionism in 1835," *Gulf States Hist. Mag.,* 2 (1903), 26–34.

25. Richard Yeadon, *The Amenability of Northern Incendiaries As Well to Southern as to Northern Laws, without Prejudice to the Right of Free Discussion* (Charleston: T. A. Hayden, 1835).

26. The resolutions of the Committee of 21 are reprinted in *Niles Weekly Register,* 22 Aug. 1835; see also the position of a Richmond, Virginia mass meeting, reprinted ibid.

27. See Resolution of 26 Dec. 1831, in *Acts of . . . Georgia . . . 1831 . . .* (Milledgeville: Prince & Ragland, 1832) (offer of $5,000 reward for conviction of Garrison or anyone circulating papers "of a seditious character"); joint resolution of 21 Jan. 1832, *Acts of . . . Alabama . . . [1831] . . .* (Tuscaloosa: Wiley, M'Guire & Henry, 1832) (request to free states to suppress antislavery publications).

28. Tennessee: Act of 13 Feb. 1836, ch. 44, in *Public Acts . . . of . . . Ten-*

Alabama peremptorily demanded northern censorship of antislavery publications, associations, and meetings.[29] Referring to state constitutional guarantees of freedom of speech, North Carolina maintained that northern states "have no right to disable themselves from [suppressing antislavery] by an organic law, more than to refuse its performance by an ordinary act of legislation."[30] In other words, the northern states would have to amend their constitutions to comply with slave-state concepts of civil liberties.

But the clarion for southern constitutional response came, naturally, from South Carolina, whose governor, the perfervid ex-nullifier George McDuffie, laid out the definitive southern agenda.[31] He first demanded that northern state legislatures make antislavery agitation a capital offense. Admitting that the southern states did not have a "right" to such legislation under the federal Constitution, McDuffie like Yeadon found the source of northern obligation in the principles of international law, which, as he interpreted it, made it a cause of war for one nation to tolerate its citizens' provoking civil unrest in another. Except for his demand for the death penalty, McDuffie had not ventured too far beyond what his contemporaries were thinking.[32]

The electrifying part of McDuffie's speech came in his defense of slavery as a positive good. "No human institution . . . is more manifestly consistent with the will of God, than human slavery," McDuffie advised the legislature, because blacks "are utterly unqualified not only for rational freedom, but for self-government of

nessee, 1835–6 (Nashville: S. Nye, 1836); Maryland: Act of 2 April 1836, ch. 325, in *Laws . . . of . . . Maryland . . . 1836* (n.p., 1836); Missouri: Act of 1 Feb. 1837, in *Laws of . . . Missouri . . . [1836] . . .* (Jefferson City: Calvin Gunn, 1837); Mississippi: Ch. 66, title 7, art. 2, in *Laws of . . . Mississippi . . . 1839* (n.p., 1839).

29. South Carolina resolution of 16 Dec. 1835, in Ames, ed., *State Documents on Federal Relations,* 216–219; Senate resolution, 22 Dec. 1835, in *Acts of . . . Georgia . . . 1835* (n.p., 1836); resolutions of Virginia, 16 Feb. 1836, in *Acts . . . of . . . Virginia . . . 1835–36 . . .* (Richmond: Thomas Ritchie, 1836); Alabama, 9 Jan. 1836, in *Acts . . . of . . . Alabama [1835]* (Tuscaloosa: Meek and M'Guire, 1836).

30. Resolutions of 1835 in *Acts . . . of North Carolina . . . 1835* (Raleigh: Philo White, 1836).

31. Message to legislature, 1835, reprinted in *Journal of the General Assembly of . . . South Carolina . . . 1835* (n.p., n.d.), 5–9.

32. See messages of governors William Schley of Georgia and David L. Swain of North Carolina, excerpted in *Niles Weekly Register,* 21 Nov. 1835 and 5 Dec. 1835 respectively.

any kind." Slavery was an immense social boon. Every society must have its menial laborers, and when these were free men "a dangerous element is obviously introduced into the body politic. Hence the alarming tendency to violate the rights of property by agrarian legislation" in states with universal suffrage and without slavery. "Domestic slavery, therefore, instead of being a political evil, is the cornerstone of our republican edifice."

James G. Birney and other abolitionists had little trouble refuting this southern intrusion into the regulation of civil liberties in the north, but the governors of Pennsylvania, Ohio, Massachusetts, New Jersey, and New York responded sympathetically to southern demands.[33] A few northern polemicists dismissed abolitionist claims to protection of the First Amendment as a "licentious extension" of liberties of speech and press.[34] The northern state legislatures, however, refused to take any actions that would stifle the abolitionists. New York and Ohio replied formally but equivocally to their southern sister states, condemning abolitionists but noting that in New York mobs made legislative action unnecessary and in Ohio the state constitution made it impossible.[35] In Pennsylvania, after incoming Governor Joseph Ritner had condemned his predecessor's message, the House Judiciary Committee, chaired by Thaddeus Stevens, vindicated the right of Pennsylvanians to free speech.[36] A select joint committee of the Massachusetts General Court, though hostile to antislavery, gave abolitionists an invaluable forum in which to present their case, and took no action on southern demands.[37] Vermont, as

33. See generally Dumond, *Antislavery*, ch. 24.
34. "A Northern Man" [Calvin Colton], *Abolition a Sedition* (Philadelphia: Geo. W. Donohue, 1839), 25; T. R. Sullivan, *Letters against the Immediate Abolition of Slavery; Addressed to the Free Blacks of the Non-Slave-Holding States. Comprising a Legal Opinion on the Power of the Legislatures in Non-Slave-Holding States to Prevent Measures Tending to Immediate and General Emancipation* . . . (Boston: Hilliard, Gray, 1835).
35. New York: Senate resolution reprinted in Ames, ed., *State Documents on Federal Relations*, 220; Ohio: *Journal of the Senate of . . . Ohio . . . 1835* . . . (Columbus: James B. Gardner, 1835), 990–991.
36. Ritner's message is quoted in *Fourth Annual Report of the American Anti-Slavery Society . . . 1837* . . . (New York: William S. Dorr, 1837), 44; on Stevens' role, see Fawn M. Brodie, *Thaddeus Stevens: Scourge of the South* (New York: Norton, 1959), 64–65.
37. *An Account of the Interviews Which Took Place . . . between a Committee of the Massachusetts Anti-Slavery Society, and the Committee of the*

always in the vanguard of state opposition to slavery, adopted a joint resolution stating that "neither Congress nor the state Governments have any constitutional right to abridge the free expression of opinions, or the transmission of them through the public mail."[38] In the climate of 1836, this was a decidedly antislavery position. At the time, Birney sighed in relief: "We have already passed our most fearful crisis," but one of his correspondents warned him that "the triumph of the liberty of the press and free discussion . . . is not identical with the triumph of abolition . . . you do not seem to have made much progress in abolition proper."[39]

The mail campaign was soon submerged in the more heated controversy over the gag rule, but the proponents of mail censorship had won a short-run de facto victory. In 1859, Virginia Attorney General John Randolph Tucker opined that states retained full control over distributing mail once it reached its geographical destination, an opinion welcomed by United States Postmaster General Joseph Holt.[40] United States Attorney General Caleb Cushing at the same time upheld the enforceability of southern laws prohibiting circulation of abolitionist literature by assuming that all antislavery publications were incitements to insurrection. He shrugged off First Amendment claims of abolitionists as "but words of rhetorical exaggeration."[41]

The trauma of the mails campaign, together with contemporary abolitionist mobbings in the north, induced in abolitionists a manichaean outlook on the struggle between antislavery and slavery. The founders of the New York State Anti-Slavery Society declared in 1835 that "the time has come to settle the great question whether

---

Legislature (Boston: Massachusetts Anti-Slavery Society, 1836); [William Goodell], *A Full Statement of the Reasons . . . Why there Should Be No Penal Laws Enacted, and No Condemnatory Resolutions Passed by the Legislature, respecting Abolitionits* [sic] *and Anti-Slavery Societies* (Boston: Massachusetts Anti-Slavery Society, 1836).

38. Resolution of 16 Nov. 1836, in *Acts . . . of . . . Vermont . . . 1836* (n.p., 1836).

39. Birney to Lewis Tappan, 17 March 1836, and John Green to Birney, 2 Nov. 1836, in Dwight L. Dumond, ed., *Letters of James Gillespie Birney, 1831–1857* (New York: Appleton-Century, 1938), I, 312, 369–371.

40. The Tucker and Holt opinions are in *Congressional Record*, 53 Cong. 2 sess. app. part 1, pp. 4–6.

41. Opinion of 2 March 1857 in 8 *Official Opinions of the Attorney General*, 489–502; quotation at 496.

the north shall give up its liberty to preserve slavery to the south, or whether the south shall give up its slavery to preserve liberty to the whole nation."[42] Abolitionists saw themselves as a secular saving remnant of Israel, surrogates for the cause of liberty of all men, black and white. As Birney saw it, "The contest is becoming—has become—one, not alone of freedom for the black, but of freedom for the white. . . . The antagonist principles of liberty and slavery have been roused into action and one or the other must be victorious."[43] This sense of a dualist opposition between the causes of liberty and repression was reinforced by another blow to abolitionists' civil liberties, the petition and gag controversy, in which abolitionists saw trampled not only their rights but those of their representatives in Congress as well.

This controversy affected antislavery constitutionalism in three ways. First, it strengthened the ties between the antislavery movement and the cause of civil liberties. This has been ably treated in the works of Dwight Dumond, Russell Nye, and Gilbert Barnes,[44] and needs no further elaboration here. The second impact had as great a significance. The most common subjects of abolitionist petitions in the late thirties were congressional power over slavery in the District of Columbia and the annexation of Texas. Leaving the Texas question aside for the time being, the issue of slavery in the District raised questions about legislative power over slavery everywhere that abolitionists stumbled upon almost unwittingly. To them, it was obvious that Congress had a plenary power over slavery derived from the broad wording of the federal district clause of Article I, section, 8; but this was not axiomatic to their opponents. So abolitionists went the long way around logically, and proved congressional power over District slavery by proving the power of any legislative body over slavery in its jurisdiction, and then coming back to the question at hand by showing that Congress had exclusive legislative power over the District. In the course of the detour, though, a few of them noticed that slavery anywhere was vulnerable to constitu-

42. *Proceedings of the New York Anti-Slavery Convention . . . and New York Anti-Slavery Society . . . 1835* (n.p., n.d. [1835]), 16.
43. Birney to Gerrit Smith, 13 Sept. 1835, *Birney Letters*, I, 343.
44. Russell B. Nye, *Fettered Freedom: Civil Liberties and the Slavery Controversy, 1830–1860*, rev. ed. (East Lansing: Michigan State Univ. Press, 1963); Dumond, *Antislavery*, chs. 28–29; Barnes, *Antislavery Impulse*, ch. 13.

tional attack. Some abolitionists, the radicals, quickly left the gag and District questions behind and explored the possibilities of an all-out constitutional assault on slavery in the states.

Third, the petition campaign proved to be a warm-up exercise for political-action abolitionists. The temporary failure of petitioning because of the gags led this group to see that all antislavery efforts could be blunted everywhere if legislative bodies simply ignored grassroots pressures. Something more would be needed to give petitioning its point, and that something more became ever-widening political action that brought abolitionists directly into participatory politics.

Antislavery petitions of one sort or another had flowed into Congress since Benjamin Franklin's 1790 effort. Unless they provoked a southern outburst, they were routinely referred to an appropriate standing committee to languish. But in 1829 Pennsylvania Federalist Charles Miner used a petition urging abolition of slavery in the District as the occasion for a rousing antislavery speech, and southern members thereafter sought to squelch petitions more effectively.[45] Boston abolitionists kept the pressure on;[46] the *Emancipator,* the *Liberator,* and the AA-SS all endorsed petitioning. But it was not until the postal campaign was smashed by southern intransigence that abolitionists appreciated the tactical advantages of petitions over mailings. Keeping in mind Lewis Tappan's calculating insight that the point of petitioning was not "so much to convert members of congress, as their constituents,"[47] the AA-SS instructed its agents in the field to divert their efforts into garnering signatures on petitions. This activity required extensive personal involvement and commitment, both for persons taking around petitions and for those signing them; contrasted with this, distributing pamphlets seemed coldly impersonal. It provided a hitherto untapped outlet for women's activism. Finally, the petition campaign was inexpensive, relying on volunteer labor or agents already in the field. The only direct costs were the minor ones of printing and mailing form petitions.

The initial southern attack on the stepped-up petition drive, which

45. Benton's *Abridgment,* X, 299–300 (6 Jan. 1829), 306–311 (7 Jan. 1829).
46. Samuel E. Sewall to Nathan Appleton, 22 Dec. 1831, in Nathan Appleton Papers, Massachusetts Historical Society, Boston.
47. Lewis Tappan to John Quincy Adams, 3 May 1837, Adams Papers, Massachusetts Historical Society (microfilm).

in 1835 concentrated on abolition of slavery and the slave trade in the District, immediately became dissipated by southern factional infighting caused by political realignments following the failure of Nullification three years earlier.[48] Responding to some District petitions, James Henry Hammond, then in the House, raged that he would not "see the rights of the Southern people assaulted day after day, by the ignorant fanatics from whom these memorials proceed," and moved that the House refuse to receive the petitions.[49] But South Carolinians were divided among themselves over the politics of the gag and produced some important constitutional hair-splitting.

The Carolinians were being pressured heavily by southern legislatures and the people-out-of-doors to adopt a position that Congress should not or could not abolish slavery in the District.[50] So Calhoun in the Senate and his allies in the House adopted a double-barreled strategy to deal both with the petitions and with the substance of their demand. They demanded that Congress resolve that it had no power whatsoever over slavery in the District, except, of course, to establish it there, as Congress had done. This would have been a self-denying ordinance by which Congress was to declare that it did not have the power expressly given it by the Constitution.[51] Second, Calhoun demanded that Congress not even receive the petitions, rather than receive them and table them automatically or shunt them to the oblivion of the District of Columbia Committees.[52] Not the least advantage to this maneuver was that it placed Vice-President Martin Van Buren, then presiding over the Senate and heir-apparent to President Jackson, in a dilemma. If the Little Magician supported

48. William W. Freehling, *Prelude to Civil War: The Nullification Controversy in South Carolina, 1816–1836* (1965; rpt. New York: Harper & Row, 1968), ch. 10.

49. *Register of Debates*, 24 Cong. 1 sess. col. 1967 (18 Dec. 1835).

50. Memorial of the Alabama General Assembly, 9 Jan. 1836, in *Acts . . . of . . . Alabama* [1835] (Tuscaloosa: Meek and M'Guire, 1836); Virginia Resolutions of 16 Feb. 1836 in *Acts . . . of . . . Virginia, 1835–36* (Richmond: Thomas Ritchie, 1836); "A Calm Appeal from the South to the North," reprinted from Richmond *Enquirer* in *Emancipator*, Oct. 1835.

51. Art I, §8: "The Congress shall have Power . . . To exercise exclusive Legislation in all Cases whatsoever, over such District (not exceeding ten Miles square) as may, by Cession of particular States, and the Acceptance of Congress, become the Seat of the Government of the United States. . . ."

52. Senate speech of 9 March 1836, in Richard K. Cralle, ed., *The Works of John C. Calhoun* (New York: D. Appleton, 1888), II, 484.

the Carolina position, he would lose northern support, but if he opposed it, he would suffer in the South.

The foxy Van Buren, however, out-maneuvered Calhoun by riding around the trap on the so-called "Pinckney Resolutions." Henry Laurens Pinckney, son of Charles Pinckney and former editor of the Charleston *Mercury,* represented a Charleston district in the House. He moved what, from Van Buren's perspective, were moderate compromise resolutions, consisting of three points: (1) Congress had "no constitutional authority" to abolish slavery in the states; (2) Congress "ought not to interfere" with slavery in the District; and (3) "all petitions . . . relating in any way . . . to the subject of slavery . . . shall, without being either printed or referred, be laid on the table, and that no further action whatever shall be had thereon." In a carefully drawn report on his resolutions, Pinckney claimed that congressional abolition in the District would violate the natural-law limitations on legislative power that Justice Samuel Chase had catalogued in *Calder* v. *Bull,* but he did not go quite so far as to say that Congress utterly lacked constitutional authority over slavery in the District, the point that Calhoun strove to establish.[53]

Hammond, representing Calhoun's position, heaped scorn on Pinckney's report. "Does he think he can paste it on his shield, and that, like the Gorgon's head, it will turn to stone all who look upon it? I can assure him it will be powerless with Tappan, Garrison, and the rest of the gang."[54] The House nonetheless adopted the Pinckney gag and proved Hammond right: it only stimulated abolitionists to mount a more intense petition campaign. The *Anti-Slavery Bugle* of Salem, Ohio, promised that they would "take possession of Congress and turn it into a vast Anti-Slavery Debating Society, with the whole country as an audience."[55] The antislavery societies poured out petitions that in 1837–1838 got half a million signatures. In addition to requesting the abolition of slavery in the District, the petitions opposed the admission of Arkansas or any other new slave states; condemned the gags; demanded abolition in all federal territories; called for abolition of the interstate slave trade; insisted that northerners of both races be protected while traveling in the south; op-

53. "Slavery in the District of Columbia," *H. R. Report,* 24 Cong. 1 sess., ser. 295, doc. 691 (1836).
54. *Register of Debates,* 24 Cong. 1 sess. col. 2494 (8 Feb. 1836).
55. Quoted in Nye, *Fettered Freedom,* 46.

posed statehood for the Republic of Texas; and asked for protection for free blacks in the District.

Disgusted with what he considered Pinckney's betrayal of principle, Calhoun carried the constitutional dialogue a step further in the Senate. He insisted that supporters of the Pinckney gag mistook the issues at stake, the more basic of which was Congress' control over the influx of petitions, not its power over the District. He drew an almost physical line between the First Amendment right of the people to send in a petition and the Article I right of the Senate to regulate its own proceedings.[56] This did not convince his Senate colleagues, who adopted Pinckney-type resolutions offered by Pennsylvania's James Buchanan. This proved to Calhoun that drastic steps were necessary to recall the Senate to its sense of obligation to the South.

First, Calhoun presented his famous positive-good thesis: slavery, far from being a political and moral curse, was a positive blessing to both races.[57] Second, he brought his gag effort to its constitutional culmination with his renowned six resolutions on the Union, which he introduced on 27 December 1837.[58]

1. The states adopting the federal Constitution in 1788–89 (and later) acted as "free, sovereign, and independent states" to achieve their internal security.

2. "Any intermeddling" by a state or people of a state with the domestic institutions of another is "not warranted" by the federal Constitution and is "subversive" of the objectives for which the Constitution was adopted.

3. The federal government was instituted by the states "as a common agent" with strictly delegated powers to protect the states' security; as such, it was bound to exercise its powers to give increased stability to the domestic institutions of the states, and to resist all efforts by one section of the union to attack the institutions of another.

4. Slavery, as a domestic institution of the southern states, was "recognized as constituting an essential element in the distribution

56. *Register of Debates,* 24 Cong. 1 sess. cols. 765–779 (9 March 1836); Art. I, §5, cl. 2: "Each House may determine the Rules of its Proceedings."

57. Cralle, ed., *Works of Calhoun,* II, 625–633, a version of his Senate speech of 6 Feb. 1837 that is superior to the versions in the congressional reports.

58. *Globe,* 25 Cong. 2 sess. 55–59 (27 Dec. 1837). Because my paraphrase does not do justice to the rich rhetorical impact of Calhoun's resolutions, the reader is referred to their full text, reproduced in the Appendix.

of its powers among the states"; thus no change of opinion in one section on the morality of slavery could justify attacks on slavery. Such attacks violated the mutual pledge given by the states in the formation of the union.

5. Any interference by Congress with slavery in the District of Columbia or the territories "would be a direct and dangerous attack on the institutions of all the slaveholding states."

6. The maintenance of the federal union depends on "an equality of rights and advantages among its members." Congress therefore could not discriminate among the states in extending these advantages, and the equality of rights would be violated if Congress refused to extend slavery into new territories, or to acquire new territories for slavery.

These resolutions were a momentous restatement of the nature of the federal union; if taken seriously they would have changed the basis of American federalism, and have given the slave states a decisive predominance in the federal government. Calhoun's colleagues did not see it that way, though; for whatever reason, the Senate in the course of long debates that lasted until 12 January 1838 accepted the first four resolves but rejected the last two. In their place, it adopted two watered-down versions promoted by Henry Clay that (1) suggested that Congress not abolish slavery in the territories because the people of the territory at the time of their admission as a state could decide the question for themselves, an early version of the doctrine later popularized by Lewis Cass and Stephen A. Douglas known as popular or squatter sovereignty; and (2) stated that abolition of slavery in the District of Columbia would violate the understanding implied in the Virginia and Maryland cessions.

Though the mails and gag controversies resulted in short-term victories for slavery, abolitionists in the thirties scored some successes too, at least in the northern states. Moreover, despite mobbings directed against them that culminated in 1835 and tapered off for the rest of the decade, opponents of slavery were able to disseminate their arguments to an ever wider and slightly more receptive audience. Finally, abolitionists discovered the force and usefulness of constitutional dialectic.

This new development, with its emphasis on constitutional doctrines, began with a spin-off of the petition and gag campaign. On 23 and 24 February 1837, George S. Hilliard and Henry B. Stanton, on behalf of the Massachusetts Anti-Slavery Society,[59] addressed a special committee of the Massachusetts General Court on the related problems of slavery in the District and the right of petition. Stanton maintained not only that Congress had power to abolish slavery there—a position endorsed by the Vermont legislature later that year,[60]—but that Congress' original establishment of it there violated the common-law preference for liberty as the natural condition of men. Here *Somerset* principles resurfaced in American constitutional discourse, transmuted into a libertarian, Americanized doctrine that we may call "neo-*Somerset*." Stanton maintained that "on the principles of the common law, slavery is everywhere null and void. Common law operates as an abolition act whenever it comes in contact with slavery. By it, every slave is free."[61] Going a step further the next year, the Massachusetts Society concluded that slavery in the District "exists in express violation of the letter and spirit of the American Constitution." Reinterpreting the federal consensus in an antislavery direction, the Society claimed that "the doctrine of the South, properly understood, that Congress has no right to meddle with slavery is sound. It follows that that body had no right to accept of that which it could not constitutionally touch."[62]

While Stanton and the Massachusetts Society were working out these doctrines in Boston, Theodore Dwight Weld was reaching similar conclusions in New York. Weld had given up field work in 1836 because his voice failed from overwork, and he joined the staff at AA-SS headquarters. Doing research in primary sources for information on slavery to incorporate into antislavery petitions, Weld compiled material for two remarkable books, *The Power of Congress over the District of Columbia* (1838) and *American Slavery as It Is*

59. Formerly the N-EA-SS, which changed its name in 1836 in acknowledgement of new antislavery societies in other New England states.

60. The Vermont legislative resolutions are reprinted in *Fifth Annual Report of the Executive Committee of the American Anti-Slavery Society . . . 1838* (New York: William S. Dorr, 1838), 57.

61. *Remarks of Henry B. Stanton . . . before the Committee of the House of Representatives of Massachusetts, to Whom was Referred Sundry Memorials on the Subject of Slavery* (Boston: Isaac Knapp, 1837), 11.

62. *Sixth Annual Report of the Board of Managers of the Massachusetts Anti-Slavery Society . . . 1838* (Boston: Isaac Knapp, 1838), 12.

(1839).[63] The latter, a pastiche of clippings from southern newspapers and other publications, revealed the inhumanity of slavery from eyewitness accounts. Harriet Beecher Stowe drew on it for materials for *Uncle Tom's Cabin*. But *The Power of Congress* had a greater impact on abolitionist constitutional thought.

The influence of Weld's tract derived from his argument that Congress had not only the power but the duty to abolish slavery in the District. He first argued that Congress, as the sole legislature for the District, had full sovereign legislative power over it, from the nature of things, by the terms of the Maryland and Virginia cession, and by the federal district clause. Like Stanton he escalated his argument by insisting that Congress tolerated slavery in the district in derogation of common law, which was "a universal, unconditional abolition act." Then Weld turned to the due process clause of the Fifth Amendment, claiming that the establishment of slavery deprived the slaves of liberty and property without due process, considered both substantively and procedurally. Congress also took property—self-ownership—not for public purposes, and without compensation. Weld concluded that "protection [of the laws] is the constitutional right of every human being under the exclusive legislation of Congress who has not forfeited it by crime." In these remarkable due process and protection arguments, Weld anticipated the following thirty years of antislavery constitutionalism, and hit upon the precise mode that antislavery Republicans would choose to destroy the vestiges of slavery.

More than that, Weld's tract was a signpost for his contemporaries, pointing to doctrines that would lead some of his fellow abolitionists to conclude in a few years that slavery was everywhere illegitimate. (Weld himself seems never to have accepted this extrapolation of his ideas.) If the Weld-Stanton doctrine was correct, and slavery had somehow been established despite, or in violation of, the common law, perhaps this meant that it could never enjoy a legitimate existence in any Anglo-American jurisdiction. Less radically, Weld's and Stanton's ideas could be developed to mean that slavery could exist nowhere but in the states that sanctioned it by positive law. In any

63. [Theodore Dwight Weld], *The Power of Congress over the District of Columbia* (New York: AA-SS, 1838); quotations that follow are from pp. 13, 45. [Weld], *American Slavery as It Is: Testimony of a Thousand Witnesses* (New York: AA-SS, 1839).

event, Stanton's legislative address and Weld's tract promoted constitutional dialogue among abolitionists.

Simultaneously, the same ideas were broached in the West, but in different forums and different contexts. In July 1836, an antiabolitionist Cincinnati mob destroyed the press that James G. Birney used to publish his antislavery newspaper, the *Philanthropist,* and threw his fonts in the Ohio River. Birney resumed publication immediately, and with associates in the Ohio Anti-Slavery Society, resorted to the courts to propagate abolitionist doctrine. A member of the OA-SS and the owner of the press sought damages in a civil action in Ohio courts. Birney then chose a rising young Cincinnati attorney, Salmon P. Chase, to represent the plaintiffs. Chase was as important an inductee to the antislavery cause as Birney had been a few years earlier. He soon became a leader of the movement in the West and went on to become United States Senator, Secretary of the Treasury, and Chief Justice of the United States. Chase and Birney, both competent lawyers, together worked out the arguments used in this litigation, and were successful.[64]

Their victory was a prelude to a more spectacular constitutional effort, the "Matilda" case, in which they fought vainly to prevent the kidnaping-recapture of Matilda Lawrence. Matilda was a nearly white young woman who had left her master, a Missourian named Larkin Lawrence (who was rumored to have been her father as well) when the steamboat they were aboard put in at Cincinnati.[65] She worked as a maid for the Birneys until she was suddenly captured by John M. Riley, a Cincinnatian reputed to be a slave catcher. Birney determined to defend her by seeking a writ of habeas corpus from an Ohio Common Pleas court (the lowest level of trial court in that state), but decided that he would be a poor choice for counsel because of local hostility to him. So he persuaded Chase to undertake Matilda's defense, and again supplied him with arguments.

The Birney-Chase arguments for Matilda demonstrated how flexible and protean antislavery constitutionalism had become.[66] Chase began and ended his effort skillfully with a sweeping reconsideration of the

64. Gamaliel Bailey to James G. Birney, 27 May 1837, in *Birney Letters,* I, 385.
65. Fladeland, *Birney,* 149–154.
66. *Speech of Salmon P. Chase, in the Case of the Colored Woman, Matilda . . . 1837* (Cincinnati: Pugh & Dodd, 1837).

nature of slavery derived from Mansfield's *Somerset* dicta. He claimed that the right to hold a slave "can have no existence beyond the territorial limits of the state which sanctions it, except in other states whose positive law recognizes and protects it. . . . The moment a slave comes into [a free state] he acquires a legal right to freedom." Concluding on the same spacious theme, Chase insisted that slavery violated a natural right to individual liberty, a right "proclaimed by our fathers, in the Declaration of Independence, to be self-evident and reiterated in our state constitution as its fundamental axiom, that all men are born 'equally free.' "

Between these broad appeals Chase developed a workmanlike construction of the role of state courts and the writ of habeas corpus as guarantors of individual liberty. Chase's argument proceeded on two levels of generalization, with both levels appealing to those already converted to antislavery, and the narrower accommodating those who had not yet been. The narrow ground was that Matilda, having been brought by her master voluntarily into a free state, had not "escaped" as the fugitive slave clause required, and hence could not be re-captured under any fugitive slave statutes, state or federal, whatever their constitutional validity. This point had important ramifications that abolitionists explored in ensuing debates in northern states over sojourners laws. If Chase's argument had been accepted, it would have effectively prevented slaveholders from voluntarily bringing slaves as personal servants into free states on business trips or to watering places like Saratoga Springs and Newport.

The broader ground of Chase's argument derived from the radical implications of the *Somerset* dicta. Going back to the loose maxims of the common law, abolitionists since Granville Sharp had insisted that a slave becomes free the moment he sets foot on free soil, at least if brought there voluntarily by his master. Only positive munic-ipal law, as Mansfield had said, could create and sustain an institution so odious to Christianity and natural law. The Northwest Ordinance having forever forbade enactment of such laws in Ohio, Chase argued that nothing kept Matilda oppressed in the unnatural status of slavery, once she laid claim to her natural condition, freedom.

Chase then attacked the constitutionality of the federal Fugitive Slave Act, ignoring broad hints by the judge that he was trying the court's patience in pursuing that line of argument. Chase claimed that the federal constitution was in part a compact between sovereign states, and that the federal statute tried to impose a duty on what was a compact relation that was independent of federal regulatory authority. The act also violated the Fourth Amendment's guarantee against unreasonable searches and seizures, the Fifth Amendment's due process clause, procedurally considered, and the Northwest Ordinance's guarantees of jury trial and habeas corpus.

The Matilda argument was a noble failure; Matilda Lawrence herself was hustled off by her captors, sent down to New Orleans on a riverboat, and sold into historical obscurity. Despite this personal tragedy, though, the episode marked an important milestone in the development of antislavery constitutionalism. Birney and Chase both derived the same insight from their joint effort and their use of *Somerset* arguments: slavery was an unnatural relation, created only by artificial legal, constitutional, and political arrangements. But from this insight they reached divergent conclusions, leading Chase to moderate constitutionalism and Birney toward radicalism. Chase rested content with the federal consensus arrangement, and was willing to let the slave laws remain in the states that had created them, if only the federal government could be separated from its unconstitutional support of those laws. The impetus of neo-*Somerset* arguments carried Birney further, and led him to see that slavery was so unnatural a relation that it could be nowhere legitimate, even if it were sanctioned by local law.

Birney and Chase managed to squeeze one small victory out of the Matilda defeat. Birney's antagonists had him prosecuted and convicted under Ohio's black code for harboring a slave. Glad for the chance to test the constitutionality of the black code and to be given another propaganda forum, Birney appealed, securing Chase to argue the appeal in the Ohio Supreme Court. The court disappointed him, however, by reversing his conviction on what amounted to a technicality: the indictment failed to aver that at the time he harbored Matilda Lawrence, he had *scienter,* a knowledge of the guilty character of his act.[67] But to reach this result, the court had to hold that in Ohio, color was no presumption of slave status, a ruling useful to conductors of Ohio's Underground Railroad who could thereafter associate more freely with their passengers.

Fugitive slave cases like Matilda's led abolitionists in the thirties

---

67. *Birney* v. *State,* 8 Ohio 230 (1838).

to think that one of the principal constitutional issues they faced was repelling the invasion of slavery in the free states. United States Senator Thomas Morris of Ohio, though not an abolitionist, bespoke their state of mind in 1839 when he claimed that the "slave power is seeking to establish itself in every state, in defiance of the constitutions and laws of the states within which it is prohibited. In order to secure its power beyond the reach of the states [that sanctioned it by positive law,] it claims its parentage from the constitution of the United States."[68] Constitutional issues concerning the status of extra-domiciliary slaves kept cropping up in the northern states, giving abolitionists repeated opportunities to test constitutional theories derived from their reading of *Somerset.*

One fruitful source of abolitionist constitutional argument was the problem of sojourners' slaves. By 1830, it was seemingly settled in the slave states that a master taking his slave for permanent residence in a free state or territory thereby liberated the slave, who could not be reenslaved upon being brought back to a slave state.[69] To this limited extent, *Somerset* principles had been absorbed into southern case law. But would they extend further, so as to liberate sojourners in the free states? This question had been dealt with only erratically by the statutory and case law of American jurisdictions before 1830.

Several northern states, among them Pennsylvania and New York, had enacted "sojourners' statutes" which permitted sojourning slaveholders to retain slaves for limited periods of residency. Pennsylvania's act was inconsistently construed. Bushrod Washington, as Presiding Justice of the United States Circuit Court for the District of Pennsylvania, applied it strictly against Senator Pierce Butler, freeing one of his slaves because a jury had found him to be a resident of Pennsylvania, where he lived while attending sessions of Congress when they met in Philadelphia, rather than of South Carolina, where he maintained only a nominal residence.[70] On the other hand, Chief Justice William Tilghman of the state Supreme Court construed it leniently

68. *Speech of the Hon. Thomas Morris, of Ohio, in the Senate of the United States, February 6, 1839, in Reply to the Hon. Henry Clay* (New York: Piercy & Reed, 1839), 16.

69. *Lunsford* v. *Coquillon,* 14 Martin 465 (La. 1824); *Harry* v. *Decker & Hopkins,* Walker (1 Miss.) 36 (1818); *Rankin* v. *Lydia,* 2 A. K. Marshall 468 (Ky. 1820).

70. *Butler* v. *Hopper,* 4 Fed. Cas. 904 (No. 2241) (C.C.D.Pa. 1806).

in favor of Representative Langdon Cheves of the same state, who was permitted to keep a personal servant enslaved in Pennsylvania even when the capital was no longer located in Philadelphia.[71] In the West, the Supreme Court of Missouri had held that a master's voluntary removal of a slave to Illinois for permanent residence freed the slave, but that mere passage through Illinois, or even residence there by the master while the slave was worked in Missouri, did not free the slave.[72] These incongruities could be tolerated in American case law before 1830 because the slavery controversy had not yet hardened attitudes and because too few cases involving sojourning or transistory slaves came up to the supreme courts to raise the issue to the level of substantial controversy.

Massachusetts abolitionists in 1835 saw the opportunity that this unsettled state of the law provided. A group of Yankee women, organized as the Boston Female Anti-Slavery Society, decided, as they put it, to "disinter the law of Massachusetts" on behalf of slaves coming temporarily into the Bay State.[73] Since Massachusetts did not have a sojourners statute, they hoped to secure a common-law decision embodying neo-*Somerset* that would liberate all slaves (except fugitives) coming onto Massachusetts soil. They persuaded Ellis Gray Loring and Rufus Choate to secure a writ of habeas corpus on behalf of a six-year-old black girl, Med, who had been brought by her mistress to Massachusetts for a brief visit.[74]

Choate and Loring in argument recited every element of Mansfield's opinion and even some points from Hargrave's argument to demonstrate that Med was free when her mistress voluntarily brought her into Massachusetts, and that a Bay State court need not respect the claim of property right in her under the principles of comity. Benjamin R. Curtis, on the other side, suggested to the court that *Grace*, rather than *Somerset*, was determinative, dismissing Mans-

71. *Commonwealth* ex rel. *negro Lewis* v. *Holloway*, 6 Binney 213 (Pa. 1814).

72. *LaGrange* v. *Chouteau*, 2 Mo. 20 (1828).

73. [Maria Weston Chapman], *Right and Wrong in Boston, in 1836. Annual Report of the Boston Female Anti-Slavery Society: Being a Concise History of the Cases of the Slave Child, Med . . .* (Boston: Isaac Knapp, 1836), 63–71; quotation p. 48.

74. Leonard W. Levy, *The Law of the Commonwealth and Cheif Justice Shaw: The Evolution of American Law, 1830–1860* (1957; rpt. New York: Harper & Row, 1967), ch. 5.

field's words as "highly figurative and declamatory language." Judges and lawyers immediately perceived the significance of the Med case, because it gave one of the most distinguished American courts the opportunity either of adopting the principles of *Somerset* entirely or of acquiescing in the intrusion of slavery into the free states. Justice Story even expected that it might eventually come before the United States Supreme Court for definitive resolution.[75]

Chief Justice Lemuel Shaw of the Supreme Judicial Court was indifferent, if not hostile, to the antislavery appeal of Med's intercessors, but he was even more hostile to the extension of slavery into Massachusetts. After a long and historically inaccurate review of the abolition of slavery in Massachusetts, Shaw concluded that the provisions of Article I of the 1780 Massachusetts Declaration of Rights could scarcely be "more precisely adapted to the abolition of negro slavery." He declared slavery to be so repugnant to natural law that it could only be established by positive municipal law. Although he did not regard slavery as contrary to the *jus gentium,* Shaw stated that Massachusetts would recognize by comity only property relationships in things, not in persons. Hence the *lex domicilii* of slavery in Louisiana did not extend into Massachusetts, and a master had no power to compel a slave to return to a slave jurisdiction.[76] Thus the Med decision represents an almost complete absorption of *Somerset* into American law. The Boston ladies paid a curiously effective tribute to Mansfield by renaming the little girl whom his ideas had freed "Med Maria Sommersett."

For abolitionists, sojourning slaves were only half the problem of slavery's extension into the free states; the other half were runaways. In the 1830s, aside from the Matilda case in Ohio, abolitionists came at the runaway issue through efforts to create, strengthen, or use personal liberty laws to prevent the kidnaping of free blacks and the recapture of actual fugitives. In Massachusetts, this produced an 1837 personal liberty act and a legislative committee report that marked the first time a political body composed of nonabolitionists adopted antislavery constitutional principles as the basis of legislative action.

75. Story to Ellis Gray Loring, 5 Nov. 1836, in Story, ed., *Life and Letters of Joseph Story,* II, 235.
76. *Commonwealth* v. *Aves,* 18 Pick. (35 Mass.) 193 (1836); for a comparable result in Connecticut the next year, but on narrower grounds, see *Jackson* v. *Bulloch,* 12 Conn. 38 (1837).

In New York, after some equivocal sparring in the courts, abolitionists secured a personal liberty law in 1840. But in Pennsylvania and Ohio they suffered reverses, with blacks being disfranchised in the first and oppressed by an anti–personal liberty law in the second.

In 1823, Chief Justice Isaac Parker of the Massachusetts Supreme Judicial Court had held the 1793 federal Fugitive Slave Act constitutional on the grounds that liberties secured in the federal and state bills of rights (jury trial, freedom from unlawful searches and seizures, and so on) did not pertain to slaves because they were not parties to the constitutional compact.[77] But he suggested obliquely that the statute would be unconstitutionally applied if it caused a free person to be seized and remitted to a slave jurisdiction. Seeing their opportunity in this concession, Massachusetts abolitionists, with the assistance of James C. Alvord, a rising young attorney, strove to have restored the writ of homine replegiando, which had been abolished in a general revision of Massachusetts laws in 1835. They were successful in 1837.[78] This was an important accomplishment, because the other writ of personal liberty, habeas corpus, did not carry with it a right to jury trial of any factual issues raised by the writ. Homine replegiando did, a procedural advantage of considerable importance in communities where popular hostility to slave catchers was widespread.

In his report for the legislative committee that recommended restoration of homine replegiando, Alvord adopted a position on the constitutional problems of state involvement in fugitive recapture proceedings that abolitionists had sketched three years earlier.[79] Defenders of the 1793 federal fugitive slave statute claimed that the federally authorized hearing did not determine the status of the black as slave or free, but only his identity, and, in a preliminary but not conclusive way, the validity of the master's claim in the first instance. The black could litigate his status, if he chose, upon his return to the master's state. Alvord, arguing from Chief Justice Parker's concession, replied that the fugitive slave clause of the federal Constitution pertained only to actual slaves, and that it could never be constitutionally applied, even in a preliminary hearing, to free men; only

77. *Commonwealth* v. *Griffith,* 2 Pick. (19 Mass.) 11 (1823).
78. Act of 19 April 1837, ch. 221, in *Laws of . . . Massachusetts . . . 1837 and 1838* (Boston: Dutton and Wentworth, 1839).
79. "The Constitution of the U. States and Slavery," *Emancipator,* 4 Nov. 1834.

"Person[s] held to Service or Labour" could be the subjects of the federal proceeding. Hence, Alvord reasoned, a black had a right to have his vital issue determined by a court in the state where he was seized before he was shipped off to a slave state where color gave rise to a presumption of slavery. Alvord further maintained, *contra* to Parker, that the federal act was unconstitutional as an intrusion on the prerogatives of the states.[80]

Abolitionists elsewhere built on Alvord's argument.[81] Elizur Wright, in a report for the AA-SS in the same year, demonstrated how far the antislavery movement had gone toward constitutional argument and political action.[82] He claimed that if a person were in fact "held to Service or Labour in one State, under the Laws thereof," it could be only by contract or a judicial determination that met the procedural requirements of the Fifth Amendment to the federal Constitution. (Wright was unaware of, or ignored, *Barron* v. *Baltimore* (1833)[83] in which the United States Supreme Court had held the provisions of the first eight amendments of the Constitution inapplicable as re-straints on state power.) The validity of this claim or adjudication had to be tested somewhere, with the burden resting on the claimant, who had to demonstrate either a contractual *quid pro quo* or the record of a judicial determination. Then, in a striking aside, Wright stated that "it is not sufficient for [the master] to prove that the laws of his state permit slavery. Slavery is unknown to the [federal] Con-stitution, which declares that no person shall be deprived of liberty without due process of law." This was the starting point of radical constitutionalism, though Wright seems to have been unaware of the significance of his argument at the time he wrote the report (May 1837).

Abolitionists elsewhere did not enjoy the same success. Although New Jersey enacted a jury-trial statute for alleged fugitives in 1837,[84] New York refused to do so at the time. The status of New York's 1828 personal liberty law was confused in the thirties by conflicting

80. James C. Alvord, "Trial by Jury, in Questions of Personal Freedom," *Am. Jurist and Law Mag.,* 17 (1837), 94–113.
81. "The Right of Trial by Jury," *Anti-Slavery Record,* Aug. 1837, 163.
82. *Fourth Annual Report of the American Anti-Slavery Society . . . 1837 . . .* (New York: William S. Dorr, 1837), 116–117.
83. 7 Pet. (32 U.S.) 243 (1833).
84. Act of 15 Feb. 1837, in *Acts of . . . New Jersey . . .* [1836] (Tren-ton: n.p., 1837).

decisions from federal and state courts. A state case, *Jack* v. *Martin* (1834)[85] held the New York statute invalid because it conflicted with the preemptive federal act of 1793. After this decision, Justice Smith Thompson of the United States Supreme Court, sitting on circuit, upheld the constitutionality of the federal act, but refused to rule explicitly on the constitutionality of the 1828 state act's procedures.[86] When *Jack* v. *Martin,* the state case, came on appeal to the New York Supreme Court for the Correction of Errors (a body composed of the Supreme Court, the Chancellor, and the state senate), it produced two conflicting opinions. One, by Senator Isaac Bishop, supported Nelson's lower-court opinion; but a concurrence by Chancellor Reuben Walworth threw out extensive dicta claiming that the federal act was unconstitutional and that an alleged fugitive had a right to jury trial to determine his status.[87]

Leaders of the New York State Anti-Slavery Society, including Elizur Wright, William Jay, Gerrit Smith, and Henry B. Stanton, then resorted to a petition campaign aimed at getting the state legislature to guarantee jury trial to alleged fugitives, as Pennsylvania and New Jersey had just done. They were unsuccessful, because most Democratic and Whig political leaders spurned their petitions. In 1840, however, the New York legislature met some of the most important demands of the NYSA-SS, requiring jury trials in all state fugitive proceedings, providing counsel to alleged fugitives, and prohibiting state officials from issuing certificates of removal except in accordance with state procedures.[88]

Prospects were gloomier elsewhere. In Pennsylvania, Chief Justice John Bannister Gibson, one of the nineteenth century's most eminent jurists, disfranchised the state's black population on the grounds that they were not "freemen" as that term was used in the state constitution.[89] Despite efforts by white and black abolitionists to rebut Gib-

85. *Jack* v. *Martin,* 12 Wend. 311 (New York Supreme Court, 1834); see generally Morris, *Free Men All,* 65–69, 79–84.
86. In re *Martin,* 16 Fed. Cas. 881 (No. 9154) (C.C.S.D.N.Y. [1835?]). This case was unrelated to *Jack* v. *Martin;* the similarity of names was a coincidence.
87. *Jack* v. *Martin,* 14 Wend. 507 (New York Court for the Correction of Errors, 1836).
88. Act of 6 May 1840, ch. 224, in *Laws of . . . New York . . . 1840* (Albany: Thurlow Weed, 1840).
89. *Hobbs* v. *Fogg,* 6 Watts 553 (Pa. 1837).

son's unsupported holding,[90] the state constitutional convention refused to re-enfranchise blacks, and the state legislature declined to add a jury trial provision to the 1826 Personal Liberty Law.[91] The state of Ohio retrogressed on the subject of fugitive slaves. The legislature was controlled by Democrats so singlemindedly proslavery that in 1839 they vindictively refused to elect Thomas Morris, a Democrat, to the United States Senate because he had criticized the proslavery views of Whig Henry Clay. The Ohio Democrats consistently rejected efforts by the Ohio Anti-Slavery Society to secure a modification or repeal of the state's harsh black code, and in 1839 enacted fugitive recapture legislation that supplemented the federal law by providing an alternative state remedy to help slave catchers.[92]

The 1830s demonstrated that the federal consensus, in its original form, had become too simplistic to be serviceable much longer as a pillar of the Union. It now represented a middle ground, flanked on either side by reinterpretations that tugged it in pro- and antislavery directions. On the proslavery side, Calhoun's 1837 resolutions represented an extreme reinterpretation of the consensus, extending it in two ways to protect slavery. First, had Calhoun's views been adopted, the consensus would have lost its mostly neutral character, and become proslavery, in the sense that the federal government could do nothing inimical about slavery, but had to protect it and promote its expansion. Second, Calhoun would have extended this proslavery innovation to the territories.

Two antislavery reinterpretations of the consensus offset Calhoun's views. The first, a purely defensive and geographically restricted one, was embodied in the personal liberty laws. Though not challenging the constitutionality of the federal fugitive slave act, these statutes reflected a northern belief that the federal government could not over-

90. John F. Denny, *An Essay on the Political Grade of the Free Coloured Population under the Constitution of the United States, and the Constitution of Pennsylvania* . . . (Chambersburg: Hickock & Ward, 1836); [Robert Purvis], *Appeal of Forty Thousand Citizens, Threatened with Disfranchisement, to the People of Pennsylvania* (Philadelphia: Merrihew and Gunn, 1838); *Remarks on the Constitution, by a Friend of Humanity, on the Subject of Slavery* (Philadelphia: Evening Star, 1836).
91. *Report of the Committee on the Judiciary Relative to* . . . *the Colored Population of this Country* . . . (Harrisburg: Boas & Coplan, 1839).
92. "An Act relating to Fugitives from Labor or Service from other States," 26 Feb. 1839, in *Acts of a General Nature* . . . *1838* (Columbus: Samuel Medary, 1839).

ride traditional state police powers that protected the liberty of their citizens. A more radical view, embryonic in the writings of Weld, the speech of Stanton, and the legal arguments of Birney and Chase, was that the federal government had to be impeded from taking any action in support of slavery. Like Calhoun's polar-opposite theory, this too would have applied to the territories.

Meanwhile, as the thrust and parry of slavery and abolition went on in the east, General Sam Houston secured the independence of the slaveholding republic of Texas in 1836. Though Benjamin Lundy and other abolitionists promptly denounced it as a slave power conspiracy,[93] they did not foresee its long-run significance, nor did they have any idea that the consequences of the drive to annex Texas to the United States would destroy the Union, annihilate proslavery constitutionalism, and embed major elements of antislavery constitutional thought in the United States Constitution. But in 1837, just at the most inopportune of times, fissionating and sectarian pressures began to split apart the antislavery movement.

93. [Benjamin Lundy], *The War in Texas: A Review of Facts and Circumstances, Showing that This Contest Is the Result of a Long Premeditated Crusade against the Government [of Mexico] Set on Foot by Slaveholders, Land Speculators, &c., with the View of Re-Establishing, Extending, and Perpetuating the System of Slavery and the Slave Trade in the Republic of Mexico . . .* (Philadelphia: Merrihew and Gunn, 1836).

CHAPTER 9

Moderate Constitutional Antislavery:
Abolition *Manquée*

Of the three antislavery groups that emerged from the decade of schisms, 1837–1847, the moderate constitutionalists represented the mainstream of abolitionist effort. They were the dominant element of the Liberty party (fl. 1840–1847) and formed the party creed in the mold of their constitutional beliefs. When they saw that Liberty was no longer serviceable, they played a major role in forming the Free Soil coalition of 1848. Moderates provided what basis there was for the Republican party's reputation for opposing slavery in the late 1850s. Being a centrist group, they clung to the United States Constitution and used conventional modes of political effort to attract nonabolitionist northern voters to their program. This characteristic, however, gave both their political organization, the Liberty party, and their constitutional doctrine a centrifugal tendency. Clear and distinct at their cores, both the party and its program tended to dissipate at the peripheries, losing voters to the regular parties and sacrificing principles for political power. As abolitionists, the moderates seemed *manqué:* unrealized, unfulfilled. The closer they approached conventional power in the northern states, the more they confused their reason for being. Rescued from irrelevance thanks to the political furor caused by the Kansas-Nebraska Act of 1854, which repealed the Missouri Compromise, they drifted into that menage of former Whigs, nativists, Independent Democrats, and Free Soilers, the Republican party.

The unified antislavery movement of 1833–1837 was put under stress by two forces simultaneously: the disruptive tendency of antislavery political action, and the controversies swirling around William

Lloyd Garrison. The first appeared when a group of abolitionists in upstate New York began to politicize what had been, till then, a benevolent reform movement. This immediately provoked opposition by Garrisonians and by some non-Garrisonian abolitionists, who feared the consequences of antislavery politics. At the same time, Garrison and his critics came to a falling out, due partly to Garrison's attack on the political-action abolitionists, and partly to the criticism of Garrison mounted by his opponents in and outside the movement. (We will examine this second tendency in the ensuing chapter.)

Certain forms of abolitionist political action were neither novel nor controversial in 1837. Ever since endorsing "moral and political action, as prescribed in the Constitution of the United States" in the 1833 AA-SS Declaration of Sentiments, abolitionists had pursued various goals by political methods at the national, state, and local level. They memorialized Congress and the state legislatures, testified before state legislative committees, and litigated at all levels of the state court system. Recognizing that Americans were "eminently a political people," some abolitionists hoped to make abolition "a practical question, something more than just an abstract theory."[1] The most promising way of achieving this seemed to be by political efforts aimed at repealing state and national laws that succored slavery. "Slavery is the creature of legislation, upheld & supported by law," resolved a Massachusetts local auxiliary of the AA-SS in 1839, "and is to be abolished by law & by law only."[2]

Non-Garrisonian abolitionists believed that political action was not only morally legitimate, but even a duty. John Pierpont, a Boston Unitarian minister and abolitionist, set forth the theological bases for antislavery politics:

Political action . . . embraces all that we do in reference to human laws: not only the enacting, the judicial declaring or exposition, and the executive administration or application and enforcing of laws; but also

1. Joshua Leavitt to Myron Holley, 12 July 1839, L. P. Noble to Myron Holley, 4 Dec. 1840, in Myron Holley MSS., N-YHS.
2. Resolutions of Worcester County North Division A.S. Society, 3 Jan. 1839, in Massachusetts Anti-Slavery Papers, N-YHS; see also "Address of the Rochester Anti-Slavery Society," *Emancipator*, 14 Jan. 1834; report of debate in NYSA-SS convention, 1837, in Cincinnati *Philanthropist*, 7 Nov. 1837; resolutions of the Warsaw, New York, Friends of Abolition convention, 13 Nov. 1839, reprinted in *Birney Letters*, I, 512; "Political Action against Slavery," *Friend of Man*, 8 Aug. 1838.

all steps or measures that, as Citizens, we adopt, either independently or in association with those whose sympathies and preferences are the same as our own, with a view to seeing that proper men are chosen to enact, declare, or administer them; [and] all that we will ourselves do, as subjects upon whom those laws are to act; as whether we will or will not obey them. . . . It is not merely my right—it is my duty . . . to obey [God] in using my political influence, my elective franchise, in his service, by placing those in political office who, I believe, will be faithful in his cause;—in other words, I am bound to act in behalf of morality through political instrumentalities.[3]

The principles Pierpont set out cathechetically had already impelled New York abolitionists in the direction of electoral politics. In their efforts (1837–1838) to secure passage of a jury trial statute for fugitive slaves, Elizur Wright, William Jay, Gerrit Smith, and Henry B. Stanton quickly moved from merely petitioning the legislature (which proved futile) to the tactic known as "questioning," that is, formally interrogating candidates for state office to sound out their position on specific slavery-related issues. Questioning implied that abolitionist voters had a duty to vote only for candidates who answered correctly.[4] This soon raised the problem of political frustration: what should an abolitionist voter do when no candidate responds satisfactorily? Political-action abolitionists at first agreed with Garrison that the voter should "scatter" his vote, i.e., cast a write-in vote as a way of protesting the nonchoice presented to him.[5] But they soon abandoned that tactic because proslavery dominance of both the regular parties meant virtual self-disfranchisement for abolitionist voters.[6]

Contemplating the dilemma of wasting their political power or being absorbed in the proslavery parties if they voted their convictions or their party affiliation on nonslavery issues, abolitionists began

---

3. John Pierpont, *Moral Rule of Political Action. A Discourse Delivered in Hollis Street Church . . . 1839*, excerpted in Dumond, *Antislavery*, 291, 404.
4. "Political Action," *Emancipator*, 19 April 1838; "Political Action Against Slavery No. 2," *Emancipator*, 13 Sept. 1838.
5. AA-SS resolution of 11 July 1838, copy in Elizur Wright Papers, LC.
6. Richard H. Sewell, *Ballots for Freedom: Antislavery Politics in the United States, 1837–1860* (New York: Oxford Univ. Press, 1976), 12–20; *passim*, for an evaluation of Liberty and Free Soil political action that differs from that presented here. See also Aileen Kraditor's survey, "The Liberty and Free Soil Parties," in Arthur M. Schlesinger, Jr., ed., *History of U.S. Political Parties* (New York: Chelsea House, 1973), I, 741–763.

to think, not in terms of the individual voting as a personal moral act, but of abolitionists voting *en masse* as a group political tactic. If abolitionists could concentrate their vote, they might elect someone sympathetic to their views or at least hold the balance of power, thereby providing an incentive for one of the regular parties to adopt their program or nominate acceptable candidates in the next election. But again the problem of frustration arose: what if the parties ignored them? Advanced proponents of political action in 1838 responded by recommending that abolitionists run their own candidates. By 1839, Alvan Stewart, Joshua Leavitt, Myron Holley, and Gerrit Smith called for abolitionist nominations, Smith even going so far as to urge putting up an entire abolitionist slate, the "Freeman's ticket."[7]

This tactic, known as "independent nominations," proved to be a preliminary to the organization of an antislavery third party. Alvan Stewart recommended formation of such a party to the Executive Committee of the New York State Anti-Slavery Society in February 1839,[8] but even in that nursery of political action, upstate New York, this was premature, and the society took no action at the time. Undeterred, Stewart and Holley continued working throughout 1839 to promote the third party. Both were upstate New York lawyers, Holley having been trained in the law office of Chancellor James Kent and Stewart in the office of Kent's successor, Chancellor Reuben Walworth. Holley, who had served as a state assemblyman and as a commissioner of the Erie Canal, came to antislavery out of the anti-Masonic movement.[9] Stewart, on the other hand, began his reform career with the teetotalling wing of the temperance crusade. A competent though not brilliant lawyer, he practiced in Utica, where he lost

7. Alvan Stewart to Francis Jackson, 23 July 1838, William Lloyd Garrison MSS., Department of Rare Books and MSS., used by courtesy of the Trustees of the Boston Public Library; Alvan Stewart, speech in New York City, 24 Oct. 1839, reprinted in *Emancipator*, 21 Nov. 1839; *Emancipator*, 26 Dec. 1839; Smith's proposed Freeman's ticket is reprinted in Fladeland, *Birney*, 179.

8. William Goodell, *Slavery and Anti-Slavery: A History of the Great Struggle in Both Hemispheres; With a View of the Slavery Question in the United States* (New York: Wm. Harned, 1852), 469; Goodell to Luther R. Marsh, n.d., quoted in Luther R. Marsh, ed., *Writings and Speeches of Alvan Stewart, on Slavery* (New York: A. B. Burdick, 1860), 27.

9. Elizur Wright, *Myron Holley; and What He Did for Liberty and True Religion* (Boston: for the author, 1882), 234 and *passim*; John W. Chadwick, *A Life For Liberty: Antislavery and Other Letters of Sallie Holley* (New York: Putnam's, 1899), 21–25.

some of his clients because of his abolitionist activities and his prominence in the formation of the NYSA-SS, of which he served as president. He moved quickly from immediatism to both third-party political action and radical constitutionalism.[10]

Stewart insisted that action within the existing parties was futile because slaveholding influence permanently nullified abolitionist efforts in them.[11] This argument proved persuasive in New York state, and momentum for a third party built up quickly. An antislavery convention in Warsaw, New York (12 November 1839) nominated Birney for president and Francis J. LeMoyne of Pennsylvania as his running mate. Both declined, but a subsequent convention in Albany on 1 April 1840 formally created the Liberty party, renominated Birney, who accepted this time, and chose another Pennsylvanian, Thomas Earle, as its vice-presidential candidate. In keeping with contemporary practice, the convention did not adopt a platform. What ensued was a noncampaign, because Birney spent the summer and fall in England at the World Antislavery Convention. The result was foregone: in all the northern states, the Liberty candidate got less than one percent of the vote.[12]

The Liberty party was the organizational home for moderate abolitionists for seven years, and its political efforts provided some of the principal occasions for working out moderate constitutional theory. It did not enjoy the support of all abolitionists, however; Garrisonians condemned it on grounds of tactics as well as principle, and even some non-Garrisonians sympathetic to political action criticized it or held aloof from its activities. Francis LeMoyne, William Jay, Lewis

10. With the exception of tenBroek's *Equal under Law*, a brief appreciative notice in Dumond, *Antislavery*, 293–295, and Sewell, *Ballots for Freedom*, Stewart has been overlooked by modern historians of abolition. Though less well known than Garrison, Birney, Weld, the Tappans, et al., his influence was pervasive and he badly needs a modern biography. For contemporaneous evaluations, see Levi Beardsley, *Reminiscences; Personal and Other Incidents; Early Settlement of Otsego County* . . . (New York: Charles Vinten, 1852), 155–175; introductory essay in Marsh, ed., *Writings of Stewart*, 9–39; handwritten notes of Luther R. Marsh in Alvan Stewart Papers, New York State Historical Association, Cooperstown, New York.

11. Alvan Stewart to Edwin W. Clarke, 14 Sept. 1839 and 17 Oct. 1840, Misc. MSS. Slavery; Stewart to Myron Holley, 16 Dec. 1839, Myron Holley MSS.; Stewart to Samuel Webb, 21 Nov. 1838, Alvan Stewart Papers; all N-YHS.

12. Figures are from a table in Theodore C. Smith, *The Liberty and Free Soil Parties in the Northwest* (New York: Longmans, Green, 1897), 46.

Tappan, Gamaliel Bailey, and John G. Whittier warned that the party would split the movement because it could not avoid taking positions on issues not related to slavery, which could only have a divisive effect among abolitionists.[13]

Neither such criticism nor their meager showing in 1840 daunted the Libertymen. They reconvened in New York City on 12 May 1841, renominated Birney for president, and adopted a proto-platform condemning the "slave power" as the cause of most of the country's troubles.[14] The party subordinated the staple issues of contemporary American politics—subtreasury, tariffs, public lands, and so on—to the overriding question of abolition. Historians refer to this as the "One Idea" platform. Some Libertymen soon found One Idea constrictive, and began insisting that the party adopt a position on non–slavery-related issues, partly as a matter of moral obligation to the extent that these issues had some moral significance, however attenuated, and partly to attract the interest of regular Whigs or Democrats. Birney and other Michigan abolitionists attacked One Idea vigorously in 1845. For a time, moderates encouraged this impulse within the party. The Cincinnati *Philanthropist* in 1844 had claimed that "the distinguishing feature of the Liberty Party is intended to be a regard for the moral influence exerted through the elective franchise. We design this not only in regard to slavery, but to apply in every other respect."[15]

But the alternative to One Idea was dangerous, for taking a stand on extraneous issues quickly presented two problems. On one hand, political-action abolitionists might adopt expediential positions and trim their abolition principles to widen the appeal of antislavery by diluting it. On the other, positions on nonslavery issues were divisive,

13. LeMoyne to Birney, 10 Dec. 1839, in *Birney Letters*, I, 511–514; Jay to Committee of Arrangements of Connecticut Anti-Slavery Society (1840) reprinted in Tuckerman, *William Jay*, 98–101, and to Gerrit Smith, 25 July 1840, John Jay MSS., Columbia University; Lewis Tappan to Gamaliel Bailey, 24 Oct. 1839, Lewis Tappan Papers, LC; Bailey to Birney, 23 Jan. 1840, 21 Feb. 1840, 3 March 1840, 30 March 1840, 18 April 1840, *Birney Letters*, I, 519–523, 531–532, 535–538, 545–548, 556–558 respectively; Whittier to Birney, 16 April 1840, ibid., 555. Despite his misgivings, Bailey urged abolitionists to vote for Birney in 1840: Cincinnati *Philanthropist*, 22 Sept. 1840.

14. "Address of the National Antislavery Convention," Cincinnati *Philanthropist*, 16 June 1841.

15. "Morality in Voting," Cincinnati *Weekly Herald and Philanthropist*, 24 June 1844.

because they would necessarily appeal either to Whigs or to Democrats. Once the political abolitionists began experimenting with non-slavery questions, they lapsed into multifariousness and inconsistency, adopting positions on both sides of issues ranging from the immediate and practical (e.g. homesteads and public lands policy) to the utopian (abolition of military forces). For these and other reasons, the Liberty party did not do well in later electoral contests.[16] But lack of success did not deter Libertymen from working out a constitutional theory that complemented their political program. Liberty politics until 1845 derived from their constitutional theory. Rarely in American history has a political party's platform been so integrally shaped by constitutional thought.

The moderates of the Liberty party revered the federal consensus as the touchstone of their program. Speaking for the Liberty party in 1844, Arnold Buffum repulsed the charge that Libertymen meant to free slaves in the southern states: "We intend no such thing. . . . In relation to slavery in the states, politically we claim no right to interfere."[17] Salmon P. Chase explained that the framers of the Constitution in 1787 "had no power to change the personal relations of the inhabitants of any State to each other, but were charged with the duty of framing a general system of government for the people of all the States, leaving those relations untouched [. I]t was equally impossible for them to abolish slavery in the states where it existed."[18] Libertymen inserted into their Free Soil platform of 1848 a plank definitively proclaiming that "slavery in the several States of the Union which recognize its existence, depends upon the State laws alone, which cannot be repealed or modified by the Federal Government, and for which laws that government is not responsible. We therefore propose no interference by Congress with Slavery within the limits of any State."[19] In twelve years, this evolved into a Re-

16. Kraditor, *Means and Ends,* 146–157.

17. Arnold Buffum, "Lecture Showing the Necessity for a Liberty Party, and Setting Forth Its Principles, Measures, and Objects" (1844), excerpted in William H. Pease and Jane H. Pease, comps., *The Antislavery Argument* (Indianapolis: Bobbs-Merrill, 1965), 424; Cincinnati *Philanthropist,* 6 Jan. 1841, 16 Feb. 1842.

18. Resolutions of the Ohio Liberty party (1843), quoted in J. W. Schuckers, *The Life and Public Services of Salmon Portland Chase . . .* (New York: Appleton, 1874), 48.

19. Kirk H. Porter and Donald B. Johnson, comps., *National Party Platforms, 1840–1960* (Urbana: Univ. of Illinois Press, 1961), 13.

publican guarantee for the security of slavery in the South. The Republican platform of 1860 promised to maintain "inviolate the rights of the states, and especially the right of each state to order and control its own domestic institutions according to its own judgment exclusively."[20]

The correlative to a lack of a federal power to abolish slavery in the states was the lack of a federal power to establish it there—or anywhere else. Consistently in their platforms (Liberty 1844, Free Soil 1848, Free Democracy 1852), the moderates insisted that "the General Government has, under the Constitution, no power to establish or continue slavery anywhere," "no more power to make a slave than to make a king; no more power to institute or establish slavery, than to institute or establish a monarchy. No such power can be found among those specifically conferred by the Constitution, or derived by just implication from them."[21] "Congress can neither create nor continue slavery anywhere, & in all places under the exclusive jurisdiction of Congress slavery is constitutionally impossible," Chase assured Lewis Tappan. "All practically important constitutional positions for antislavery men to [illegible] are the logical consequences of this."[22]

Moderates denied federal power to establish slavery on two grounds. First, adopting the doctrine of "strict construction" usually associated with Jefferson's position in the Kentucky Resolutions (1798–1799), moderates claimed that neither explicit clauses nor implied powers "delegated" this capacity to the federal government, and the Tenth Amendment specifically reserved it to the states.[23] Second, the Fifth Amendment's due process clause was a restraint on federal authority.[24] Since enslavement deprived a person of liberty and property, Congress could not establish slavery in the District of

20. Porter and Johnson, comps., *National Party Platforms*, 32–33.

21. Porter & Johnson, comps., *National Party Platforms*, 5, 13, 18.

22. Chase to Lewis Tappan, 18 March 1847, Salmon P. Chase Papers, LC, ser. 1, cont. 12.

23. Joshua R. Giddings, *A Letter from Hon. J. R. Giddings upon the Duty of Anti-Slavery Men in the Present Crisis* (Ravenna: William Wadsworth, 1844), 3. (Giddings was a Whig, not a Libertyman, but his constitutional views were identical with those of the moderates).

24. Liberty party platform of 1844, in Porter & Johnson, comps., *National Party Platforms*, 4; Salmon P. Chase to Lewis Tappan, 18 March 1847, in Chase Papers, LC, ser. 1, cont. 12.

Columbia, protect it in the territories, admit new slave states, or provide a federal mechanism for the recapture of fugitive slaves.[25]

Their reading of the framer's intentions fortified moderates in this conviction. Unlike the radicals, they conceded that the draftsmen of the Constitution deliberately included securities for extant slavery in the text;[26] unlike the Garrisonians, they viewed these concessions as a pledge that the national government should not be concerned in any way with the establishment or preservation of slavery.[27] Seeing slavery "interwoven with domestic habits, pecuniary interests, and legal rights," the framers did not attempt to abolish it, for the perfectly good reason that they had no power to do so even if they had had the inclination. But they attempted to subordinate their proslavery concessions to the more exalted libertarian principles of the Revolution and the Constitution. The framers meant to "keep the action of the national government free from all connection with the system; to discountenance and discourage it in the states; and to favour the abolition of it by state authority—a result then generally expected; and, finally, to provide against its further extension by confining the power to acquire new territory, and admit new States to the General Government."[28] They therefore avoided use of the words "slave" or "slavery" in the document and inserted their true libertarian aspirations into the Northwest Ordinance.

Given this antislavery impulse, though, what had happened since 1787 that caused the framers' expectations to be so sadly betrayed? Surely Madison and the others had not meant to create a national authority that would wage war on unoffending Mexico to extend the power of the slave states? The moderates found their answer to these questions in the conception of a Slave Power. On the reality of this power, all abolitionists agreed. Francis Jackson, a Garrisonian, defined it as "a body of men, which, however it may be regarded by the Constitution as 'persons,' is in fact and in practical effect, a vast

25. [Salmon P. Chase], "Address of the Southern and Western Liberty Convention, Held at Cincinnati, June 11 and 12, 1845. To the People of the United States," in Charles D. Cleveland, ed., *Anti-Slavery Addresses of 1844 and 1845* (Philadelphia: J. A. Bancroft, 1867), 86.

26. Cincinnati *Philanthropist,* 17 Feb. 1841.

27. Ohio Liberty party, "Address to the People of Ohio," reprinted in Cincinnati *Philanthropist,* 11 Jan. 1843; "Relations of the Federal Constitution to Slavery," *New Englander,* 3 (1845), 595–600.

28. [Chase], "Address of the Southern and Western Liberty Convention," 84.

moneyed corporation, bound together by an indissoluble unity of interest, by a common sense of a common danger; counseling at all times for its common protection; wielding the whole power, and controlling the destiny of the nation."[29] Taking advantage of unwise concessions to slavery made by the epigone who succeeded the framers, such as the Fugitive Slave Act of 1793 or the toleration of slavery in the Louisiana Purchase area, the Slave Power "has overleaped its prescribed limits, and usurped control of the National Government."[30] Seeing such power in the hands of their enemies, Garrisonians thought conventional political opposition "impossible or powerless,"[31] but moderates disagreed. Harking back to the original justifications of antislavery political action, moderates maintained that slavery was a creature of law, and hence could be abolished only by repeal of laws supporting it.[32] This could best be accomplished by placing abolitionists in legislatures and would require leading the American people to a true understanding of constitutional principles.[33]

In order to inculcate these principles, moderates turned to *Somerset*, and particularly to Mansfield's statement that "the state of slavery is of such a nature, that it is incapable of being introduced on any reasons, moral or political; but only positive law, which preserves its force long after the reasons, occasion, and time itself from whence it was created, is erased from memory: It's so odious, that nothing can be suffered to support it but positive law."

From this opinion the moderates concluded that slavery could be created by positive law, and had been in the southern states. But where it had not been so created, or where the positive laws necessary to sustain it could not have been enacted because the proper

29. Francis Jackson to Gov. George N. Briggs, 4 July 1844, reprinted in [Wendell Phillips, ed.], *The Constitution a Pro-Slavery Compact: or, Extracts from the Madison Papers, Etc.* (New York: AA-SS, 1844), 115; Henry Wilson, *History of the Rise and Fall of the Slave Power in America* (Boston: Osgood, 1872–77).
30. "Address of the Liberty Convention to the People of Ohio" (Dec. 1841), reprinted in *Emancipator and Free American,* 27 Jan. 1842.
31. [Stephen S. Foster], *Revolution the Only Remedy for Slavery* (New York: AA-SS, [1855?]), 15.
32. "Political Action against Slavery," *Friend of Man,* 8 Aug. 1838; resolutions of the 1839 Warsaw, New York, convention, reprinted in *Birney Letters,* I, 512; "How Abolitionism May Be Considered a Political Question," Cincinnati *Philanthropist,* 30 Dec. 1836.
33. Henry B. Stanton to Salmon P. Chase, 6 Feb. 1844, in Chase Papers, LC, ser. 1, cont. 8.

legislative authority lacked power to pass them, slavery could not exist. "Slavery is a creature of positive law," declared Pennsylvania Libertymen, "and exists within those limits, and within those limits only, where the laws that sanction it have force."[34] An upstate New York abolitionist, Edwin W. Clarke, wrote that slavery "does not spring up like noxious weeds spontaniously [*sic*], requiring positive enactments to suppress it. Except when it is created and sustained by positive statutes it is unknown, it cannot in the nature of things otherwise exist."[35] This was the constitutional and political heart of the Liberty position.

Libertymen in their political and forensic efforts played endless variations on this idea. The two most important variations were neo-*Somerset* ideas relating to extradomiciliary slaves and to slavery in areas under federal jurisdiction. A proper application of neo-*Somerset* in these two areas, moderates predicted, would interdict slavery's expansion and confine it to the southern states. The belief that slavery would stagnate and eventually die if confined strictly to the states where it existed as of 1840 was crucial to Liberty constitutional thought. Moderates proposed a "quarantine of slavery"[36] in the expectation that slavery could not survive if it could not expand. Libertymen further assumed that the power of the federal government to impose this quarantine was conceded by all, a naive attitude in the light of southern resistance to territorial restriction in 1820 and to abolition in the District of Columbia in 1836.

Neo-*Somerset* as applied to extradomiciliary slaves was meant by moderates to lop off the penetration of slavery into the free states by masters either pursuing fugitive slaves or bringing in sojourning slaves. "If you choose to cling to such a system [slavery],—cling to it; but you shall not cross our line; you shall not bring that foul thing here," declaimed the Pennsylvania Liberty party to the South.[37] The constitutional basis of this position was Birney and Chase's Matilda argument of 1837, which had comprehensively set forth all arguments necessary to inhibit recaptures and demonstrated the unconstitution-

34. "Address of the Liberty Party of Pennsylvania to the People of Pennsylvania," 1844, in Cleveland, *Anti-Slavery Addresses of 1844 and 1845*, 21.
35. MS. draft, 29 March 1842, in Edwin W. Clake MSS., N-YHS.
36. The phrase is Richard H. Sewell's, *Ballots for Freedom*, 121; see p. 171 for elaboration.
37. "Address of the Liberty Party of Pennsylvania," in Cleveland, ed., *Anti-Slavery Addresses of 1844 and 1845*, 45.

ality of the 1793 federal fugitive statute. Moderates, led by Chase, insisted through the 1850s that when slaves leave a slaveholding jurisdiction, they "become free, whenever and however they get out of a slaveholding state, simply because they are out."[38] Under this interpretation, fugitives, sojourners, and *in transitu* slaves were freed, permanently, the moment they left slave jurisdictions. Moderates embraced the doctrine enunciated by southern supreme courts in *Harry* v. *Decker & Hopkins* (Mississippi, 1818), *Rankin* v. *Lydia* (Kentucky, 1820), and *Lunsford* v. *Coquillon* (Louisiana, 1824) that "slavery is against natural rights, and strictly local, and that its existence and continuance rest on no other support than State legislation."[39]

On these central tenets, Liberty moderates saw eye-to-eye with an important group of individuals, predominantly Whigs, who did not belong to abolitionist organizations or the Liberty party, but who opposed the expansion of slavery outside the extant slaveholding states. (Whether these individuals should be considered abolitionists is a definitional problem that need not be resolved here; what is important is that they agreed with many or all points in the Liberty party's moderate constitutional program.) Early in 1842, Chase, on behalf of the Liberty party, wrote to the foremost Whig opponent of slavery's expansion, Joshua R. Giddings, who represented the Ashtabula district of northeastern Ohio in the United States House of Representatives, and who, together with John Quincy Adams, led a small Whig antislavery bloc known as "The Insurgency" there. "Slavery is a creature of state law," Chase insisted to his fellow Ohioan, "local—not to be extended or favored, but to be confined within the States which admit and sanction it."[40] Giddings, from his own constitutional position, agreed with this idea, and soon found an opportunity to introduce it, in elaborated form, into full-dress debate in the House.

The House had been in an Insurgency-induced ferment for several months. Giddings had carried on a one-man crusade against further

38. [Chase], "An Important View," Cincinnati *Weekly Herald and Philanthropist*, 5 Nov. 1844; [Chase], "Address of the Southern and Western Liberty Convention," 85; autograph draft copy of Chase speech, 29 Dec. 1842, in Chase MSS., Historical Society of Pennsylvania, Philadelphia.

39. Liberty Party platform of 1844 in Porter & Johnson, comps., *National Party Platforms*, 5.

40. Salmon P. Chase to Joshua R. Giddings, 15 Feb. 1842, in Joshua R. Giddings Papers, LC.

federal support for the Second Seminole War, which he correctly saw as being waged by the federal government to protect the security of slavery on its southern flank by exterminating maroon colonies in northern Florida, expelling their Indian members to the west, and selling their black members back into slavery. In his Seminole War arguments, Giddings anticipated Chase's point by arguing that since slavery was exclusively a matter for state control under the Tenth Amendment, the federal government had no power to wage war or police territories to enhance its security.[41] The gag was still in force, but the Insurgency, particularly Adams, had evaded and flouted it to the point where proslavery representatives tried, unsuccessfully, to censure Adams for twitting them about it. This failure had put the proslavery majority of the House in a foul mood at just the time Giddings chose to introduce moderate abolitionist ideas into congressional debate despite the gag.

Giddings seized on a spectacular incident, the *Creole* mutiny (1842), to promote the constitutional principles he shared with Libertymen. An American vessel, the *Creole,* was carrying some Virginia slaves on the high seas to New Orleans in the coastal slave trade. Somewhere outside Virginia's territorial waters, the slaves mutinied, seized the ship, killed a passenger, and sailed the vessel to Nassau, in the Bahamas. There British authorities detained nineteen of the slaves suspected of the murder, but set free the rest because slavery had been abolished in the British colonies. Officials of the Tyler administration, including Secretary of State Daniel Webster and Minister to England Edward Everett, demanded compensation for the freed slaves' owners from the British government.[42] This prompted James G. Birney (then an exponent of the moderate position) to write an article, which Representative Seth Gates, another member of the Insurgency, secured for publication in the New York *American.* Birney denounced executive efforts to uphold an extraterritorial continuation of the slave relationship onto the high seas and into a foreign nation's colonial holdings where slavery had been abolished.[43]

41. *The Florida War, Speech of Mr. Giddings . . . in the House of Representatives, February 9, 1841* (Hallowell: Bangor Female Anti-Slavery Society, 1841), 6–7.
42. See the untitled Senate document, 27 Cong. 2 sess., ser. 397, doc 137 (21 Feb. 1842), including a letter from Webster to Everett, expounding the administration's proslavery position.
43. The article is reprinted in *Birney Letters,* II, 667–670; see also William

Giddings then combined Birney's argument with some ideas of his own and presented them as the "Creole Resolutions" on the floor of the House. The resolutions centered around the moderates' neo-*Somerset* theory that the slaves became freemen once outside Virginia waters. The federal government had no power to extend their slave status onto the high seas or protect it there, because slavery existed only by force of Virginia's municipal laws and "is necessarily confined to the territorial jurisdiction of the power creating it." The slaves, in mutinying, had merely assumed their normal status—freedom—and had resisted efforts to reenslave them. Though Giddings and other moderates did not know it, such views found a sympathetic audience in an unlikely place, the United States Supreme Court. Joseph Story, writing an implicit rebuke to Webster, insisted that whether a jurisdiction chooses to recognize the property status of slaves coming into it by accident is entirely a matter of comity, not a right that the claimant or his jurisdiction may demand.[44]

Democrats and proslavery Whigs then compounded the propaganda value of the Creole Resolutions by moving a censure of Giddings for expounding such doctrines. Having learned a lesson from the effort to censure Adams, they immediately moved the previous question, a parliamentary trick that had the effect of prohibiting Giddings from speaking in his own defense. With Giddings and other antislavery Whigs thus gagged, censure passed easily, but Giddings turned his enemies' sword back on them.[45] He resigned his seat, returned to his Ashtabula district, campaigned for reelection, and was returned by a landslide—eighteen to one over his Democratic opponent. His reelection was the first instance in national elections when voters could be said to have voted in a referendum on an issue relating exclusively to slavery. Giddings' triumphal return to his seat, together with the failure of the Adams censure, assured the demise of the gag, which was repealed in 1844.

E. Channing, *The Duty of the Free States; or, Remarks Suggested by the Case of the Creole* (Boston: William Crosby, 1842); *The Creole Case, and Mr. Webster's Despatch* . . . (New York: American, 1842); and "J.C.," "Case of the Creole," *Am. Jurist & Law Mag.*, 27 (1842), 79–110.

44. *Globe*, 27 Cong. 2 sess., 342 (21 March 1842). Story to Daniel Webster, 26 March 1842, in C. H. Van Tyne, ed., *The Letters of Daniel Webster* (New York: McClure, Phillips, 1902), 263–266.

45. James B. Stewart, *Joshua R. Giddings and the Tactics of Radical Politics* (Cleveland: Press of Case Western Reserve Univ., 1970), 73–76.

The constitutional affinity between the Whig Insurgency and the Liberty moderates in 1842 had important consequences for both. It led both groups to consider the possibility of coalition. Giddings earnestly wooed Libertymen, hoping to entice them into the Whig fold. In public and private correspondence, he reminded them that it had been Democratic administrations that had been the true enthusiasts for proslavery measures, whereas Whigs respected states' and individuals' rights. Whigs, he argued, supported the Liberty program of "the preservation of our own [state's] rights; the repeal of all acts of Congress, passed for the support of slavery or the slave trade; to separate the Federal Government, and the free States, from all unconstitutional connexion with that institution, and to leave it with the individual States, where the Constitution placed it."[46] On the Liberty side, Chase and others also considered fusion. Absorption into the Whig party would have been unacceptable to Chase, who remained a lifelong crypto-Democrat, but fusion in a new antislavery party had much appeal to disaffected moderates who were disheartened by Liberty's prospects at the polls.

While Chase and others were contemplating fusion, they continued to elaborate and extend their original Liberty principles, to tolerate occasional semiofficial restatements of Liberty views that placed them in the radical camp, and to work harmoniously with the radicals in their ranks. Even Chase, in private correspondence in 1844, went so far as to proclaim himself "a full convert to the [radical] doctrine that slavery and the Constitution are incompatible."[47] This impulse carried Liberty moderates a long way toward radicalism, as where they insisted that property rights in slaves did not enjoy the ubiquitous protection of natural law extended to ordinary property.[48] Their constitutional position, which Chase in 1856 called the "denationalization of slavery entire,"[49] suggested many programmatic political applications: abolition of slavery in the District of Columbia; abolition of

46. "Pacificus" [Joshua Giddings], *The Rights and Privileges of the Several States in regard to Slavery; Being a Series of Essays, Published in the Western Reserve Chronicle (Ohio) after the Election of 1842* (n.p., n.d. [1842]); Giddings to Salmon P. Chase, 30 Oct. 1846, in Chase MSS., Historical Society of Pennsylvania.
47. Chase to Lewis Tappan, 3 April 1844, in Chase Papers, LC, ser. 1, cont. 8.
48. "Constitutional Law," *Emancipator and Free American,* 28 April 1842.
49. Quoted in Sewell, *Ballots for Freedom,* 285.

the slave trade; congressional prohibition of removal of slaves out of their domiciliary state; abolition in the territories; refusal to admit new slave states; refusal to call up the militia of other states to put down slave insurrections; refusal to protect the carrying of slaves on the high seas; refusal to use slave labor in public works; selection only of abolitionists for federal appointive office; denial of the right of citizens of any but the original thirteen states to recapture fugitive slaves; denial of federal diplomatic and military power to support the interests of slaveholders anywhere outside the United States; and prohibiting slaveholding on federal properties like forts and ships.[50]

The constitutional doctrines of the moderates had their political counterparts. Picking up a suggestion made in 1835 by abolitionists in Maine, moderates demanded that the federal Constitution be "wrested from the polluting and unholy alliance with slavery." To achieve this, they sought "the absolute and unqualified divorce of the General Government from slavery."[51] Divorce was a many-planked platform, sometimes aggressively antislavery, and broad enough in its appeal to hold the loyalty, for a time, even of the radicals. It embraced all the policy goals just noted, and differed from the radical position in only two particulars, though those two were crucial: the universal illegitimacy of slavery and the power of the federal government to abolish it in the states.

Moderates adopted the most comprehensive expression of their constitutional and political views in the 1844 Liberty platform, the lengthiest platform adopted by any American political party in the nineteenth century. They extolled "human brotherhood," called for "the restoration of equality of rights, among men, in every State where the party exists," promised that they would "carry out the principles of Equal Rights, into all their practical consequences and applications, and support every just measure conducive to individual and social freedom," called for laws prohibiting slaveholding in all

50. "Moderatus," *Review of . . . President Wayland's Valuable Treatise on the Limitations of Human Responsibility . . . in relation to the Slavery Question* (Providence: n.p., 1840); Salmon P. Chase to ?, 15 Aug. 1846, Chase Papers, LC, ser. 1, cont. 11; [Chase], "Address of the Southern and Western Liberty Convention," 98; and see William Goodell's summary of the moderate program in *Slavery and Anti-Slavery,* 566–569.

51. "Address" of the Portland Anti-Slavery Society, reprinted in *Liberator,* 3 Oct. 1835; Liberty platform of 1844, Porter and Johnson, comps., *National Party Platforms,* 4.

areas under federal jurisdiction including the high seas (an indirect attack on the interstate slave trade), demanded repeal of the federal number and fugitive slave clauses of the Constitution, urged repeal of racially discriminatory state laws, and "cordially welcome[d] our colored fellow citizens to fraternity with us in the Liberty Party, in its great contest to secure the rights of mankind."[52]

These bold egalitarian statements, the uttermost Liberty salient toward radicalism the party ever achieved, were virtually repudiated within a year as the party's western wing rose to dominance. After 1841, the eastern leadership of the party disintegrated. Some easterners began an irreversible drift toward radicalism that left them a minority in the party by 1847; these included Alvan Stewart, Gerrit Smith, William Goodell, and James G. Birney. Myron Holley and Charles T. Torrey died prematurely.[53] Elizur Wright and Henry B. Stanton dropped out of antislavery temporarily. Joshua Leavitt went to Washington in 1841 as a correspondent of the *Emancipator* where he worked with Theodore Dwight Weld as an abolitionist apostle to the Whigs. After the 1844 national elections, westerners dominated Liberty affairs, led by Ohio's Salmon P. Chase. The Ohio Libertymen included Gamaliel Bailey, editor of the Cincinnati *Philanthropist,* Sam Lewis, Stanley Matthews, future justice of the United States Supreme Court, the brothers Edward and Benjamin F. Wade, James H. Paine, Edward S. Hamlin, and Leicester King. In Illinois, Zebina Eastman, editor of the Chicago Western *Citizen,* and Owen Lovejoy, congressman and brother of the murdered abolitionist editor Elijah Lovejoy, spoke for the party.

The westerners, soon called "the expedients" by their opponents, rejected the radicals' broad political platform as impractical and their constitutional theory as unsound. They hoped either to convert one of the regular parties to antislavery or to amalgamate with elements from both the parties to form a new antislavery political coalition having the moderate program as its constitutional platform, and therefore did not want to scare off potential nonabolitionist allies. The emergence of western and moderate leadership within the Liberty

52. Porter & Johnson, comps., *National Party Platforms,* 5–8.
53. Holley died of natural causes in 1841. Torrey died in 1846 of consumption contracted while imprisoned in Maryland for his role in helping fugitives escape, and, in the movement's hagiology, was accorded martyr status second only to Elijah Lovejoy.

party was signalized by the Southern and Western Liberty Convention, held in Cincinnati, 11 and 12 June 1845, which had been called by Chase in an effort to broaden Liberty's appeal to Whigs and Democrats.

The Southern and Western Convention adopted a firmly moderate platform drafted by Chase. Vestiges of abolition appeared in planks calling for divorce, abolition of slavery in the territories, and interdiction of the interstate slave trade. But a new and distinctly western emphasis appeared in a plank declaring that the whole point to antislavery was "to discourage and discontinue the system of work without wages," an oblique anticipation of the later Free Soil position.[54] Emphasizing this Free Soil posture, which appealed to the self-interest and even racism of whites, was the striking absence of the previous year's platitudes about equal rights and brotherhood. The westerners would have no nonsense about "cordially welcom[ing] our colored fellow citizens to fraternity with us"; the cordial welcome was to white Whigs and Democrats. This doubtless represented a politically sensible and expedient concession to the prevalent racism of the time,[55] but it was a retrograde movement from the 1844 platform and did reflect western, antiradical views.

After 1845 the idea of divorce gave way to Free Soil, which in turn became transmuted into the slogan-doctrine "Freedom national, slavery sectional," a catchy restatement of neo-*Somerset* principles adapted to the American federal union. Adopted as the core of the Republican position in 1856, Freedom-national embodied the idea that freedom, the natural condition of men, should pertain everywhere except in jurisdictions that had established slavery by positive law. This doctrinal transformation, with its implication for narrowing the constitutional scope of the antislavery attack, can best be explained by the political hopes of the western moderates. As early as 1842, Chase had urged a plank of "Protection to Free Labor" as an element of the Liberty program,[56] arousing Birney's suspicions that

54. Resolutions of the Southern and Western Liberty Convention, quoted in Joseph G. Rayback, *Free Soil: The Election of 1848* (Lexington: Univ. Press of Kentucky, 1970), 106.

55. Sewell, *Ballots for Freedom,* 160.

56. "Address of the Liberty Convention to the People of Ohio," *Emancipator and Free American,* 27 Jan. 1842; Chase to Lewis Tappan, 15 Sept. 1842, Chase Papers, LC; Joseph G. Rayback, "The Liberty Party Leaders of Ohio: Exponents of Anti-slavery Coalition," *Ohio Arch. & Hist. Q.,* 57 (1948), 165–178.

he planned to dissociate abolition from Liberty efforts.[57] Chase for his part, had opposed Birney's renomination in 1844 and had never tried to conceal his own Democratic leanings. He had little faith in the staying power of the Liberty party as a political entity. "As fast as we can bring public sentiment right," he explained to New Hampshire Senator John Parker Hale, "the other parties will approach our ground and keep sufficiently close to it, to prevent any great accession to our numbers."[58]

As Chase was putting these ideas on paper in 1846–47, most Libertymen had by then decided that One Idea no longer sufficed. The real question for the Liberty party was not whether One Idea should be modified, but whether it should be diluted or supplemented. Radicals wanted to supplement it with broad, universal-reform planks, while Chase and his supporters hoped to dilute it as part of an appeal to nonabolitionist Democrats and Whigs. This determination suddenly hardened as moderates perceived the widespread popularity of the Wilmot Proviso (1846), which they considered "by far more important than any movement on the subject of slavery" since the Missouri debates.[59]

The Wilmot Proviso prohibited the extension of slavery into any territory acquired as a result of the Mexican War; in all such territory before Mexico's forced cession, slavery had been abolished under the Mexican Constitution. Supporters of the Proviso correctly feared that slavery would follow the American flag. Nicholas Trist, President Polk's commissioner treating with Mexican envoys to end the war, reacted to their demand that slavery be excluded from any ceded territory by assuring them

that the bare mention of the subject in any treaty to which the United States were a party, was an absolute impossibility: that no President of the U.S. would dare to present any such treaty to the Senate; and that, if it were in their power to offer me the whole territory described in our project, increased ten-fold in value, and in addition to that, covered a

57. James G. Birney, diary entry of 22 April 1842, James G. Birney Papers, LC.
58. Chase to John P. Hale, 12 May 1847; see also Chase to ?, 15 Aug. 1846, both in Chase Papers, LC; Chase to Charles Sumner, 24 April 1847, in "Diary and Correspondence of Salmon P. Chase," Am. Hist. Assn. *Annual Report 1902* (Washington: GPO, 1903), II, 113–116.
59. "The Triumph," Cincinnati *Weekly Herald and Philanthropist,* 19 Aug. 1846.

foot thick all over with pure gold, upon the single condition that slavery should be excluded therefrom, I could not entertain the offer for a moment, nor think even of communicating it to Washington.[60]

But the Wilmot Proviso was not the result of an outburst of abolitionist idealism. Rather, it was a response by northern Democrats, and specifically by New York Barnburners, to southern efforts to control the Democratic party and force slavery into the territories. Under heavy pressure from their constituents, and pilloried as catspaws of the Slave Power, Democratic congressmen and their colleagues in all the northern state legislatures backed the Proviso as the least painful way of defusing the slavery controversy, which they saw as endangering the Union.[61]

The Wilmot Proviso and the Free Soil appeal were antislavery at its most ambivalent. On the one hand, the Proviso was, as its Democratic supporters touted it, "the White man's resolution."[62] The exclusion of slavery from the territories was for some Freesoilers only the prelude to ridding America completely of black people by colonization. The heart of the issue raised by the Proviso was the "question of the white man against the Ethiopian."[63] But on the other hand, for many non-Democratic Freesoilers, the Proviso was just one logical early step in the progression toward a more thoroughgoing attack on slavery. Gamaliel Bailey saw it as a temporary stop on the way to complete divorce; Charles Sumner went further, seeing the conversion of some Democrats to Free Soil as sustaining "a broader conclusion, that is, the duty of no longer allowing the continuance of the evil any where within our constitutional action. They must become Abolitionists."[64] Perhaps one source of the Proviso's appeal lay in this ambivalence.

60. Trist to Secretary of State James Buchanan, 4 Sept. 1847, in William R. Manning, ed., *Diplomatic Correspondence of the United States: Inter-American Affairs, 1831–1860* (Washington, D.C.: Carnegie Endowment, 1925–39), VIII, 939.

61. Eric Foner, "The Wilmot Proviso Revisited," *J. Am. Hist.,* 66 (1969), 262–279.

62. Sewell, *Ballots for Freedom,* 172–173; Eric Foner, "Politics and Prejudice: The Free Soil Party and the Negro, 1849–1852," *J. Negro Hist.,* 50 (1965), 239–256; Frederick J. Blue, *The Free Soilers: Third Party Politics, 1848–1854* (Urbana: Univ. of Illinois Press, 1973), 87–88.

63. H. C. Trinne to Lyman Trumbull, 15 Dec. 1859, quoted in Larry Gara, "Slavery and the Slave Power: A Crucial Distinction," *Civil War Hist.,* 15 (1969), 5–18 at 16.

64. Bailey and Sumner as quoted in Sewell, *Ballots for Freedom,* 153–154.

The Proviso furnished a common ground on which Liberty moderates could join hands with nonabolitionists from the regular parties. Late in 1846, Massachusetts Whig Charles Sumner invited Chase to participate in "a new chrystallization of parties, in which there shall be one grand Northern party of Freedom."[65] Moderate leaders responded warmly; Stanton and Stanley Matthews urged Chase and the Libertymen to accept a nonabolitionist as presidential candidate of a fusion party on a Wilmot Proviso platform.[66] Chase leapt at the chance, admitting in private correspondence that "I have always regarded the Lib. organization as a means to this end [the overthrow of slavery]; I now regard it as nothing more. I feel ready therefore to give up the Lib. organ. at any time when I see that the great object can be accomplished without the sacrifice of principle in less time by another agency."[67]

Fusion became a realistic possibility after 1846 because of the wide popular support in the north for the Wilmot Proviso. Factions from the regular parties had been cut loose by the dominant proslavery majorities in both, and by the Texas-annexation and war policies of the Tyler and Polk administrations. The Democracy was splitting in the states. Voters in the southern part of Ohio had already sent the maverick antislavery Democrat Jacob Brinkerhoff to the House, the first Democratic opponent of slavery in Congress since the ouster of Ohio Senator Thomas Morris in 1839. In Massachusetts, potentially antislavery Democrats Marcus Morton and George Bancroft grew uneasy under Doughface party leaders like Benjamin Henshaw, Benjamin Hallett, and Robert Rantoul—and even Rantoul came around to antislavery in the 1850s. The New York Democracy was divided between William Marcy's proslavery Hunker faction, favored by Polk in patronage matters, and the angry Barnburner followers of former president Martin Van Buren, who had been denied the 1844 presidential nomination because of his opposition to Texas' immediate annexation.[68]

65. Sumner to Salmon P. Chase, 12 Dec. 1846, in Chase Papers, LC, ser. 1, cont. 12.

66. Stanton to Chase, 6 Aug. 1847 and 6 June 1848, Chase Papers, LC, ser. 1, cont. 13 and 14 respectively; Cincinnati *Weekly Herald and Philanthropist,* 21 April 1847.

67. Chase to John Thomas, 24 June 1847, "Diary and Correspondence of Chase," II, 118–120.

68. Charles G. Sellers, *James K. Polk, Continentalist: 1843–1848* (Princeton:

The most serious defection occurred in New Hampshire and produced an antislavery Democratic leader of national stature, John P.
Hale.[69] Before annexation, the New Hampshire Democracy had been
dominated by the Doughface leadership of Franklin Pierce, Senator
Charles Atherton, who gave his name to one of the early gags,[70] Levi
Woodbury, and that ardent Jacksonian with the unlikely name of
Edmund Burke. But Hale, backed by an amorphous antiannexationist
group called the "Independent Democrats," opposed annexation
in 1845 and was elected with Whig support, first as speaker of the
state house and then to the United States Senate. What was known
in Granite State politics as the "Hale Storm" had national
repercussions.

Texas annexation also forced a split in the Massachusetts Whig
party between a group known first as "Young Whigs" and the party
regulars.[71] (The terms "Conscience" and "Cotton" did not come into
common use until 1846.) The Young Whigs included an extraordinary group of men: Charles Francis Adams, who was taking the
baton passed on by his failing father; Charles Sumner, later a
towering figure in the Senate during war and Reconstruction; Henry
Wilson, later vice-president of the United States; Samuel Gridley
Howe, an M.D. who had fought in the Greek revolution of 1827–
1828 and who pioneered prison reform, public school education, and
education of the blind and the mentally retarded; John Gorham
Palfrey, former editor of the *North American Review;* Ebenezer
Rockwood Hoar, future Attorney General of the United States; and
Richard Henry Dana, Jr., author of *Two Years Before the Mast* and
of *The Seaman's Friend,* a standard work on maritime law that at-
tested to his considerable abilities as a lawyer.

Princeton Univ. Press, 1966), 3–212; O. C. Gardiner, *The Great Issue . . .
Being a Brief Historical Sketch of the Free Soil Question in the United
States . . .* (n.p., n.d. [1848]) is a useful contemporary documentary history
of the origins of Free Soil fusion.

69. See Richard Sewell's superb political biography, *John P. Hale and the
Politics of Abolition* (Cambridge: Harvard Univ. Press, 1965), chs. 4–5.

70. By one of the many ironies in the history of antislavery, the Atherton
of the gag was the grandson of the antifederalist Joshua Atherton who had
opposed ratification of the Constitution in 1788 because of its proslavery
character; *Emancipator,* 24 Jan. 1839.

71. Kinley J. Brauer, *Cotton versus Conscience: Massachusetts Whig Politics
and Southwestern Expansion, 1843–1848* (Lexington: Univ. Press of Kentucky,
1967).

Joining in transideological coalition with Garrison and Wendell Phillips on one hand, and John Greenleaf Whittier and Elizur Wright on the other, the Young Whigs started an antiannexation newspaper and organized conventions dedicated to keeping Texas out. At the September 1846 state Whig convention, the Conscience faction promoted four specific antislavery points: nonsupport of candidates who did not favor abolition of slavery in the states "by all constitutional means," a vague qualification conceivably reaching into the periphery of the radicals' position; abolition of slavery in the District of Columbia and the territories; prohibition of the interstate slave trade; and refusal to admit new slave states—a live rather than an abstract issue since the question of whether Texas was to be cloned into five separate slave states had not yet been settled.[72] Sumner, addressing the convention, insisted that the Whigs go beyond mere nonextension to oppose "the larger continuance [of slavery] under the Constitution and Laws of the Union. . . . Emancipation should always be presented as the cardinal object of our national policy."[73] But in 1847 the Conscience faction adopted the Wilmot Proviso as their central goal, retreating from their broader platform of the year before, and placed themselves in a position to coalesce with the moderates.

Thus by the summer of 1847, three groups were open to coalition or fusion: Conscience Whigs, Barnburner Democrats, and Liberty moderates. On 20 October 1847 the Liberty majority chose the independent Democrat, Hale, as its nominee for the presidential race next year. In June, 1848, the Barnburners nominated ex-President Martin Van Buren while the Libertymen called for a national Free Soil convention to meet in Buffalo on 9 August 1848.

In preparation for the fusion convention, the abolitionist component of the nascent Free Soil coalition downplayed their antislavery views. In March 1848, Joshua Giddings urged Chase, who needed no prodding in that direction, to organize the forthcoming Buffalo con-

72. Such cloning was provided for in the joint resolution on annexation, 1 March 1845, 5 Stat. 797. One hundred thirty years later, another southern conservative, Rep. James M. Collins (R., Tex.) proposed reviving the subdivision idea to increase the number of presumably conservative southern members as a means of offsetting liberal northern votes. *New York Times,* 1 March 1975, p. 19, col. 5.

73. *The Works of Charles Sumner* (Boston: Lee and Shepard, 1875–83), I, 313.

vention solely on the basis of the Wilmot Proviso. "I would say nothing about abolition or anti-slavery," Giddings cautioned, "as these terms frighten many people."[74] There were only two real questions to be settled at Buffalo: who would be the Free Soil presidential candidate and how much vestigial antislavery would survive in the platform.

The nomination was the more difficult question. Martin Van Buren had made a career out of opposition to antislavery measures, and was better known to his new Free Soil associates as "the northern man with southern principles" than by his conventional political nicknames, the Red Fox of Kinderhook or the Little Magician. Abolitionists could not forget that, as Democratic presidential candidate in 1836 and 1840, he had campaigned on a promise to veto any bill for the abolition of slavery in the District of Columbia and had approved the gag.[75] The faction promoting him, the Barnburners, were the most avowedly negrophobic and antiegalitarian of Free Soil coalition.[76] Van Buren was a peculiar candidate for a fusion party to any degree antislavery, but he had one insuperable advantage: he and Hale were the only realistic fusion candidates, and most people, including Hale himself, thought that Hale was just warming the seat for the eventual Free Soil nominee.

The situation was ready for a logroll; Chase for the Liberty element and Benjamin F. Butler for the Barnburners did the rolling. They came up with a package that everyone (excepting a few forlorn radical abolitionists present) could at least live with, and for which some principled delegates could work up enthusiasm. Van Buren got the nomination, and Charles Francis Adams was chosen as his running mate, a graceful gesture to the Whig Conscience group. The platform, composed by Chase and Barnburner Preston King, conceded two Liberty points, nonextension and divorce, abstractly formulated; it gave the Whigs and westerners internal improvements and free homesteads, and the Barnburners a revenue tariff. Thus Free Soil was born, and went into the campaign under the revealingly equivocal slogan "Van Buren and Free Soil, Adams and Liberty."

74. Giddings to Chase, 16 March 1848, Salmon P. Chase MSS., Historical Society of Pennsylvania.
75. Joshua Leavitt to Salmon P. Chase, 7 July 1848, Salmon P. Chase MSS., Historical Society of Pennsylvania.
76. Eric Foner, "Racial Attitudes of New York Free Soilers," *New York Hist.*, 46 (1965), 311–329.

Van Buren then watered down the Free Soil antislavery formula even more. In his letter of acceptance, he reinterpreted the platform to imply "a spirit of considerate forbearance towards the institution [of slavery] in localities where it was placed under the control of Congress," except the territories.[77] With this, the coalition scrapped what little potential it had had to become an egalitarian party prepared to face the problem of race relations in a society where slavery had been abolished, and instead opted for a western empire free for white men by being kept free of black men. The predictions of the opponents of independent political action in 1839 were realized: the moderates seemed to sell their libertarian heritage for a mess of political pottage.

Yet abolition sentiments among the Freesoilers were not wholly snuffed out. In 1849, the Boston *Republican,* edited by Freesoiler Henry Wilson, insisted that the party would abolish slavery in the territories and the District of Columbia; abolish the slave trade; repeal the 1793 fugitive act; and "exercise all its constitutional power to discourage, localize, and destroy slavery." The Ohio ex-Libertyman Edward S. Hamlin insisted to Chase in 1850 that "our [Free Soil?] mission is to overthrow slavery *in the States,* as well as to keep it out of the territories." To do this, Hamlin proposed to "make war upon the institution of slavery itself wherever it exists; and, when we have strength to legislate for its overthrow in the States, I think we shall find Constitutional powers through which to exert that strength."[78] No radical abolitionist could ask for more.

But such reassurances did not satisfy abolitionist opponents of the moderates. They saw divorce, potentially so aggressive, as it was in the 1844 Liberty platform, shrivel to nonextension. "Non-extension is not abolition," warned the executive committee of the then-radical American and Foreign Anti-Slavery Society; the true mission of the Liberty party was to stand by "the great anti-slavery principles we avow, viz.: the entire divorcement of the national government from slavery."[79] In 1842, Garrisonian Lydia Maria Child had predicted that "where the accession of numbers can be gained by compromise,

77. Quoted in Goodell, *Slavery and Anti-Slavery,* 481.
78. Wilson and Hamlin as quoted in Sewell, *Ballots for Freedom,* 198, 190 (italics in original).
79. *Address to the Friends of Liberty, by the Executive Committee of the Amer. and For. Anti-Slavery Society* (n.p., n.d. [1848]), 4.

compromise will be made."[80] Radical constitutionalist Lysander Spooner verified her prediction after the Liberty party picked the nonabolitionist Hale as its presidential candidate in 1847: "While they have gained a candidate, they have lost their party. I do not see that they can do anything but join the Wilmot Proviso and anti-war men. They obviously have dared avow no principles that can avail in a contest for the abolition of slavery." These were the consequences, Spooner believed, of accepting the constitutional doctrines of the "nincompoop" Chase.[81]

The sourness of Spooner's attitude may have reflected the envy of an outsider as much as divergence of principles. But the outsiders of the movement in their own way made a significant contribution to abolition, and did so without the dissimulation of the Liberty moderates of 1848. In examining the outsiders' constitutional theories, we can learn much about how Americans have confronted legally sanctioned injustice.

80. Lydia Maria Child to Ellis Gray Loring, 25 Jan. 1842, in Lydia Maria Child, Personal Miscellaneous Papers, Manuscripts and Archives Division, The New York Public Library, Astor, Lenox and Tilden Foundations.
81. Spooner to George Bradburn, 8 Nov. 1847, Lysander Spooner Papers, N-YHS.

CHAPTER 10

The Garrisonian Critique

Where both radical and moderate constitutionalists adhered to the American Constitution, William Lloyd Garrison and his coworkers repudiated it as a "proslavery compact," the "covenant with death" and "agreement with hell" mentioned in Isaiah.[1] They denounced the American union, called on individual Americans to repudiate their loyalty to it, and advocated secession by the northern states. "No Union With Slaveholders," which had begun as an ecclesiastical program, became a secular political objective. Garrisonian constitutional theories influenced non-Garrisonian abolitionists, even if negatively. But those theories are easy to misunderstand and criticize, and can be appreciated only in the context of Garrison's thought as it developed between 1835 and 1845. If not integrated with its nonconstitutional components, Garrisonian constitutionalism seems to be the absurd and self-defeating jumble of sophistries criticized by Gilbert H. Barnes and Dwight L. Dumond.

Garrisonians developed their constitutional ideas only after they had worked out theories of perfectionism and nonresistance. Garrison and his associates elaborated a program of political action in response to the innovations of their opponents within the antislavery movement, then they developed parallel and consonant constitutional dogmas, which were little more than rebuttals of radical and Liberty political ideas. Hence a bald restatement of Garrisonian constitutionalism, wrenched out of the totality of Garrison's thought, would be misleading and implicitly false.

In the years from 1832 to 1838 Garrison dabbled in constitutional antislavery to such an extent that in 1838 Ellis Gray Loring thought

1. Isaiah 28:18.

he was allied with Alvan Stewart in believing that slavery was unconstitutional everywhere.[2] He promoted various programs of political action, including the petition campaign and selective voting for candidates sympathetic to antislavery.[3] Yet in the same period Garrison excoriated the government of the United States, the American people, and the Christian denominations as hopelessly corrupt; he also toyed with schemes of nonresistant pacifism.[4] While all this was going on, his asperity was building up a reservoir of ill will among fellow abolitionists, to say nothing of persons outside the movement.

In 1836, Garrison simultaneously antagonized fellow abolitionists in theological and political quarrels, and began the development of his nonresistance theories. Both proved divisive to the movement. The quarrel between Garrison and others in the movement dates from Garrison's condemnation of the well-intentioned but paternalistic American Union for the Relief and Improvement of the Colored Race, a short-lived resuscitation of the old Abolition Societies, and from Garrison's skepticism about the divine institution of the Sabbath.[5] These controversies had a dual impact. For Garrison, they jolted him loose from his religious orthodoxy and left him free to explore perfectionism. On the other side, it provided an occasion for conservative clergy to anathematize Garrison. A group of orthodox ministers in Massachusetts issued a "Pastoral Letter" in 1837, de-

2. Garrison to Thomas Shipley, 17 Dec. 1835, in Walter M. Merrill, ed., *I Will Be Heard, 1822–1835* (vol. I of *The Letters of William Lloyd Garrison*) (Cambridge: Harvard Univ. Press, 1971), 584 (hereinafter cited: *Garrison Letters I*); "Important Decision," *Liberator*, 16 April 1836; Garrison to Isaac Knapp, 23 Aug. 1836, in Louis Ruchames ,ed., *A House Dividing against Itself, 1836–1840* (vol. II of *The Letters of William Lloyd Garrison*) (Cambridge: Harvard Univ. Press, 1971), 170 (hereinafter cited: *Garrison Letters II*); "U.S. Circuit Court," *Liberator*, 19 Oct. 1838; Ellis Gray Loring to William Jay, 15 March 1838, John Jay Papers, Columbia University.
3. See Garrison to George W. Benson, 11 Jan. 1836, *Garrison Letters II*, 7; Garrison to Dutee J. Pearce, 26 Feb. 1836, ibid., 48; Garrison to Samuel J. May, 17 Jan. 1836, ibid., 14; printed form letter "To Friends of the Anti-Slavery Movement," 18 April 1836, ibid., 84; Garrison to Henry E. Benson, 16 Jan. 1836, ibid., 9; Garrison's speech reported in *Fourth Annual Report of the American Anti-Slavery Society*, 23.
4. *Liberator*, 29 Dec. 1832; Garrison to Peleg Sprague, in *Liberator*, 12 Sept. 1835; Garrison to George Benson, 21 Oct. 1835, *Garrison Letters I*, 540; Garrison to Mary Benson, 27 Nov. 1835, ibid., 563; Garrison to Isaac Knapp, 5 July 1836, *Garrison Letters II*, 138; Garrison to Samuel J. May, 23 Sept. 1836, ibid., 178.
5. *Liberator*, 17 Jan. 1835; 31 Jan. 1835; 7 Feb. 1835; "Lyman Beecher," ibid., 23 July 1836.

nouncing the practice of bringing extraneous lecturers on controversial topics into churches without the consent of the minister, and condemning the practice of women lecturing in public. The Pastoral Letter, which did not allude to Garrison by name, was shortly followed by the "Appeal of the Clerical Abolitionists," which explicitly rebuked Garrison's harsh language and critical attitude toward all who disagreed with him.[6]

This challenge from orthodoxy came at a juncture in Garrison's personal development. In early 1837, Garrison had been, as he told the perfectionist John Humphrey Noyes, "heaving on the subject of Holiness and the Kingdom of Heaven."[7] Pacifism appealed to him, and he wrote to the nonresistant Henry C. Wright that "in the kingdom of God's dear Son, holiness and love are the only magistracy. It has no swords . . . no chains, for all are free. And that kingdom is to be established upon the earth."[8] Eagerly endorsing the command to Isaiah, Garrison urged, " 'Cease from man'; beware of a worldly policy."[9] With the line from the Lord's Prayer, "Thy kingdom come," in mind, he concluded that "if that kingdom be within us, if that will be truly obeyed by us, we enjoy, as to times and seasons, a liberty in Christ Jesus, unknown to those under the first covenant."[10] From thence, perfectionism was only a short way off.

Restated summarily, Garrison's perfectionist beliefs by 1840 comprised several tenets. God made man capable of perfection, a state in which man was free from sin and from the vicious tendencies of human nature. Through His Son Jesus Christ, He called all men to this state of perfection: "Be ye therefore perfect, even as your Father which is in Heaven is perfect."[11] Men could attain perfection on earth, before their death, and could do so by an act of faith and will that transformed their actions. In this state, they would not only leave off sinning; they would be incapable of sinning, just as Jesus Christ was.

6. "Appeal of Clerical Abolitionists on Anti-Slavery Measures," reprinted in *Liberator,* 11 Aug. 1837.

7. Quoted in Garrisons, *William Lloyd Garrison,* II, 145.

8. Garrison to Henry C. Wright, 16 April 1837, *Garrison Letters II,* 257.

9. Isaiah 2:22; Garrison to Samuel J. May, 17 Jan. 1836, *Garrison Letters II,* 17–21.

10. Garrison to editor of *New England Spectator,* 30 July 1836, reprinted in *Garrison Letters II,* 148.

11. Matthew 5:48.

Garrison carried these premises to a millenialist conclusion.[12] Criticizing the Millerite premillenarian craze of 1842, Garrison insisted that the second coming had already occurred circa 60 A.D. and that the kingdom of God had therefore already been established on earth, rather than being something yet to come.[13] He reasoned: "Let Christ fulfill his mission, for the government is laid on his shoulders; and he (in the persons of his followers, of course,) shall put down all rule, and all authority and power."[14] His parenthetical qualification indicated that the true followers of Christ—presumably perfectionists—in themselves embodied God's reign on earth, and that all secular government should dissolve before them.

Momentous consequences followed from these perfectionist and millenialist beliefs. All earthly institutions, even those that Garrison had formerly thought basically good or capable of being turned to good ends, like the church and human government, were adapted to man in his sinful, preperfected state. They were necessary to restrain men from harming other men by giving in to their vicious propensities, but, like the state in Marx's communist society, they would wither away when the cause of them, man's sinfulness, disappeared. "If all men would come into the obedience of Christ," Garrison wrote in 1837, "there would be no need of prisons, or of penal enactments, or military bands, for there would be no criminals, and therefore none to punish."[15] When men had become perfect, all, including females and blacks, would coexist as equals. The distinctions of rank, place, and function that set one man above others in the church or state would be swept away. So would the practices of church and state derived from the old Mosaic dispensation, such as Sabbath observance, taxation, and so forth.

Church and state necessarily had repressive arms—episcopal or clerical authority, jails, armies, taxes, courts—all of which relied at bottom on force or the threat of force, by which some men compelled other men to behave in ways ordained by those who controlled the instruments of force. These arms, like the church and state them-

12. On the meaning of millenialism and its distinction from millenarian beliefs, see Ernest L. Tuveson, *Redeemer Nation: The Idea of America's Millenial Role* (Chicago: Univ. Chicago Press, 1968), 34–35.
13. "The Second Advent. No. II," *Liberator,* 17 Feb. 1843.
14. *Liberator,* 20 Sept. 1842.
15. *Liberator,* 23 June 1837.

selves, became perverted into roadblocks to men traveling along to perfection. Because human institutions obstructed men from their divine goal of perfection, and because they rested on the sanction of force, perfectionist doctrine led finally to nonresistant pacifism.[16]

Garrison and fellow nonresistants rejected not only war but the entire apparatus that sustained governments in power. He summarized this position in a programmatic outline, the "Declaration of Sentiments Adopted by the Peace Convention . . . 1838," a nonresistance manifesto renouncing allegiance to all human government. Nonresistants disabled themselves from holding "any office which imposes upon its incumbent the obligation to compel men to do right," including all political office. This carried with it a rejection of voting: "If we cannot occupy a seat in the legislature or on the bench, neither can we elect others to act as our substitutes in any such capacity."[17] The extreme logical outcome of this principle appeared in a remark of Henry C. Wright, who stated that he would not vote, even if by his one vote he could free all the slaves.[18]

Perfectionism thus came out, via nonresistance, as opposition to political action, a stance its opponents called "no-human-government." Garrison was annoyed at the label, preferring "the divine government theory" instead.[19] What divided him from his opponents within the antislavery movement was his belief in the possibility of universal moral regeneration. Only when all men were brought to a state of spiritual perfection would true "abolition" take place—abolition from the enslavement of one person to the will of another, whether this subjection took the form of slaveholding, military command, tax-collecting authority, or the magisterium of the church. Garrison summed up this theory in announcing a change in the editorial direction of the *Liberator* in December 1837.[20] This editorial note was the manifesto of Garrisonian protestantism within the one antislavery church. True or "universal" emancipation meant "the emancipation

16. On perfectionism and nonresistance generally, see Kraditor, *Means and Ends*, ch. 4; Lewis Perry, *Radical Abolitionism: Anarchy and the Government of God in Antislavery Thought* (Ithaca: Cornell Univ. Press, 1973), ch. 3; and John Demos, "The Antislavery Movement and the Problem of Violent Means," *New Eng. Q.*, 37 (1964), 501–526.

17. Reprinted in Garrisons, *William Lloyd Garrison*, II, 230–234.

18. Henry C. Wright, "Ballot-box and Battle-field," *Liberator*, 23 March 1842.

19. *Liberator*, 26 Oct. 1838.

20. "Prospectus of the Liberator Volume VIII," *Liberator*, 15 Dec. 1837.

of our whole race from the dominion of man, . . . and bringing them under the dominion of God, the control of an inward spirit, the government of the law of love, and into the obedience and liberty of Christ." Any other or more limited reform, such as temperance or the abolition of slavery, was merely temporizing and limited. A perfectionist could not content himself with any partial reform, any more than he could dally with halfway measures like gradualism, for the success of any temporary expedient would still leave men unregenerated and prone inevitably to fall into the sin of force, into allegiance to the kingdoms of this world. From a perfectionist viewpoint, political-action antislavery was dangerous because it used corrupt instrumentalities to effect only a limited modification of mundane society, and stopped far short of the government of God, the only real universal emancipation.

Despite Garrison's self-absolving professions of meekness and his labored efforts to explicate his thought beyond the possibility of mis understanding, his abolitionist critics became convinced that he was anticlerical, anarchistic, and divisive. They saw his ideas as a diversion from the exigent needs of the movement, a gratuitous *folie d'extrème*. The New York abolitionists decided that it was time to take drastic action against the Boston heresiarch, his *Liberator,* and his Massachusetts Anti-Slavery Society. Elizur Wright objected to Garrison's supposed linkage of antislavery, perfectionism, and nonresistance: "You can't drive a three tined fork through a hay mow, though turn it t'other end to, and you can drive in the handle."[21] Gamaliel Bailey and William Goodell condemned Garrison's nonresistance "heresies," Goodell claiming that they were incompatible with "that essential feature of primitive [1833] abolitionism" as defined in the AA-SS Declaration of Sentiments.[22]

Garrison responded by seeing a conspiracy among the writers of the Pastoral Letter and the Clerical Appeal, procolonizationist clergy, and the New York abolitionists.[23] He detected the priestly hands of the Reverends Orange Scott (Methodist), Charles T. Torrey (Con-

21. Wright to A. A. Phelps, 5 Sept. 1837, in Elizur Wright Papers, LC.
22. Gamaliel Bailey to A. A. Phelps, 2 Nov. 1837, in Amos A. Phelps MSS., and William Goodell to Henry B. Stanton, 5 Feb. 1839, Department of Rare Books and MSS., used by courtesy of the Trustees of the Boston Public Library.
23. Garrison to George W. Benson, 20 Oct. 1837, *Garrison Letters II*, 311–313.

gregationalist), Alanson St. Clair (Unitarian), and Nathaniel Colver (Baptist) in a supradenominational plot, abetted by Henry B. Stanton, James G. Birney, Joshua Leavitt, Elizur Wright, the Tappans, and William Goodell, to subvert his leadership of the movement in Massachusetts. Of the movement's leaders in 1837, only Gerrit Smith, William Jay, Alvan Stewart, and Theodore Dwight Weld held aloof from the controversy.

Garrison was not entirely wrong. The New York leadership tried, with litttle success, to create rival state and local antislavery societies and a rival newspaper that would be, as Torrey put it, more "in accordance with our original principles of association."[24] When Garrison exposed such scheming, the New York leaders of the AA-SS decided on a fight to the finish, and Garrison accepted the challenge.[25] A special committee of the AA-SS transferred its organ, the *Emancipator,* to the NYCA-SS, safely in control of Garrison's opponents. The AA-SS itself was bankrupt, and its Executive Committee planned to disband it. Garrison, however, seized control by bringing a boatload of his supporters to attend its annual meeting in May 1840. Lewis Tappan then led the New York group in a secession from the AA-SS and organized the rival American and Foreign Anti-Slavery Society (A&FA-SS). The schism was complete, and the animating spirit that had sustained organized antislavery in the 1830s was dead. After the schism, Garrison and some of his associates elaborated on their nonresistance principles to develop a theory of political action that would counter the rationale of their opponents, who were by then committed to third-party antislavery politics.[26] It was out of these theories of political action that Garrisonian constitutionalism sprang.

A nonresistant, as Garrison had concluded in the Peace Convention manifesto of 1838, could not vote as a matter of principle, though he or she could participate in such things as petitioning, interrogating,

24. Charles T. Torrey to "Dear Sir," 7 Jan. 1839, Charles T. Torrey Papers, Congregational Library, Boston.
25. John L. Thomas, *The Liberator: William Lloyd Garrison: A Biography* (Boston: Little, Brown, 1963), chs. 12–13; Walter M. Merrill, *Against Wind and Tide: A Biography of Wm. Lloyd Garrison* (Cambridge: Harvard Univ. Press, 1963), ch. 12; Kraditor, *Means and Ends, passim;* Wyatt-Brown, *Lewis Tappan,* ch. 10; Dumond, *Antislavery,* ch 34.
26. For a succinct analysis of Garrisonian political theory, see Wyatt-Brown, *Lewis Tappan,* 269–272.

and urging others to vote for "friends of the slave."[27] In 1839, Garrison insisted, "I have always expected, I still expect, to see abolition at the ballot-box, renovating the political action of the country . . . modifying and rescinding all laws which sanction slavery. But this political reformation is to be effected solely by a change in the moral vision of the people."[28] What would be sinful for nonresistants would not necessarily be so for other abolitionists; hence an abolitionist could vote, providing that he cast his ballot only in conformity to the principles of the AA-SS Declaration of Sentiments. A voting abolitionist would be "recreant to his duty" if he voted for a candidate who was sympathetic to slavery or who did not support antislavery positions, or if he failed to vote for a candidate who would support antislavery positions. For such abolitionists, voting and other forms of political action were not questions of principle, but rather of expediency, the wisdom of which was to be determined on expediential grounds.[29]

It was the problem of political frustration that decisively split Garrison from his opponents. Garrison insisted, as his opponents originally had, that the best response to the nonchoice of two proslavery candidates was either scattering (the write-in vote) or abstention. From there abolitionists could act as a balance-of-power group, which would in turn induce one of the parties to appeal to their program by putting up acceptable candidates next time. Thus abolitionists would swing one or the other of the regular parties around to an antislavery platform.[30]

Antislavery third-party politics appalled Garrison as a matter of theory and tactics, and his abhorrence was increased when he noted that those most enthusiastic for political action were his personal enemies, the secessionists of 1840. He felt that abolitionists would best serve the cause of political antislavery by remaining in the two major parties, to purify them from within, and to bear with frustration patiently in the meantime. Further, since abolitionists of all persuasions were a minority of the American electorate, withdrawing

27. Wendell Phillips, "The No-Voting Theory," *Liberator*, 26 July 1844.
28. *Liberator*, 28 June 1839.
29. "Dying Away—Another Richmond in the Field—Political Action," *Liberator*, 1 Oct. 1841.
30. "Anti-Slavery Political Party," *Liberator*, 26 June 1840; "The Balance of Power," reprinted from the *Herald of Freedom*, in *Liberator*, 1 Jan. 1841; *Liberator*, 5 Aug. 1842.

to form a third party would condemn them to permanent exclusion from political effectiveness, a form of self-disfranchisement worse than scattering or abstention.

An antislavery third party would split the movement and dilute antislavery principles by dragging them into the political gutter, where they would be kicked around like any other question relating to banks, tariff, distribution, and the other sordid, trivial staples of routine party politics. Because abolitionists differed among themselves on these nonslavery staples, some being Whigs, others being Democrats, and some being independents with strong feelings about individual issues, the cause of the slave would be abandoned as the antislavery party fell apart because of wrangling among its membership on nonslavery issues. This would turn the antislavery party into just another collection of log-rolling, back-scratching, demagogic hacks. "Adventurers" would invade the party in hopes of spoils, and the force of antislavery would be dissipated.[31]

Thus Garrisonian abolition as of 1841. Then it began to undergo another transformation that led it to a new stance, one in which Garrisonians claimed that the Constitution was a proslavery document and therefore advocated personal disallegiance and sectional disunion. To Garrison, disunion was not a break from his prior thought, but a logical culmination of it.[32] It is necessary to discriminate carefully and not confuse disunion with perfectionism, nonresistance, and other aspects of Garrisonian political theory.

Garrisonian disunion grew out of internal and external pressures on the antislavery movement in the 1840s. The come-outer impulse led many abolitionists, including some non-Garrisonians, to abandon parties, societies, and churches as corrupt.[33] Memories of the violence of the thirties—mobbings, lynchings, rifling of mail—still rankled. Texas annexation and the war on Mexico led many, again including non-Garrisonians, to weigh the value of the union. Finally, the

31. Board of Managers of Massachusetts Anti-Slavery Society, quoted in Cincinnati *Philanthropist,* 12 Nov. 1839; *Liberator,* 31 Jan. 1840; 30 Oct. 1840; 6 March 1842; 11 March 1842; 22 March 1844.

32. "The Constitution—Political Action No. 1," *Liberator,* 17 April 1846.

33. Derived from Revelation 18:4: "Come out of her, my people, that ye be not partakers of her sins, and that ye receive not of her plagues." See William Goodell, *Come-Outerism. The Duty of Secession from a Corrupt Church* (New York: AA-SS, 1845).

Latimer incident in 1842 convinced Boston abolitionists that slavery existed in Massachusetts as well as South Carolina.

In October 1842, a Boston constable seized George Latimer as a runaway slave under the federal statute of 1793 and held him in a Boston jail.[34] The antislavery community, electrified, pursued several courses of action. They created a paper, the *North Star and Latimer Journal,* edited by Henry I. Bowditch, antislavery physician and brother of William I. Bowditch.[35] They sent monster petitions to the General Court and to Congress, demanding that the Bay State dissociate itself from fugitive recaptures; and through legal pressure in state courts, they so impeded efforts at Latimer's rendition that his supposed master relinquished his claim for four hundred dollars.

For the emergence of Garrisonian constitutionalism, the highlight of the Latimer episode was a rally held at Faneuil Hall on 30 October 1842. Among the speakers was Wendell Phillips, already acknowledged the movement's premier orator. He suggested dramatically that the true source of Boston's discomfiture was the United States Constitution itself.

There stands the bloody [fugitive slave] clause in the Constitution—you cannot fret the seal off the bond. The fault is in allowing such a Constitution to live an hour. . . . When I look on these crowded thousands and see them trample on their consciences and the rights of their fellow men at the bidding of a piece of parchment, I say, my curse be on the Constitution of these United States! (Hisses and shouts.)[36]

The Constitution was obviously a quasi-sacred symbol that one profaned at his risk, even among abolitionists. This led Phillips to muse on its relationship to slavery and, within a few years, to produce the ablest defence of the Garrisonian "agreement with hell" thesis.

Garrisonian constitutional thought was also influenced by disunion ideas. Disunion in Garrisonian ideology was an ambiguous idea, or rather, set of related ideas. It began in the early thirties as an ecclesiastical program summed up in the phrase "No Union With Slaveholders," a demand that northern churches dissociate themselves from the proslavery ministry of the South and exclude slaveholders

34. Levy, *Shaw,* 78–85; Morris, *Free Men All,* 109–117.
35. A full file of this ephemera, together with the most complete collection of materials anywhere relating to the Latimer episode, may be found in the Massachusetts Historical Society, Boston.
36. *Liberator,* 11 Nov. 1842.

from the sacramental community.[37] But it took on a secular connotation as Garrison reread Isaiah 28:14–18:

Wherefore hear the word of the Lord, ye scornful men, that rule this people which is in Jerusalem. Because ye have said, we have made a covenant with death, and with hell are we at agreement . . . your covenant with death shall be disannulled, and your agreement with hell shall not stand; when the overflowing scourge shall pass through, then ye shall be trodden down by it.

Tied to ideas of the Slave Power, the religious notion of disunion led Garrison to the insight that "as a component part of the union, [slavery] is necessarily a national interest. Divorced from Northern protection, it dies; with that protection, it enlarges its boundaries, multiplies its victims, and extends its ravages."[38]

Garrison at first suggested disunion, in the sense of a breakup of the American federation of states, as an alternative to emancipation in the south, but by 1844 he demanded disunion *per se*.[39] Disunion in this sense meant a secession by the free states of the North from the American union, and an individual's personal repudiation of his or her allegiance to the United States government. Disunion thus had a double rationale. By disavowing the union as an individual act, a northern abolitionist would clear himself from complicity with the system; and to the extent that the union supported slavery—as it did in Garrisonian constitutional theory—disunion would remove that constitutional buttress.[40] Putting his idea in the form of an aphorism, Garrison adopted this slogan as an editorial masthead for the *Liberator* after 1842: "A repeal of the union between northern liberty and southern slavery is essential to the abolition of the one and the preservation of the other." (He overlooked the fact that his

37. [Evan Lewis], *An Address to Christians of All Denominations on the Inconsistency of Admitting Slave-Holders to Communion and Church Membership* (Philadelphia: S. C. Atkinson, 1831); [George Bourne], *An Address to the Presbyterian Church Enforcing the Duty of Excluding All Slaveholders from the 'Communion of the Saints'* (New York: n.p., 1833).

38. *Liberator,* 6 May 1842.

39. Compare Garrison to Elizabeth Pease, 2 July 1842, in Walter M. Merrill, ed., *No Union with Slave-Holders, 1841–1849* (vol. III of *The Letters of William Lloyd Garrison*) (Cambridge: Harvard Univ. Press, 1973), 89, with *Liberator,* 24 May 1844.

40. "Progress of Anti-Slavery Movement," *Liberator,* 28 Jan. 1842; "Gerrit Smith's Constitutional Argument No. III," *Liberator,* 4 Oct. 1844.

literary parallellism misfired syntactically, so that disunion would bring about the abolition of northern liberty and the preservation of southern slavery.)

Garrison made it clear that he demanded not merely a moral, token, or symbolic act, but actual personal disallegiance and actual secession from the Union by the free states.[41] This carried Garrisonians well beyond their original beliefs, for a time at least. They now condemned voting by anyone, not just nonresistants, on the grounds that to vote for any public official, local, state, or federal, would be to endorse someone who would have to take an oath to uphold the United States Constitution, which supported slavery.[42] Any act of allegiance to a government whose constitution supports slavery "means either to undertake myself to execute the law which I think wrong, or to appoint another to do so."[43] Garrison declared voting to be "of Satanic origin, and inherently wicked and murderous. We must cease to sanction it . . . voting for men to have discretionary power over the lives and liberties of their fellow-men must be put in the same category with rum-drinking, profanity, lewdness, and every evil work."[44]

Disunion was premised on the theory that the United States Constitution was a proslavery compact. Garrison and others arrived at this view in three ways. First, textual exegesis proved that the documentary Constitution was a bulwark of slavery in at least four particulars. Second, they took advantage of the publication in 1840 of the so-called "Madison Papers," James Madison's record of the 1787 Philadelphia debates.[45] This was a traumatic revelation to abolitionists, for Madison's detailed coverage of the debates confirmed abolitionists' suspicions that the framers consciously wrote guarantees for slavery into the Constitution. Third, Garrison and his colleagues

41. "Protest" of the Massachusetts Anti-Slavery Society, *Liberator,* 2 Feb. 1844; Garrison's speech at Faneuil Hall antiannexation convention (1845), reprinted in *Liberator,* 7 Feb. 1845.
42. "Address" of Adin Ballou, *Liberator,* 22 Sept. 1843.
43. Wendell Phillips, "The No-Voting Theory," *Liberator,* 22 Sept. 1843; Edmund Quincy, *An Examination of the Charges of Mr. John Scoble & Mr. Lewis Tappan against the American Anti-Slavery Society* (Dublin: Webb and Chapman, 1842), 7.
44. *Liberator,* 20 Sept. 1842.
45. "Notes of Debates in the Federal Convention of 1787 Reported by James Madison," first published as part of H. D. Gilpin, ed., *The Papers of James Madison* (Washington, D.C.: Langtree and O'Sullivan, 1840).

were pursuing their principal opponents, the supporters of the Liberty party, and were trying to controvert every Liberty position, theoretical as well as tactical. They entered with zest into the task of demolishing the Liberty construction of the Constitution as actually or potentially antislavery. After Texas and Latimer had sensitized them to the nefarious potential of the Union and the Constitution, they channeled their analysis doggedly into a proslavery interpretation and did it so effectively that the proslavery Alabama politician John A. Campbell suggested to John C. Calhoun that Wendell Phillips' *The Constitution a Pro-Slavery Compact* was "an able pamphlet . . . [which] we might circulate to great advantage excluding a few paragraphs."[46]

Garrisonian constitutionalism was a *post-hoc* rationalization for disunion. Unlike radical and moderate arguments, most of the Garrisonian output was compiled hastily and was not refined by exposure to courts or legislative bodies. Wendell Phillips, for example, belittled his influential pamphlet, *The Constitution a Pro-Slavery Compact,* in correspondence with an Irish friend: "As for my poor little thing—it was scissored and patched into existence in one day—and printed almost as quick to circulate at our annual meeting and keep Abby Kelley from teasing me awhile—she wanted something to sell after her lectures and I had to provide it."[47] Garrisonian constitutionalism was nevertheless a respectable, internally consistent, coherent attempt to explain the relationship between slavery and the American constitution.[48]

Garrisonians, and Phillips in particular, began their inquiry with a positivist jurisprudential assumption: law is "a rule of civil conduct prescribed by the supreme power of a state, commanding what its subjects are to do, and prohibiting what they are to forbear," or, more simply, "a rule prescribed."[49] This axiom was central to Gar-

46. Campbell to John C. Calhoun, 20 Nov. 1847, in J. Franklin Jameson, ed., *Correspondence of John C. Calhoun* (vol. II of *Annual Report* of Am. Hist. Assn. 1899) (Washington, D.C.: GPO, 1900), 1143.

47. [Wendell Phillips, ed.], *The Constitution a Pro-Slavery Compact. or Selections from the Madison Papers, &c.* (New York: AA-SS, 1844); subsequent editions came out in 1845 and 1856. All quotations below are from the first edition. Phillips to Richard D. Webb, 25 Feb. 1845, quoted in Oscar Sherwin, *Prophet of Liberty: The Life and Times of Wendell Phillips* (New York: Bookman, 1958), 149.

48. See generally the following surveys of Garrisonian constitutionalism: Kraditor, *Means and Ends,* ch. 7; Stanley B. Bernstein, "Abolitionist Readings of the Constitution," Ph.D. diss., Harvard University, 1969, ch. 4.

49. Wendell Phillips, *Review of Lysander Spooner's Essay on the Un-*

risonian constitutionalism; reject it, and the whole structure of Garrisonian legal thought collapses. Garrisonians did not deny the existence of a higher law or its primacy; they merely insisted that natural and municipal law be not confused with each other, and that only the latter be recognized as the law that earthly courts administer. In this view, they were in accord with the jurisprudential postulates of proslavery constitutionalism, especially as expounded by the American Hegelian, John Codman Hurd.[50] Laws may be immoral and violative of higher law, yet still be of binding authority, as far as the judicial agents of the state were concerned. A judge may not consult his notions of natural law; rather, he must apply the law as given, without reference to postulates of morality.[51] Nathaniel Bouton, an antiabolitionist minister, extended this idea even to private individuals, who he thought had to obey all laws, whether consonant with higher law or not. Squaring statutes with natural law was exclusively a function of legislators; both courts and individuals were bound to obey all enactments, whatever their personal moral reservations might be.[52]

Any interpretation of law that deviated from this rigid positivism led to the "practical anarchy" of each man being a law unto himself.[53] The real no-government men were those who pushed an interpretation of the American constitution that deviated from the canonical. Courts, particularly the United States Supreme Court, can apply "only the legal standard of morality."[54] If a judge found himself obliged to administer an unjust law, he must resign. It was partly

---

constitutionality of Slavery . . . (Boston: Andrews & Prentiss, 1847), 7; [Wendell Phillips], *Can Abolitionists Vote or Take Office under the United States Constitution?* (New York: AA-SS, 1845), 18.

50. John C. Hurd, *Topics of Jurisprudence Connected with Conditions of Freedom and Bondage* (New York: D. Van Nostrand, 1856), 38, citing extensively from Hegel's *Grundlinien der Philosophie des Rechts.* (The *Topics* was the first part of Hurd's magisterial *The Law of Freedom and Bondage in the United States,* published in 1858.)

51. Cf. [Peleg W. Chandler, an antiabolitionist Boston legal writer], "The Latimer Case," *Law Reporter,* 481–498 (1843).

52. Nathaniel Bouton, *The Good Land in Which We Live: A Discourse Preached . . . on the Day of Public Thanksgiving . . .* (Concord: McFarland & Jenks, 1850).

53. Phillips, "The No-Voting Theory," *Liberator,* 26 July 1844.

54. "Constitutionality of Slavery," *Mass. Q. Rev.,* 4 (1848), 463–509 at 464. Though sometimes attributed to Phillips, internal evidence (see fn., p. 494) indicates that Phillips was a friend of the author. The author, whoever he was, seems to have been a lawyer, well versed in jurisprudence and the English precedents.

on this basis that the Garrisonian Francis Jackson resigned his commission as a Massachusetts justice of the peace.[55] Judges must consider themselves bound, not by absolute standards of justice, which have not yet been attained on earth, nor by standards of relative justice, which are constantly changing and subject to conflicting interpretations, but by the intentions of the framers of the laws and the common understanding of that intention as embodied in precedent and the uniform practice of the people and their representatives.[56] Courts administer "the general system of National Law under which they sit"; to fulfill that trust, their interpretation must be ultimate and authoritative, and not open to challenge.[57]

In the Garrisonians' positivism lies an irony. Elsewhere they and their latter-day supporters defended their tactics by an agitational rationale: it was necessary to adopt advanced positions to bring all men to a heightened awareness of their moral obligation. Yet they failed to see the same agitational value in the beliefs of their radical constitutionalist opponents, an opportunity for using ethical and legal precepts constructively to bring men out of an unquestioned reverence for extant law and forward to a demand that mundane laws square with natural justice. Under positivist assumptions, men were doomed to accept the law as they found it, with all its deformity, and abolitionists were precluded from working for change through and with extant law and legal systems. The Garrisonians' postulates locked them into a legal status quo that could be changed only by a millenial and universal shift in public sentiment. In this way, as in others, Garrisonian theory led functionally to de facto conservatism.

Rules of interpretation were another element of the Garrisonian argument. They insisted that the Constitution be "expounded in its plain, obvious, and common sense," and that ambiguities be resolved by a resort to contextual analysis enlightened by the social conditions of the framers.[58] Seen in this light, the Constitution obviously did

55. Jackson to Gov. George N. Briggs, 4 July 1844, reprinted as an appendix to [Phillips], *The Constitution a Pro-Slavery Compact*.
56. "Constitutionality of Slavery," 487.
57. Phillips, *Review of Spooner's Essay*, 15, 57; William I. Bowditch, *Slavery and the Constitution* (Boston: Robert F. Wallcut, 1849), 145. The latter portion of this pamphlet, the constitutional argument, was reprinted anonymously as *The United States Constitution* (New York: AA-SS, [1855?]).
58. "Constitutionality of Slavery," 483; Bowditch, *Slavery and the Constitution,* 117.

secure slavery in at least four respects, and did embody a one-sided proslavery compromise. As Garrison said, in a layman's misstatement of contract law, "The intent of a bargain is the bargain, whatever may be the language used, and I would not try to get rid of an obligation, however unjust, by a false interpretation of the instrument."[59] This part of the Garrisonian argument was its least assailable historically, and it made nonsense of those parts of the radical constitutionalist effort that disingenuously construed away the slavery clauses.

Phillips heaped ridicule on the strained efforts of the radicals: "If the unanimous, concurrent, unbroken practice of every department of government, judicial, legislative, and executive, and the acquiescence of the people for fifty years, do not prove which is the true construction, then how and where can such a question be settled? If the people and the courts of the land do not know what they themselves mean, who has authority to settle their meaning for them?"[60] Americans "may well take the Constitution to be what the courts and nation allow that it is, and leave the hair-splitters and cob-web spinners to amuse themselves at their leisure."[61] Such rhetoric had a superficial plausibility, but it was rebutted by William Howard Day, a delegate to the 1851 State Convention of Colored Citizens of Ohio, who pointed out that the Garrisonians fell into the error "of making the construction of the constitution of the United States, the same as the constitution itself."[62]

Having laid a jurisprudential and interpretive groundwork, Garrisonians then surveyed the origins and establishment of slavery in America to rebut the historically oriented arguments of their opponents. Relying on the dictum of Mansfield in *Somerset,* as elaborated by Chief Justice Shaw in *Med,* they insisted that modern as well as ancient custom was a legally sufficient origin of slavery. The "positive law" that Mansfield had said was necessary to the creation of slavery included custom: "Positive law is the term usually employed to distinguish the rules, usages, and laws which are made by man, from those which God has implanted in our nature. It matters not whether

59. William Lloyd Garrison, *"No Fetters in the Bay State!" Speech . . . in Support of the Petition Asking for a Law to Prevent the Recapture of Fugitive Slaves . . . 1859* (Boston: R. F. Wallcut, 1859), 10.
60. Phillips, *Can Abolitionists Vote,* 14.
61. Phillips, *Review of Spooner's Essay,* 93.
62. Quoted in Aptheker, ed., *Documentary History of the Negro People,* I, 318.

these rules and laws are written or unwritten, whether they originate in custom or are expressly enacted by Legislatures."[63] Statutory law merely codified what custom had created. This explained away the radicals' argument that only positive—that is, statutory—law could create a system in derogation of natural right.

Phillips and others then turned to the problem of *Somerset.* First, they construed the case narrowly and limited its impact to England. Whatever its impact on the common law in the metropolis, it did not and could not affect the status of slavery in the colonies. Common law did not survive the sea crossing unchanged; rather, it was received in America only insofar as it was compatible with the customs and systems of law in the colonies. Thus if the colonial customs and laws had established slavery, *Somerset* left the institution unaffected. Further, like the proslavery legalists, the Garrisonians considered *Grace* to be the definitive reinterpretation of *Somerset.*[64] Slavery existed in the mainland colonies by virtue of custom as ratified by legislative enactments of the colonial assemblies.

Independence no more altered slavery's legitimacy than did *Somerset.* The laws of the provincial and state legislatures and the new state constitutions continued slavery intact. As to the Declarations of Rights in the early state constitutions, stating that all men are created free and equal, their impact was necessarily differential, depending on the social circumstances of the state. In a commonwealth like Massachusetts, where slavery was moribund by 1780, such a declaration recognized the freedom of all citizens; but in a commonwealth like Virginia, where nearly half the population was enslaved, a comparable clause applied only to freemen, with slaves being an implicit exception to its scope.[65]

Since slavery was the creature of the states, national action could not disestablish it. Neither the Continental Congress that framed the Declaration of Independence nor the Confederation Congress that drew up the Articles was empowered by the states to meddle with their internal social institutions. Hence neither instrument could affect slavery or have any impact on municipal law concerning it. Black

63. Phillips, *Review of Spooner's Essay,* 85; see also "Constitutionality of Slavery," 466–467, 470.
64. Phillips, *Review of Spooner's Essay,* 81; "Constitutionality of Slavery," 466–477.
65. "Constitutionality of Slavery," 472, 488, 490.

slaves were an exception to the Declaration. Anticipating Taney's *Dred Scott* opinion, Phillips wrote that slaves "were regarded as an unfortunate, but still a very inferior portion of the human race. With this estimate of them, it was impossible, of course, for those who framed the Constitution to concede to them any of its privileges."[66]

Thus Garrisonian analysis got to its long suit, construction of the four proslavery clauses of the Constitution itself. Here the publication of the Madison Papers in 1840 became critical, revealing as it did in the words of John Quincy Adams, "the saturation of the parchment with the infection of slavery, which no fumigation could purify, no quarantine could extinguish."[67] The relevant clauses, ambiguously worded, became quite clear in the light of the Philadelphia debates and the arguments in the state ratifying conventions. The "all other Persons" of the three-fifths clause were obviously slaves, and the clause itself was the touchstone of the Slave Power.[68] The word "importation" in the 1808 clause could refer only to slaves, since its contextual correlative, migration, necessarily implied free agency.[69] The fugitive clause, interpreted in the light of its textual matrix, the Northwest Ordinance, clearly referred to slaves in the phrase "Person held to Service or Labour."[70] Finally, the insurrections and domestic violence clauses pertained to the uprisings of slaves as well as to other sorts of upheaval.

Evaluating the impact of the Constitution, Garrisonians concluded that "our fathers were intent on securing liberty to themselves, without being very scrupulous as to the means they used to accomplish their purpose. . . . [T]hough they recognized occasionally the brotherhood of the human race, in practice they continually denied it. They did not blush to enslave a portion of their fellow man . . . while they were . . . boasting of their regard for the rights of man."[71] The

66. "The Madison Papers," *Liberator*, 13 Sept. 1842; "Constitutionality of Slavery," 482, 494; Phillips, *Review of Spooner's Essay*, 87.

67. John Quincy Adams, address at North Bridgewater, Mass., 6 Nov. 1844, quoted in [Phillips], *The Constitution a Pro-Slavery Compact*, 123.

68. *Disunion. Address of the American Anti-Slavery Society; and F. Jackson's Letter on the Pro-Slavery Character of the Constitution* (New York: AA-SS, 1845), 12–16.

69. [Bowditch], *United States Constitution*, 2.

70. Phillips, *Review of Spooner's Essay*, 60–80.

71. *Disunion*, 7. See also Theodore Parker, *An Address . . . before the New York City Anti-Slavery Society, at Its First Anniversary, Held at the Broadway Tabernacle, May 12, 1854* (New York: AA-SS, 1854), 21–22.

Constitution took slavery "out of its former category of municipal law and local life, adopted it as a national institution, spread around it the broad and sufficient shield of national law, and thus gave to slavery a national existence."[72] Garrisonians endorsed John Quincy Adams' assertion that "the preservation, propagation, and perpetuation of slavery [is] the vital and animating spirit of the national government."[73]

The Garrisonian critique, despite its rejection of the Constitution itself, affected American constitutional development. It was correct in seeing that each of the clauses singled out for criticism had to be expunged or made a dead letter—which is what was done by the adoption of the Thirteenth through Fifteenth Amendments and supportive legislation—before the libertarian potential of the Constitution could be realized. The Garrisonians were most successful in pointing out the obvious, namely, that the clauses they noted not only related to slavery but secured and protected it. The Garrisonians were also on point when they insisted that a mere change in laws, even to the extent of legally abolishing the institution of slavery, would be an insufficient reform, a half-way measure that would not eradicate the evil, but merely palliate it. In seeking to reform the public sentiment that lay behind laws and constitutions and that inspirited them, the Garrisonians struck at the source of the problem.

Phillips insisted that the only path to justice "is over the Constitution, trampling it under foot; not under it, trying to evade its fair meaning."[74] There he pithily summed up the difference between the Garrisonians and the political-action constitutionalists, and raised pertinent questions about the processes of constitutionalism. Must a just person reject an imperfect constitution, or even one that sanctioned and protected an evil like slavery, to work effectively for constitutional reform and to abolish injustice? Or is it possible to regard the constitution as an imperfect but amendable instrument of social organization, with defects to be excised and spongy areas to be improved, but still the only thing available in the here and now of a heterogeneous secular society that can serve as a means of changing a society's goals and structure? Whatever the agitational or inspirational value of insisting on universal moral regeneration and abso-

72. *Disunion*, 22.
73. Quoted in [Bowditch], *United States Constitution*, 12.
74. Phillips, *Review of Spooner's Essay*, 35.

lutist goals, is there a place in a democratic society for a legal order that accepts and incorporates the society's evils as well as its good? Can men in good conscience choose to work within that defective legal order for its betterment, or must they seek only its overthrow in the service of absolute justice? The Garrisonians insisted endlessly—and rightly so—on the uselessness of condemning slavery in the abstract, but is it equally useless to strive for perfect justice in the abstract, the kingdom of Christ on earth? Is there a place for less total ends and less absolute means?

The weaknesses of Garrisonian constitutional thought lay in their brittle assumptions. The origin of Garrisonian constitutionalism was disunion. But is disunion the only moral response to an evil social order? As a posture, it had obvious shortcomings: it promoted a solipsistic outlook, it encouraged moral narcissism, and its dogmatism repelled, rather than convinced, the unconverted. Another assumption was the legal positivism that informed Garrisonian constitutional thought. By rejecting the radicals' innovative use of natural law, the Garrisonians threw away, without trial, what might have been a powerful motive for change. Garrisonians denied the possibility of legal flexibility and adaptation. By insisting that the only acceptable change was total and revolutionary, they disdained more limited, yet more tangible, evolutionary change. To be specific: why should a justice of the peace like Francis Jackson, or lawyers like Wendell Phillips, Nathaniel Rogers, and David Lee Child necessarily have to resign their commissions or abandon their practice? Why not pursue the law from the bench or the bar as William Jay, Ellis Gray Loring, or Salmon P. Chase had done, working to rescue a fugitive slave in courts here or getting a sojourners law repealed there? Law and lawyers performed a useful office even when they did not hold out for the unattainable absolutes of Garrisonism.

The greatest defect of Garrisonian constitutionalism lay in its similarity to the jurisprudential assumptions of Taney's *Dred Scott* opinion. Both insisted that the Constitution was locked rigidly in the social and intellectual world of the 1780s; that its language was insusceptible of changing interpretation; that its categories could not be modified and eroded by time; that a constitution is a rigid, static, concrete instrument, rather than a plastic, fluid, and growing one. The Constitution was more ambiguous, more susceptible to interpretive modification, than the Garrisonians allowed. Its zones of obscurity, including the fugitive slave and insurrections clauses, invited meliorist solutions. Lawyers, judges, and others could serve their sense of justice by interstitial modification. "Law is always becoming," Robert Cover has recently written. "We must speak of direction and weight as well as of position."[75] But Phillips and Garrison saw only position: what the law had been. This catatonic Garrisonian constitutional posture best served the interests of the Slave Power.

75. Cover, *Justice Accused,* 6.

CHAPTER 11

Radical Constitutional Antislavery: The Imagined Past, the Remembered Future

Sir Lewis Namier could have been writing about the controversy over slavery in America when he remarked on the perverse inclination of people to "imagine the past and remember the future."[1] When they thought and wrote about some historical problem, such as the framers' actual intentions, abolitionists (and defenders of slavery, too) imagined the past in terms of their contemporary values, if not in terms of their wishful thinking. When they tried to descry and influence the future, they "remembered" it along the synthetic lines sketched by their historical imagining. In doing so, radical abolitionists produced a flawed and disingenuous constitutional program. But though a failure in the short run, radical constitutionalism contained prescient ideas about the American libertarian heritage. Some of these ideas passed into the mainstream of postwar constitutional development, and those that were not so absorbed remained as a reminder of how far American social reality fell short of our democratic goals.

The radicals were either independents, with no previous or subsequent affiliation with any branch of organized antislavery, or belonged to a splinter of the Liberty party. A disaffected group within the party began to coalesce in the early forties, at first over nothing more tangible than dissatisfaction with the party's failure to come to grips successfully with specific issues. These potential dissidents remained in the Liberty party through the 1844 national elections because of their distaste for the choice between the proslavery Whig Tweedle-

---

1. Lewis B. Namier, "Symmetry and Repetition," in *Conflicts: Studies in Contemporary History* (London: Macmillian, 1942), 70.

dum, Henry Clay, and the Democratic Tweedledee, James K. Polk, that the regular parties offered them.

Increasingly, however, they balked at Liberty moderation and the emergent tendency in western Liberty leadership toward amalgamation politically and constitutionally with nonabolitionists. The radicals' restiveness erupted at the Port Byron, New York, Liberty party state convention (25 and 26 June 1845). William Goodell there delivered a formal address, which the convention refused to adopt, that condemned One Idea platforms and the prevalent assumption that the Liberty party was a temporary expedient to be abandoned as soon as one of the regular parties could be converted to antislavery. Goodell argued that the depredations of the Slave Power, abetted by the subservience of the regular parties, made it necessary for the Liberty party to become a permanent party advocating the cause of all human rights, and to take a stand on all issues that were the legitimate objects of governmental power.[2] Where the moderates were simultaneously trying to dilute the Liberty program in order to broaden its appeal, the radicals sought to extend it to embrace all reform issues.

Though rejected in 1845, Goodell's proposal remained in circulation for two years and became the platform of a rump faction that seceded from the Liberty party in 1847. This group, resisting the imminent sell-out to the Free Soil movement by the Liberty majority, gathered in a convention at Macedon Lock, New York (8 to 10 June 1847) in response to a convention call drafted by Goodell that repeated the premises of the 1845 address.[3] The delegates to the Macedon convention renamed themselves the Liberty League, nominated Gerrit Smith for the presidency, and adopted a platform written by Goodell, the "Address of the Macedon Convention."[4] The "Address" jettisoned One Idea and called for repeal of all tariffs, including those for revenue; abolition of the army and navy; an immediate end to the Mexican war; limitations on the amount of land that could be held by individuals and corporations; free public lands to actual

2. [William Goodell], *Address Read at the New-York State Liberty Convention, Held at Port Byron, on Wednesday and Thursday, July 25, and 26, 1845* (Albany: Patriot, [1845]).
3. "Call for a National Nominating Convention," reprinted in *Birney Letters*, II, 1047–1057.
4. *Address of the Macedon Convention by William Goodell; and Letters of Gerrit Smith* (Albany: S. W. Green, 1847).

settlers; inalienability of homesteads; abolition of the federal government's post office monopoly; cheap postage and abolition of franking privileges; and the exclusion of slaveholders from public offices.

After their decisive rebuff at the Buffalo Free Soil convention in August 1848, the Leaguers reorganized themselves as the "Liberty Party Abolitionists" and ran Smith as an abolitionist alternative to the Van Buren-Adams ticket. They made an insignificant showing, since only dedicated purists would throw away their vote as a gesture of protest against the shortcomings of Free Soil. The League resurfaced again in 1852 as the National Liberty party, when it ran, the shadow of a shadow, in opposition to the Free Democracy's candidate, John P. Hale.[5] After lackluster conventions at Buffalo (1851) and Syracuse (1852 and 1855), the group rejuvenated a little, reorganized itself as the Radical Political Abolitionists, a party, and the American Abolition Society, a reform organization and successor to the A&FA-SS. These tandem groups contained an unusual assortment of veteran abolitionists: Goodell, their chief propagandist and editor of the party's organ, the *Radical Abolitionist;* Frederick Douglass, editor of the *North Star,* organ of the National Liberty party in 1852; Lewis Tappan, along with Smith the chief financier of the movement, who had reluctantly and slowly been converted to political action out of a sense of the futility of nonparty groups like the A&FA-SS; black abolitionists James McCune Smith and Jermain W. Loguen; and Amos Dresser, one of the earliest and best-known victims of anti-abolitionist violence. Disheartened by the political stresses of the 1850s and by the covertly racist program of the Republicans, the radicals reorganized for one last try in 1860 as the Free Constitutionalists. Their pathetic objective—"to procure the defeat of the Republicans" which among the parties was "the most thoroughly senseless, baseless, aimless, inconsistent, and insincere"—was a measure of the frustrations of consistent and principled men.[6]

The radicals rejected the disunion and the de facto political quietism of the Garrisonians because both "seek to separate the free States from the slave States, and to leave the slave States, so far as concerns

5. Nomenclature is misleading here. Neither the Liberty Party Abolitionists of 1848 nor the National Liberty party of 1852 should be confused with the Liberty party, which went out of existence after its 1848 merger in the Free Soil party.

6. *Address of the Free Constitutionalists to the People of the United States* (Boston: Thayer & Eldridge, 1860), 53, 41.

the political power of the free States, at perfect liberty to continue their oppression and torture of the black man." "Dissolve the Union on this issue," they challenged the Garrisonians, "and you delude the people of the free States with the false notion that their responsibilities have ceased, though the slaves remain in bondage. Who shall stand up as deliverers, then?" They forthrightly rebutted the moral premise of the disunionist posture: "They sometimes demand of us whether we would maintain a political connection with robbers to put down robbery, and with adulterers to put down adultery? We readily answer them, yes. This is precisely the thing we are doing in respect to all crimes. Civil government is founded on this very idea."[7]

Radicals also rejected the allure of major-party politics because they believed that the true function of an antislavery political party was to hold aloft egalitarian principles, not to embrace halfway measures like the Wilmot Proviso. Nor were they any more satisfied with other limited objectives of moderate constitutionalism. "We are not merely warring against the extension of new slave territory," the Western Anti-Slavery Society insisted in 1851, "nor against any fugitive slave law constitutional or unconstitutional; nor for the writ of habeas corpus, or the right of trial by jury for recaptured slaves, but we are waging eternal war against the doctrine that man can ever under any possibility of circumstances, hold property in man."[8]

Some of the ideas of radical constitutionalism had been broached early in the nineteenth century. In 1806, John Parrish had claimed that "there is no just law to support [slavery]; it is against the essence of the Constitution," whose "leading features" were determined by the Declaration of Independence. Jesse Torrey in 1817 and James Duncan in 1824 had hinted at radical constitutional arguments based on concepts of the protection of the laws and republican government.[9] In 1837, Elizur Wright and an anonymous black abolitionist used

7. *Proceedings of the Convention of Radical Political Abolitionists, Held at Syracuse, N.Y., June 26th, 27th, and 28th, 1855: Slavery an Outlaw—And Forbidden by the Constitution, Which Provides for Its Abolition* (New York: Central Abolition Board, 1855), "call" of convention and pp. 42–43.

8. Quoted in Larry Gara, "Slavery and the Slave Power: A Crucial Distinction," *Civil War History*, 15 (1969), 5–18 at 5.

9. John Parrish, *Remarks on the Slavery of the Black People; Addressed to the Citizens of the United States, Particularly to Those Who Are in Legislative or Executive Stations in the General or State Governments . . .* (Philadelphia: Kimber, Conrad, 1806), 30–31; Torrey, *Portraiture of Domestic Slavery*, 59; Duncan, *Treatise on Slavery*, 30, 53.

due process arguments to condemn the federal Fugitive Slave Act of 1793.[10] At the same time, at the annual convention of the N-EA-SS, a range of radical opinion surfaced: William Goodell claimed vaguely that slavery was "unlawful"; Nathaniel Colver, a Massachusetts clerical abolitionist, argued that the Constitution did not recognize any right of slaveholding; and the Reverend Orange Scott went all the way: "The whole system of slavery is unconstitutional, null and void, and the time is coming when the Judges of the land will pronounce it so. So far from the Constitution authorizing or permitting slavery, it was established to guard life, liberty, and property."[11] The business committee of the Massachusetts Anti-Slavery Society in the next year fatuously urged southern slaves to petition Congress for a redress of their grievances, and, if they were unsuccessful, "then we will lend them our aid in bringing their cause before the [Supreme] court of the United States to ascertain if a man can be held in bondage agreeably to the principles contained in the Declaration of Independence of the Constitution of our country."[12]

But these tentative expressions were not representative of the thinking of those who were to become radicals. Gerrit Smith bespoke their orthodoxy on the federal consensus when he wrote New York's Governor William Marcy early in 1836, affirming categorically that "the federal constitution, by which we are bound, . . . leaves 'the right to abolish slavery where only it could be safely left; with the respective states, wherein slavery existed.' We are glad, that this right belongs exclusively to those states; and the abolitionists do not meditate the least encroachment on it."[13]

This orthodox position was first challenged by two unlikely figures, Samuel J. May and Nathaniel P. Rogers—unlikely because both became Garrisonians for a time after the schism, and Garrisonian thought was the inveterate enemy of radical constitutionalism. May and Rogers published articles in the *Quarterly Anti-Slavery Magazine*

10. *Fourth Annual Report of the American Anti-Slavery Society,* 116–117; an excerpt from the black abolitionist's essay, first printed in the *Colored American,* was reprinted in *Friend of Man,* 23 Aug. 1837.
11. *Proceedings of the Fourth New England Anti-Slavery Convention, Held in Boston, . . . 1837* (Boston: Isaac Knapp, 1837), 79, 17, 18.
12. The committee's resolution is quoted in Tuckerman, *William Jay,* 86.
13. Smith to Gov. William Marcy, 14 Jan. 1836, printed in New Richmond *Philanthropist,* 26 Feb. 1836.

in 1836 and 1837 that contained several elements of radical theory.[14] May agreed with Charles Olcott, an Ohio protoradical, that the Constitution did not establish slavery, but simply ignored it or left it alone.[15] Such a position was still compatible with the federal consensus, since it left the legitimacy of slavery to be determined by the states. Even Alvan Stewart at the time maintained that the Constitution was "neutral" as to slavery or that "it leans many degrees in favor of liberty, and against slavery as a system."[16] But the pattern of thinking in May's, Olcott's, and Stewart's writing represented a trajectory away from the federal consensus, a trajectory best described by Lewis Tappan in 1844: "Not long since almost every person supposed the C[onstitution] of the U.S. guaranteed slavery. Now most men believe it merely permits it, while an increasing number are persuaded that the Constitution is altogether an anti-slavery document, and will put an end to American slavery."[17] Rogers, in his article "The Constitution," and in an earlier speech to the New Hampshire Anti-Slavery Society,[18] went considerably further, concluding that slaveholding "is contrary to the Constitution of the United States." This conclusion might have been startling at the time (1837) had it not been for the rhetorical tone of Rogers' argument, which merely iterated conclusions with little analysis or supportive reasoning.

The Rogers and May pieces went unnoticed in the national antislavery press, partly because of a more sensational event in 1837: Alvan Stewart's open repudiation of the federal consensus. On 20 September 1837, in a speech before the second annual meeting of the

14. Samuel J. May, "Slavery and the Constitution, *Quarterly Anti-Slavery Mag.,* 2 (1836–1837), 73–90, 226–238; Nathaniel P. Rogers, "The Constitution," *ibid.,* 145–153.

15. Charles Olcott, *Two Lectures on the Subjects of Slavery and Abolition, Compiled for the Special Use of Anti-Slavery Lecturers and Debaters . . .* (Massillon, Ohio: for the author, 1838), 78; see also editorial, presumably by Birney, in New Richmond *Philanthropist,* 4 March 1836; Elizur Wright's "Report" for the AA-SS Executive Committee in *First Annual Report of the American Anti-Slavery Society . . . 1834 . . .* (New York: Dorr & Butterfield, 1834), 58.

16. Stewart, "Response to the Message of Gov. Marcy" (1836), and Stewart to Lewis Tappan, 11 Feb. 1836, in Marsh, ed., *Writings of Stewart,* 76, 19; speech to Rochester, New York antislavery convention, 10-12 Jan. 1838, in *Friend of Man,* 31 Jan. 1838.

17. Tappan to William Jay, 11 Oct. 1844, Lewis Tappan Papers, LC.

18. "Speech of N. P. Rogers, Esq. Before the N.H. Anti-Slavery Society," *Emancipator,* 30 June 1836.

NYSA-SS, Stewart shocked the entire movement by arguing that the due process clause of the Fifth Amendment empowered the federal government to abolish slavery in the states. This speech marked the dramatic debut of radical antislavery constitutionalism. Stewart published his argument a month later as "A Constitutional Argument on the Subject of Slavery,"[19] and then carried his argument to its logically necessary conclusion by moving that the AA-SS, at its fifth annual meeting (1838), delete from its constitution the clause affirming the society's adhesion to the federal consensus.

Both Garrisonian and orthodox political-action abolitionists denounced Stewart's innovation. An incensed William Jay demanded that he be drummed out of the AA-SS for "this vile heresy."[20] Birney condemned Stewart's argument at the 1837 NYSA-SS meeting,[21] and he was joined by Jay, Loring, Wendell Phillips, Wright, and Leavitt at the AA-SS meeting in 1838, who presented a wide array of substantive and tactical objections to the due process arguments.[22] In spite of this denunciation, Stewart thought he had won an "immense victory" at the AA-SS.[23] In reality, he had not, at least not in the short run. Though he secured a majority for his repeal motion at the AA-SS meeting, it fell short of the two-thirds necessary to amend the Society's constitution, and the AA-SS affirmance of the federal consensus remained intact. From their different perspectives, William Jay, Gamaliel Bailey, and Wendell Phillips then issued long written rejoinders to Stewart's argument, insisting that Stewart had given the due process clause an unwarranted extrapolation.[24]

19. *Friend of Man*, 18 Oct. 1837, conveniently reprinted in tenBroek, *Equal under Law*, Appendix B, 281–295. Portions of this address not contemporaneously reported were printed in *Emancipator*, 17 May 1838. All citations to this speech below will be to an abbreviated form of its *Friend of Man* caption: Stewart, "A Constitutional Argument," with page citations to *Equal under Law*.

20. Jay to: Elizur Wright, 13 April 1838 (quoted); Joshua Leavitt, 13 March 1838; Lewis Tappan, 28 March 1838; E. G. Loring, 29 March 1838; Abel Libolt, 28 Jan. 1839; A. H. Williams et al., 17 April 1840; all in John Jay MSS., Columbia University.

21. *Emancipator*, 7 June 1838.

22. "The Constitutional Debate" summarizes their arguments in *Emancipator*, 17 May 1838.

23. Stewart to wife, 7 May 1838, in Alvan Stewart Papers, New York State Historical Association, Cooperstown.

24. See "Judge Jay's Examination" and "Remarks of Wendell Phillips, Esq. on the Same Subject," in *Friend of Man*, 13 June 1838. Bailey's arguments are in Cincinnati *Philanthropist*, 22 May 1838, 30 April 1839, 10 Dec. 1839.

In the same year (1838) that Stewart's effort to amend the AA-SS constitution failed, Weld brought out his *Power of Congress over the District of Columbia,* which, though limited to a moderate objective (abolition in the District) contained arguments of much wider applicability that were better grounded in history and legal precedent than Stewart's argument. Henry B. Stanton at the next annual meeting of the AA-SS reversed Weld's procedure, seeking a radical end, total and immediate abolition, by a moderate mode, amendment of the federal Constitution: as "a dernier resort we will alter the Constitution and bring slavery in the States within the range of federal legislation, and then annihilate it at a blow."[25]

In 1841, George W. F. Mellen published *An Argument on the Unconstitutionality of Slavery,* the first book-length exposition of the radical argument.[26] Despite its chronological priority, Mellen's work was not particularly significant, and was seldom cited by other radicals, partly because Mellen was an embarrassment to more conventional abolitionists. He was flamboyantly eccentric, if not mad. Mellen was a namesake of George Washington, and at times thought he *was* Washington. Accordingly, he appeared at antislavery conventions dressed in the military uniform of the Revolution.[27] Impressed by the fact that his grandfather, a Revolutionary-era congressman, had emancipated his slaves, Mellen reinvestigated the federal and state constitutional and ratifying conventions to prove that slavery was established in the southern states in contravention of the federal Constitution. His book was an unsuccessful attempt to neutralize the impact of the Madison Papers.

The banner years for radical constitutionalism were 1844 and 1845; within a few months of each other there appeared three comprehensive arguments denying the legitimacy of slavery in the states. First was Alvan Stewart's "New Jersey argument" wherein he put his 1837 theory to practical application in a freedom suit. New Jersey in 1804 and 1820 had enacted *post-nati* emancipation statutes, by

25. Speech of Henry B. Stanton, 7 May 1839, reported in *Sixth Annual Report of the . . . American Anti-Slavery Society . . .* (New York: William S. Dorr, 1839), 16; see also "Ohio and a National Convention," Cincinnati *Philanthropist,* 1 March 1842.

26. G. W. F. Mellen, *An Argument on the Unconstitutionality of Slavery, Embracing an Abstract of the Proceedings of the National and State Conventions on This Subject* (Boston: Saxton & Pierce, 1841).

27. Henry B. Stanton, *Random Recollections* (New York: Harper, 1887), 70.

which all persons born slaves before 4 July 1804 would remain slaves for life, and all children born of such slaves after that date were free but were held as apprentices by their "owners," males till age twenty-five, females till twenty-one. In two companion cases, *State* v. *Van Buren* and *State* v. *Post* (1845),[28] Stewart and Jersey abolitionists sought writs of habeas corpus for a pre-1804 slave and a child of such a slave apprenticed to her master. They contended that the new state constitution of 1844 abolished slavery because it contained an "all-men-are-by-nature-free-and-independent" clause patterned after Article I of the 1776 Virginia Declaration of Rights and Article I of the 1780 Massachusetts Constitution.[29] For the first time, radical constitutionalism had been brought into a courtroom.[30]

Next came the publication of William Goodell's compendium, *Views of American Constitutional Law*.[31] Though disjointed in its organization, Goodell's volume was a synopsis of the radical argument. He elaborated on it in subsequent pamphlet, book, and newspaper writings, but his 1844 *Views* embodied the principal ideas of the radical constitutionalists, especially since Goodell remained at the center of their activities through 1860.

The third of the comprehensive radical arguments of 1844–1845 was the Massachusetts lawyer Lysander Spooner's *Unconstitutionality of Slavery*.[32] Even in a movement that attracted individualists and eccentrics, Spooner stood out.[33] His earliest publications dealt with free thought and postal reform, but he soon moved on to antislavery,

28. *State* v. *Post*, 20 N.J. Law 368 (1845). Stewart's effort was unsuccessful; the court, by a 3–1 vote (Hornblower, C. J., dissenting without opinion), held that the abstract propositions of the states' new Declaration of Rights did not derange the extant social or legal orders.

29. "Argument, On the Question Whether the New Constitution of 1844 [of New Jersey] Abolished Slavery in New Jersey," in Marsh, ed., *Writings of Stewart*, 272–367; henceforth cited: Stewart, "New Jersey Argument."

30. For a thoughtful reconsideration of this case from the viewpoint of the majority judges, see Cover, *Justice Accused*, 55–60.

31. William Goodell, *Views of American Constitutional Law, in Its Bearing upon American Slavery* (Utica: Jackson & Chaplin, 1844). A second and revised edition, which I have used here, was published in 1845 at Utica by Lawson & Chaplin.

32. Lysander Spooner, *The Unconstitutionality of Slavery* (1845). I used the 4th ed. (Boston: Bela Marsh, 1860). The first and second editions (the latter 1847) consisted only of what was called "Part I" in subsequent editions. The third (1853) and fourth (1860), contained a "Part II," which was an elaboration of some of the points made in Part I, and which seems to have been drafted in response to Wendell Phillips' *Review of Spooner*.

33. For estimates of his place in American reform, see Perry, *Radical*

and his long treatise was accepted as a text of radical constitutionalism. In reality, the views of Goodell and Stewart probably had a greater impact, but Spooner's lengthy, heavily annotated, well-organized study rivalled them in its influence. Spooner disseminated his tract widely among legislators in hopes that it would convert them to radical premises, but he had no success.[34]

Spooner supplemented his *Unconstitutionality of Slavery* with an anonymous article in the 1848 *Massachusetts Quarterly Review,* "Has Slavery in the United States a Legal Basis?"[35] and two years later produced a legalistic attack on the fugitive slave laws.[36] Relentlessly pursuing his ideas to their extreme logical conclusions, he next turned to the role of the common-law jury as a guarantor of individual liberty against the oppression of majorities and of the state, and argued that juries must be judges of both fact and law.[37] He defended John Brown after the Harpers Ferry raid, and after the war became a leading exponent of antistatist thought, second only to Josiah Warren in his influence on American anarchism.

The Macedon Convention and the formation of the Liberty League in 1847 further stimulated radical constitutionalist efforts. The Liberty League's presidential nominee, Gerrit Smith, restated radical constitutionalism as a political platform in a public challenge to the leader of the moderates, Salmon P. Chase.[38] Of more intellectual sub-

---

Abolitionism, 194–208; James J. Martin, *Men against the State: The Expositors of Individualist Anarchism in America, 1827–1908* (Colorado Springs: Myles, 1970), ch. vii; and A. John Alexander, "The Ideas of Lysander Spooner," *New Eng. Q.,* 23 (1950), 200–217.

34. Spooner to George Bradburn, 30 Jan. 1847, in Lysander Spooner Papers, N-YHS.

35. [Lysander Spooner], "Has Slavery in the United States a Legal Basis?" *Mass. Q. Rev.,* 1 (1848), 145–168, 274–293. These articles will henceforth be cited: [Spooner], "Legal Basis." The attribution to Spooner is made by Charles M. Haar, *The Golden Age of American Law* (New York: Braziller, 1965), 271. However, Merton L. Dillon, in *The Abolitionists: The Growth of a Dissenting Minority* (DeKalb: Northern Illinois Univ. Press, 1974), 217, attributes the articles to Richard Hildreth. For our purposes, it does not matter which of these attributions is correct.

36. Lysander Spooner, *A Defense for Fugitive Slaves, against the Acts of Congress of February 12, 1793 and September 18, 1850 . . .* (Boston: Bela Marsh, 1850).

37. Lysander Spooner, *An Essay on the Trial by Jury* (Boston: John P. Jewett, 1852).

38. *Letter of Gerrit Smith to S. P. Chase, on the Unconstitutionality of Every Part of American Slavery* (Albany: S. W. Green, 1847).

stance was a series of articles in the *Albany Patriot* in 1847 contributed by James G. Birney.[39] Birney was by then disillusioned with his former associates. Suspicious of the sort of expediential politics that was irresistible to the Liberty moderates, he worked out for himself anew the premises of radical constitutionalism. Finally, in 1849 Joel Tiffany, reporter of the New York Supreme Court and a lawyer raised in that extraordinary nursery of abolitionist and Radical Republican theorists, Lorain County, Ohio, rounded out the work of the radical systematizers with his *Treatise on the Unconstitutionality of Amercian Slavery.*[40]

Where the jurisprudential base of Garrisonian thought had been positivism, the foundation of radical constitutionalism was its opposite: an emphasis on the legally binding force of natural law. Quoting Blackstone, who had naturalized this semitheological concept into English law, radicals claimed that "this law of nature, being coeval with mankind, and dictated by God himself, is, of course, superior in obligation to any other. It is binding all over the globe, in all countries, and at all times. No human laws are of any validity, if contrary to this. And such of them as are valid, derive all their force, and all their authority mediately or immediately, from this original."[41] In a more secular form, natural law inhered in "natural justice," "men's natural rights," "natural principles of right," "human conscience," or "principles existing in the nature of things."[42]

Radicals converted the moral "ought" directly to the legal "must"

39. James G. Birney, "Can Congress, under the Constitution, Abolish Slavery in the States?" *Albany Patriot,* 12, 19, 20, 22 May 1847, reprinted in tenBroek, *Equal under Law,* app. C., 296–319. All citations to this series below will be in this form: Birney, "Can Congress," with the page citation being to tenBroek, *Equal under Law.*

40. Joel Tiffany, *A Treatise on the Unconstitutionality of American Slavery; Together with the Powers and Duties of Federal Government in Relation to that Subject* (Cleveland: J. Calyer, 1849).

41. Blackstone, *Commentaries,* I, *41. Among those citing this passage are: Tiffany, *Treatise,* 23; Spooner, *Unconstitutionality,* 16; William Goodell, "The American Jubilee," broadside prospectus [1854] in Birney Papers, Clements Library, Univ. of Michigan.

42. Gerrit Smith, *Substance of the Speech Made by Gerrit Smith, in the Capitol of the State of New York . . .* (Albany: Jacob T. Hazen, 1850), 4 (hereinafter cited: Smith, *Constitutional Argument,* which was its cover title); Spooner, *Unconstitutionality,* 6; [Spooner], "Legal Basis," 146; Goodell, *Views,* 151; Theodore Parker, *A Sermon on the Dangers Which Threaten the Rights of Man in America . . .* (1854: rpt. Boston: Old South Leaflets, n.d.); Weld, *Power of Congress,* 3.

because natural law, whether embodied in secular or religious form, was of anterior and superior obligation to manmade law. As such, it was both the source of individual human rights and a limitation on the powers of government. Governments existed to secure individual liberty; no government could deprive men of liberty, security, and property (a Blackstonian triad), nor permit other men to do so. Hence any governmental act infringing human liberty was ipso facto void, of no obligation, and incapable of being legitimated.[43] Radicals rejected Garrisonian positivism as a standard of legitimacy because it grounded law in force, whereas to the radicals conventional law had to be measured against a superior gauge of morality and justice.[44] Reversing Phillips' criticism of their natural-law position, Spooner and Goodell insisted that it was conventional law that was unstable, dependent as it was on the changing whims of whoever happened to be in power. According to a common law maxim, *jura naturae sunt immutabilia,* it was the laws of nature that were stable, unchanging, universal, and certain.[45]

The radicals' natural-law emphasis was not an alien graft on American constitutionalism.[46] Justice Samuel Chase had acclimated it in his *Calder* v. *Bull* opinion (1798),[47] and Chief Justice Marshall reiterated it in *Fletcher* v. *Peck* (1810), where he voided a state statute both because it conflicted with a specific clause of the federal Constitution and because it was contrary to "general principles which are common to our free institutions."[48] Story echoed Marshall im-

43. Speech of Myron Holley, 28 Feb. 1839 at Penn Yan, N.Y., antislavery convention, reported in *Friend of Man,* 3 April 1839; [William Goodell], *The Constitutional Duty of the Federal Government to Abolish American Slavery: An Expose of the Position of the [American] Abolition Society* (New York: American Abolition Society, 1856), 3; Birney, "Can Congress," 310; Samuel J. May, *Speech . . . to the Convention of Citizens, of Onondaga County . . . 1851 . . .* (Syracuse: Agan & Summers, 1851), 18.
44. Leonard Bacon, *The Higher Law. A Sermon, Preached on Thanksgiving Day, November 27, 1851* (New Haven: B. L. Hamlen, 1851), 8.
45. Spooner, *Unconstitutionality,* 6, 137–146; Goodell, *Views,* 100.
46. Edward S. Corwin, "The Basic Doctrine of American Constitutional Law," *Mich. L. Rev.,* 12 (1914), 247–276; Ferenc M. Szasz, "Antebellum Appeals to the 'Higher Law', 1830–1860," Essex Institute *Historical Collections,* 110 (1974), 33–48.
47. For the text of this opinion, see Appendix 1; see also Justice William Paterson's Circuit Court opinion in *Van Horne's Lessee* v. *Dorrance,* 2 Dall. 304 (C.C.D.Pa. 1795).
48. 6 Cranch (10 U.S.) 87 (1810) at 139.

plicitly in *Terrett* v. *Taylor* (1815) and explicitly in *Wilkinson* v. *Leland* (1829),[49] though Marshall had abandoned the natural-law branch of his argument in *Dartmouth College* v. *Woodward* (1819).[50] Natural-law principles were vigorously applied by state court judges in the next generation and were reabsorbed into U.S. Supreme Court thinking by Taney's *Dred Scott* opinion in 1857, whence they passed on, via the due process clause, into modern constitutional discourse in the late nineteenth century. In the 1840s, radicals, like contemporary conservative judges on the state benches, were attuned to the judicial formulation of natural-law doctrine, and cited *Calder* v. *Bull* to support limitations on the power of all governments to interfere with individual liberty.

Natural law was not the only source of higher law. The common law also embodied its principles, and constituted another limitation on the power of states to authorize enslavement. "The common law is the grand element in the United States Constitution," Weld argued; "all its fundamental provisions are instinct with its spirit." "Its principles annihilate slavery wherever they touch it. It is a universal unconditional abolition act."[51] Radicals recurred to Mansfield's *Somerset* opinion, which they considered to be the definitive exposition of the common law as it pertained to slavery. They maintained that *Somerset* had held slavery to be incompatible with the common law, and had sanctioned legal mechanisms—habeas corpus and, in the United States, jury trial and homine replegiando—by which individuals could secure judicial protection of their liberty.[52]

The impact of *Somerset* was not spent in the metropolis; it extended to the colonies as well. If the common law was the basis for the colonial constitutions and legal order, and if slavery was void

---

49. 9 Cranch (11 U.S.) 43 (1815) and 2 Pet. (27 U.S.) 627 (1829), respectively. See also Johnson and Graham's Lessee v. M'Intosh, 8 Wheat. (21 U.S.) 543 (1823) at 572.

50. 4 Wheat. (17 U.S.) 518 (1819).

51. Weld, *Power of Congress*, 13; *Remarks of Henry B. Stanton . . . before the Committee of the House of Representatives of Massachusetts . . .* (Boston: Isaac Knapp, 1837), 11; Goodell, *Views*, 97–102; [Spooner], "Legal Basis," 164–167.

52. "An American Citizen" [Jesse Chickering], *Letter Addressed to the President of the United States on Slavery, Considered in relation to the Constitutional Principles of Government in Great Britain and the United States* (Boston: Redding & Co., 1855), 1; Spooner, *Unconstitutionality*, 23, 27–28; Stewart, "New Jersey Argument," 295.

under the common law of the metropolis, then it followed that it was just as invalid in the colonies. Here radicals recurred to Sharp and one of his favorite common-law maxims, *debile fundamentum, fallit opus.*[53] To Sharp, this maxim had meant that slavery's illegitimate origins in force had destroyed the structure of laws that supposedly supported it. To his American disciples, however, the *fundamentum* was the legitimacy of slavery in the colonies under the common law, and the *opus* was the legal structure of black codes that maintained slavery.

Another variant of the common-law argument derived from the provisions found in the charters of all the colonies stating that the power of the colonial legislatures did not extend to enacting laws repugnant to the law of England. Seizing on these repugnancy clauses, the radicals claimed that the colonial-era black codes could not have created slavery in America because slavery was repugnant to the common law. Moreover, the colonies constitutions had embedded in them guarantees of English liberty (jury trial, habeas corpus) that Americans claimed as their constitutional birthright, and slavery was blighted by these too.[54]

To radicals, only some absolutely explicit statute, such as the hypothetical suggested by Justice John McLean, "And be it enacted that slavery shall exist," could have been the positive law that Mansfield had said was necessary to the establishment of slavery.[55] But no such law had ever been enacted; at most, the colonial black codes had merely recognized the existence of slavery in society, somewhat in the way that laws taxing alcoholic beverages recognized the use of liquor. Hence even a constricted and conservative reading of *Somerset* delegitimated slavery, and rendered it "sheer usurpation and abuse, from beginning to end; a nuisance, demanding judicial (not to say legislative) removal. Every slave held in America is unlawfully held, and in defiance of American Constitutional Law.[56]

53. Loosely, "the foundation being weak, the superstructure collapses."

54. Richard Hildreth, *Despotism in America; An Inquiry into the Nature, Results, and Legal Basis of the Slave-Holding System in the United States* (Boston: John P. Jewett, 1854), 203 (this book was originally published in 1840 under a slightly different title); Spooner, *Unconstitutionality,* 21; *Address of the Free Constitutionalists,* 17–19.

55. McLean suggested this hypothetical only to reject the argument summarized in text: *Miller v. McQuerry,* 17 Fed. Cas. 335 (No. 9583) (C.C.D.-Ohio 1853). He stated that immemorial custom provided the requisite positive-law basis.

56. Goodell, *Views,* 101 (quotation); Goodell, *Constitutional Duty,* 4–6;

When radicals turned from abstract theory to the Constitution itself, they immediately confronted an inconvenient obstacle: the Madison Papers, which seemed to be incontrovertible proof of the proslavery intentions of the framers. To get around this, radicals turned to common-law maxims for rules of construction that might provide a way through the less clear places in the Constitution. Spooner was the leading exponent of this method, and he devoted whole chapters of his *Unconstitutionality of Slavery* to exegetical ground rules.

Spooner and others suggested these rules of interpretation: construe the document by "the prevailing spirit, the general scope, the leading design, the paramount object, the obvious purpose" of the instrument; resolve ambiguities in favor of liberty and justice; do not construe words so as to give effect to fraud or injustice; look to "the general common established meaning of the words used, in a dictionary, or other works where the true signification of the words may be found." This last rule was particularly important because the words "slave" and "slavery" do not appear in the document.[57]

Thus armed, the radicals were ready to tackle the difficult question of the framers' intentions. They insisted above all that these intentions be gleaned from the words of the document themselves, taken in their literal meaning. "Extraneous" historical evidence (i.e. the Madison Papers) they dismissed as "worthless" or at least as insufficient to overthrow the literal meaning of the text.[58] This, however, was not enough to neutralize the impact of the Madison Papers, and some radicals fell back on a conspiracy theory to explain how the proslavery intent of the framers could have been so imperfectly realized by the ambiguous language they used. They "chose rather to trust to their craft and influence to corrupt the government . . . after the constitution should have been adopted, rather than ask the necessary authority [to establish slavery] directly from the people." The Con-

Spooner, *Unconstitutionality*, 32; resolutions offered by Goodell at 1859 Church Anti-Slavery Society convention in *Proceedings of the Convention Which Met at Worcester* . . . (New York: John F. Trow, 1859), 26.

57. Spooner, *Unconstitutionality*, 44, 157–205; Tiffany, *Treatise*, 47–48; Goodell, *Views*, 81.

58. Spooner, *Unconstitutionality*, 58, 62, 123–124; Tiffany, *Treatise*, 46, 50; Theodore Parker, *The Relation of Slavery to a Republican Form of Government: A Speech Delivered at the New England Anti-Slavery Convention* . . . (Boston: Kent, 1858), 11; Stewart, "New Jersey Argument" and letter to Liberty Party (1847), in Marsh, ed., *Writings of Stewart*, 334, 43.

264   *Antislavery Constitutionalism*

stitution, Goodell maintained, had an intrinsically "honest character" that the framers perverted after ratification.[59]

But this conspiracy explanation did not satisfy radicals either. Most of the framers, after all, were on record as having mild antislavery sentiments, so the radicals tried to reconcile these with the words of the Constitution. This was the focus of Mellen's work, the first radical treatise to appear. The benign reinterpretation of the framers' intent began with their known desire to establish liberty for themselves and their posterity. According to the radicals, they viewed slavery as an anomaly, an obsolete retrograde system inconsistent with the empire of liberty they had established. The framers expected slavery to pass away shortly, hastened toward its end by moral pressure and state political action. They chose their circumlocutions carefully to avoid any inference that the Constitution secured slavery, and even inserted into the Constitution numerous provisions that might in time insure its demise.[60]

Having thus partially exculpated the framers, the radicals could then get on with construing their handiwork. They began with the Declaration of Independence and comparable Bill of Rights provisions in the state constitutions. Was it literally a self-evident truth that all men are born free and equal? Or were there implicit exceptions for black people, women, aliens, and others? Americans would be forced anew to determine what their republic was to be; they would have to rediscover themselves.

Before 1840, Americans viewed the Declaration as being rhetorical or hortatory, rather than as a substantive and operative component of the constitution. Radicals, on the other hand, insisted that it was *the* constitution until 1782, when the Articles of Confederation were ratified, or at least that its principles were "the basis of the Constitution."[61] So elemental was the Declaration that compared to it the Constitution was but "the mere outward form, the minutely

59. Spooner, *Unconstitutionality*, 119; Goodell, *Address of the Free Constitutionalists*, 14.
60. Mellen, *Argument*, 61, 129, 125, ch. 2 *passim*; Tiffany, *Treatise*, 9, 18–19; "Sixty Years Since," *Friend of Man*, 11 April 1838.
61. "A Constitutional Argument," *Emancipator*, 4 Jan. 1838; James P. Miller, *The Constitution & Slavery: A Lecture . . . in Which the Question "Does the Constitution Sanction Slavery?" Is Investigated* (Albany: Graves & Herrick, 1844), 2–8; Spooner, *Unconstitutionality*, 36–37; Smith, *Constitutional Argument*, 9.

detailed provisions . . . the instrument, of which those principles [of the Declaration] are the living spirit and substance. To accept [the Constitution] as a substitute for the [Declaration] . . . would be to accept of the shell, and throw the kernel away,—to idolize the instrument and spurn the blessings it was intended to procure for us."[62] The Declaration overrode all inferior laws, including statutory enactments, court decisions, and inconsistent provisions in the federal and state constitutions. It was of its own force an act of abolition.[63] As both a source of principles and as substantive constitutional law, the Declaration supplemented natural law as a limitation on the power of government and a guarantor of individual liberty.[64]

Radicals then scrutinized the Constitution for documentary proof that slavery was illegitimate. By 1864, their search was so successful that William Goodell's annotated text of the Constitution, *Our National Charters,* listed almost half its clauses as actually or potentially antislavery.[65] They relied primarily, though, on three sources: the due process clause of the Fifth Amendment, the privileges and immunities clause, and the guarantee clause.

Alvan Stewart was the chief architect of antislavery due process. His interpretation transformed the clause in two ways. First, he insisted that it was a limitation on state, as well as federal power; and second, he gave it a substantive, rather than procedural, reading. Stewart began with the orthodox procedural interpretation of the clause in Joseph Story's *Commentaries on the Constitution,* which held the clause to be

but an enlargement of the language of Magna Charta . . . (neither will we pass upon him, or condemn him, but by the lawful judgment of his peers, or by the law of the land.) Lord Coke says that these latter words "per legem terrae" (by the law of the land), mean by due process of law, that is, without [sic] due presentment or indictment, and being brought in

62. Goodell, *Views,* 138.
63. [Goodell], *Address Read at the New-York State Liberty Convention, Held at Port Byron,* 6; [Goodell], *Constitutional Duty,* 6.
64. Tiffany, *Treatise,* 9–10, 29; Stewart, "Report of a Speech Delivered before a Joint Committee of the Vermont Legislature," and "Address to the Abolitionists of the State of New York," in Marsh, ed., *Writings of Alvan Stewart,* 177, 86–107 respectively.
65. William Goodell, *Our National Charters: For the Millions* . . . (New York: J. W. Alden, 1864).

to answer thereto, by due process of the common law. So that this clause, in effect, affirms the right of trial according to process and proceedings of common law.[66]

But in his 1837 "Constitutional Argument," and in the New Jersey argument of 1844,[67] Stewart blurred the distinction, so familiar to American lawyers, between procedural and substantive due process. In Stewart's hands, the distinction became meaningless (as, indeed, it intrinsically is) because procedure shaded off imperceptibly into substance. If a person had a procedural right not to be enslaved unless he was held to be a slave under the traditional forms of common-law criminal proceedings, that right could itself be enforceable as a substantive one. Stewart therefore concluded that no person anywhere in the United States was constitutionally enslaved because none had been declared to be a slave in common-law proceedings, and all had a substantive right to liberty.

In its time, Stewart's due process argument was fatally defective in three ways. First, he accounted for the presence of the due process clause in the Constitution by a benevolent conspiracy theory: the framers supposedly felt obliged to counterbalance their concessions to slavery by insisting that the victims of those concessions be only those who were held to be slaves by due process of law. When Stewart first made his due process arguments in 1837, he labored under the handicap of not having access to Madison's notes, which were not published for another three years, so this argument was not at first as preposterous as it later appeared. Second, he made the incredible error of assuming that the due process clause was drawn up at the Philadelphia convention of 1787! Nowhere in his later arguments did he repudiate this. This may have been a lapse attributable to zeal, but it did his reputation as a lawyer no credit. Third, Stewart ignored the doctrine enunciated by the United States Supreme Court in *Barron* v. *Baltimore* (1833), which held the first eight amendments to the federal Constitution inapplicable as restraints on the states.[68] Stewart was swimming upstream against the current of a nearly unanimous understanding that the Fifth Amendment did not bind the states.

66. Joseph Story, *Commentaries on the Constitution of the United States,* 4th ed. (Boston: Little, Brown, 1873), §1789.
67. Stewart, "A Constitutional Argument," 284–285; Stewart, "New Jersey Argument," 331, 345–346.
68. 7 Pet. (32 U.S.) 243 (1833); reaffirmed in *Permoli* v. *First Municipality of New Orleans,* 3 How. (44 U.S.) 589 (1845).

Yet Stewart's due process argument may not have been quite the folly that the foregoing suggests. For one thing, he may have been understandably unaware of the existence of the *Barron* precedent. At that time, it was not unusual or discreditable for attorneys to lack the means for familiarity with the holdings of distant courts that the modern lawyer enjoys thanks to twentieth-century innovations in legal communications like advance sheets, loose-leaf and pocket supplements, and the Shepards service. If Stewart was ignorant of *Barron,* he was in good company. The Illinois Supreme Court in 1846 considered the due process clause of the Fifth Amendment to be binding on the states.[69] In the same year as the *Barron* decision, Henry Baldwin, one of the justices of the United States Supreme Court that handed down that unanimous decision, sitting on circuit, felt himself bound by another provision of the Bill of Rights (the First Amendment religion clauses) in interpreting state law.[70]

Alternatively, Stewart and other radicals who used the due process clause may have been aware of *Barron* and may have chosen to repudiate it as bad law. Gerrit Smith did so explicitly in 1850, claiming that the Court was wrong and that only the First, Ninth, and Tenth Amendments were exclusively restrictions on federal power.[71] The other amendments (Two through Eight), he argued, were restraints on both the states and the federal government. Smith's argument had two plausible bases: the language of the amendments (only One and Ten are by their phrasing related to federal authority), and the history of the period of their adoption. His historical understanding may have been better than the Supreme Court's; the framers of the Amendments did seem at times to be thinking of inherent limitations on all governmental power or of universal safeguards for individual liberty. Amendments Two through Ten are written in the passive voice, leaving open the syntactical possibility that they were universally applicable.[72]

The second basis of radical constitutionalism was a conglomeration

69. *Rhinehart* v. *Schuyler,* 7 Ill. 473 (1846) at 522.
70. *Magill* v. *Brown,* 16 Fed. Cas. 408 (No. 8952) (C.C.E.D.Pa. 1833) at 427.
71. Smith, *Constitutional Argument,* appendix.
72. Cp. William W. Crosskey, *Politics and the Constitution in the History of the United States* (Chicago: Univ. of Chicago Press, 1953), 1056–1081, with Charles Fairman, "The Supreme Court and the Constitutional Limitations on State Governmental Authority," *U. Chi. L. Rev.,* 21 (1953), 40–78.

of concepts: protection of law, equality of status, and the privileges and immunities of citizenship. Its doctrinal source was the privilege and immunities clause. The second Missouri crisis, *Corfield* v. *Coryell,* and the Prudence Crandall controversy provided radicals with an ample fund of ideas on which to draw in their effort to secure for both free and enslaved blacks the rights that whites enjoyed. But none of these aboriginal civil rights controversies had established a definitive meaning for the privileges and immunities clause, and the field beckoned invitingly to radicals.

"A Constitution springs from our weakness and need of protection," Stewart argued in the New Jersey case, "and is a covenant of the whole people with each person, and of each person with the whole people, for the protection and defence of our natural rights, of life, liberty, and the pursuit of happiness." He bundled together the objects of government as set forth in the Preamble to the United States Constitution, the natural rights theory, and the concept of protection by law.[73] Radicals agreed that "allegiance and protection are inseparable" and that since slaves owed allegiance to the government that compelled their obedience, "protection is the constitutional right of every human being."[74] In claiming protection for all men, the radicals were attuned to jurisprudential values that dominated their time. The nineteenth-century American legal order placed a high premium on the creative capacity of the individual and protected him in his exercise of it.[75] Illinois abolitionists bespoke the spirit of the age when they declared that "the great end of all systems of legislation" is "to aid each individual member of society to gain the great end of his being, in accordance with the laws of his nature, and to maintain and defend those rights which are essential to enable him to do so."[76] This could only be done if the law provided equal opportunity to all men to realize their creative capacities.

The concept of equal protection aimed at securing blacks' "civil rights" in the nineteenth-century sense of that phrase: the right to

73. Stewart, "New Jersey Argument," 339.
74. Birney, "Can Congress," 317; Weld, *Power of Congress,* 42; William Yates, *Rights of Colored Men to Suffrage, Citizenship, and Trial by Jury . . .* (Philadelphia: Merrihew & Gunn, 1838), 37.
75. James Willard Hurst, *Law and the Conditions of Freedom in the Nineteenth-Century United States* (Madison: Univ. of Wisconsin Press, 1967), ch. 1.
76. Illinois State Anti-Slavery Society, Minute Book, 22, Chicago Historical Society.

own property, marry, move about, not be commanded by a master, etc. Eventually, though, radicals recognized that their egalitarian logic compelled them to accord full political rights—the vote—as well, and they did not flinch from this position, despite the violent opposition they knew it would arouse. Goodell's Port Byron address of 1845 frankly stated that the right to vote was protected under the privileges and immunities clause, and Smith, as Liberty League candidate of 1848, saw the ballot as a right equivalent with rights of social equality "in the school, or the house of worship, or elsewhere."[77]

When radicals atempted to tie down their vague concepts of equality and protection to a specific clause, the privileges and immunities clause seemed the most likely candidate, and Joel Tiffany became its prime exegete. In order to make this work, however, Tiffany and others first had to demonstrate that slaves were citizens in the terms of the clause, and then to demonstrate that equal protection was one of the rights of citizenship. They did this by construing the word "citizen" as it was used the second time in the clause as having the implicit qualification "of the United States," so that slaves enjoyed a national citizenship by reason of their American nativity.[78]

This was a strained argument, even for the radicals, and it exposed a weakness inherent in the clause. The clause cut both ways, and could work against the abolitionist position as well as for it. For example, a free New York black seaman imprisoned in Charleston under the Negro Seamen's Acts had no right to complain under the clause, because he was treated just as South Carolina would treat any of its own free black "citizens" suspected of inciting disaffection among slaves and other blacks. These considerations suggested that the tangled, obscure, and difficult question of citizenship would be a weak reed for abolitionists to lean on, and encouraged them to rely instead on the third of their major arguments against slavery in the states, the guarantee clause.

Article IV, section 4, of the Constitution contains the enigmatic provision: "The United States shall guarantee to every State in this

77. Goodell, *Address Read at the New-York State Liberty Convention*, 7; Gerrit Smith to L. K. Ingalls, 15 Aug. 1848, (broadside) in Birney Papers, vol. 18, Clements Library, Univ. of Michigan.

78. Tiffany, *Treatise*, 57, 92, and ch. 12 *passim*.

Union a Republican Form of Government." Again sensing possibilities in textual ambiguity, radicals read into the vague phrases of the
clause a command that the federal government abolish slavery in
the states.[79] They devoted most of their attention to defining "a
republican form of government." Such a government, they argued,
was one dedicated to the ideals of the Declaration of Independence,
"that authenticated definition of a republican form of Government."[80]
In a republican government, all men must be secure in the enjoyment
of their rights to life, liberty, property. "The very pith and essence
of a republican government . . . [is] the protection and security of
those rights."[81] The guarantee clause incorporated the whole scope
of natural rights, the ideals of the Declaration, and the objectives of
the Preamble.

Radicals referred to Madison's classical definition of a republic in
Federalist Number 39:

> a government which derives all its powers directly or indirectly from the
> great body of the people. . . . It is essential to such a government, that
> it be derived from the great body of the society, not from an inconsider-
> able proportion, or a favored class of it.[82]

From this statement they inferred that a government had to be
majoritarian, in the sense that the whole people constituted the basis
of society, not a "favored class" of slaveholders who held a large
minority in bondage. The principle of popular self-government inherent in the majoritarian idea was violated by enslavement.[83]
Radicals also drew on an even older tradition that lay behind the
origins of the guarantee clause in 1786–1787: an observation in

79. See generally Wiecek, *Guarantee Clause*, chs. 3–5.
80. William Goodell, *The Rights and the Wrongs of Rhode Island; Com-
prising Views of Liberty and Law, of Religion and Rights, as Exhibited in the
Recent and Existing Difficulties in That State* . . . (Whitesboro, N.Y.,
Christian Investigator No. 8, 1842), 27.
81. Goodell, *Views*, 39, 49 (quotation); Stewart, Letter to [Gamaliel]
Bailey, April 1842, in Marsh, ed., *Writings of Stewart*, 268; Stewart, "New
Jersey Argument," 336, 345; Smith, "To the Friends of the Slave in the Town
of Smithfield" (1844, broadside) in Gerrit Smith Collection, New York State
Historical Association, Cooperstown; Theodore Parker, *The Relation of Slavery
to a Republican Form of Government* . . . (Boston: William L. Kent, 1858),
8–14.
82. *The Federalist*, Number 39, 251.
83. Goodell, *Our National Charters*, 62–65; Goodell, *Views*, 46–57; Mellen,
Argument, 87; "Address of the Liberty Party Convention, Held at Peter-
boro . . . ," *Emancipator and Free American*, 10 March 1842.

Montesquieu's *Spirit of the Laws* that in a republican federation, all constituent members must be republican, lest an aristocratic or monarchic member overthrow the free institutions of the others. This seemed to foretell exactly the policies of the governments of the southern states. It further implied a power in the central authority to control the social institutions and internal policies of the states to check antirepublican tendencies.[84] The verb "guarantee" was a plenary grant of power, and the phrase "the United States" was a clear designation of who should exercise it.

Radicals found power to abolish slavery in the states in lesser clauses, too. The common defence and general welfare clause was violated by an institution that depressed the welfare of all classes and endangered the United States in time of war.[85] A nonabolitionist, John Quincy Adams, had argued that Congress' war power might be used to liberate slaves, and radicals improved on this idea by suggesting both war- and peacetime modes for incorporating blacks into the army and militias or for liberating slaves in a theater of military operations.[86] Radicals saw the commerce clause as a means of expanding federal power over the states, presciently anticipating one of the most expansive sources of federal power in the twentieth century.[87] They argued that Congress' power over interstate commerce was plenary, and read the 1808 clause as confirming commerce power over the slave trade by a negative pregnant, i.e., that the withdrawal of one limited segment of congressional power for twenty years implies an otherwise unlimited power over the whole subject.[88]

84. Smith, *Constitutional Argument*, 20–21; Goodell, *Views*, 46–57; [Goodell], *Address of the Macedon Convention*, 3; Spooner, *Unconstitutionality*, 105–114; *Address of the Free Constitutionalists*, 10; Goodell, *Our National Charters*, 62–65.

85. Olcott, *Two Lectures*, 88; Mellen, *Argument* 73; [Spooner], "Legal Basis," 292.

86. Smith, *Constitutional Argument*, 20; [Goodell], *Constitutional Duty*, 9; Spooner, *Unconstitutionality*, 96–97; "Its First Public Advocate," Cincinnati *Philanthropist*, 13 April 1842. Adams broached his war-power theory on the floor on the House: *Globe*, 27 Cong. 2 sess. 429 (15 April 1842).

87. Stewart, "Report of a Speech Delivered before a Joint Committee of the Vermont Legislature," and "Address to the Abolitionists of the State of New York," in Marsh, ed., *Writings of Stewart*, 177, 86–107.

88. Stewart, "Address to the Abolitionists of the State of New York," in Marsh, ed., *Writings of Stewart*, 105–107; Goodell, *Views*, 43–46; Spooner, *Unconstitutionality*, 95–96; Tiffany, *Treatise*, 134. In *A View of the Constitution of the United States of America*, 2d ed. (Philadelphia: Philip H. Nicklin, 1839), 117, William Rawle, a prominent nonabolitionist constitutional commentator, supported the negative-pregnant argument.

The supremacy clause of Article VI was important to the radicals' argument, since they read it as establishing the superiority of federal power over the states.[89] Rebutting Calhoun's 1837 resolutions, radicals saw the federal Constitution with all its antislavery potential as the "supreme act of the sovereign people . . . paramount to the constitutions, laws, or usages of any single state."[90] Finally, several provisions of the Bill of Rights, including the jury trial, search and seizure, cruel and unusual punishment, and the taking of property without compensation clauses, and all the First Amendment liberties, were violated by slavery.[91]

Having investigated the antislavery provisions of the Constitution, radicals then took up the four clauses alleged to be guarantees of slavery. They were of two minds about these clauses. Some admitted that the clauses did in fact refer to slaves, but argued that they need not be honored, or could easily and legitimately be evaded by the free states. These clauses were also examples of the framers' strained effort to keep slavery out of the Constitution. Radicals again emphasized that the words "slave" and "slavery" did not appear in the document. Some of them agreed with John Quincy Adams that "circumlocutions are the fig leaves under which these parts of the body politic are decently concealed," and therefore saw the proslavery clauses as something to be gotten around.[92] Others maintained that each of the clauses might be applied to something other than slavery. Mellen, reviewing the federal number clause, thought that "it would seem as if some one had worded this phrase in such a manner that it would not require an alteration of the Constitution for the purpose of having representatives chosen, or taxes collected, provided the system of slavery should be done away, and were careful

---

89. Art. VI, cl. 2: "This Constitution, and the Laws of the United States which shall be made in Pursuance thereof; and all Treaties made, or which shall be made, under the Authority of the United States, shall be the supreme Law of the Land; and the Judges in every State shall be bound thereby, any Thing in the Constitution or Laws of any State to the Contrary notwithstanding."

90. Stewart, "Constitutional Argument," in tenBroek, *Equal under Law,* 290; Goodell, *Views,* 41–43, 106–114; Birney, "Can Congress," 312.

91. Mellen, *Argument,* 77, 88; Goodell, *Views,* 91; Spooner, *Unconstitutionality,* 102; Smith, *Constitutional Argument,* 20.

92. *Argument of John Quincy Adams, before the Supreme Court of the United States, in the Case of the United States, Appellants vs. Cinque* (New York: S. W. Benedict, 1841), 39; L. Bonnefoux, *The Constitution Expounded, respecting Its Bearing on the Subject of Slavery* (New York: Wilmer & Rogers, 1850), 6.

to have it worded as to exclude the idea, as much as possible, that they had anything to do with it."[93] In this interpretation, the federal number clause was actually a disincentive to the maintenance of slavery, a "penalty," or a "premium in favor of human liberty."[94] Other radicals argued that the negative correlative of the "free Persons" mentioned in the clause was not slaves, but rather aliens and Indians not taxed. By this argument, slavery disappeared entirely from the clause.[95]

Radicals also gave the 1808 clause differing interpretations. Mellen conceded that it did apply to slaves, but others argued that even if it did, it was an antislavery authorization to Congress, giving it power to abolish both the international and interstate trade.[96] Whatever sanction for slavery might be read into the clause applied only to the original states and lapsed with the abolition of the trade in 1808.[97] Alternatively they argued that the clause referred only to federal authority over the in-migration of free persons like indentured servants, who could in a sense be said to be "imported."[98]

Radicals maintained that the fugitive slave clause did not apply to slaves for two reasons. First, under *Somerset*, once a slave left the jurisdiction under which he was held, his slave status fell away.[99] Second, a slave was not "held to service" and his labor was not "due" his master under the laws of the southern states. The black codes disbarred slaves from entering into a contractual relationship, and since the quoted phrases implied a contract, the clause applied only to

93. Mellen, *Argument*, 66; see also [Spooner], "Legal Basis," 286.

94 Tiffany, *Treatise*, 65; Stewart, "Response to the Message of Govr. Marcy" (1836) in Marsh, ed., *Writings of Stewart*, 75; Goodell, *Views*, 89; Mellen, *Argument*, 71; Smith, *Letter to Chase;* Daniel Foster, *The Constitution of the United States . . . Showing that a Fair Interpretation and Application of Said Constitution Will Abolish Slavery and Establish Liberty* (Springfield, Mass.: Samuel Bowles, 1855).

95. Mellen, *Argument*, 66; Spooner, *Unconstitutionality*, 73–81, 237–270; Goodell, *Constitutional Duty*, 13; *Address of the Free Constitutionalists*, 14; Smith, *Constitutional Argument*, 14.

96. Mellen, *Argument*, 75; Tiffany, *Treatise*, 64; *Remarks on the Constitution, by a Friend of Humanity, on the Subject of Slavery* (Philadelphia: Evening Star, 1836).

97. Goodell, *Views*, 28–30; Stewart, "Response to Marcy," in Marsh, ed., *Writings of Stewart*, 74.

98. Miller, *Constitution & Slavery*, 10.

99. Tiffany, *Treatise*, 68, 80; Miller, *Constitution & Slavery*, 12; F[rancis] C. Treadwell to Gerrit Smith, 16 May 1840, Gerrit Smith Collection, Syracuse University.

indentured servants and apprentices or other forms of labor that are based on a contractual relation.[100] As to the pair of clauses that arguably pertained to slave uprisings, the insurrections and domestic violence clauses, radicals argued that putting down an uprising for liberty would be wrongful; that a slave uprising is not an "insurrection"; and that slaveholding itself is the "domestic violence" against which the federal government must protect the states.[101]

This was obviously the weakest part of the radicals' argument, justifying William Jay's harsh judgment that radical constitutionalism was a mere "verbal quibble."[102] However necessary it may have seemed to radicals to construe slavery out of the Constitution, they appeared only obtuse or dishonest for the effort, and weakened their posture vis-à-vis moderates and Garrisonians.

In the short run, radical constitutionalism was a failure. Northern opposition to slavery became channeled into the Free Soil and Republican effort and the radicals, both in their constitutionalism and their politics, were left stranded in a backwater where they became increasingly unrealistic and sectarian. But their long-term impact was more substantial. They were the antebellum era's leading exponents of a theory of natural-law limitations on governmental power. Alvan Stewart outlined the premises of this "modern" natural-law approach in 1836:

There is a class of rights of the most personal and sacred character to the citizen, which are a portion of individual sovereignty, never surrendered by the citizen. . . . The legislatures of the States and Union are forbidden by the constitutions of the States and Union from touching those unsurrendered rights; no matter in what distress or exigency a State may find itself, the legislature can never touch those unsurrendered rights as objects of legislation.[103]

However imperfectly realized, this view has become prevalent today. Modern libertarian constitutional thought, using the Fourteenth

100. Mellen, *Argument,* 83; Spooner, *Unconstitutionality,* 67–73; Theodore D. Weld, *Persons Held to Service, Fugitive Slaves &c.* (Boston: J. W. Alden for the New England Anti-Slavery Tract Association, n.d. [1842?]); Goodell, *Views,* 21–28; "Persons Held to Service," *Emancipator and Free American,* 30 March 1843; speech of Gerrit Smith to NYSA-SS convention, 1839, reported in *Friend of Man,* 9 Oct. 1839.

101. [Spooner], "Legal Basis," 293; Tiffany, *Treatise,* ch. 18.

102. William Jay to A. A. Phelps, 3 July 1846, in Lewis Tappan Papers, LC.

103. Stewart, "Response to Marcy," in Marsh, ed., *Writings of Stewart,* 65.

Amendment's due process and equal protection clauses as vehicles, has transmuted natural-law concepts into working guarantors of individual freedom. Ideas of substantive due process, equal protection of the laws, paramount national citizenship, and the privileges and immunities of that citizenship were all first suggested by the radicals. They did not contribute directly to the triumph of their ideas; that was, ironically, the work of the Republicans whom they came so heartily to despise. But it was the radicals who first opened up the possibilities realized by their foes.

Epilogue: Beyond Free Soil

Constitutional debate concerning slavery after 1848 had a peculiar, shadow-boxing quality about it: men seemed to be discussing issues that were real only to them, not to their opponents. Those who opposed any limits to slavery's expansion into the territories, foreign areas, and the free states, and those who supported limits of some sort, failed to come to grips with each other's arguments, for a reason that appears obvious with the benefit of hindsight. Freesoiler Republicans seeking to constrain slavery's expansion assumed that the federal consensus was still a workable constitutional principle; those who opposed these constraints saw that the consensus was dead, and would have to be replaced by something radically different.

As the heirs of moderate constitutional antislavery, the Republicans preserved a strong attachment to the consensus. The original Thirteenth Amendment, endorsed by leading Republicans and actually sent out by Congress to the states for ratification, was to be an irrepealable provision that:

No amendment shall be made to the Constitution which will authorize or give to Congress the power to abolish or interfere, within any state, with the domestic institutions thereof, including that of persons held to labor or service by the laws of said State.[1]

In his first inaugural address, Abraham Lincoln claimed that the point was already "implied constitutional law," but that it would do no harm to put the federal consensus explicitly into the Constitution.[2]

1. Joint resolution of 2 March 1861, 12 Stat. 251.
2. "First Inaugural Address," in Roy P. Basler, ed., *The Collected Works of Abraham Lincoln* (New Brunswick: Rutgers Univ. Press, 1953–55), IV, 270.

But as Lincoln spoke, it had become obvious that the consensus no longer sufficed. The meager showing of the Constitutional Union party in 1860—which, of the four factions running presidential candidates, was the one most dedicated to restoring pre-Wilmot Proviso constitutional arrangements—together with the failure of the Crittenden Compromise and the Old Gentlemen's Conference, proved that the old constitutional world had disappeared, and that in the new one, old assumptions were beside the point. Secessionist leaders correctly saw that the federal consensus embodied in the original Thirteenth Amendment, once the capstone of the constitution, had become a meaningless anachronism.

The federal consensus was a casualty of the Mexican War. "The United States will conquer Mexico," wrote Ralph Waldo Emerson in 1846, "but it will be as the man swallows the arsenic, which brings him down in turn. Mexico will poison us."[3] The territorial acquisitions of the Treaty of Guadaloupe Hidalgo (1848) proved to be Emerson's poison. Fundamental constitutional readjustments had resolved the first three crises of the Union, but after the Mexican War, Congress could achieve only unstable, short-run compromises in 1848–1850 and 1854. The terminal crisis of 1860–1861 demonstrated just how fragile those compromises were. Bernard De Voto overstated for dramatic purposes when he wrote that "at some time between August and December, 1846, the Civil War had begun,"[4] but he was not essentially wrong.

The war had such a disruptive impact because, in effect, it produced a new American nation. The territory the United States acquired after 1845 as a result of the annexation of Texas (1845), the Oregon settlement (1847), the Mexican cession (1848), and the Gadsden Purchase (1853) was considerably larger than either the Louisiana Purchase or the original United States of 1783.[5] The Civil War would probably not have occurred—and certainly not in 1861—had the dispute over slavery been argued out in a stable, nonexpanding nation. White Americans before 1846, and after as well, were willing to go a long way toward repressing blacks and their white friends in the

3. Edward W. Emerson and Waldo E. Forbes, eds., *Journals of Ralph Waldo Emerson* (Boston: Houghton Mifflin, 1909–14), VII, 206.
4. Bernard De Voto, *The Year of Decision 1846* (Boston: Houghton Mifflin, 1942), 496.
5. In hundreds of thousands of square miles, the figures are: original United States, 847; Louisiana Purchase, 822; 1845–53 acquisitions, 1234.

interests of social and sectional harmony. Had slavery been confined to the states where it existed as of 1844, other issues, such as those over fugitive recaptures, personal liberty laws, and the interstate slave trade, would have remained as manageable and negotiable as they had been until then.

Writing to William Seward shortly before his inauguration, Lincoln insisted that his party hold fast to the idea of nonextension. But "as to fugitive slaves, District of Columbia, slave trade among the slave states, and whatever springs of necessity from the fact that the institution is amongst us, I care but little, so that what is done be comely, and not altogether outrageous."[6] Slavery alone was not the efficient cause of the Civil War. Neither was territorial expansion. Both before and after the Mexican war, the American nation had been able to absorb large acquisitions of territory without being torn apart by severe internal strain. It was the conjunction of slavery and imperial expansion that brought on the war. Together, and only together, they were its cause.

Abolitionist constitutionalism was relevant only to a political system that was stable and equilibrated. Before 1846, men in politics operated within a geographically finite polity, whose constitutional workings could be premised on the assumption that the basic relationship of political and sectional forces within it would not suddenly be changed in fundamentals. In such a constitutional system, political questions were susceptible of being resolved in the ordinary course of politics and there were no problems that were insoluble except by surrender of the basic position of one party or section. The Mexican War destroyed the stability and equilibration requisite to the functioning of such a system.

In contrast to the obsolete core of Republican constitutional thought, slavery's proponents offered a sweeping and compelling program for the new order. First, they completed the task of assuring the internal security and permanence of slavery in the extant slave states. Next, they toyed with ambitious schemes to expand slavery into foreign territories, by military conquest if necessary. At the same time, they extended slavery's reach into the free states so much that some northerners thought that southerners intended to nationalize

6. Lincoln to William Seward, 1 Feb. 1861, in Basler, ed., *Collected Works of Lincoln,* IV, 183.

slavery, making it legitimate everywhere. Finally, they demanded that the federal government actively force slavery into all the territories.

The process of shoring up slavery's security in the states where it existed, which had been going on since the Revolution, culminated in a provision inserted by amendment into the Kentucky Constitution in 1850:

The right of property is before and higher than any constitutional sanction; and the right of the owner of a slave to such slave, and its increase, is the same, and as inviolable as the right of the owner of any property whatever.[7]

Slavery here took on a meta-constitutional status, removed even beyond the sovereign power of the people to control or abolish it.

Thus secured in its home base, slavery then turned outward, even beyond the bounds of the United States.[8] "The south can never consent to be confined to prescribed limits," insisted Virginia's Governor William Smith in 1847. "She wants and must have space."[9] The exuberance of this imperial thrust was best expressed by Mississippi Senator Albert Gallatin Brown in 1858:

I want Cuba . . . Tamaulipas, Potosi, and one or two other Mexican States; and I want them all for the same reason—for the planting or spreading of slavery. And a foothold in Central America will powerfully aid us in acquiring those other States. If any one desires to know why I want a foothold in Central America, I avow frankly it is because I want to plant slavery there; I think slavery is a good thing *per se* . . . Yes, I want these Countries for the spread of slavery. I would spread the blessings of slavery, like the religion of our Divine Master, to the uttermost ends of the earth, and rebellious and wicked as the Yankees have been, I would even extend it to them.[10]

7. Art. XIII, §3, in Thorpe, ed., *Federal and State Constitutions*, III, 1312.
8. Eugene D. Genovese, *The Political Economy of Slavery: Studies in the Economy and Society of the Slave South* (New York: Vintage, 1967), ch. 10; Robert E. May, *The Southern Dream of a Caribbean Empire, 1854–1861* (Baton Rouge: Louisiana State Univ. Press, 1973); Ronald Takaki, *A Pro-Slavery Crusade: The Agitation to Reopen the African Slave Trade* (Glencoe: Free Press, 1971).
9. Message of Gov. William Smith to Virginia legislature, excerpted in *Niles National Register*, 8 Jan. 1848.
10. "Speech at Hazelhurst, Mississippi . . . 1858" in M. W. Cluskey, ed., *Speeches, Messages, and Other Writings of the Hon. Albert G. Brown . . .* (Philadelphia: James B. Smith, 1859), 588–599.

This southern lust for *lebensraum* was trumpeted by the publication of the Ostend Manifesto in 1854, a document signed by the American ministers to Spain, France, and England, urging the United States to pressure Spain to cede Cuba on the grounds that it might "be Africanized [i.e. that slavery might be abolished or overthrown] and become a second St. Domingo, with all its attendant horrors to the white race, and suffer the flames to extend to our own neighboring shores." By way of bolstering this internal security rationale, the ministers rattled the saber and threatened that the United States might seize Cuba by force if Spain proved reluctant to sell, on the grounds that the United States had to resort to "self-preservation."[11]

This was not a vapid threat, as William Walker's filibustering expeditions to Baja California, Nicaragua, and British Honduras between 1853 and 1860 suggested. In these three areas, Walker, despite the formal opposition of the United States government, tried to incite an insurrection so as to annex the territory to the United States and introduce slavery. Kansas territorial governor Robert Walker (no relation) urged President James Buchanan to acquire Puerto Rico to extend the American slave domain and Congressman Owen Lovejoy even suspected the slave states of similar designs on the Sandwich Islands (modern Hawaii).[12] A nation that had only recently gone to war with Mexico for more slave territory, and that had considered absorbing all of that nation despite revulsion at the race and religion of its indigenous population, might easily burst its borders once more.

Senator Brown, probably with tongue in cheek, had recommended extending slavery's blessings to the wicked and rebellious Yankees. His Georgia colleague, Robert Toombs, was widely quoted as boasting that he would call the roll of his slaves at the foot of Bunker Hill.[13] They thereby confirmed northern fears that slavery was entering the free states and converting them into virtual slave states. The 1850 Fugitive Slave Act, the Kansas-Nebraska Act, and President

11. The Ostend Manifesto is reprinted in "The Ostend Conference, &c.," 33 Cong. 2 sess., ser. 790, doc. 93 (1855), 127–132.

12. Robert Walker is quoted in Filler, *Crusade against Slavery,* 251; Owen Lovejoy to Gerrit Smith, 21 Jan. 1854, Owen Lovejoy Papers, Clements Library, University of Michigan.

13. Pleasant A. Stovall, *Robert Toombs: Statesman, Speaker, Soldier, Sage* (New York: Cassell, 1892), 119. Toombs denied having said this, insisting that he was being misquoted in an abolitionist canard.

James Buchanan's complicity in proslavery politics convinced some Republicans that there was "a continuous movement of slaveholders to advance slavery over the entire North."[14] One especially ominous symptom of this proslavery conspiracy was the willingness of the federal government to use its ultimate legal weapon, criminal prosecutions for treason, to deal with the nuisance of abolitionists' resistance to the fugitive slave acts. In 1850, Daniel Webster and Massachusetts Democratic leader Benjamin Hallett demanded that resistance to enforcement of the 1850 act or assistance to black runaways constituted "an act of clear treason."[15]

This was not claptrap. United States Attorneys, with the approval of Washington, contemplated or actually began treason prosecutions in two spectacular 1851 fugitive rescues: the Jerry rescue in Syracuse, New York, and the so-called "Christiana massacre" in southeastern Pennsylvania. In the latter, a former Jacksonian, United States District Court Judge John Kane redefined treason in a way that did violence to the definitive exposition of the subject, Chief Justice Marshall's opinion in the Aaron Burr treason prosecution (1807). Rejecting Marshall's strict and libertarian construction of the treason clause, Kane instructed a grand jury that treason consisted not merely of levying war, but also of forcible opposition to the enforcement of a federal statute, or instigating opposition if accompanied or followed by forcible opposition.[16] Not since the days of the Sedition Acts (1798–1800) had so repressive a stance been taken by national authorities toward resistance to national policy. Like the mobbings of the thirties, these treason prosecutions and the heavy-handed federal enforcement of the fugitive slave laws persuaded many nonabolitionist northerners that the freedom of white men was being sacrificed to slavery.

But it was into the territories that slavery's proponents seemed most determined to expand the peculiar institution. The Wilmot Proviso, with its extensive popular support in the north, came as an

14. Quoted in Sewell, *Ballots for Freedom,* 258.
15. Speech of Benjamin F. Hallett in *Proceedings of the Constitutional Meeting at Faneuil Hall, November 28, 1850* (Boston: Beals & Greene, 1850), 21–23; "Speech to the Young Men of Albany" (1851), in *The Works of Daniel Webster* (Boston: Little & Brown, 1851), II, 577–578.
16. "Charge to Grand Jury, Treason," 30 Fed. Cas. 1047 (No. 18276) (C.C.E.D.Pa. 1851); but see *U.S. v. Hanway,* 26 Fed. Cas. 105 (No. 15299) (C.C.E.D.Pa. 1851)

unpleasant surprise to southern leaders. Calhoun recognized that his 1837 resolutions had already been by-passed by events, and updated them by a new set he introduced in 1847. Rejecting the conception of federal power that underlay the Wilmost Proviso, Calhoun insisted that (1) the territories are the joint property of all the states; (2) Congress had no power to deprive the states or their citizens of the right to exercise property rights in the territories; and (3) Congress could not foreordain what sort of a constitution a territory's inhabitants might draw up when they were ready for statehood.[17]

These resolutions, however, were only temporizing, a tactic to gain time against the constitutional assault of the Wilmot Proviso, until a more comprehensive position could be worked out. Alabama fire-eater William Lowndes Yancey carried the southern position further in 1848 with the "Alabama Platform," in which he maintained the affirmative right of all citizens to take their property to the territories. (Calhoun had only inveighed against federal repression of this right.) Yancey demanded federal protection of this property right for the duration of territorial status.[18]

Southern jurists were at the same time repudiating the doctrines of *Somerset* and finding a legitimating origin of slavery in the colonial period.[19] From this conceptual point, proslavery commentators reversed the "Freedom national" doctrine then popular among Free-soiler Republicans in favor of a concept of "Slavery national": "What is local and municipal is the abolition of slavery. The states that are now non-slaveholding have been made so by positive statute. Slavery exists, of course, in every nation in which it is not prohibited."[20] Given this universal legitimacy, any effort by the federal government to keep slavery out of the territories would be unconstitutional. The only appropriate role for the federal government concerning slavery in the territories was protection and promotion. Richard Yeadon,

17. *Globe,* 29 Cong. 2 sess. 455 (19 Feb. 1847).
18. The Alabama platform is excerpted in John W. DuBose, *The Life and Times of William Lowndes Yancey* (1892; rpt. New York: Peter Smith, 1942), I, 212–214.
19. *Neal* v. *Farmer,* 9 Ga. 555 (1851); Thomas R. R. Cobb, *An Inquiry into the Law of Negro Slavery in the United States of America* . . . (Philadelphia: T. & J. W. Johnson, 1858), 170; George S. Sawyer, *Southern Institutes; or, An Inquiry into the Origin and Early Prevalence of Slavery and the Slave Trade* . . . (Philadelphia: Lippincott, 1858), 321–322.
20. J. H. Thornwell, *The State of the Country* . . . (Columbia: Southern Guardian, 1861), 12.

editor of the Charleston *Courier,* maintained in 1857 that "[the Constitution] not only recognized, sanctioned, and guaranteed [slavery] as a state institution, . . . but also [went] so far as to foster and expand it, by federal protection and agency, wherever it was legalized, within State or Territorial limits. [Slavery was] exclusively within State jurisdiction and beyond the constitutional power of Congress or of the General Government, except for guarantee, protection, and defence."[21]

This required nothing less than a federal law, not only protecting slavery in the territories, but forcing it on them. Senator Jefferson Davis of Mississippi demanded this in resolutions he introduced in the United States Senate in 1860:

Neither Congress, nor a territorial legislature, whether by direct legislation or legislation of an indirect and unfriendly nature, possess the power to annul or impair the constitutional right of any citizen of the United States to take his slave property into the common territories; but it is the duty of the Federal Government there to afford for that, as for other species of property, the needful protection; and if experience should at any time prove that the judiciary does not possess power to insure adequate protection, it will then become the duty of Congress to supply such deficiency.[22]

These were subsequently adopted by the Breckinridge faction of the Democratic party as its core position in the 1860 election.[23]

Between the Free Soil and slavery protection concepts a range of proposals surfaced as a substitute for the federal consensus. They were nominally neutral, in that their proponents claimed that they neither encouraged nor inhibited the spread of slavery into the territories. The simplest, which attracted almost no support apart from Whig opponents of Polk's war policy, was for the United States to take no territories as a result of the war. This flew in the face of Manifest Destiny and became nugatory after 1848.[24] Any realistic suggestion would have to assume American territorial aggrandize-

21. Richard Yeadon, *An Address Delivered before the Euphemian and Philomathean Literary Societies of Erskine College . . . 1857* excerpted in Theodore Parker, *The Present Aspect of Slavery in America and the Immediate Duty of the North . . .* (Boston: Bela Marsh, 1858), 17–19.
22. *Globe,* 36 Cong. 1 sess. 658 (2 Feb. 1860).
23. Porter and Johnson, comps., *National Party Platforms,* 31.
24. The no-territories proposal is discussed in Rayback, *Free Soil,* 122, and Sewell, *Ballots for Freedom,* 142.

ment. One such idea was to extend the old Missouri Compromise line of 36°30′ all the way to the Pacific. James Buchanan, then a United States Senator from Pennsylvania, first proposed this in 1847.[25] Some southerners found it attractive; Justice John Catron of the United States Supreme Court endorsed it privately in 1848, and the Nashville Convention, called to consider secession proposals in the midst of the 1850 crisis, recommended it if northerners found Yancey's Alabama Platform unacceptable.[26] Though irrelevant and unconstitutional after the Kansas-Nebraska Act and *Dred Scott,* the proposal was exhumed by Kentucky Senator John J. Crittenden during the winter of secession as part of the "Crittenden Compromise."

The superficially appealing alternative of "popular sovereignty" was first touted by northern Democrats in 1847, including Michigan Senator Lewis Cass and Vice-President George M. Dallas.[27] In his "Nicholson Letter" of 1847–1848, Cass suggested that the Wilmot Proviso was an unnecessary irritant, since the federal government could not control slavery in a territory once it had became a state. Therefore he recommended "leaving the people of any territory . . . the right to regulate [slavery] themselves, under the general principles of the constitution."[28] Stephen A. Douglas picked up the idea and popularized it to soothe northern feelings during the fifth crisis of the Union, but it was destroyed in the Kansas bushwhacking that ensued.

Next was something called a "compromise," though "evasion" would have been a more suitable word. It was urged in 1848 by Senator John Clayton of Delaware, and is known as the "Clayton Compromise." He recommended that after California and New Mexico Territories were organized, the question of slavery there be determined by the territorial supreme court, with a right of appeal from its decision directly to the Supreme Court of the United States.[29]

25. James Buchanan to Charles Kessler, 25 Aug. 1847 (the "Old Berks" letter), in John Bassett Moore, ed., *The Works of James Buchanan* (Philadelphia: Lippincott, 1908–11), VII, 386.
26. John Catron to Daniel Graham, 12 July 1848, James K. Polk Presidential Papers, LC (microfilm, ser. 2); resolutions of the Nashville Convention are excerpted in Commager, ed., *Documents of American History,* I, 324–325.
27. Chaplain W. Morrison, *Democratic Politics and Sectionalism: The Wilmost Proviso Controversy* (Chapel Hill: Univ. of North Carolina Press, 1967), 87–89.
28. The Nicholson letter is reprinted in *Niles National Register,* 8 Jan. 1848.
29. A bill embodying the substance of Clayton's recommendations, "A Bill

In modified form, the Clayton Compromise became a part of the Compromise of 1850, in the New Mexico and Utah territorial acts.[30] Congress created these territories without prohibiting or establishing slavery there, and provided an appellate mechanism by writs of error from the United States Supreme Court for habeas corpus determinations of the territorial supreme courts involving the status of slaves. The whole point to the Clayton Compromise and 1850 measures was to get the United States Supreme Court to resolve the problem of slavery in the territories. As such, it was an implicit admission that political processes had broken down, and that the dominant political question of the period had proved beyond the capacity of the political system to resolve.[31] The Supreme Court took the tendered invitation in *Dred Scott*, with results so calamitous that any political solution at all might have been better.

For northerners who sought to limit slavery's spread into the territories and the free states, *Somerset* remained as significant as the federal consensus. One *Somerset*-based proposal attracted an unusually broad range of support in the decade after it was first suggested. A New York judge, Greene C. Bronson, proposed in 1848 that Congress exclude slavery from the territories simply by not enacting a slave code for a territory during its first stage of territorial government. Since, under *Somerset's* doctrine, slavery cannot exist in the absence of positive law, "if the owner of slaves removes with, or sends them into a country, state, or territory, where slavery does not exist by law, they will from that moment become free men."[32] It was not surprising that this theory was endorsed by Justice John McLean of the United States Supreme Court, whose opposition to the territorial expansion of slavery was well known.[33] But even the proslavery Alabama lawyer John A. Campbell, who was a delegate to the Nashville Convention and who joined McLean on the high court in 1853, admitted the validity of the idea, conceding that slavery is "purely a

to Establish the Territorial Governments of Oregon, New Mexico, and California," is printed in *Globe*, 30 Cong. 1 sess. 1002–1005 (26 July 1848); the "compromise" is in §24.

30. Act of 9 Sept. 1850, ch. 49, §10, 9 Stat. 446; Act of 9 Sept. 1850, ch. 51, §9, 9 Stat. 453.

31. Wallace Mendelson, "Dred Scott's Case—Reconsidered," *Minn. L. Rev.*, 38 (1953), 16–28.

32. Quoted in Rayback, *Free Soil*, 253.

33. McLean was quoted in "Territorial Government," *United States Magazine and Democratic Review*, n.s., 23 (1848), 191–192.

municipal institution" that Congress could exclude from the territories by simple inaction.[34] Senator Stephen A. Douglas adopted the idea ten years later as the so-called "Freeport Doctrine" in the Lincoln-Douglas debates (1858), despite Lincoln's insistence that *Dred Scott* had made it untenable.

Unlike the federal consensus, *Somerset* could prove equally serviceable in repelling slavery from the states. Northern courts relied on it in questions dealing with sojourners' slaves and fugitives. In *Lemmon v. The People* (1860), the New York Court of Appeals liberated slaves who were in transit from Virginia to Texas via the port of New York.[35] Rejecting the proslavery implications of *Dred Scott* in favor of the right of the states to regulate the status of persons within their jurisdiction, a majority of the New York judges declined to read into the United States Constitution any warrant for the power of the southern states to control the status of persons in the free states (except fugitives). In *Anderson v. Poindexter* (1857), the Ohio Supreme Court adopted neo-*Somerset* principles to free sojourners' slaves in that state, holding slavery to be "repugnant to reason and the principles of natural law." For good measure, the court refused to adopt the *Grace* reattachment principle.[36]

Northern courts and legislatures affirmed principles of individual freedom more forcefully in fugitive slave issues. The extreme of northern judicial resistance to slavery's penetration occurred in the Wisconsin *Booth* cases, where the supreme court of that state twice issued writs of habeas corpus to free abolitionist Sherman Booth from the custody of the United States Marshal.[37] It also held the 1850 Fugitive Slave Act unconstitutional. When the United States Supreme Court directed its writ of error to the state court, the Wisconsin judges ordered the clerk to ignore the writ and to refuse to send up the papers in the case, an unprecedented defiance of federal judicial authority.[38]

34. John A. Campbell to John C. Calhoun, 1 March 1848, in Chauncey S. Boucher and Robert P. Brooks, eds., "Correspondence Addressed to John C. Calhoun, 1837–1849," Am. Hist. Assn. *Annual Report . . . 1929* (Washington, D.C.: GPO, 1930), 431.

35. 20 N.Y. 562 (1860); Maine judges similarly rejected *Dred Scott:* Opinion of the Justices, 44 Me. 505 (1858).

36. 6 Ohio St. 623 (1857).

37. In re *Booth*, 3 Wis. 1 (1854); In re *Booth and Rycraft*, 3 Wis. 144 (1855).

38. *Ableman v. Booth*, 21 How. (62 U.S.) 506 (1859).

The Vermont legislature went even further in constitutional ance. In the Freedom Act of 1858,[39] it rejected the constit doctrines of *Dred Scott* by declaring that every slave coming it Green Mountain state, with or without his master, was free; by making it a misdemeanor to try to hold such a person as a slave; by declaring that no person in Vermont should be vendible or held as a slave, or be deprived of liberty or property without due process of law, defined in a procedural sense; by granting jury trials to all alleged fugitives; and by holding that neither slavery nor previous state of slavery should be grounds for denying state citizenship to any person.

Vermont's Freedom Act was a partial culmination of antislavery constitutionalism. If we compare it in its main features with its antithesis, the *Dred Scott* case that provoked it, we can draw some instructive lessons about Everyman's Constitution. The Freedom Act was a policy decision made by that branch of government, the legislature, that most intimately represented the sovereign people. *Dred Scott*, by contrast, was a failed prophylaxis of popular decision-making power by nonelected judges. In Arthur Bestor's acute judgment, the United States Supreme Court "was under no obligation to reflect the views of popular majorities. Policy would be made *for* the nation, but not *by* the nation. Power would be neatly divorced from accountability, action from deliberation."[40] Where Vermont made policy for her people at the state level, *Dred Scott* represented the centralizing, power-accumulating thrust of proslavery constitutionalism that sought to rule the nation and the western empire from Washington.

Ultimately, the north's peaceable resistance failed. The future of slavery was resolved, not by legal and constitutional action, but by the strong arm. Six hundred thousand American soldiers died in the war, plus an unknown number of civilians. "That these dead shall not have died in vain," as Lincoln said at Gettysburg, the American people recreated their Constitution, embedding in its Thirteenth and Fourteenth Amendments the elements of antislavery constitutionalism.

39. No. 37, "An Act to Secure Freedom to All Persons within This State," in *Acts and Resolves of . . . Vermont . . . 1858* (Bradford: Joseph D. Clark, 1858), 42–44.

40. Arthur Bestor, "State Sovereignty and Slavery: A Reinterpretation of Proslavery Constitutional Doctrine, 1846–1860," *J. Ill. State Hist. Soc.*, 54 (1961), 117–180 at 167 (italics in original).

Appendix 1

Excerpt from opinion of Justice Samuel Chase.
Calder v. *Bull,* 3 Dall. (3 U.S.) 386 (1798) at 387–388.

Whether the legislature of any of the states can revise and correct by law, a decision of any of its courts of justice, although not prohibited by the constitution of the state, is a question of very great importance, and not necessary now to be determined; because the resolution or law in question does not go so far. I cannot subscribe to the omnipotence of a state legislature, or that it is absolute and without control; although its authority should not be expressly restrained by the constitution, or fundamental law of the state. The people of the United States erected their constitutions or forms of government, to establish justice, to promote the general welfare, to secure the blessings of liberty, and to protect their persons and property from violence. The purposes for which men enter into society will determine the nature and terms of the social compact; and as they are the foundation of the legislative power, they will decide what are the proper objects of it. The nature, and ends of legislative power will limit the exercise of it. This fundamental principle flows from the very nature of our free republican governments, that no man should be compelled to do what the laws do not require; nor to refrain from acts which the laws permit. There are acts which the federal, or state legislature cannot do, without exceeding their authority. There are certain vital principles in our free republican governments, which will determine and overrule an apparent and flagrant abuse of legislative power; as to authorize manifest injustice by positive law; or to take away that security for personal liberty, or private property, for the protection whereof the government was established. An act of the legislature (for I cannot call it a law), contrary to the great first principles of the social compact, cannot be considered a rightful exercise of legislative authority. The obligation of a law, in governments established on express compact, and on republican principles, must be determined by the nature of the power on which it is founded.

A few instances will suffice to explain what I mean. A law that punished a citizen for an innocent action, or, in other words, for an act, which, when done, was in violation of no existing law; a law that destroys or impairs the lawful private contracts of citizens; a law that makes a man a judge in his own cause; or a law that takes property from A and gives it to B; it is against all reason and justice, for a people to intrust a legislature with such powers; and therefore, it cannot be presumed that they have done it. The genius, the nature and the spirit of our state governments, amount to a prohibition of such acts of legislation; and the general principles of law and reason forbid them. The legislature may enjoin, permit, forbid and punish; they may declare new crimes; and establish rules of conduct for all its citizens in future cases; they may command what is right, and prohibit what is wrong; but they cannot change innocence into guilt; or punish innocence as a crime; or violate the right of an antecedent lawful private contract; or the right of private property. To maintain that our federal, or state legislature possesses such powers, if they had not been expressly restrained; would, in my opinion, be a political heresy, altogether inadmissible in our free republican governments.

Appendix 2

Globe, 25 Cong. 2 sess. 55 (27 Dec. 1837).
Mr. Calhoun then submitted the following resolutions.

Resolved, That in the adoption of the Federal Constitution, the States adopting the same acted, severally, as free, independent, and sovereign States; and that each, for itself, by its own voluntary assent, entered the Union with the view to its increased security against all dangers, *domestic* as well as foreign, and the more perfect and secure enjoyment of its advantages, natural, political, and social.

Resolved, That in delegating a portion of their powers to be exercised by the Federal Government, the States retained, severally, the exclusive and sole right over their own domestic institutions and police, and are alone responsible for them, and that any intermeddling of any one or more States, or a combination of their citizens, with the domestic institutions and police of the others, on any ground, or under any pretext whatever, political, moral, or religious, with the view to their alteration, or subversion, is an assumption of superiority not warranted by the Constitution; insulting to the States interfered with, tending to endanger their domestic peace and tranquility, subversive of the objects for which the Constitution was formed, and, by necessary consequence, tending to weaken and destroy the Union itself.

Resolved, That this Government was instituted and adopted by the several States of this Union as a common agent, in order to carry into effect the powers which they had delegated by the Constitution for their mutual security and prosperity; and that, in fulfillment of this high and sacred trust, this Government is bound so to exercise its powers as to give, as far as may be practicable, increased stability and security to the domestic institutions of the States that compose the Union; and that it is the solemn duty of the Government to resist all attempts by one portion of the Union to use it as an instrument to attack the domestic institutions of another, or to weaken or destroy such institutions, instead of strengthening and upholding them, as it is in duty bound to do.

Resolved, That domestic slavery, as it exists in the Southern and Western States of this Union, composes an important part of their domestic institutions, inherited from their ancestors, and existing at the adoption of the Constitution, by which it is recognised as constituting an essential element in the distribution of its powers among the States; and that no change of opinion, or feeling, on the part of the other States of the Union in relation to it, can justify them or their citizens in open and systematic attacks thereon, with the view to its overthrow; and that all such attacks are in manifest violation of the mutual and solemn pledge to protect and defend each other, given by the States, respectively, on entering into the Constitutional compact, which formed the Union, and as such is [*sic*] a manifest breach of faith, and a violation of the most solemn obligations, moral and religious.

Resolved, That the intermeddling of any State or States, or their citizens, to abolish slavery in this District, or any of the Territories, on the ground, or under the pretext, that it is immoral or sinful, or the passage of any act or measure of Congress, with that view, would be a direct and dangerous attack on the institutions of all the slaveholding States.

Resolved, That the union of these States rests on an equality of rights and advantages among its members; and that whatever destroys that equality, tends to destroy the Union itself; and that it is the solemn duty of all, and more especially of this body, which represents the States in their corporate capacity, to resist all attempts to discriminate between the States in extending the benefits of the Government to the several portions of the Union; and that to refuse to extend to the Southern and Western States any advantage which would tend to strengthen, or render them more secure, or increase their limits or population by the annexation of new territory or States, on the assumption or under the pretext that the institution of slavery, as it exists among them, is immoral or sinful, or otherwise obnoxious, would be contrary to that equality of rights and advantages which the Constitution was intended to secure alike to all the members of the Union, and would, in effect, disfranchise the slaveholding States, withholding from them the advantages, while it subjected them to the burthens, of the Government.

Index

300   *Index*

insurrections clauses (Art. I, sec. 8, Art. IV, sec. 4), 63, 80–81, 175, 245, 248, 274
internal improvements, 130, 132, 148
international law, 179, 180
interposition, 176
interpretation of statutes & constitutions, 242–243, 263–264
Iredell, James, 64–65, 76, 77
Isaiah, 228, 230, 238

Jack v. Martin, 199
Jackson, Andrew, 125, 139, 175
Jackson, Francis, 210, 242, 247
Jackson, James, 94, 104
Jackson v. Bulloch, 196n
Jay, John, 111–112, 154
Jay, William, 101, 153–154, 156, 161, 199, 204, 206, 234, 247, 255, 274
Jefferson, Thomas, 51, 53, 60, 75, 97, 125
Jennison v. Caldwell, 46
Jerry rescue, 281
Jesus Christ, 168, 230, 231
Jocelyn, Simeon S., 153, 154, 161, 167
Johnson, Oliver, 154, 160
Johnson, William, 133–136
Judson, Andrew T., 163, 166
jury trial, 86, 157, 159, 193, 197–200, 252, 258, 261, 262, 272, 287
jus gentium, 148, 196

Kane, John, 281
Kansas-Nebraska Act, 202, 280, 284
Kendall, Amos, 174–175
Kenrick, John, 150–151
Kentucky, 91, 103, 279
Kentucky Resolutions, 75, 130, 209
Kentucky v. Dennison, 99
Key, Francis S., 127
kidnaping of blacks, 50, 54, 88, 96, 100, 102, 156–159, 196
King, John P., 177
King, Leicester, 218
King, Preston, 225
King, Rufus, 61, 71, 80, 111, 120, 141
Knapp, Isaac, 173
Knight v. Wedderburn, 33
Knox, Alexander, 147

LaGrange v. Chouteau, 195
Lane Theological Seminary, 162

Latimer, George, 237
law. See conflict of laws; natural law; positive law; slavery, law of
Lawrence, Matilda, 191, 193
Lay, Benjamin, 41
Leavitt, Joshua, 154, 161, 170, 205, 218, 234, 255
Lee, Henry, 96
Leigh, Benjamin W., 145, 148
Lemmon v. People, 286
LeMoyne, Francis J., 206
Letter on Colonization, 153–154
Lewis, Evan, 167
Lewis, Sam, 218
Lewis, William, 87
Lewis v. Stapleton, 28
Liberator, The, 153, 173, 174, 184, 232, 233, 238
Liberty League, 250, 258, 269
Liberty party, 17, 39, 202, 206–209, 216–219, 240, 249–251, 259
Liberty Party Abolitionists, 251
Lincoln, Abraham, 276–278, 286, 287
Lincoln, Levi, 46
Lloyd, John, 146
lobbying, 85–86, 158
Loguen, Jermain, 251
Long, Edward, 32–33
Loring, Ellis G., 160, 195, 228, 247, 255
Louisiana, 91, 103, 110, 126, 140
Louisiana Purchase, 103–104, 107
Lovejoy, Owen, 218, 280
Lowndes, Rawlins, 64
Lucas, John B., 96
Lundy, Benjamin, 152, 154, 161, 201
Lunsford v. Coquillon, 143, 194, 213
Lynch, Thomas, 57
Lynch v. Clarke, 166

McCrummell, James, 167
McDowell, James, 146
McDuffie, George, 180–181
McKean, Thomas, 87
McKim, James M., 167
McLean, John, 262, 285
Madison, James, 55, 64, 69, 73–74, 77, 78–79, 81, 94, 112, 113, 114, 115n, 127, 145, 239, 270
"Madison Papers," 81, 239, 245, 256, 263, 266
Magill v. Brown, 267

Library of Congress Cataloging in Publication Data
(For library cataloging purposes only)

Wiecek, William M   1938–
    The sources of antislavery constitutionalism in America, 1760–1848.

    Includes bibliographical references and index.
    1. Slavery in the United States—Law—History. 2. United States—Con-
stitutional history. I. Title.
KF4545.S5W53   346'.73'013   77-6169
ISBN 0-8014-1089-4

The Sources of Antislavery
Constitutionalism in America, 1760–1848

Designed by R. E. Rosenbaum.
Composed by York Composition Company, Inc.,
in 10 point Linotype Times Roman, 2 points leaded,
with display lines in Weiss Roman and Italic.
Printed letterpress from type by York Composition Company
on Warren's Number 66 text, 50 pound basis.
Bound by John H. Dekker & Sons, Inc.
in Joanna book cloth
and stamped in All Purpose foil.

Moore, Harry Thornton.
    Henry James [by] Harry T. Moore. New York, Viking
Press [1974]

    128 p. illus. 24 cm. (A Studio book) $7.95

    Includes bibliographical references.

    1. James, Henry, 1843–1916.

PS2123.M63 1974   813'.4 [B]   73–21499
ISBN 0–670–36755–9   MARC